Love Like Hate Adore

A Place of Stones

That Childhood Country

Falling for a Dancer

Francey

Sky

Deirdre Purcell

Love Like Hate Adore

MACMILLAN

First published 1997 by Macmillan

an imprint of Macmillan Publishers Ltd
25 Eccleston Place, London SW1W 9NF
and Basingstoke

Associated companies throughout the world

ISBN 0 333 63704 6 (Hardback)
ISBN 0 333 72650 2 (Trade Paperback)

1 3 5 7 9 8 6 4 2

A CIP catalogue record for this book is available from
the British Library.

Typeset by CentraCet, Cambridge
Printed and bound in Great Britain
by Mackays of Chatham plc, Chatham, Kent

In memory of Nellie

✦ Acknowledgements ✦

As always, profound gratitude is due to many people. To my sister-in-law, Mary Purcell, who helped with research and who was assisted by my terrific brother, Declan. To Aldiscon Information Ltd, and Barry White, SC, who gave generously of their time and expertise. To my mother, Maureen, who found the correct words of 'Kitty from Coleraine'. To the dedicated person – you know who you are – who helped with detail about Mountjoy Park. To Joe from Cheekys Kissing Telegram Company, to the long-suffering Fiona from Reprocentre, to the three Pats – the brilliant Pat Brennan, loyal Patricia Byrne, ever-loving Patricia Scanlan.

Thanks to my agents Charles Pick, Martin Pick, Treasa Coady – and to Amanda Kiely of Townhouse. To my superb editor, Suzanne Baboneau of Macmillan, to Hazel Orme, and to Ian Chapman who bemused me with his enthusiasm.

Huge thanks to Aoife Cronin who spent a whole day at Christmas time in carrying the manuscript to London – and to Roger and Carol who assisted.

Finally, much love to all my kind, supportive friends. And to my family, particularly Simon, Adrian and Kevin.

→ One ←

Every second of this summer hammered a spike into my memory. It is bizarre that so much could have happened. It is still August and the first intimations of disaster came on a Saturday in early May. Three months. As slow as a century.

I thought I'd tell it all to you before the finer details blow away like dandelion clocks.

By the way, you'll forgive me if sometimes I use what you might think are inappropriate words. Or at least words above my station! I'm not all that educated and my grammar or tenses may not always be the best, although I do watch out for the inflexible rules, like, *never a comma after an 'and'* — and so forth. But I adore the words themselves, always have, they're piled higgledy-piggledy in my brain. In ordinary life, or what passes for it nowdays, I have to squish a lot of them when they pop into my mouth in case people think I'm showing off. I learned this lesson early, where I grew up, in the flats.

That was some tough area of Dublin. There you didn't dare be different or you'd be in danger of getting your head chopped off. I got used to kids shouting after me, There goes Angela Devine, she swallowed a dictionary. I'd die. I'd pretend I didn't care, but I'd die.

Well, I still love dictionaries. They're so fat and full of possibilities. And I'll tell you another thing, I'm a natural speller. For some reason, I never had one bit of difficulty with spelling, right from the start-off at school in Low Babies. It's something to do with the sound and the shape of words on the page. I can even see some of them, some are like smooth Christmas balls that you can't resist touching and stroking and holding up to the light so they glitter.

I don't want to go on about it. Just take it that however it happened, from the very beginning, my brain sort of hoovered up every word it could find and stored it like you'd store good wine or cheeses. (Strange as it may seem, I know a bit about wines and cheeses. It's because of one of my jobs – of which more anon . . .)

Enough apologias. To get to the story.

Day one, that Saturday. Afternoon.

The bus was crammed as usual. I was coming home from one of my jobs, the Saturday morning one in the deli – a southside deli – and I was wrecked because we had been particularly busy.

You know the type who rush into these delicatessen shops as if they're on their way to a fire? They usually have the small-bore Merc or Volvo runaround – Beemers are now *out*, apparently – parked with one wheel on the footpath outside. Stuck at about age thirty-four, sound like they're asking for poppyseed rails instead of rolls. Designer track suits, the smoothed wide-eyed look that gives them all faces like Dolly Parton. They're the type who give out about the price of balsamic vinegar even though it's far from balsamic vinegar many of them were reared. I call them Samanthas. Marks, if they're men.

Because it's Saturday the Marks wear Nikes or Adidas runners and waxed jackets.

Now, in fairness I have to say I have met one or two real people named Samantha and Mark and they've been grand. But you know what I mean. It's my personal shorthand.

That morning we'd had a lot of Samanthas and Marks and by the time I'd had to run across to the jewellers' for the fifth time to change the fifth twenty-pound note, I was ready to scream. What's more, it was raining that day and on the way home I'd had to wait thirty-five minutes for the bus.

I could have walked, often do — because we live very close to town — but as I told you I was wall-falling with tiredness, soaked to the skin, and my feet were killing me from all the standing and from my new shoes. Which got even tighter in the bus. It's funny how your feet swell in buses, isn't it?

I defy you to tell the difference between chain-store shoes and shoes from a real shoe shop. I suppose I should feel guilty about them, though. They're real leather and at the price I bought them they had to have been manufactured by some tiny little boy or girl in Bangladesh or East Timor or somewhere. Who was probably whipped into producing them. Literally.

So as you can imagine, I could have done without any more hassle that day.

When the bus eventually came, the omens were not good. The minute you stepped inside you were assaulted with the smell of damp and wet feet. And buggies and crying babies, and dozens of crabby, snotty toddlers — not to speak of exhausted women with Roches Stores' bags clamped between their ankles to stop them spilling over every time the bus went around a corner. You couldn't see a sausage through the windows with all the steam from the coats and the umbrellas and the breath.

Actually, the way those bus drivers throw these double-deckers around corners, I find it amazing that they don't keel over. What's big and green and lies in a ditch? A dead bus. That's the only joke I ever remember Mammy telling. Of course that's when the buses were all green, that long ago I can only vaguely remember them. Now they're like mobile funderlands, painted all over with brilliant colours. I love the Birds Eye one with the peas tumbling over it from top to bottom.

By the time we got to my stop, I was glad to get off, I can tell you.

Mountjoy Square is going all yuppie these days and it seemed to happen overnight. Trees growing out of windows one day and then, shazam! next day there are acres of phoney frontages with apartments behind them. Some of these apartments cost more than a four-bedroomed house. Half the space for a hundred times the rent.

I have to admit the Square is not a bad environment to live in if you're forced to rent privately. At least it's very nice outside. We have a terrific park in the middle of this square.

But why anyone would want to live in a flat, even when it's called an apartment, is beyond me. Call me a snob but I certainly wouldn't live in an apartment if I had the choice of buying a house.

Even that day I wouldn't have been surprised if Reddy, our so-and-so of a landlord, came to tell us he wanted to get us all out of our place. I'd say given half the chance, he'd knock our whole place down. He could probably get some kind of a grant for knocking it and building an eggbox like all the other eggboxes around here because this is a tax-designated area. I've never quite understood what that is, but it seems people who have money to invest in Ireland can buy apartments in the inner city and can then rent them out, paying no tax at all. Like in Temple Bar. Temple Bar is the new centrefold of Dublin that we're all supposed to be very proud of, full of pubs and trendy restaurants and as for the yuppie apartments across there! People queued all night to buy them at *huge* prices.

Not that I'd know. I've never been to Temple Bar, even though it's less than a mile from where we live. Temple Bar is not for people like me. I hear from James, who's nineteen, that it's a young person's place, full of tourists and English fellows puking at their weekend stag parties and kids as young as fourteen drunk on three beers sprawled all over the footpaths. You see articles in the paper about it all the time — it's supposed to be our Left Bank.

Well, that day I would have wished Reddy luck with trying to get us out. At the time in question I was, speaking generally, full of vim. Even though he had given us only a month to month lease, if he'd tried anything, if there'd been a peep out of him, I would have been prepared to take him to the Supreme Court. To Europe if necessary. We were going when we were good and ready and not a day before. In this country, thank God, the courts always take a lenient view of people like us when it comes to the landlord–tenant relationship.

And anyway, even if he did try something, it takes donkey's years for anything even to get near a court. James and I would have had plenty of time to find somewhere decent of our own.

As I walked away from the bus stop I saw there was a sale on in Discount Electrical. Nothing unusual, there always seems to be a sale on there. Another one in D.I.D. Electrical a few houses away. (That electrical

business is cutthroat in Dublin. You'd think that everyone in Ireland has enough tellys and microwaves by now.
But no. Soon they'll be giving them away with pounds of
rashers.) At least it had stopped raining.

When I got to the steps leading to the front door of
our place James's bike was not locked into its usual place
on the railings. I'll tell you who James is in a minute,
you'll be hearing a lot about him. This is his story I'm
going to be telling you, not mine. I always hated that
bike. He came off it more than once — I was always
telling him that those Kawasakis are too powerful, and
half the time he wouldn't wear his crash helmet. He had
to when he was working, he's a courier by profession,
but he thought it was cissy to wear it when he wasn't on
duty even though it's the law that he has to. Once or
twice I had thought of reporting him to the cops to
frighten him into it, but then I'd think of his face in the
police station and I couldn't.

I knew I'd have to get over thinking of him as a baby.
I'd already started working on it.

It was a bit odd that the bike was gone that day,
because normally on a Saturday an earthquake wouldn't
wake him. I half thought it might have been nicked, but
when I got inside, I saw he was gone all right. Amazing.
Only three o'clock! I'm not being sarcastic here,
honestly, James always tended to stay in bed a lot if he
didn't have to do anything. (And sometimes even when
he did. For instance, I had to go on at him or he would
have slept away his appointments at the dental hospital.
He has great teeth and I aimed to keep them that way.)

I suppose if I'd had more money, I probably should
have been sending him to a counsellor, or at least
someone who would identify if there was anything wrong
with him. Like, was this behaviour normal for a nineteen-
year-old? I mean, I wasn't competent to decide whether

or not his long silences, black moods, staying in bed a lot, would qualify as depression or what. There's a lot about James I can't precisely pin down, he's a loner, certainly, but a loner who goes out to clubs and parties and stuff. Who seems to have friends. And yet whose loneliness you can feel almost a hundred per cent of the time when he's in the same room as you. Does that make sense?

Counsellors are all the rage these days but in our circumstances where we'd have to go public, it was a non-starter because you'd be waiting years for an appointment. So we had to muddle along the best we could.

About money. I'm prepared to admit that I have an ambivalent attitude towards money. With all my jobs, we should probably have been doing better than we were at that stage – but I was saving hard. Probably too much. (Although as you'll see I haven't succeeded all that well. Twenty years' working and only a few thousand to show for it! However, it's something . . .) I was putting it away towards that place of our own. And for something else that I find hard to talk about. For some reason, I find it very difficult to spend money on myself, even when I have a few bob over. I sort of have to put it away towards the future. I've analysed this and I think it has a great deal to do with security. Some day James was going to go off on his own and I've always known – from day one – that I couldn't rely on him to look after me if I got sick or anything. I wouldn't have asked him to anyway. Having seen the state of Mammy for so many years, who could? Enough said.

He has a very strong personality as you will see. It can be difficult living with someone like that when they're under your feet a lot. Don't get me wrong, though, I adore that kid.

That first Saturday, when I got in and found him gone, I have to admit it was nice to know I'd have a bit of peace for a while.

Now I'd like to be able to say that when I let myself into the flat I was aware that something was amiss. That's what you read always in books. The main character always finds something amiss when he lets himself into his home. Mind you, there's usually blood smeared all over the walls or a funny smell of gas or something. Not in this case. Everything looked normal. Like a tornado blew through the window and out through the front door. Typical. I always found it like that when James went out and I hadn't been there to nag at him.

I always got a bit of a kick in the teeth when I let myself into the flat. Somehow, when I was out, I managed to develop this sort of rosy feeling about going back home again. You know, looking forward to snuggling back into my own little nest. Well, each time I actually did get in – I leave it to your imagination.

If I was to use words like damp or brown or peeling, would they fill in the picture for you?

I did my best. I've a lot of books and the bookshelves were arranged in front of the worst of the wallpaper. And I'd hidden what upholstery there was under white candlewick bedspreads I bought (for half-nothing – fair play!) at the Daisy Market.

I picked up the wet towels in the facilities – Reddy's word, not mine, it's a cubbyhole partitioned off the room but the so-called walls are so flimsy you can hear *everything*. (I usually turned up the radio or the telly when James went in. You have to have a little bit of privacy in your life.)

Then I kicked off the famous shoes and did a bit of tidying before I put the kettle on and laid out the bits of grub I'd brought home from the deli. I look forward to that on a Saturday. Have myself a posh little picnic. I'm allowed take the heels of cheese and the bits of salami that fall off the slicer, stuff like that. On Saturdays I make an exception to my miserly instincts, I buy myself a couple of rolls. I vary them. Sesame. Tomato. Onion. Garlic. Et cetera. I have a special tray that I use, it's Chinese laquered, with a lovely picture of a spreading willow tree, green on black — more turquoise really or, that lovely word, aqua. The colour of the sea just before a storm.

Isn't it amazing how life works out? Every so often I stop and wonder how someone like me, Angela Devine from the flats, came to be able to talk knowledgeably about chorizo and prosciutto. And even more than that, came to be eating it *by choice*. God, if Mammy could see me now. Of course James wouldn't be caught dead eating any of it. He's into fast foods, like them all at his age. Personally I can't stick burgers any more, especially since I saw on the telly that when you're eating them in some places you're eating cow's abscesses. Yuck.

I should have sat down immediately that day and started to study. I was preparing for my Leaving Cert — I'm doing it bit by bit as a mature student — and with the exam so near I had no business behaving like the Queen of Sheba with my tray and my little bits of finger food. But I was so damp and cranky, I couldn't face into the books straight off.

Anyhow, I was pretty well on top of things. *Hamlet* was on our cycle this time in English, although during the course of that year our teacher, Mr Elliott, had made us study *Macbeth* as well. We weren't all that keen, of course, because it was not going to come up in the paper, but he insisted. It would be greatly to our benefit, he told us, to know more than one play if we were to have any idea of the context in which Shakespeare was writing.

According to him, studying just the Shakespeare on the curriculum is simply not getting a proper education and this school, he goes, puffing out his chest like a cockatoo, prides itself on not being merely a crammer. Whatever. I just wanted to get the exam. I was dreading it, of course, the weeks were flying by. I did OK in maths last year. Pass paper naturally, but I got a C3. High normal. Not bad for someone who never went to secondary school, if I do say so myself.

On that Saturday in May I was still continuing to study Irish as well, although looking back on it now, I was mad ever to think I could do Irish and English in the same year. I suppose it was because at the rate of only one subject a year it'd be the millennium before I got the bloody certificate. It's beyond me how kids can do six or seven subjects all together.

Here's another thing – I'm quite glad it's only at this age (I'm thirty-six) I got into Shakespeare. Because if I was doing those plays when I was sixteen or seventeen, like normal kids have to do them, I don't think I'd have understood half of what was going on. Ireland is a very peculiar country. There's people all over the place giving out about porno videos and *Playboy* magazine and all the rest of it but do they know what their kids are studying in English for the Leaving Cert? Do they have any idea what *Hamlet* and *Macbeth* are all about? Like incest?

Anyway, I said feck it to the books and turned on the telly. I took my tray and my cup of coffee over to sit in front of it. There's usually a good Bette Davis or Cary Grant on BBC2. I love Kirk Douglas. We got the cable last year, it's expensive but I think it's worth it, you have to have some nice things in life and it was mostly for James. I put my foot down, though, about us getting Sky Sports. Over my dead body. Twenty-four hours a day of Italian bobsledding or motocross? No way.

But we might as well have had Sky Sports that Saturday, it was nothing but sport, sport, sport. Even BBC2 had cricket. God help us, I thought, when the Olympics start in July.

At least Sky News had one of those fashion programmes, this one was from Milan. It was fantasy gear, stuff I wouldn't wear in a million years. Couldn't. You'd have to be seven feet tall like Naomi Campbell or Elle MacPherson. They all come to Dublin a lot, you know, or at least they used to when Naomi was engaged to Adam Clayton. Dublin is where it's all at these days, I keep reading it in the paper. For fun and music and clubs and stuff. And they're all making millions out of the music. That Cranberry girl is a millionaire already in her early twenties.

But what I think is really gas is that they all make the money out of giving out. Their childhoods and their upbringings and their abuse and their deprivation. The whole shebang.

In that case I should be a billionaire. I should give a seminar.

I must have dozed off looking at the telly because suddenly there's one of those American news programmes on and I didn't even remember the end of the fashion one. Still no sign of James. I'll kill him, I thought. He was supposed to be here this afternoon, I'd extracted a promise out of him to help me bring a bunch of stuff down to the launderette. Winter duvets and covers. They're not all that heavy but they're very bulky and it's a fairly long walk.

I was damned if I was going down to that snooker hall again to haul him out of it. He had too much loose change from his job, in my opinion. But I just couldn't help being so soft with him. I mean, he grew up not remembering one iota about Mammy. How could he? He wasn't even three months old when she died. I mean, with all her troubles, she was his mother and everyone needs a mother. All these years, even when he was in nappies, I never let him call me Mammy. He'd had a mammy and it wasn't me.

I made sure he knew all about her, all the good bits. I didn't hide the truth from him, I couldn't anyway, even if I wanted to, not with all the social workers around. But I made a point of telling him how nice she was underneath.

I should have insisted he gave me his paypacket and then I'd give him back pocket money. Mind you, even though he was old enough to vote and to get a mortgage he was still a child, really – and I suppose I was so thrilled he had found a job that he continued to get out of bed for, I didn't want to rock the boat too much.

Speaking of being just a child, in some ways I quite often feel like one too, if I'm being honest. I don't know how I got to be this age, I really don't. When you look at it, I'm only two years younger than Mammy was when she died. God, I wonder how she felt when she was thirty-six. Did she know she had only two years left? Too far gone, I suppose.

One day I'll always remember about Mammy. I was going in the bus along O'Connell Street – as far as I can recall I must have been about ten or eleven. I'd seen Francesca and Justine and Nicola on an access visit and I was in the bus with my own social worker going back to her office. The three had all just been moved from one foster home to two separate ones, Francesca in one, the other two in another. Nicola, in particular, was pretty upset and she had started to cry when she saw me. Then the other two had started as well. It had been a real waterworks party.

Anyway, I'm going along in this bus afterwards and

I'm not feeling the greatest, as you can imagine, and I look out through the window beside me and, my God, there she is. Mammy. Absolutely straight. Walking perfectly, no wobbling. And she has a kind of suit on, an outfit I never saw before. It's a lovely sunny day, I remember. Her hair is shining, it looks as shiny as a crow's wing. Tears come into my eyes for some reason, and I remember thinking, My mammy is beautiful. I look hard at all the other women in O'Connell Street – we're just outside Clery's – and I'm thinking, None of them, not one of those other women, is a patch on her. It gives me the most extraordinary feeling.

The social worker sees there's something going on with me. Is everything all right, Angela? she asks.

Fine, I say. I don't want to tell her I saw Mammy. I can't explain even now why not. It was something to do with keeping the perfection of it.

To this day I don't know whether she was really there or whether it was a vision. For instance, I never saw that suit again. Like, I get home a few hours later after spending a while with the social worker in her office. Mammy's in her usual slacks and jumper and the wobble is back in the walk. I saw you in O'Connell Street, I go, that was a lovely suit, Mammy, where'd you get it?

But she just looks at me. Blank. No one home.

Ah well, I thought, that Saturday sitting in front of Sky News, no point dwelling on the past. So I was thirty-six. Big deal. We were managing OK and we weren't having to humiliate ourselves by being on the Labour. And at least I wasn't looking at the world through the bottom of a bottle or the butt of a syringe. I certainly could be. Funny how I'd managed to keep James straight too, I thought. Not funny at all, pretty damned lucky.

It started to spill again and never stopped for the rest of that whole day. You couldn't even see out with the

condensation on the window, and the bucket under the
drip in the ceiling of the facilities was nearly full. There
was something new too – a patch of damp over the sink,
spreading by the minute so that by half past seven it was
as big as a small continent.

Another thing for Reddy for next Friday night, I
thought, adding it to the list, which included not only the
drip but the blown ring on the breakfast cooker. It was
only a two-ring one. You try cooking a full meal with
one ring! It always gave me great satisfaction to withhold
some of Reddy's money until he fixed things. There was
nearly always a reason to withhold. These were going to
do nicely for this week.

I love that phrase. I wonder what it would be like to
have an American Express card. (Of course, James would
probably take it and buy himself a Harley Davidson.
That's all I'd need.)

My second job was being a kissogram person and I had
a 'bunny girl' gig that night so I couldn't spend any more
time lounging around.

Before you jump to conclusions, I have to assure you
it's not as seedy as you might think. Some very
respectable people (like me!) do the work only because
they need the money.

By eight o'clock I was almost ready, I had my raincoat
on over my outfit and I was just putting my ears and
other bits and pieces into my bag when I heard his key in
the lock. Where were you? I'm sounding aggrieved
before I can stop myself. Even though I know as sure as
eggs that it's the worst possible thing I can say and the
minute I've said it I regret it.

I'm also thinking how hilarious this would look to an
outsider – this deranged woman in a raincoat and a cheap
rabbit's outfit, giving out to this big six-foot hunk in
leathers.

Nowhere, he says and pushes past me into his room. He got the bedroom in the flat — it was only right, I suppose, raging male hormones et cetera — while I used the bed-settee in the lounge.

I was tempted to barrel in after him but I knew that I might as well save my breath to cool my porridge. I'd smelled the Heineken off him. I consoled myself that this was not too bad, at least it wasn't spirits. So I contented myself with just hmmphing and glaring and slamming about a bit.

Before I left, I took the precaution of lifting his keys from where he threw them on the table. If he went out again he wouldn't kill himself on that bike.

Please God, I thought as I left for the gig, he'll go asleep now and stay asleep until I get home. I had only three kissogram calls booked in — so I wasn't going to be home too late.

✦ Two ✦

The third job at the beginning of this summer – I still had it then – was by far the most fun. Myself and my friend, Patsy Jennings, had been doing gigs for a few years, singing at weddings, if we could get them (big party-weddings seem to be going out fashion in this country) but mostly pubs. Sunday mornings, that sort of thing.

She's brilliant, Patsy. A really strong voice and she plays three instruments, keyboards, guitar and clarinet. Although to tell you the truth, the clarinet isn't much use. It's too soft for the kind of clientele we play to. I felt privileged to be singing with her because my own voice is not a patch on hers, a bit above average, I suppose, although I did once get a second place in the Feis Maitiú when I was about nine.

I suppose I shouldn't boast but kids came from all over the city for that Feis, so it was a bit of a feather in my cap. It was held in the Father Matthew Hall in Church Street (I suppose that's why they called it the Feis Maitiú). Being on the north side, it wasn't as posh as the Feis Ceoil, and not as specialized, because the Feis Ceoil did only music whereas ours had compeititions for Irish dancing and elocution and God knows what else.

Patsy wasn't in for it that day, lucky for me or I would have only got third! I sang Kitty From Coleraine. Those days you had to act out the songs so the nuns found me a little three-legged stool and a milking bucket but they had to show me what to do with a cow. I couldn't *believe* that you actually have to put your hands on. Yuck.

When beautiful Kitty one morning was tripping
With a pitcher of milk to the fair of Coleraine,
When she saw me she stumbled
And the pitcher it tumbled,
And all the sweet buttermilk watered the plain.
'Twas hay-making season, I can't tell the reason,
Misfortune never comes single 'tis plain.
For very soon after poor Kitty's disaster,
The divil a pitcher was whole in Coleraine!

Picture it. Me sitting on this little stool milking this imaginary cow into my pitcher before standing up and tripping. Nobody seemed to mind that we'd got completely the wrong end of the stick. That song is supposed to be sung by a boy. A boy from the country. The adjudicator never mentioned it.

The nuns put ringlets in my hair for the occasion because, of course, the way poor Mammy was at the time she wouldn't have been able to twist a ringlet if you'd paid her a tenner. But those days you had to have ringlets if you were to have any chance of a medal. And little white socks.

Even though I only got second, the way Sister Marita was carrying on you'd think I'd won the Nobel Prize for Singing. It was a brilliant day. She brought me and another girl who got a Highly Commended down into town and we had chips and a Wimpy and as much Coke as we liked. I still have the medal somewhere. The winner got a plaque. In a way I'd prefer medals, I think plaques are a bit vulgar.

Patsy and I called ourselves PA System. Get it? P for Patsy, A for Angela. On a good day with the light behind her, as the fella says, Patsy would pass for Goldie Hawn. She's tall and blonde. 'Statuesque'. We'd known each other since High Babies.

We did lose touch for a few years after national school but then she turned up at Mammy's funeral. She told me one of the nuns rang her. I know people give out about nuns and how narrow-minded they were during that era but in my experience they were brilliant. With one notable exception, which I'll come to soon.

That Sunday morning, the second day of this story, PA System had no gig lined up so I was free to potter about in the flat. It was so small, you could fix it up in a trice but sometimes I liked to play house. You know, when it's real peaceful, and maybe raining outside, or even when it's sunny like it was that morning, you polish and hoover and shine everything up and when you stand back and look at it, the place sort of talks back to you. I always imagined the lounge twinkling and saying, 'Thanks, Ange!' I was using a brand new yellow duster, the kind you get as free offers with Flash. I love them, they're so soft, like the kind of gloves you'd buy only in Brown Thomas's. And the colour is so pure. I'd always planned that when James and I got a place of our own I was going to paint the walls that colour because then there'd be sunshine all the time *inside* the house. No more wallpaper. I hate frigging wallpaper.

I hate going into Brown Thomas's. I feel everyone there is looking at me and asking themselves who let me in.

Now it may have been poxy in the damp and drips department but we had a lovely high ceiling in that flat.

Georgian. Dublin's famous all over the world for being Georgian. I went to the Abbey once to see *Shadow of a Gunman* by Seán Ó Casey – one of the things that's great about living in Mountjoy Square is that the two best theatres in Ireland are right on your doorstep. I nearly fell out of my standing when I went into the Abbey that night and saw the stage. The room that the gunman was staying in? You'd think they'd copied the décor from our gaff. Right down to the peeling wallpaper.

I believe that in all those new apartments the ceilings are so low they're oppressive.

Well, that Sunday morning, as I told you, I was really enjoying myself tipping around. *Hamlet* was sitting there reproachfully on the arm of the bed-settee. I was ignoring him. That man's heart was too dark by half for such a lovely atmosphere. As a finishing touch, I put fresh water and a Disprin into the vase of motorway daffodils James nicked for us and then I put them inside the net curtains, between them and the glass. Patsy made those curtains for me on her electric machine. They're ruched and that morning, maybe it was the ruching, maybe it was the sun outside, they instantly turned gold when I placed the daffs behind them. The effect looked brilliant. You wouldn't see it in a magazine.

People are always giving out yards about Dublin Corporation and the County Councils and so on, but I think credit where credit is due. They've done a fantastic job with those motorways. I remember the first spring I saw the way they were planted, we were on our way to a gig in Patsy's car and I couldn't believe the sight of my own eyes, four wide ribbons of flower stretching for miles and miles, like four Yellow Brick Roads.

Years ago, in primary school, we did that poem by Wordsworth about daffodils. I thought it was useless, to tell you the truth.

I have another memory about daffodils, which is not
great. I was only about eight, and here we come to that
bitch of a nun, Sister Concepta, the only termagant nun
I've ever come across in my whole life. That nun hated
me. Well, maybe she didn't, in fairness. But when I was
eight, I was *sure* she hated me. She was always sucking up
to the kids who had money. At least, that's what it
seemed like to me. Most of us in High Babies came from
the flats but there were a few who came in from private
estates in places like Glasnevin and Fairview. I suppose,
looking back, their parents were socialists or something.
They were the pets and you'd want to see the shop
flowers they brought in for the May altars. (I suppose
sucking up goes two ways.) When it came to that altar,
the rest of us had make do with robbing Michaelmas
daisies or snapdragons or tulips out of people's gardens.
That was in the days before the motorways.

I'll give you an example of this one's bitchery, it has to
do with daffodils, that's probably why I'm remembering
her at this point. I wrote the word jonquils in a
composition for her. Now remember – I was eight years
old.

You mean 'daffodils', she says to me. How often do I
have to tell you that you don't use big words just because
they're big? Stop looking for notice.

I blush to the roots of my hair and insist that I mean
jonquils. That jonquils are a different species to daffodils.
I say I saw it in a gardening book.

Big mistake.

What gardening book? she pounces.

One I got out of the library, Sister. Now I'm in real
deep. And I'm terrified.

Oh, the *library*, is it? she goes, is that right? Well, Miss
Notice Box, bring it in so we can all see.

Of course there was no gardening book and I'd used

jonquils because I loved the sound of it. I have no idea where I heard it. How was I to know it was the French for daffodil? In my mind a jonquil was as different from a daffodil as a daisy from a dandelion. A jonquil was soft and quiet with petals like ferns.

She wouldn't let it go. She pursued me on it day after day. And of course I ended up getting slapped because of looking for notice and lying.

But the worst of all was the day she announced that the school was having a jumble sale in aid of Biafra or some other unfortunate place, I can't really remember, and that our class was having its own stall. She asked us – looking down at the pets – to bring in our unwanted toys and unused household items.

That was a laugh where I was concerned. Unwanted toys? Crap tyres and chipped steelies and bits of frayed rope from the docks which we used as skipping ropes. And as for unused household items, the mind boggles.

Mind you, we weren't all that deprived. Those steelies were lethal against real glass marbles. (A friend of mine was friends with McHugh Himself, the bicycle man, who gave her the best part of a bucketful of ballbearings he didn't need. Fair dues to her, she divvied them out.) And our dock ropes lasted a hell of a lot longer than the cissy skipping ropes you'd buy in a shop. Particularly when they were used for swinging around lamp-posts. They killed your hands, though.

But to get back to Concepta, I did have one lovely thing, my pride and joy. One of our social workers had given me a doll. I didn't even play with her, I didn't dare in case I ruined her. Her frock was made of stiff organdy in pale blue and she had real hair on her eyelashes. I called her Susie and I kept her hidden from the others. I hate to say this, because it sounds disloyal, but I didn't let even Mammy know where I kept her. Because you know what would have happened. Susie would have gone down to me uncle's in ten seconds flat and that'd be the end of her. Poor Mammy. The pawn was always her best friend.

So when Sister Concepta asked us about our unwanted toys—

I know, I know . . . You're way ahead of me here.

It wasn't even a struggle. I didn't even have to imagine how awful it was for the poor children of Biafra or wherever it was.

I don't know what got into me. I suppose deep down I was insecure enough to want her to like me. Whatever.

I ran home at little lunch, even though we weren't supposed to leave the grounds of the convent under pain of *death*. The flats were nearly a mile from the school and when I say I ran, I mean I really legged it. Little lunch was only twenty minutes.

I must have got home in about six or seven minutes because I could barely breathe when I was going up the steps to our door. And wouldn't you know it, just my luck, Mammy had a friend there.

She looks up all bleary-eyed when I run in the door and I can see him there on the sofa behind her, even more bleary-eyed. I ignore the both of them and run straight to where I'd hidden the doll.

On the way out they don't even look up. But the baby, it had to be Justine at the time, she's sitting in the middle of the floor with that look on her face, which meant she was probably going to cry in a minute. She smells, too, but I don't have time to change her nappy. I just put her soother back in her mouth and run.

I get a stitch half-way back and I have to stop. A very nice lady asks me if I'm all right and I have so little puff I can barely answer her that I am. When the stitch eases up a bit I have to run as though my life depended on it.

Which in a way it did. We were always strapped for being late. Even half a minute.

I manage to get back in without being noticed. Things were freer then, nobody worrying about baby-snatching or drugs in school playgrounds or suchlike, and the double gates were always wide open. The bell is just ringing for the end of little lunch and they're all going back inside. And as soon as I get inside the classroom I run straight up to Sister Concepta and give Susie to her.

Thanks, she says, and turns around to chalk something on the blackboard.

Thanks!

All during the rest of the day, I couldn't take my eyes of that doll where she'd put her beside the duster and the bell on top of the cófra. Yes, that same cófra where she kept not only the chalk and the copies and things like that but her best stick, her strap, and our knitting bags (I *hated* knitting with a *passion*), also the toilet paper you had to ask her for when you were going outside, making a show of you. That cófra symbolized everything I hated about that nun. And there was my beloved Susie sitting on it. A prisoner. Not only that, she was looking at me all the time. *How could you?*

Thanks.

It would be hard to exaggerate the effect that incident had on me. It was trivial, I suppose, and it happened so long ago, I should be able to let it go, shouldn't I? But it genuinely haunts me. I can still feel all the feelings, fresh as the day they arrived. Rage, sorrow, misery, and an overwhelming sense of injustice. I was also furious with myself for being such an eejit.

To get back to the Sunday in question. I had the radio playing low. 2FM.

I'm a big radio fan, as you'll discover. One of the stations, Classic Hits – or was it FM104? – used to have

The Golden Hour on Sunday mornings, I used to listen any time I could because it was a complete programme of the songs from the seventies and eighties that Patsy and I always used in our act. But now they're all doing chart shows. I just can't take techno or dance. I hate it.

All the time I was keeping an eye on the bedroom door. He likes to get up and go to meet some of his pals in the Millrace for a few pints before Sunday dinner. When PA System has no gig, I like to have Sunday dinner, the real thing, with Bisto and marrowfat peas. It makes me feel we're like a proper family.

So, sure enough, the door opens on schedule, about a quarter to twelve. I keep my mouth shut. Because I want him to come home for the dinner. The moods he's been in lately, you'd never know how he'd react if you said anything at all. A joke can be taken as an insult. You can't look crooked at him. All he's looking for is an excuse to storm out. And with the motorbike, I'm always afraid.

How'ya, I say to him, I know I'm walking on eggshells here and I try to place my tone just right. Not too cheery, no hint of enquiry in case he thinks I'm being intrusive.

He just grunts back and despite my best intentions, I get goaded. Oh, very nice, I say. Yes, Angela, I'm fine, thank you for asking. And what a lovely day it is outside and how are you doing yourself?

There's no point, I'm talking to myself. He's already gone into the facilities.

When he comes back out I ask him if there's anything wrong.

Nothing, he says.

I know better than to go on at him. Whatever chance I have of him coming round, I've none if I nag. Those hormonês, probably. I have to make allowances, I know that.

Although I used to think naïvely that at nineteeen he should have been over the worst of them. I kept on telling myself that some people are just late developers, yet sometimes during that period, I used to find myself fantasizing we were having a real chat like real people. You know, having a laugh about the kissograms or the gigging or the cleaning (my main job) or the Samanthas and Marks I've met that week. And then he would be telling me about funny things that happened to him on his deliveries.

There had to have been some crack to be got out of that job of his. I've seen bunches of those courier lads sitting in their leathers, chatting and smoking there along the canal near where Patrick Kavanagh is supposed to have sat. (According to Mr Elliott we should all be making pilgrimages to that spot. Apparently Kavanagh wrote some of his best poems about that district around there and he used to spend a lot of time in some bookshop on Baggot Street Bridge.)

Now he grabs a heel of a loaf and eats it raw.

Will he have an egg or a rasher? Or even cornflakes?

I'm to get off his back and leave him alone.

At least he does say he will be home for the dinner. Well, so long as he stays on the Heineken, I suppose it'll be all right.

I tell him to be back for half two on the dot. He says he might.

A peculiar thing is that during that period I prayed a lot (if you could call it prayer, because I'm not practising and I'm not a bit religious. I don't even much believe in God, to tell you the truth). But I found myself all the time saying stuff like, 'God, if you're up there, please keep him safe . . .'

I worried a lot about drugs. Not for myself, because since I was old enough to notice the kind of thing that was going on around me, the last thing in the world I ever wanted to see was a cap or a syringe. To this day I try to manage without tablets when I have a toothache. It's sort of a principle with me. But there's no getting away from it in this city and where we're concerned, of course, there's heredity. Genes. Apart from Mammy altogether, I'd be willing to bet that James's father was a druggie. It stands to reason. From the time he was about twelve, I searched James's bedroom on a regular basis when he was out and once or twice I did find cigarettes broken up but I didn't really worry about that. That meant only hash. They all do that.

I'm humming away to myself over the dinner when he comes in about ten to three. Not late enough for a row but not on time either – tardy enough to show me I can't be interfering in his life.

I remember thinking, that day, God help his wife – and then wondering how I'd get on with her. A fantasy . . . Even at that stage I'd figured he did have a girlfriend although I hadn't dared open my mouth about her. There were little signs.

What little signs? Big signs! Like condoms in his jeans pockets. And him asking me to bring him back Lynx deodorant when I went to the shops.

The dinner went OK that day – he even talked to me a bit about some of his pals. There was one, Ferdia, who had a car, he worked for his father's computer business, and on the odd time I've met him he seemed to be a decent bloke. James tells me that they're all planning to go down the country, to Wicklow, to stay in a mobile home that Ferdia's parents have near Brittas Bay.

That brought me back. I was there once on the August Bank Holiday. One of the social workers arranged a supervised access visit for Mammy with the three in care and she let me go with them. She had a new Toyota car — well, new to her — and we all fitted in quite comfortably. She'd even brought a proper tartan rug so we could all sit down on it together.

Brittas Bay that day was crawling with kids, frolicking in and out of the waves and digging for shells and making moats for the tide to fill. I was fascinated to see the way the water came into the little channels, creeping in like fingers wearing white lace gloves. Although I'd been to Dollymount a few times I'd never noticed this before because every time I was there the tide was so far out you'd need binoculars to see any water.

Yes, it was brilliant. Mammy was grand that day, she even paddled with us. And on the way back she sat in the front holding Francesca on her knee and the whole lot of us were on our best behaviour.

I'd love to live somewhere nice like that. One of my biggest fantasies is of winning money in the Lotto. I'm not looking for a fortune, half a fortune would be enough! Patsy got three and a bonus once. Great lot of use eight quid was to her when she estimated that over the years she must have spend hundreds.

I've always concentrated on the scratch cards myself, I feel the odds are better. And I've won loads of two poundses, two fours and once even an eight. But I have to tell you getting those three Frees is useless. You're wasting your time going back in to claim the free card. It's just a way of prolonging the agony. But James got a twenty-five just before Christmas.

No matter what happened or happens to me I never lose sight of my belief that one day I'll get the three stars. Then I'll go on *Winning Streak* and I'll win that quarter of a million. Funny how most of the people on the programme are from the country. I suppose they've more money to spend on the scratch cards. The EU and all the rest of it. Headage. You'd have to laugh. Here's me from the inner city and I could hold my own with the best of the culchies in the matter of slurry and first-cut silage and headage grants. Isn't the telly very educational all the same?

By the way when I do get to go on *Winning Streak* I'm going to be very strict as to what my supporters in the audience can put on my posters to wave for me. Some of those posters are really stupid. 'Go for it, Deccie', or Joe or Nessa. Stupid. What do those people think the contestants are going to do? Not go for it? Why do they think they're on the ruddy programme?

Maybe we'll have our own mobile home in Brittas Bay someday, I say to James, as I'm ladling out the gravy. You know, of course, that I'm going to win the Lotto——

Huh, he goes. You and what army?

You just wait and see, I say. Maybe you'll be married by then, and have a couple of kids and I can mind them in the mobile home while you and your wife go to the pub for a bit of a break.

He lets me know what he thinks of that little scenario with a look that'd kill an elephant. So I shut up. Typical, give me an inch and I'll take a mile.

Three

D on't laugh, but there was a time when I was in
danger of getting married myself. I was just turned
seventeen. Nowadays seventeen would be seen as far too
young, and of course it is, but it would have been a great
way to go, eh? And it was legal. We're allowed to get
married when we're fourteen, they've to wait until
they're sixteen although maybe they've changed it now.
Last I heard about it they were talking about raising the
age of both sexes although, being a bit lax as far as being
a Catholic is concerned, I'm not up to date on it.

I met him at the zoo, of all places. It was another
Sunday and James was in hospital. It was just before
Mammy died and he'd been taken in the day before 'for
observation'. I knew what that meant. He was going into
care too, like the other three. He was only two months
old. He had been left with us as a sort of trial to see how
Mammy'd get on.

But what did they expect?

There'd been murder in the flat that Friday night, the
night before the zoo. Mammy wouldn't give James to the
social worker and the police had to be called to get him
away from her. I was screaming at them to get out, she
was screaming, the social worker was screaming, that rat
of a boyfriend was screaming. He pulled a knife on the

social worker, and the police jumped on him. Complete bedlam.

The neighbours in on the act, gawking in through the open door. It was most likely one of them that reported us. Busyfeckingbodies. Sorry for the language but that kind of nosiness really gets on my wick.

I can still feel sick when I think of that night. I ran out of the place to get away from it. From them all. Afterwards when I realized I'd left them all to it I nearly died with the guilt. Any of them could have been killed. At least when I was there they'd listen to me. Most of the time anyway.

I spent that Friday night walking the streets but I did manage to get a bit of a kip down at the Irish Life Mall, there are a lot of nooky places in there and you'd be amazed who you'd meet. The Simon people came on their food run but I hid. I didn't trust them not to report me. I've always looked younger than I am.

But when I went home the next morning to face the music no one was there. I really panicked then. I was afraid to go to the police station and there was no way in the world that I was going to go down to Killarney Street to the social workers. Not yet. So for some reason that to this day I can't fathom, I got on the 10 bus and went up to the zoo.

I suppose I felt I'd be safe. They'd never think of the zoo – they'd know I'd be starving and they'd probably be looking for me in fast-food joints. I knew the zoo had a café and I did have a bit of money in my pocket to cover food and the entrance fee – I was working in the stockroom at Dunne's at the time and we'd just got paid.

Even still, I think that something stronger than the ordinary made me go to the Phoenix Park that day. It was like fate.

I saw Tom Bennett the minute I walked in through the stiles. He was gorgeous, in a chunky kind of way. His hair was slicked back straight in a DA and, although the Brylcreem darkened it, you could see it was red. Wet-coppery. I went weak at the knees. I always go for the Viking-type – you know, freckles, reddish or blond thick hair. And shoulders. Kind of like Brendan Gleeson or Liam Neeson. And if they wear glasses, particularly granny glasses, I'm done for. Don't ask me why. He was wearing glasses, black horn-rims. Like James Dean, or was that Buddy Holly?

He was with another bloke and a girl and they were strolling along by the lake there on the left-hand side, not the one with the flamingoes, the one with the ordinary swans and ducks. There were loads of seagulls there that day too, I remember. I suppose they were hoping for a free meal.

I walked casually after them, watching them. I don't know what I thought I was doing. I mean, my whole life was upside down and I knew that sooner or later I'd have to go to the police or the Eastern Health Board or at least Temple Street – although I hate hospitals with a passion – to find out what was happening with James, but here I was, passing the time of day in the zoo like a real person. I even forgot I was hungry while I was trying to work out whether "my" fella or the other bloke was the one with the girl. She was a bit of a chrissie, to tell you the truth, a bottle blonde with very thick kohl around her eyes and the platforms she was wearing made her spindly little legs look like ants' feelers. I would have been very disappointed in him if he'd been with her.

I needn't have worried. The other bloke, whom I subsequently found out was called Jason, kissed her and put his arm around her shoulders and since there was no aggro about it, I knew then that the fella I was interested in was free.

They stopped at the monkey house and he said something to the other two and then he laughed. Not sneering laughing, like you'd hear from a smart alec, but real, chuckly laughing, like he was saying something appreciative of the monkeys.

I dawdled along beside them, holding on to the metal rail in front of the cage and pretending to read the notice that told you what kind of monkeys they were.

And then the miracle. He turned around to me and he asked me if I'd like to join them. Just like that.

I was flabbergasted. I mean, I didn't even know he'd noticed I was there.

Well, you *are* all on your own, aren't you? he goes.

I can't remember what I said. Since then I've gone over that scene in my mind trillions of times but, as God is my judge, I could have answered him with the ten times table as far as I can tell. And the funny thing is that later, when we tried to remember together, he had no idea what I said either. We agreed it must be lurve!

Anyway, I joined them and the four of us had coffee and chips in the café. It turns out I was right about the girl. Common. No manners at all. She and Jason were eating each other – and this is with kids all over the place watching. And when they weren't eating each other they were bopping monkey nuts off each other's faces – that was in the days when you could buy monkey nuts in little twists of paper.

I was very embarrassed and I think so was Tom. It turned out that he wasn't a close friend of either of them, they were all just part of a big gang of people who knew each other and who had been supposed to go to the zoo that day. Only these three had turned up. So the two of us ignored the two of them as best we could and got on with getting to know each other. He had brilliant eyes. Dark blue.

I'm going all over the place with this, aren't I? So I suppose I'd better get back to what happened on day two of this summer story, that Sunday.

Despite the contretemps about me talking about James's future wife, the dinner had been as much of a success as I could have hoped for. He ate everything, the bit of lamb and potatoes, stewed apple and custard for sweet. Even the marrowfats, and he normally gives out about those. He even helped me with the dishes afterwards – picked up the dishcloth to dry without waiting to be asked. Yes, he was mellow for the first time in what seemed like weeks. I was being careful though, chatting to him about this and that and asking him the odd question but in a casual sort of way because I didn't want him to think that I was prying into his private affairs.

Out of the blue, he tells me he's planning on staying in that night. You could have knocked me over with a feather. The last weekend night James Devine stayed in by choice was the night after he was mugged on Harcourt Street after coming out of a club. Because he gets paid on a Friday, if he has two pennies to rub together he's off. But I must admit he's pretty good at managing his money. Not that he's saving or anything, but he's always good for a few bob if I run short myself.

By the way we're all called Devine. That was Mammy's name. Wouldn't it be a howl if all five of us pursued our five fathers to get their names off of them? The Eastern Health Board is running some sort of a tracing service now for natural parents. Fat chance we'd have. But I was building myself up to do it some day.

What's the matter? I say. Lose all your money on the horses or what?

No, he says, I'm just tired of that crowd. Anyway there's Italian soccer on the telly.

I'm so pleased he's going to be here that I don't even bother to object to having to sit watching a bunch of poncy Italian footballers for the night.

And then the knock comes to the door.

You know the way you're off your guard, lulled into a 'false sense of security'? When I think of it now . . .

There were two of them there and I knew immediately who they were. You can smell a policeman at a hundred yards. Maybe it's their shoe polish.

James Devine?

From behind me I hear James make a little noise. I can't describe it accurately, but you know in films when a train pulls into a station and it stops and there is an extra little whoosh of air? That kind of noise, but very quiet.

Who's asking for him? I say. My heart starts going like it's in a conga line. Don't I know full well who's asking for him.

They come in and ask to speak to him alone.

What can I do? When you know as much about cops as I do — coming from where I do it's the main part of your education — you know it's as well to be polite. At the beginning, anyway. They can do you for anything they like if you're not. So it's as well to play along until you see which way the wind is blowing.

James is as pale as the moon now. I go over to him and I touch him on the arm. It'll tell you how worried he is when he doesn't even flinch. Normally if you touch him, even accidentally, it's like you've put electric wires into him. Don't worry, I go, I'll just be in the bedroom. I glare over at the cops. Suddenly the room seems awfully small. Did you ever notice how even one policeman can fill up a room?

Seeing the way James is I'm not at all as confident as I'm trying to portray.

I pick up *Hamlet* ostentatiously. I won't be far away, I make the point again as loud as I can without sounding as if I'm trying to start an argument with the cops. I don't say anything more but I hope these two get the message that I know what's what and I won't tolerate any messing. I've long had the impression they pick on fellas James's age just out of spite.

Then I go into the bedroom and close the door.

Here I'd like to be able to write that I could only hear a murmur through the closed doors, or that I had to strain to hear what was being said. It would probably sound more like a real story. But not a bit of it. It's not only the facilities, all of Reddy's walls are like tissue-paper. They're only partitions. James threw a saucepan once — he was angry about something, I forget what — and it made a huge dinge. The wallpaper tore and there were splinters all over the cooker. I had to get a mirror down at the Daisy Market to cover the hole. I'm going to leave the mirror to Reddy when we move out of here, pretend I forgot it. He'll be so delighted to get something for nothing he won't bother to check under it. Otherwise he'd probably dun us for every penny of the security deposit.

And the doors are the cheapest you can buy.

I could hear perfectly what was going on.

I can't write here what was said. I just can't. It's too hard. The words were like brass knockers on my skull and still are. I can't put them in proper sentences on paper because I'd dissolve.

Sexual asssault. Police station. That's all I can manage.
Even that's after taking me ten minutes.

I nearly collapse when I realize. I'm holding *Hamlet* so
hard that the cover has got hot. I can't stand it any
longer. I crash out through the door. What's going on?

The two policemen look across at me as though I'm
someone they'd never seen before. But I'll never forget
James's face. Never. He's staring at me with eyes like
craters in the middle of this white moon of a face and he
looks about three years old. Like he did the first time I
brought him to that Eastern Health Board playgroup and
had to leave him there. I want to batter those cops to
within an inch of their lives and take him in my arms and
hug him to pieces and never let him go for as long as both
of us lived. How dare they. Who do they think they are.

Will someone tell me what's going on, please?

The taller of the two stands up and says that they have
to bring James to the station to ask him a few questions.
That there had been allegations.

What allegations? I say.

They tell me. Some girl has filed a complaint. Rape.

That was the word I couldn't write before. It's still
difficult.

James, I go, tell them. Come on, tell them—

He can't say anything. He's still looking at me with
those eyes, like an alien, he's getting younger-looking by
the minute. And the odd thing is, I notice for the first
time that his jeans are pressed. How come I never
noticed that earlier, when he got up or when we were
washing the dishes. Who ironed your jeans I? say.

Still he can't answer. And it's only then that the penny
drops. This is a boy who up to a few weeks ago wouldn't
even wash a sock of his own.

Ironed jeans.

He'd pulled a few all-nighters recently, telling me it's

twenty-firsts and parties and clubs and so on. I should have taken the condoms and the deodorant more seriously.

We have to go now, says the smaller cop. Sorry, Missus, he says to me.

Something happens to me inside, a sort of cool wash feeling, and I get very sharp. I'm getting him a solicitor, I say. He's entitled to a solicitor.

Thanks be to God for the telly.

Hang in there, I say to James and for the first time he blinks. I see the rims of his eyes have gone all red. It nearly does me in but I manage to hold on. I wouldn't lower myself in front of these other two gougers.

That's your prerogative, says policeman one. But at this stage we only want to ask your son a few questions.

He's not my son, I say. They look a bit surprised at that. Maybe I'm not as young-looking for my age as I think I am.

It's the small things, isn't it? My image of him being taken away is of the back of his neck with the collar up on one side.

Wouldn't you know it, the first phone I try is out of order although it wasn't vandalized, just ordinary out of order. It used to be awful, you could never get a phone that worked, but since they got card phones in Dublin and put in those steel cables and took out the glass in the boxes, the gurriers don't seem to bother. They still smash the glass in those nice new bus shelters, though. Why they do that I don't know, because you'd think they wouldn't want to get wet any more than the rest of us. Maybe they don't travel in buses. It's probably faster for them to get where they want to go if they rob a car.

The next phone box is OK. I'm still thinking sharp. Since it's a Sunday, I know there's only a duty social worker on and I know there's no point in ringing her.

They're always snowed under with work and they take
the emergencies first so problems like mine are always
sliding down the queue. The best thing is to go straight
to whom I want. Luckily I have Pat McCartan's number
still, from the time he sorted James out with that bit of
trouble he got into when he was sixteen. I don't care that
he was a politician as well as a solicitor at the time. I'm
not one of those begrudgers that says people shouldn't be
allowed to make millions. If they're good at what they
do they deserve everything they make and, as far as I'm
concerned, Pat was great that time. He got the Probation
Act for James. And James hasn't been in one bit of
trouble since.

Unfortunately he was out that Sunday but whoever
was there, I don't know if it was his wife, she gave me
the number of another solicitor to ring. This fella's name
is Patrice Murphy. I find it hard to believe that this is a
real name. He was probably a Patrick and had to change
it to distinguish himself from all the other Pat Murphys.

I don't want to go on too much about the rest of that
day. I was able to keep going because I'd things to do to
help James. I got the solicitor and I have to say he was
very efficient. I mean, he came down to the cop shop at
Fitzgibbon Street right away and he had a nice car so he
had to have had a bit of success. The thing was, though,
he did look like he was only James's age. At least Pat
McCartan has grey hair even if he does have a young face.
Solicitors nearly always have young, well-padded faces,
have you noticed that?

James was arrested.

And despite Patrice Murphy's best efforts to get him
released into my custody, he was put into a cell for the
night. We were going to have to wait until the morning
until we knew whether a judge would give him bail. I

can't remember much of what the room was like where they eventually let me see him. I think it was quite small.

The cops themselves were quite good as it turned out, they let me bring in his own pyjamas and toothbrush and his ruddy deodorant. And of course I had to bring in his good clothes for the court. Luckily we'd been able to buy him a new jacket for the previous Christmas.

Neither of us can think of anything to say at first when he's brought into the room where I was told I could see him. Eventually he asks me would I ring his work first thing in the morning to say he wouldn't be in for the day. Say I'm sick, he goes.

Of course I'll ring them, I go. Although it wasn't going to be easy doing that. We're watched like hawks on the cleaning job in case we lift anything. And making free phone calls is regarded as lifting. Anyway, I wouldn't want anyone to know our business. They're nice, the crowd at work, but I like to keep a bit of distance.

Silence again.

Don't sign anything, I say to him next. It's your word against hers. Who is she anyway—

He's looking at the floor. Muttering something.

What?

He says louder that he knows there's no point in denying anything, even if what he's being charged with isn't true. That women have it all sewn up. That I'm pathetic. That I don't know what it's like in the modern world. You only have to look crooked at some girl now and she and all her mates are crying rape.

I don't know what to believe, of course, but here and in this situation is not a place to get into an argument about greater society. Tell me what happened, I go, in your own words.

You won't believe me either, he says. Sort of hopeless.

I get that feeling again, a fierce wave, where I want to smash open the walls with my bare fists and let him out of there and the two of us fly away to Spain or Timbuktu or somewhere safe.

Tell me, I say again, at least try me.

He looks at the floor. I can't, he says.

I wish there wasn't a damned policeman standing at the door only three feet away from us. Then James looks back up at me and there are now big tears in his eyes. I haven't seen tears in that fella's eyes since he was seven. It turns me inside out but I certainly don't want to start blubbing in front of him or the policeman. I stand up and say as steadily as I can that I'll see him in the court tomorrow.

Can I give him a goodbye hug? I ask the policeman, who nods.

I go around the table and I put my arms around him but he doesn't stand up. He just sits there like a rag doll. Well, not a rag doll, his shoulders and chest feel like a hollow drum. Except I can feel his insides shaking.

Just tell me one thing, I whisper to him while I'm still holding on to his shoulders. Is this why you've been in such bad humour for the last few weeks? Did you know something like this might happen?

No, not really, he says back, but I was worrying about why she suddenly changed towards me.

Well, at least that's something, I go, I wasn't just imagining things. The policeman then tells us it's time for James to leave and that moment has to rank very near the lowest in my life.

→ Four ←

Patrice Murphy comes to the flat that night. He asks me about my means and whether, if the judge grants bail, I can come up with it. He tells me I'm going to have to show that I can.

The hell I can. If I've to rob a bank I can.

Well, do I have a bank book or something to show I'm good for the money in case James skips the jurisdiction? And do I know two people who could give indpendent sureties? The usual would be about ten thousand in all.

Ten thousand? I can't believe it. My brain is skipping and hopping over the figure. To me that's Lotto money. I promise you James won't skip the jurisdiction, I say but my voice sounds as weak as a baby's. Anyway, he doesn't even have a passport.

Patrice Murphy looks at me as though I've lost it. There's England, he says, very quietly.

He won't go to England, I say. That's a definite.

Have you any means at all, bank books? Any valuables?

I tell him about my post-office bonds. As I told you, I've been putting money away, into those bonds because I believe they're the safest. There would be a couple of thousand, I go, actually two thousand eight hundred and fifty. But nothing near what we'd need—

Is there no one at all you'd know? Do you have a bank

account? Could you go to the manager? What about friends? Employers?

I shake my head. Employers? The only possibility is the deli owner but I'd be very hesitant there.

Then I think of Patsy, but I reject the thought as quickly as it's occurred to me. Patsy and I are best friends but I wouldn't even consider asking her for money. For a start she's always going on about how Martin's business is going from strength to strength, yet how as a family they never have two pennies to rub together what with the drain on them from all the children's activities.

But even if she wasn't always talking like that, I would never put myself under an obligation to her. This is a disaster. How much time do we have? I ask Patrice Murphy.

He purses his lips as though he's trying to look wise. The judge will have to be satisfied in the court tomorrow if we're to get James out after the hearing. Bring the bonds along with you tomorrow. How about valuables? Jewellery? He looks around the flat. Looks back at me. His face says it all.

I think. Review my measly possessions. Maybe another thousand, I say, one thousand two hundred?

Well, that makes four you can come up with, he says. We'll see. I'll try to talk to the other side. Bring everything with you tomorrow, will you? He's still putting on the wise act but the matter-of-fact language impresses me. He seems to know his stuff.

I see him out. Sit down to draw breath. I start feeling sorry for myself, why is it always us, what are we going to do, et cetera . . .

I catch myself at it. Hate it. Self-pity has to be by far the most destructive of emotions.

Right, I say to myself and stand up again. Shut up. Stop whingeing. James is not dead. He doesn't have terminal

cancer. He's not on heroin, he's only in trouble. And
he's just accused not convicted. Look on the bright side,
it could all be a misunderstanding, it could all be cleared
up in ten minutes. We have a great solicitor and who
knows, we might get a great judge tomorrow who'll
trust me when I say James will turn up.

And the time factor was working in our favour, so that
was in the plus column too. Carthy's Pawnbrokers in
Marlborough Street opens at half nine and James's court
appearance wasn't due until half ten. Luckily I get off
work every morning at nine. There was going to be
enough time. Just.

I do a quick mental survey of our hockable items.
James's bike is on the drip but we've paid off a mere six
months of it – anyway, he needs it for work – and the
telly's rented. So they're out.

But the haul turns out to be respectable enough. The
payments are finished on the video, and on the micro-
wave and on the coal-effect electric fire. They're ours
and we can live without them. All biz now, I make out a
list in order of preference. Jewellery and video first, I'd
get most money on them. Electric fire next – luckily it is
the summer.

Thank God I've resisted the temptation all these years
to cash in Mammy's bits and pieces. Sentimentality, I
suppose, because God knows there were times when
James and I could have used the money. I think some of
them are quite good, particularly the Victorian mourning
brooch and the rose-gold neck chain and garnet ring.
There's a silver christening spoon as well.

There's one thing that I'd part with only as a last
resort, though – a tiny marcasite brooch in the shape of a
peacock. I always wear that, I change it from lapel to
lapel. She told me once that marcasite is diamond chips
and of course I believed her until I looked it up one day in

my dictionary and found otherwise. I never told her, though, because she thought her peacock brooch was the most valuable thing she owned and she always told me it was for me after she was gone and I was to mind it.

I don't care whether it's valuable or not. It was diamonds to her.

Anyway, I have to have something left belonging to her, don't I? Just in case I can't get the rest of the jewellery back out . . .

Isn't it funny how things go in circles in your life? First of all, Carthy's was the pawn Mammy used, I had a path worn to it from our place. And second, with the exception of the peacock brooch, I never wore any of that jewellery, it just never looked right on me somehow and now I know why. It's fate. I was meant to save it. In a strange way she was saving it for me for when it was needed to help James.

It goes to show that she's still looking after us in her own way.

I bet you're surprised that she had such quality jewellery.

You see, Mammy came originally from a well-to-do family down the country in Birr, Co. Offaly. Believe it or not she was a Protestant. She never practised, of course. Where could you, if you were living in the flats? Even if she wanted to − or if they'd have her which, of course, was unlikely. And I suppose she had us baptized Catholics because it was simply easier for her. There were more people to look after us that way, like there were more schools.

One thing I have to hand to her is that with all her vicissitudes the jewellery never got hocked. Not once. (And I'd know because I'd be the one sent with it.)

She even had it hidden away from all the so-called friends. I suppose somewhere deep down she felt that to own a little bit of good jewellery would maintain some shreds of her dignity. The temptation must have been huge, though, especially when she was having a hard time and moaning for relief. Wouldn't you have to admire her?

Now here was I hocking it.

Oh well, I thought that Sunday, the stuff won't be in for long. And I reckoned that with a small amount of luck it wouldn't be necessary to give in the other electrical appliances. Like her, I wanted to keep up a certain standard if at all possible.

I suppose it's because she was a Protestant that Mammy knew unusual hymns. She had a very nice voice — that's probably where I got it. There was one time when she was just out of Coolmine and she was straight for a few weeks — that was a brilliant time, they hadn't taken Nicola, the youngest, yet — she taught me one of those hymns. Abide With Me. I believe they sang it on the *Titanic* when it was going down.

Or was that Nearer My God To Thee? I saw *A Night To Remember* on the telly the other night. I should be able to remember which hymn they sang. Wasn't it a brilliant film?

Anyway, she taught it to me and I remember she was holding Nicola on her lap at the time and feeding her like a real mother. Oh, it was fantastic. I can still remember the words, every single one of them.

But my favourite was Starbright. On her good nights she used to say it to me when she was putting me to bed. Starlight Starbright First Star I See Tonight. I Wish I May I Wish I Might, Have The Wish I Wish Tonight. And then she'd kiss me on the forehead. I can't bear to think about it.

It's funny how you remember things you learned at that age. I even remember the first verse of Wordsworth's

bloody daffodils. And An Old Woman of the Roads.
Although she was a homeless poor old thing, I was quite
easily able to put myself in her position. It's funny, but
when I got sentimental about the kind of place we were
going to get for ourselves I always saw us in a little house
with the stool and all, just like her.

> Oh to have a little house
> To own the hearth and stool and all
> The heaped up sods upon the fire
> The pile of turf again the wall . . .

Et cetera. In my imagination, the wind was always
howling outside my little house and the rain was bashing
against my snug little windowpanes. We never had sods
stacked up ourselves, of course, but our nun — *not*
Concepta, I hasten to add — described what turf should
look like and I could just see it. She said it smelled
pungent and wrote the word on the blackboard. For days
I was trying to find ways to slip pungent into sentences.

> I could be busy all the day
> Cleaning and sweeping hearth and floor . . .

Because of that poem, I even practised sweeping up in
our place. (That was a riot, you'd want to see our place!)
I'd found a brush handle outside in one of the entryways
and I pretended it had bristles. Imagination is a great
thing, isn't it?

But to get back to the jewellery. The neck chain and
the mourning brooch were Mammy's own grandmother's. That would have to make them more than a
hundred years old.

Unfortunately that Birr, Co. Offaly, branch of the
family wants nothing to do with this branch in Dublin

and I wouldn't know any of them if they stopped me in the street. I wouldn't blame them for disowning us, I suppose. Still, it must have been hard. I know she tried her best.

I suppose at this stage you're wondering why I wasn't taken into care when all the others were?

Well, I just wouldn't stay anywhere, that's the holy all of it. I kicked up murder and I ran back to her all the time. And in the beginning, anyway, things weren't too bad and they kept giving Mammy chances. I slipped through the net, sort of.

And by the way, no one could say she ever, *ever* abused me. I'd kill anyone who said that. She never abused any of us. All right, under the definition of neglect, I suppose in some ways we were neglected but she did her best. She certainly did her best when she was able to.

Some of the boyfriends weren't all that bad at the beginning either. There was one – I'm nearly sure he was Francesca's father because he was the one who lasted the longest. About three years. And Franscesa was born sometime around then. This fella, his name was Joey, he was from Kerry or somewhere and he was a bit of fun. He even bought clothes for us. The only problem was he kept disappearing for weeks at a time. And when he'd come back there's be some other fella there and there'd be an almighty row and the social workers'd come again and I'd be delivered up to my regular foster family and I'd run away after a day.

I must point out that no blame should attach to those people, the foster parents, I won't tell you their names because I'm not sure they'd want to be associated with us any more. They were kind, and they had a nice house, lovely and warm. I loved having a real bath.

I absolutely hated the real children, though. And I know they hated me. They'd hold their noses when I came in the door. Behind their Mammy and Daddy's backs, of course.

Another thing was, I could never get used to a Daddy around the place, giving orders.

I keep meaning to try to re-establish contact with Francesca for one last try, but I just haven't got around to it. I did make efforts for a while, wrote regularly, but she kept rebuffing me and eventually I lost heart. I know she's in England somewhere because she's in touch with her foster family and the mother told me a couple of years ago she was still there. The woman wouldn't give me the latest address, though, she said that'd have to come from Francesca herself.

I suppose I can understand it, she set off on her new life and she wanted a complete clean break with the old stuff. We'd all be painful reminders of what she has escaped from. She'd be about thirty now. She might even be married and I might even have nieces and nephews.

Justine and Nicola were always a twosome. They're in Australia, and although I have their addresses and I make sure to remember their birthdays, I get only a Christmas card from Nicola and maybe a postcard, once in a blue moon, from Justine. At least it's something. Neither of them is married, although in her last card Nicola dropped a hint that she had a boyfriend. Isn't it terrible the way people of the same flesh and blood – or half it, anyway – can so easily scatter?

Some day I'll go out to Australia. The girls haven't invited me yet, but I'm sure they'd be delighted. I have this lovely fantasy about my fiftieth birthday, that I'll have a bit of money put by and we'll have a real reunion, all five of us. Dream on, Ange!

It was very lonely that Sunday night without James. It was unusually quiet outside with hardly any traffic and whatever way the wind was blowing I could hear

Eason's clock chiming into the early hours, all the way from O'Connell Street. It wasn't like the times he'd pulled all-nighters, this was completely different. This time I knew where he was, you see, I could picture him. I kept seeing his white face and those big eyes, and wondering was he sleeping. I doubted it. The papers are always full of how awful these remand cells are and how kids are always committing suicide in them. I had a terrible time visualizing. Graffiti. Concrete. A really hard mattress. A toilet bowl in the corner. No seat or lid. Stink. All night I saw worse and worse things. I couldn't wait for five o'clock to come when it would be time to get up.

I'm not usually introspective but in between thinking about James I did bring up a lot about my own life all that night. And oddly enough one of the people I thought about a lot was Tom Bennett. There was never any real chance we'd get married, I see that now. But, as I think I said earlier, I did have high hopes at one stage. I thought Mrs Angela Bennett had a great ring to it.

When I got back to the flats after the zoo that first day I met him, there was nobody in our place and I had to go around asking. It killed me, you could see their little smiles and their little slitty eyes. They were all delighted that the Devines were out at last. Nobody said so, of course, with their phoney sympathy and their where-were-you-love, we-were-looking-for-you.

They were in their eye. Couldn't wait to get rid of us. As if we were the only dysfunctional family in the place.

I couldn't avoid it any longer, I had to go up to Temple Street to ask after James. To keep me determined I kept my mind fixed on a bright thing – I had a date with Tom Bennett to go to the pictures on the following Wednesday. He worked most nights, he was a shift worker in Cadbury's, but he had Wednesdays and Fridays off.

They were all right to me in Temple Street. They were used to it, I suppose.

But James was already gone. To a family, somewhere up on the Navan Road. The nurse wasn't supposed to tell me that but she was nice. She saw how upset I was, I guess. I was used to the drill by then, of course. The new family was an emergency homing; they'd keep him until he went to a proper foster home.

Something snapped in me. Over my dead body. I was old enough to look after him — all right, I wasn't his mother but I'd certainly had enough practice at it. And I was seventeen. All you had to be was sixteen for you not to have to go into care yourself. I was a responsible adult and I knew the provisions of the 1908 Children's Act. He was my little brother. I wanted to mind him and that was that.

Apart from anything else, it was something to do, a project to keep my mind off where Mammy might be or what might be happening to her. So I pushed and pushed until I managed to persuade the powers that be that he'd be better off with me than with strangers. I had a brilliant social worker that time. (She left to go to the North afterwards and I really missed her. This was the same one who brought us all on the picnic to Brittas Bay with the tartan rug.) She was always on at me that I had to develop a life of my own and stop worrying about all the others, but when she saw I was absolutely set about James, she came on my side and some way or other she managed to get her bosses to give me a chance.

She got James back out of the emergency foster home and I was allowed bring him home with me on a trial basis. It was the same evening I was to meet Tom Bennett and she even babysat for me when I went down to explain that I wouldn't be able to go to the pictures with him as we had planned. I bet that was against the rules of the Eastern Health Board. That's why she was brilliant. She used her noggin instead of always going by the book. I know they have to have rules because otherwise they might be left holding the baby. Joke. Ha ha. But I'm not like that and she knew. She trusted me.

I rush to Eason's to meet Tom Bennett. All the way down I'm peppering. I wouldn't blame him if he did a runner. I mean, who wants to take on a girl with a two-month-old baby? Especially in that era — this was nineteen years ago.

He's here, waiting already — and he looks fabulous. He has on this crocodile jacket and a black polo-neck and very, very tight jeans. He isn't wearing his glasses. He wears contacts because he plays football. I'm very flattered, I can tell you, that he put in the contacts just because he was meeting me. (Even though, of course, I love fellas in glasses as I told you already.)

And he's great about what's happened, he really is. (I never blamed him afterwards. It was nobody's fault that it didn't work out with Tom Bennett and me.)

I explain the whole thing to him. Well, not the *whole* thing. I don't tell yet about Mammy being missing again, and the boyfriend, and the other three in care. I just say that, owing to circumstances beyond my control, I have to mind James for a little while. It's a desperately windy evening, and my hair keeps blowing around my face so I have to talk to him holding it back with both hands.

There's one awful moment when I'm finished and he doesn't say anything. A bit of litter blows around his legs and sticks there and he has to bend down to peel it off.

Even the top of his head is gorgeous.

Don't worry about it, he says. We can meet some other time. Then he says he understands about James. That he himself is the youngest of twelve and although his mother is still alive there are so many of them that one or other of his sisters always had to mind him too when he was growing up. (I already know they live in Finglas. There are lots of huge families up there.) When, I go, when can we meet?

In for a penny in for a pound. I'm not in a position to be shy about this, I don't have time.

He doesn't back off like most of them would have, doesn't just say, See you, or I'll be in touch. No, he makes another definite arrangement with me for the following week. I know I'm home and dry when he asks me would I have time now just for one quick coffee.

Sure, I say, although I had promised the social worker I'd only be half an hour.

We go to the nearest place, I can't remember whether it was Cafolla's or Forte's or Wimpy's or what. And as for remembering what the coffee was like, it might even have been tea.

Another plus. His manners. He makes me sit down while he goes up to the counter.

He comes back with the two cups and sits down, gives me this smile of his. It pulls me in feet first like going down a warm water slide.

We start to chat. Usually I'm the one that talks the hind legs off a donkey but I find I hardly have to talk at all (even if I could!). He doesn't ask a thing about my family and in my opinion this is very tactful. Instead, he tells me about his family and his job in Cadbury's and how he's seen so much chocolate he'll never eat another square of it for the rest of his life. You wouldn't either, he goes, if you saw what we have to deal with. Big brown lakes of the stuff. I leave it to your imagination as to what it'd remind you of.

I'd like to be tested, I say. I've always had a sweet tooth.

I don't have a sweet tooth at all, but that'll give you an idea of how I was behaving that day.

Afterwards, he kisses me goodbye, right there in the open in O'Connell Street. Not a snog, a respectful, gentlemanly goodbye kiss.

That night, when I'm alone and James is sleeping, I do the cross-off game. (I'm not sure if it's just a Dublin thing, I don't think so.) You know it? Where you write his name, and then your own name directly underneath, and then you cross off the common letters and you count off what you're left with. *Love Like Hate Adore Kiss Court Marry* . . .

It came out that for him it was Court and for me it was Love. Not great, I think you'll agree. Court is up against the wall, slam, bam and thank you, Mam.

So I redid it as Thomas Bennett versus Angela Devine. Much, much better! Almost the best of all! (Which would have been for both of us to have come out as Marry.)

Would you believe this time I came out Love and he came out Marry?

It was cheating in a way – it's supposed to be the name you're known by, but Thomas was his real name, after all.

I whirr across the floor and into bed. Two feet off the ground, like I'm an angel.

→ Five ←

James was all smiley and cuddly when I got home and the social worker had bought us a block of ripple ice cream to celebrate our homecoming and she even gave me a bag of Babygros, hardly used. She explained all about my entitlements – actually they were James's entitlements – but she needn't have bothered. I knew them backwards, everyone in the flats did.

I listened, of course, I didn't want to be impolite. It paid off. Because there was one entitlement I didn't know about – we could apply for some money to buy a little pram or a go-car. Nowadays I see them all with those Lolita buggies. Ten a penny. Fifteen- and-sixteen-year-olds (that's why we call then Lolitas) proud as punch walking in pairs down Henry Street with buggies that wouldn't disgrace a millionaire. But back then the buggy thing was still only in its infancy. Ha ha!

Poor Mammy could have done with this particular entitlement. Maybe if she'd had a buggy or a little pram she might have had something to do. You know, push us down to the river for a walk or something. But I suppose they couldn't have given her a buggy because it would have gone down to the pawn first thing.

I asked her once how she came to Dublin and why she didn't stay with her family in Birr, Co. Offaly. She said she'd tell me when I was older. She never did, of course, she was dead before I asked her again.

But there's no point in dwelling on what might have been. I believe in looking to the future. And I was born with certain advantages. Like I always knew that if I ever sincerely wanted to discover my father's identity I was in a far better position than any of the others. Their fathers flitted in and out — flies amongst flies whose names none of us really knew and who probably ended up in the morgue.

But mine wasn't one of them. She told me once I hadn't been conceived in Dublin, only born here.

And over the years she'd say other things to me when she was relatively well and feeling soft, little starry things, like teasing me about being a bit of a culchie. Or she'd warn me to watch out for romance with the boy next door. They seem to be the nicest, she'd say, but they're always the most deadly. And she'd get this wistful look on her face.

There was enough of that nature so that when I put them all together I'd have to conclude that to begin a search for my father I'd have to start in Birr, Co. Offaly.

Of course I couldn't be *absolutely* certain, only ninety-nine per cent.

But one thing for definite. I definitely knew I'd be looking for someone with fair hair, since I'm the only one of the five of us with it. Mammy's was black — did I tell you that already? Maybe it's because of my father that I always go for the Viking type! Mind you, I always figured that if I ever did find him, the first thing I'd do is I'd probably give him a dig.

Then I'd think it needn't necessarily have been his fault. He could have been very young. He mightn't even have known about me, Mammy was only nineteen when I was born, the same age James is now. My father might have been only seventeen, or even sixteen – or so I fantasized when I was in a forgiving mood. For some reason I saw him always in a meadow. With cows and daisies and buttercups and skylarks joyously trilling overhead, like in an Emma Thompson picture. Birr, Co. Offaly, had a hell of a lot to live up to in the picturesque stakes if I ever got there.

But as a matter of fact I can't stand that Ode to a Skylark by Percy Bysshe Shelley.

That Sunday night when I was lying awake in bed and picturing James in his hard, horrible little cell, I realized how much I was going to have on my plate with this court problem. So I decided I was going to pull out of doing the Irish exam. There would always be next year.

It was a great relief. Irish is too hard. In the Inter, I only wrote my name on the Irish paper. Just my name in Irish and not another comma.

At least with some of the other subjects I did try. But that time I couldn't wait to get out of school – legally you had to stay there until you were fifteen and I suppose I was just marking time. Mammy was bad during that period so I had a lot more to think about than history and geography. Certainly more than Irish.

There are too many haitches, like Devine in Irish is Ní Dhaibhín. I think they put in the haitches to keep Irish exclusive. I get the feeling that those Gaeilgeórí are a secret society, like the Masons, and their secret sign is that they all wear jumpers.

Maybe I'm prejudiced but did you ever notice that they seem to think they're comedians? Éibhear Ó Súilleabháin, our teacher, was always making a joke out of my name. Angela Devine. Divine. Angela. Angel. Get it? Angel Divine. Maybe it was Mammy's sense of humour.

But I was furious that it took someone in a jumper to point it out to me. I'm not *that* thick, am I?

Ping pong ping pong, pong ping ping pong . . . Eason's clock down in O'Connell Street again. I thought the dawn would never come that Monday morning and then, when the alarm did go off, I was afraid of the day.

James won't be in this morning because he's sick. I'm looking over my shoulder, with the telephone right up to my mouth. Thank God this particular courier company believes in starting early. It's seven o'clock and I'm standing there with the polisher going full blast, pushing it round and round in circles so this bit of lino will nearly have a hole in it by the time I'm finished. That bitch of a supervisor creeps around. I'm sure you won't believe this but she wears slippers. I swear to God, she comes in in her shoes all right but then she changes into her slippers. Real bedroom slippers with blue fur all around the uppers. You never hear her until she's right behind you.

I'm passed on to the base controller and I'm sure I can hear your woman coming so I hang up.

I polish as though my life depends on it but it turns out to be a false alarm. I move to the next desk and dial all over again. Hello, it's me again, I was holding on for the controller and got cut off.

He takes like a million years to get on. Hello, who's this?

This is James Devine's sister. He's sick and he won't be in this morning. I'm sorry for the short notice.

Heavy sighing on the other end. Look, I go, I'm just his sister. Don't shoot the messenger. And I put down the phone.

We're six floors up and the sky outside is gorgeous so I feel a bit better about the day coming up. Pink and gold. It's a late dawn because it was cloudy this morning but it's still lovely.

You may have gathered by now that yellow, and gold in particular, is my favourite colour. I love skies in the summer-time. No matter what the weather is going to be like for the rest of the day – and it could be howling when we're being picked up in the minibus – it very rarely seems to be raining when the sun comes up. We're usually working somewhere where there's a huge amount of glass. Most days, certainly from February to October, I manage to see the dawn or at least the early sun. I regard it as one of the perks of the job. (That's unless she puts me working on the western side of the building out of spite – she's caught me more than once mooning out, Dreamy Drawers, she calls me. She should talk. In her slippers.)

It makes you humble. No matter what happens, that sun will come up tomorrow morning and that sky will still be gold under whatever clouds are there. Our little problems don't amount to a hill of beans, eh?

Today is so lovely I hope it's an omen.

I'm dusting now and I can't stop wondering how James is feeling. He'll get bail anyway – that solicitor seemed very confident.

The little so-and-so, I'll kill him when I get him home. He'll tell me every last detail, I'll make sure of it. I've been in court before so I'm much better off than some poor bitch who's going in there for the first time. That was the children's court, though, which is supposed to be much better than real court.

Still, I'm quaking. I hope she won't be there. She probably won't, isn't she just a witness, or something, and don't they try to spare her until the very last minute.

I wonder what she looks like, the girl? What's her family like?

I never met Tom Bennett's family. Wait 'til you hear why!

Time and again he said he was going to bring me up there but he never did. About six months after we started going out together I asked him what was the mystery. Was he ashamed of me? Of us coming from the flats? He was really upset that I'd even think of such a thing.

Well, why not, then, I go, do you have something to hide up there, maybe? Are you all on the game or into something else hookey? I was only joking, naturally. Someone as straight and respectful as him couldn't come from that kind of a family.

It was the only occasion during the whole time we knew each other that I thought I was in danger of getting a clatter from him. He didn't, of course, but he looked like he might. If only I'd known then what I found out later I wouldn't have been making such an eejit of myself.

He dashed away from me and then came back – we were in Talbot Street, I remember – and he stood in front of me and denied vehemently that he was ashamed of me or anything like it. He was yelling. Everyone was looking and I was mortified.

Now that I think back on it, he was probably *too* upset. That usually means you've hit the nail on the head. It should have set off my alarm bells.

I let it go, though, because I didn't want to provoke him any further.

It wasn't the only row we had, of course. They never started that way, always about something else. Usually tiny little things. I remember one day we were in Bewley's. James was in a high chair and he had jam all over his face. (Tom Bennett was good about that. Half the times I saw him I had to bring James along.) We'd had a lovely day. It was a Sunday. We'd been for a bus ride all the way out to Dalkey and back. James had been as good as gold.

Anyway we started arguing about whether the sugar in the packets was Irish or English. Pathetic. A little thing like that to develop into an almighty hoo-hah! What started with packets of sugar ended up with us having a fierce row about the English still being in the North of Ireland and whether Patrick Pearse should have held the Rising or not in 1916. This is one of the reasons I hate politics in this country. You can never have a calm conversation with anyone about the subject.

Up to that moment I wouldn't have put Tom Bennett in the Republican camp. And to tell you the truth, I probably shouldn't have argued with him at all because he didn't say anything I hadn't heard a million times before in pubs or at a sing-song. Roddy McCorley's Going To Die On The Bridge Of Toome Today? How many times have you heard that one? Heard the passion? Especially from someone with the few jars on . . .

I suppose a lot of our skins are very thin in that North of Ireland department.

It later turned out that he didn't care a fig one way or the other about Patrick Pearse or the Rising. It was just argument for argument's sake. I think I must have had a bit of PMT because, looking back, my reaction was completely out of proportion. I whipped James out of the high chair and stormed out of Bewley's and I didn't give a sugar, no pun intended, what anyone thought of me. He didn't try to stop me.

Of course I was sorry by the time I got to O'Connell Bridge. I ran back straight away. He was gone. I can still see the empty chair where he'd been sitting.

I was frantic. I ran up and down Westmoreland Street and D'Olier Street and then ran the length of O'Connell

Street to where all the 40 buses left for Finglas. Poor James got a terrible bumping around in his buggy.

It was no use, Tom Bennett seemed to have vanished into thin air.

I rang Cadbury's the next day but they said he was on a day off.

He turned up at the flat the following night and even though I had my rollers in I threw myself at him the minute I saw him in the doorway, and cried and couldn't say enough how sorry I was.

That was the first night we ever had sex. And we got engaged the next morning.

Our flat that time wasn't bad, thanks to that brilliant social worker I told you about – and to the Vincent.

Poor Mammy always hated having the Vincent.

Come to think of it, maybe she didn't like them because she was a Protestant. Maybe she thought they'd put a hex on her something, or make her say the Rosary with them (of course, they never do) but I think it's more likely she hated accepting charity. Towards the end, she didn't care and ironically, the place was never better furnished than when she was too far gone to appreciate it.

She shouldn't have minded, she could have been killed in the rush. More than half the families in our flats got help from the Vincent de Paul.

That morning we got engaged, I fed and changed James and put him into his playpen and then Tom Bennett ordered me back to bed. That gave me the greatest feeling. Fluttery and excited. Even sexual. But strange, too. I wasn't so sure I was going to be able to let anyone, even Tom Bennett, boss me and James around even in a nice way.

He was taking another day off, even though he wasn't

supposed to. He didn't even ring. Feck it, he says, it's not every day a fella gets engaged.

Suppose they sack you, I go. We have to start saving up immediately and we can't have you unemployed.

Not at all, he goes back. Will you stop worrying. Leave the worrying about our future to me, I'm your man now and you'll have to trust me to take care of us all.

It was a single bed and before I got back into it, I insisted on changing the sheets. They were all stained. Sex was not like I expected. It was very smelly for a start. But it didn't hurt half as much as I'd been led to believe. I quite enjoyed it, although I believe you're not supposed to enjoy it your first time. I didn't ask him if it was his first time. I didn't care a damn – that was all in the past and the future was what was on our minds. It was pretty obvious that it was my first time so he didn't have to ask me!

The second time I was sore from the previous night but I got over it. And from then on I knew it was going to be OK. Tom was avid for it. I knew that morning I was going to have to work miracles and get a washing machine from the Vincent! Or, failing that, I thought I might try the *Gay Byrne Radio Show* fund. You do that through your social worker and they seem to specialize in washing machines, or they did at that time. I wouldn't tell them why I needed it, mind you. If they knew the reason I wanted it they mightn't think I was all that worthy a cause!

Now will you bring me up to meet your family? I say, when we're standing at the window having a cup of tea afterwards.

Of course, he says.

When?

On my next day off.

I'll never forget that moment. The window in our

place looked out over the yard and for once it was really respectable-looking, as pristine as a new twenty-pence piece. The Corporation had just removed all the graffiti, and for good measure, they'd cleaned away all the rubbish, the oil and dog dirt and broken glass, even the burned out Volkswagen that had been there for years. They'd put concrete tubs in, filled with wallflowers which, so-far-touch-wood, the gurriers had left alone. And the scent! You could have got drunk on that scent. The sun was shining after a spell of rain and those wallflowers wafted all the way up to our balcony. There were kids on the swings.

This was the Communion season and there were two little girls in their Communion outfits sitting together on one end of the see-saw, heads bent over the Communion bags as they counted their lolly. It didn't matter that morning how long the yard was going to stay like this because looking down at it all, the scene and the moment became fixed for me. I was going to meet Tom Bennett's family and at last have a real family to be part of.

The only fly in the ointment was, would they take to James. He said of course they would, there'd be no problem. Weren't they well used to kids? Anyway, who wouldn't take to him. He was at a lovely age.

He sure was. Then.

I know every mother since Eve has said, 'If only they'd stay like that . . .' And if I feel that, and I'm only a sister, I hate to think how a real mother must feel when she looks at the scowling hard chaw who's suddenly shot out of her little chuckling baby. It's like being related to The Incredible Hulk.

They were very decent at the pawn that Monday morning, they gave me exactly five hundred for the jewellery and the christening spoon and fifty for the video – although the pawnbroker himself said he should only be giving me twenty-five. They even remembered me from years before and asked after James.

Grand, I said, he's grand, never better. Stroppy, of course, you know how they all are at that age . . .

Even in the middle of my panic about the court and what was facing me in the next hour, I felt a pang parting with Mammy's jewellery. Naturally, I was going to do my damnedest to get it all back. I had six months to redeem it but I'd no illusions about how difficult it was going to be. The case probably wouldn't come up for months and months. There's a terrible backlog, according to Patrice Murphy, and not half enough judges.

I was going to have to find something else to do that'd earn money. A bit of private cleaning, maybe. The pay is lousy but it's into your hand.

Some of the women at work are always bitching about the deductions from our wages, but to tell you the truth, I don't really mind. Like, where is the Government going to get the money for the social welfare entitlements and all the rest of it if it's not from the PAYE worker? From farmers? Give us a break.

We're all socialists until we get a few bob. (Come back to me after I've won the Lotto!) But for the moment anyway, I fervently believe in helping those less fortunate than ourselves – after all, I've been there, done that, got the T-shirt. At the very least, my own deductions are an investment in our future. The old-age pension or invalidity if anything ever happened to me.

The dole is different. I'd die rather than queue up for the dole. As long as there's breath left in my body et cetera. I'd do anything, skivvy in McDonald's, *anything*. We've paid our way since I was able to and we're going to continue to do so.

Like everyone else, though, money into my hand is what I really want.

It was a quarter to ten when I got out of Carthy's and rushed over to the GPO to buy more certs and bonds with the cash. I never had that much cash before, I never *saw* that much cash before. I held on to my handbag for dear life, I can tell you. I still had sixty from my own bits and bobs of wages and from a few spare notes and coins I found in James's room so we were going to be OK. I kept ten back for us to live on until next Friday. So, all in all, I was bringing evidence that I could come up with three thousand four hundred and fifty pounds into the court. I hoped it would be enough.

I was in rag order when I got to the court because I had to run all the way down the Quays to the Four Courts.

The girl wasn't there, thank God, but her mother was. With her pussycat bow under her chin.

No, I have to be fair. The poor woman looked shattered. That's how I knew who she was immediately, that and the way she stared straight ahead the whole time and because she held her handbag upright in her lap, like a headstone. She wore a donkey-brown pull-on hat, the kind you buy for the winter and then don't wear.

She was older than me. A lot older. She was very small, like a little wren, and she had that skin that looks like creased tissue paper. In fact, she looked old enough to be the girl's grandmother. I couldn't look the woman in the eye, of course, but I was sitting at the end of the row in the public gallery and I knew I could see her if I turned my head. There was another woman sitting beside her and you could see that she was with her. I found out later she was from the Rape Crisis Centre. Apparently that's what they do, they always have someone sitting with the victim in the court cases.

It was awful to think of someone being a victim of James. Before I could go too far down that road I blanked out my mind deliberately. I had enough on my plate without feeling sorry for everyone else in the courtroom.

The public gallery is not really a gallery at all. I don't know why they call it that. It's just a row of chairs at the back of the room. And the room is nice, I was surprised. I don't know what I was expecting. Bars and a cage and whips, maybe? Like the zoo? It was actually a bit like the children's court, sort of open plan with light-coloured wood furniture. Quite like those office blocks we clean. Beigey.

At least there were no plants. I always think that poor plants absorb the atmosphere around them. A plant in a courtroom must have a terrible time.

James wasn't anywhere to be seen as the court was called to order. The Devines were never at the top of the queue for anything.

Patrice Murphy takes me outside and asks me have I arranged the bail money. He shakes his head when I show him how much I have, tells me I'll probably have to go into the box to convince the judge. He also tells me her name is Madden. The girl. Rosemary Madden.

It gives me an awful land. Mammy's name was Rose. It's also my middle name, after her.

And that's Mrs Madden inside, he goes, you may have noticed her.

Then he gives me the bad news. Apparently this Rosemary Madden has waived her right to anonymity. It's unusual, he says, highly unusual. He doesn't know what her motivation could be, doesn't want to hazard a guess. He warns me that one of the consequences of this is that sooner or later the papers are going to name James. So we're to brace ourselves.

Has he no idea at all why she's done this?

No, he hasn't. It could be because she's so angry, that very occasionally happens. It could be because she's under pressure from someone else. It could be because she's playing some complicated role within her family. But since we'll probably never know why she's doing this, he says we're not to waste time with wondering, it's not our concern, we've to take care of our own problems, keep our eyes on our own ball. This waiving will have no bearing on the trial. It's the facts and the truth that count inside the courtroom. And we're not to be distracted by the media, they won't be making any decisions, the judge and jury will.

Yeah, sure, I think, but only to myself.

Then he has to race back in for other cases so he can't tell me any more. I follow him in and if I tell you my heart is leaden it's an understatement.

The two of us had to sit there, the girl's mother and I, while the other cases came and went. They were all remand or for mention and they went up and down quickly. I hated to see those boys in their 'good' track suits or their cheap suits. They tried to look so cocky and failed miserably. There's a particular look about being poor, I don't know if you've ever noticed. They're always thin. (But it's not that, I find that the richer people are the thinner they are.) No, the poor have cheekbones like knife handles. They protrude under their eye sockets. It's an absolute mystery to me. The rich have cheekbones, of course, but they're not like knife handles. I wonder if it could be something to do with their teeth?

On the odd occasion when I've ventured into Grafton Street or the Powerscourt Centre, I've used that information to pick out who shouldn't be there. Knowledge like this comes in handy, you know when to watch your handbag.

Anyway, up they came, one after the other, those boys with the knife-handle cheeks and the pimples on the back of their necks. There wasn't one girl or woman up for anything that morning, although if you were to believe the *Evening Herald*, there are women being thrown in jail big-time every day, just for nicking something like a pair of tights.

Mrs Madden didn't move a muscle, as far as I could see.

When he came up at last he looked terrible. I could see he was trying to be calm but he was shaking. And the collar of the new jacket was standing away from the back of his neck like it was too big for him. He looked around for me and when he saw me it was pitiful, the expression on his face. I couldn't help myself, I gave him a little wave. Then I stopped my hand. I didn't want Mrs Madden thinking I was the type of person who didn't care about rape.

→ Six ←

Patrice Murphy was right on the button about the bail. Ten thousand. He gets the judge to agree to hear me.

I'm afraid I want to draw a veil over my appearance in the box, it was one of the most humiliating experiences I've ever had and I never, ever want to go through anything like it again. The judge was lovely, but in a way it didn't help. She was quite gentle and said I was obviously a hard-working woman and provided I could guarantee James would fulfil absolutely all the conditions, she would post bail at three thousand pounds and would accept me as sole surety.

I felt like a real charity case, sitting there in the silence while she was scrutinizing my pathetic little bonds and my new receipts. All those eyes. Having to admit in public how poor we were. It was like being naked in the middle of O'Connell Street.

I was still beetroot when I was signing the bail bond. I mean, I never in a million years thought I'd be in a situation where I'd be in a courtroom bailing out someone who was charged with rape. It was dreadful. The registrar was terribly matter-of-fact about it, which helped in one way and in another way made it worse. I mean, did they think we were just common criminals like the rest of the dross that were hanging around that place?

James smiles at me when we get out on to the street. The first real smile I've seen on him for weeks. I get another land because I really see the resemblance in him to Mammy. Really see it as opposed to just half noticing or taking it for granted. She had the loveliest smile and here she is, smiling at me out of James.

I have to harden my heart, though. Don't you smirk at me, I say, we're not going to lower ourselves to talk here in the street but you're coming straight home with me and you're telling me exactly what happened.

He gets stroppy immediately. Tells me to eff off.

I'm outraged. Don't you talk to me like that, I go, and for once, to my surprise, he takes me seriously. Maybe something in him recognized subconsciously that I meant it this time.

Sorry, he says.

Now that was a moment to treasure. The only other time he ever said sorry to me since he came to be a teenager was one night when he was fourteen. I'd been saving up so he could go to the Gaeltacht with the rest of the class and he stole the money out of my drawer and went out and bought a ghetto-blaster. Everyone else had a ghetto-blaster and I suppose he didn't want to be different. I was so shocked when I found out I couldn't even be angry.

I didn't need to be because he got his comeuppance in the end. When the time came, all his pals went off to the Gaeltacht without him and he was miserable for the three weeks. A lot of them got scholarships from Gael Linn. I was working, of course, and I didn't even try for a scholarship for him. That time I thought if you were working you were eligible for nothing.

We get home after the court case and after he tells me his side of the story, I don't know what to believe.

The girl, Rosemary, is a bit older than him, she's just turned twenty and she's doing a bookkeeping course on a FÁS scheme or a Youth Employment or something like that, he doesn't know which kind of scheme it is. They're all hookey, as far as I can see, just a way to keep the unemployment figures down and then you're back to square one. The family's pretty well off. The father's in the printing business and she's the only daughter.

He met her at a club, where else. According to him, she was a goer. They nearly had sex on the very first night. I have to listen to this without saying a word of criticism because who am I to cast the first stone in that regard.

I wait until he pauses for breath. What did he mean 'nearly'.

Nearly, he says, use your imagination.

Where did you do it? I go. I'm trying to strike a balance because being straight up – as if this is the kind of thing we talk about all the time – and showing him that in general casual sex is not on. He's about to tell me to eff off again, I can see it, but he stops himself. And he says, quite humbly, that where they nearly did it was in your man Ferdia's car. The whole gang of fellas were at the club that night, apparently, and two of them clicked and this fella Ferdia lent his car to both of them.

Together? I ask, and I can't help sounding scandalized. Because I am. This is the same Ferdia that wanted to take them all down to a mobile home in Brittas Bay. Over my dead body.

James looks at me as if I'm mental but then he realizes that he's not exactly in a great position to argue with me and he tells me that they took turns.

It's a relief, of sorts. Right, I say. Go on.

Well, according to him, he and Rosemary Madden 'nearly' do it again two more times. Once at a party in a free house, somebody's parents were in Majorca on holidays, then again, the day after another party. In another free house. (There was always someone in the gang whose parents were away, it seems.) The two of then went to the Furry Glen in the Phoenix Park. In broad daylight. He skived off work and she skived off her FÁS course and he took her up there on the bike. That's the time she alleges he raped her.

Now, I'm not stupid. I know about date rape and all the rest of it. The newspapers are full of it and Marian Finucane has it on all the time on the radio and not for a second would I not agree that the woman has every right to say no. Every right.

Why did she think he raped her this time? What was different? He just shrugs. I dunno, he goes. Beats me. I didn't even come.

I nearly die. Don't be so vulgar, I say. And it's not good enough just to say you don't know. What do you mean you don't know? She didn't just make it up out of thin air. Or did she?

As far as he's concerned she did.

But what about her statement? According to Patrice Murphy, her statement is totally detailed.

That's nothing to do with me, he goes. I know what happened. When they wanted me to sign a statement saying I did it—

Don't you sign *anything*, I yell at him. Look what happened to the Birmingham Six.

After I calm down I try again. There must be something to it, I say to him. You must have done *something* to her. Otherwise why would she complain—

He's definite he did nothing to her he didn't do before. Only a bit more so.

Well, for instance, did she say no? At any stage?

He can't remember. But as far as he was concerned she was definitely as willing as he was. I can feel his temper starting to go – Look, he says, we didn't do it properly – we've never done it properly.

I keep cool. Was there a tiff? He shrugs again. Nothing more than the usual.

What does the usual mean –

You know, he says, the usual. A bit of slagging. Sniping at each other, nothing serious.

Could he elaborate, please? It was nothing serious, nothing – he's getting angry now – nothing, all right?

And no matter how I cajole, I can't get any more out of him. As far as he's concerned everything was hunky-dory that day. Apparently he thought they were in love and he thought she thought so too. After the alleged rape, they came back from the Furry Glen on the bike and he left her off near her house in Drumcondra and he went back to work. End of story. And as far as he was concerned, she was probably still a virgin.

Well, I'm on dangerous territory here and I don't want to go much further into this. I mean, what am I supposed to ask him next? How did he know she was still a virgin if he says they never did it? Maybe he used a magnifying glass?

Then I think I see another avenue of enquiry opening up. If everything was so great then why was he going round with a face on him like the back of a bus for the last couple of weeks?

He has an answer for that. She wouldn't see him any more after that day and he couldn't understand it. When he went to meet her at their usual place the following weekend he waited for three-quarters of an hour before he realized he'd been stood up. He tried to ring her a few times but she wouldn't come to the phone.

His last try – even though he would have been livid if any of his mates had seen him – came when he brought a presentation-size box of Cadbury's Roses up to her house. But when he knocked on her door, the mother answered it and said none of them wanted to see him around their house ever again. And then she closed the door in his face.

Did she slam it?

No. He looks surprised. She just closed it.

I'm thinking now maybe I should go and see her. Maybe we could sort this out, woman to woman.

But Patrice Murphy, when I ring him to ask him about it, thinks that would be an awful idea. He tells me not to go near her.

Still, I don't know. Sometimes a personal approach isn't such a bad idea.

James goes out after our so-called chat and I pull out the bed-settee for a bit of a nap. I'm wrecked. No sleep the night before, as I told you, and all the drama of the morning. I bring *Macbeth* into bed with me because I have a class that night – it's the last time we're going to do *Macbeth*. After tonight we're going to concentrate on the texts for the exam itself. But Mr Elliott wants us to be so familiar with *Macbeth* that, no matter what comes up about *Hamlet*, we'll be able to show off a bit in the paper, compare and contrast.

I can't concentrate, though. We're supposed to be studying the really famous bit in the play, the bit where she's wringing her hands and thinks she can't get the blood off them. But when I crack open the book, absolutely by chance, I find myself looking at the part,

right after the murder of Duncan, when Macbeth is on
about never sleeping again.

I find that a lot. I'll be thinking about something and
then it happens. Patsy says that everyone is psychic
although they don't know it. It's only when you give in
to it that you notice all the strange things that happen.
I've long been enamoured of pathetic fallacy, it's my
favourite device of the English language. But it's not just
a device, that's what's so brilliant. If you're watching out
for pathetic fallacy in real life you'll notice that it really
does happen. For instance it usually rains when I have my
period. At least one of the days. (And no smart remarks,
please, about this being Ireland where every day would
be a lovely day if it would stop raining.) *Macbeth* is *full* of
pathetic fallacy. Maybe that's what I love about it.

It also has a terrific story, like *Pulp Fiction*. I got the
video of it out once, although when I got home I
discovered it wasn't the play at all but the opera. Opera!
But I'd paid good money for it so I watched it anyway.
There were subtitles in English and I could follow it and
guess what – the story was the exact same as in the play
and believe it or not, watching that opera helped me with
an essay Mr Elliott had given us to write. It clued me in
to the atmosphere of the time, and I got a B. It was the
first B I ever got in English and I was dead chuffed.
Actually, it was the first B I ever got in anything.

Shakespeare was a genius, there's no doubt about it.
'Sleep that knits up the ravelled sleave of care, The death
of each day's life, sore labour's bath, Balm of hurt minds,
great nature's second course, Chief nourisher in life's
feast'. Who else could come up with all that? I can
certainly identify with 'sore labour's bath'. What woman
couldn't?

I'm just drifting off to sleep and it comes to me. Maybe

the Rape Crisis Centre can help us too. After all, it's a rape crisis for us as well. Patsy did a sponsored parachute jump for them and she must know someone.

Well, maybe not. They're pretty implacable about rapists from what I hear.

Anyway, I hadn't made up my mind at that stage whether to tell Patsy or not. We tell each other a lot but not everything. Like, I have the feeling that although she goes on about how lucky she is, everything isn't all rosy in her garden. And James says he saw her husband one night in one of his clubs.

I was dreading the *Herald* that evening. I didn't normally get it on a Monday but of course I had to that day. I was praying they wouldn't use our name.

You know the way when you sleep in the afternoon sometimes you have really bright, weird dreams. That day I dreamt about Tom Bennett. After all those years. You would have thought, with all the trouble we were in, I would have dreamt about courts or jails or something like that but no.

He was a golden lion in the dream and I was there in the dream with him but I was invisible. Nothing much happened. He was just there, sitting on the grass, and I was just there, watching him, I could see him but he couldn't see me. Nevertheless it was still very vivid. I suppose the lion bit was because we met at the zoo.

Tom turned out to be an orphan.

I couldn't believe it when he told me. He left it right until the last minute. What last minute, last millisecond! We were all set, or so I thought, to go up to meet this supposed huge family of his in Finglas. I'd washed my hair until it hurt and I was wearing one of Mammy's linen dresses. She had two linen dresses that she must have brought with her from Birr, Co. Offaly, when she

came to Dublin. They were always hung up, even when
we'd no wardrobes. I only saw her wearing one of them
once, for my Confirmation.

I was the exact same size as her when I was nineteen so
both of them fitted me. They were perfect too – linen
lasts for ever. And they were shirtwaisters so they never
went out of fashion. I wore the blue one. I'd ironed it
very carefully but of course I knew it would be creased
again in ten minutes – that's the trouble with linen. Still,
it's very classy.

You'd think blue only goes with blue eyes. But oddly
enough, it really suits me. I'm one of those peculiar
people with dark brown eyes which you don't normally
get with fair hair, which, by the way, was long at the
time. For that day, I let it stay loose. I thought I looked
good, although I do say so myself. Or at least the best I
could look.

James too. I'd scrubbed and polished him to within an
inch of his poor little life, God love him. I was damned if
I was going to let Mrs Bennett, who'd reared so many of
them, think I couldn't take care of a baby properly.

It took us all morning to get ready. And that was
getting up at half seven. More fool me.

He whistled at me when he saw me. I could see he
really meant it, too. That shirtwaister did suit me, I have
to admit, because I was quite slim. I still am but I was
really slim then. And I was taller than Mammy so the
dress wasn't too long on me. In fact, it was just above
my knees, just right. And I wore my good sandals.

Are we right, he says, very jovially. I must say you
look terrific. He goes to put his arm around me but I
scream at him not to touch me or he'll crease the linen.

I have butterflies in my tummy. You'd think I was
going to see the Pope. (Not that I give a damn about the

Pope. I'd like to see him manage to live in Dublin on our income. What I earn wouldn't keep him in tassels for his throne.)

I pick up James and put him in his buggy. I've washed the upholstery of that too. Last night, so it would be dry.

I wheel James out on to our balcony and turned around expectantly so that Tom Bennett can help me carry the buggy down the steps to the yard. I freeze. He's not coming after me. He's still standing at the door. His face is crumpled up like an old orange.

I'd better come back inside. He has something to tell me.

Somehow we managed to get through that first week James was on bail. I leave it to you to imagine what his mood was like. Reluctant to go to work, that kind of thing.

At least I had the usual routines to distract me. The cleaning, a couple of night classes for the Leaving – it was such a relief not to have to show up for the Irish, it clashed with *ER* anyway – the deli on Saturday morning.

The hardest was on the Sunday. PA System had a gig, in a pub in Rathmines. I had to act my head off. Our next remand was on the Monday morning and of course I was going to run into Mrs Madden again. And that's all that I could think of even while we were singing.

By the way, all the time was I growing up I thought the southside was posh. Not any more. Not if you've played some of the pub venues we've played. The rugby crowd is by far the worst. I believe rugby is a working-class game in other countries (and in Limerick) and it's only here and across the water that it's upper class. I'm not surprised. We do everything baw-ways here. And how-

ever they behave during the matches, they certainly
lower the tone here with their working-class manners
when they've had a few scoops. Give me soccer any day.
Or even GAA, God love them, although I've heard that
the prostitutes around Fitzwilliam Square say that their
best business comes with the All-Ireland Gaelic football
finals. Must be the excitement of all those country
bachelors coming up to the Big Smoke!

The pub is already raucous when we get to it and
we're completely ignored for our first set. Come on
now, everyone, Patsy starts to yell at them, this is
supposed to be a singalong, you're all supposed to be
singing with us. Otherwise we might as well just go
home—

Big roars from the floor. None of it printable.

You have to hand it to Patsy, she rolls with it. What's
that? Keep 'er going, Patsy? We have a comedian in our
midst, do we? There's always one – oh, very droll. How
long did it take you to dream up that one, Einstein?

She rolls her eyes at me, then, now, come on, fellas,
give us a break. Everybody ready? You ready, Angela?
Dha-dhah! All together now – one two three – Keep
Your Mind On Your Driving Keep Your Hand On The
Wheel – And Keep Your Snoopy Eyes On The Road
Ahead—

I'm singing away but my brain is clicking like an
abacus. It's desperate having to pretend that I'm having a
great time. I'm really glad it's a church wedding next
weekend and not another gig like this. Right now, I hate
showbiz with a passion. I know Patsy sees right through
me. She's keeps looking at me, she's probably wondering
what's wrong. I still haven't made up my mind whether
to tell her . . . Kissin' And A Huggin' With Fred. Up a
dupp a-dum. Dee do dee dum dum, dee do dee dum
dum, dee do dee dum dum *dum*.

At least they listened that time. They're even applauding – wonders will never cease . . .

We go through the routine and get mercifully near the end. They're getting drunker by the minute. Here goes Patsy again, she's really very good at this crowd-control lark. Some of you down the back there a bit fragile from last night, eh? Or are yiz practising for tonight? Poor babies, eh, Angela? Now, let's hear you on this one. Clean out the sinuses. Right up your street, boys – and girls! One two three – *and* . . .

Two Little Boys Had Two Little Toys . . . Both Had A Wooden Horse . . . Daily They Played Each Summer's Day . . .

Poor Patsy, she's been carrying me through the whole of this gig. I can't stave her off for ever. I'll have to tell her sometime.

I like the harmonies on this. Did You Think I Would Leave You Dying, When There's Room On My Horse For Two . . . Please, Sacred Heart, be kind tomorrow at the remand. Let the *Evening Herald* not be there . . .

That was great. They're great, aren't they, Ange?

They sure are, Patsy. They were great.

Nearly there. We can go home soon.

Now, ladies and gentlemen, this next one is our penultimate song – that's the second last for those of you who don't have the Irish! But seriously, folks, we were only joking when we were giving out to you – you've been a lovely crowd. And at this point we're going to slow things down a bit. We're going to give you something from our native Irish culture. The old ones are the best, eh? And for this we need a bit of hush.

O Danny Boy, The Pipes The Pipes Are Calling . . .

*

The remand hearing next morning. She's there again, Mrs Madden. Still not looking at me although she'd want to be incredibly thick not to know who I am. She knows all right. I know she knows by the way she keeps staring straight ahead. From the minute I come into the room to the minute I leave.

I can't stick it. I make up my mind. I have to go and see her.

Seven

He was moping around in his cacks, looking at the *Big Breakfast*, when I got home from the job on the second Tuesday. So far he'd got away with being late for work on the Mondays by saying he had appointment in an outpatients' clinic.

When I had a go at him he got defensive immediately, said he couldn't face it. I bawled him out of it, told him he'd be sacked. All right, so it was only an old courier job but it was me had to go guarantor for the loan on that bike. Anyway, I told him, going to work would keep his mind off his troubles.

After I calmed down we both had a bit of breakfast.

We'd also got away with it so far where publicity was concerned. For some reason the papers weren't showing any interest in the case. Maybe rape is just ordinary now, what with all the crime against the elderly and child abuse and murders and all the rest of it. Or maybe his rape, on the scale of things, wasn't too bad when you consider the horrific injuries some poor girls have to contend with.

When we were on our second cup of tea, I told him what I was going to do and asked for the Maddens' address.

Well, he went ballistic. No way was I going to go up

there, no way. He started to throw things. It's what he does, he has a terrible temper. (But at least he always throws inanimate things if that's the right word. No one ever gets hurt. He wouldn't hurt a fly, you know, that's why this thing is so absurd. That's why I think that if I go and see Mrs Madden we'll be able to sort this thing out between us.)

Of all the boys in the world, James a rapist?

I remember when he was little, from six on, he was besotted with wildlife. We had quite a decent telly, the good old Vincent again, and he absolutely loved all those Richard Attenborough programmes. I was delighted with him. I mean, other kids were into nothing but *Star Trek* and *Neighbours* or cop programmes and the more violent the better, but the worst punishment I could ever threaten on James was not to let him watch his nature programmes. He still watches them, even in preference sometimes to his MTV. He always said that when he grew up he wanted to be a vet. Some hope he had, with the points you'd need from the Leaving. Even if we'd any chance of him staying on at school to do the damned Leaving.

I never discouraged him though. I thought it showed high aspirations. And anyway, who knows, I thought at that stage, maybe by the time he was leaving school the points would have come down and you wouldn't need to have been a farmer's son and to have gone to Rockwell or Clongowes or somewhere.

I did try to get him into Belvedere, they had a scholarship scheme for poor kids, but he didn't do well enough in the entrance exam. It's just around the corner. When he didn't get it I told myself I was just as glad, Belvedere is a rugby school and you know what I think of the rugby heads, but I was only fooling myself. I would have given my eye teeth to have got him in there. The

Jesuits give a great education but more than that, they
operate a brilliant old boys' network. I'd say if you did a
survey, you'd find very few Belvedere boys in the ranks
of the unemployed. It would have been really handy too,
he could have walked.

I wouldn't allow him to have pets when he was a kid,
and I'm sorry now. At the time I thought I'd enough to
mind, without a load of animals around the place. Mind
you, he took no notice of me, all the time bringing home
mongrel dogs and bloody kittens and I was all the time
ringing up the cruelty people to come and get them and
then there'd be murder. He'd swear he hated me and
he'd never speak to me again as long as he lived.

Once it was a hamster. He said he swapped it for a
Hallowe'en mask. I gave in and let him keep it but it
died. Died of love, I'd say. He stuffed it with food and
never let it get a minute's respite. Played with it every
blessed waking minute.

Now, does that sound like a rapist?

He wouldn't give me the address so I had to go to a
pub to look it up in a telephone directory. It wasn't hard,
they were in under Madden Colour Printers. I knew
from what the solicitor had told me that they ran the
business from behind their house.

I know Drumcondra a bit, it's not that far and Patsy
and I have done gigs at the Regency Hotel and another
pub up there near where the Lemon's factory used to be
on the river. I'm not old enough to remember Lemon's
factory but I do remember the sweets. Mammy loved the
soft chewy fruit ones, especially the lime. Her teeth
weren't great towards the end and I suppose she had a
bad taste in her mouth from the drugs. The lime taste
probably cut through it. I think now that she might have
been HIV but this was back in the time when it wasn't
heard of.

It's one of the things I keep meaning to do. I'd like to have a long chat with a doctor sometime, describe the way she was. Because I've seen a few documentaries about HIV and you'd think they were talking about Mammy. When did that HIV come in to Ireland?

She was only barely alive when I met Tom Bennett that day in the zoo. Maybe that's why I latched on to him so quickly.

Of course, I see now I'd been living in cloud cuckoo land where Tom Bennett was concerned. It did occur to me right at the beginning how peculiar it was that a fella coming from a magic family like his would have any time at all for people like us. But then I've told you I was naïve. And when Mammy died soon after I met him and when Tom found out about her and about James and didn't do a runner, I thought our luck had just turned. Simple as that.

I just stare at him when he tells me he's an orphan.

It takes me a minute. You mean there's no family? (I know I sound stupid. How can you have a family if you're an orphan?)

He shakes his head. Mumbles something. He looks ashamed, I give him that.

I look out over the yard. The concrete tubs are still there but as for the wallflowers . . . History. And someone's tastefully redecorated the tarmac with a few broken bottles. Devine's variation of pathetic fallacy. Never lets me down.

I go to wheel the buggy inside again and Tom steps out of my way. Poor James. All that scrubbing for nothing. He's looking at me — James, I mean, not Tom — like I'm off my rocker. I thought we were going out, his eyes go at me above his soother. He's too surprised to cry.

Right, I go, closing the door. What gives? I'm not yelling, not shouting. Calm as a nun.

It turns out he didn't think a girl, I quote, as good-looking unquote, as me, would go with an orphan. He was brought up in an orphanage and he thought there was a stigma attached to that. So he reinvented *The Waltons*.

Stigma? Jesus, had he taken a look around our place lately?

No relatives at all?

None that he's aware of, anyway, although he does admit that it stands to reason there must be someone he could trace if he put his mind to it. Like he knows he didn't arrive on this earth like a dalek. Even Superman had a family, according to the film. The Brothers were my family, Tom goes, as though saying it is like saying you're an alcoholic.

Now I've heard what went on in those orphanages run by the religious orders. They were brutal, in every sense of the word. So immediately I'm beginning to see the other side of it and I can't stay mad at him.

Was he traumatized? I'm already picturing him in little short pants with his poor little legs black and blue from all the beatings the children were supposed to get in those places for the slightest thing. And crying for his Mammy in his bed that night and being afraid to wet his bed in case he'll get another beating.

Before Tom can answer, James throws his soother on the ground, in protest I suppose, and starts yelling and I have to deal with him. Sit down and we'll talk about it, I go to Tom, while I'm unpeeling James's outer layer. Ah, what the hell, I'm thinking to myself, we have each other. Or so I think that day. Lord, when they made me they threw away the mould.

Drumcondra's not a bad little place although it's always stuffed with traffic going to the airport and beyond to

Belfast – my bus was crawling. I've never been to Belfast,
not yet anyway. I was going to go during the ceasefire
and Patsy was dead keen to go up to see President
Clinton when he lit the Christmas tree up there but I
couldn't go that day. So I went to see President Clinton
in College Green in Dublin the following day. It was
freezing.

She was lovely, I thought, no matter what the papers
say about her being a bossy-boots. Why wouldn't she be
bossy, what man ever got anywhere without a good,
bossy woman, eh? She looked as if she was feeling the
cold too, although, thanks be to God, the sun shone the
whole time. It's a pity they didn't bring Chelsea. I always
feel sorry for that poor kid. Did you ever, in all your
twist, see such horrific train tracks? And she has such a
little mouth. But I believe the tide is turning for her now.

Do you know what I heard from one of the women in
work? That there are actually orthodontists in America
making a *fortune* out of putting braces on kids' teeth *for
show only*! Would you believe that? They're real braces all
right, but they're not tightened because the kids don't
need their teeth straightened one iota. They're put on
just to be a status symbol.

Clinton was grand, quite handsome and much taller
than I'd imagined – but I'd put a question mark over his
hair. And he has this sort of smile where you wouldn't
know whether he's going to cry or not. Patsy thinks it's
an act, I'm not so sure. I was only a few yards away from
him and I watched him very closely and I really believe
he was sincere in what he said.

Not that he said all that much but I suppose he can't,
with the delicacy of the situation in the North. We didn't
care anyway, me and the thousands of others who turned
out to make eejits of ourselves waving the little plastic
American flags his secret-service people gave out. He

could have recited Mary Had a Little Lamb and we would have cheered him every bit as lustily. Dubliners always give visitors a great welcome. We take things personally, I think, we feel responsible for people having a good time and bringing home a good report about us.

By the end of it even those secret-service guys were smiling at us. And I hear they thought the Dublin crowd was the best of any foreign crowd he ever addressed – or so the papers said. Our own papers anyhow, I didn't read any of the rest.

President Kennedy certainly thought the Irish were the best. It's hard to believe that I was alive when he was here. That's always heartrending in the old programmes to see him telling us at Shannon that he'll be back to see us in the springtime. And waving. When now we all know when we watch it that he's standing there and he's only a few months left to live. And he's looking as though he hasn't a care in the world. Hasn't a clue about what's in store for him.

Another great occasion, apparently, was when the Pope said Mass in the Phoenix Park. I say apparently, because I wasn't there. I wouldn't bother my barney going up there to see him. He's sincere enough, I suppose, but I don't approve of his views on contraception.

Abortion is a different matter. I'd never have an abortion for myself – it's very hard to imagine how you could, once you've known what a baby really is. It'd be different if you'd never had one, I'd imagine.

I have known a fair few who've taken the boat to England, God love them. Some of them not a million miles away from work. We have a tea-break every morning and that's when the truth comes out. I think it's to do with the oceans of shiny floor all around us and us huddled in the middle like castaways with our teabags and our kettle. It makes you feel intimate.

I don't know what Patsy's views are on abortion. It's one of those things you don't really talk about with your friends, only your acquaintances.

I couldn't believe it when Patsy showed up at Mammy's funeral after us not seeing one another for nearly nine years, not since First Class. It was a pretty sad day, of course, mourners pretty thin on the ground and the church was huge. It looked like Croke Park on the day of a GAA camogie final. Patsy and I went to a camogie final once because she had a friend who played for Kilkenny so that's how I can make the comparison.

Hurling is a good game but there's something really weird about camogie. I know they put their hearts and souls into it, just the same as the men, but when you hear the thin, high-pitched shouting from the bare sidelines, it doesn't seem to match up. Does that make sense?

At the funeral the four of us girls – James was being minded – were sort of huddled together in the front row of the church with the director from the Eastern Health Board. The nuns were spread out in the row just behind us, God bless them, and behind them again a few of the social workers and the foster families who had some of their friends and relations with them. To give them moral support, I suppose. None of her so-called boy-friends showed up. Not one.

Nor was there a single relative of Mammy's, although the notices were in the papers. I'd been half hoping but I wasn't surprised.

To be fair, a good few of the neighbours did come along. I was pretty bitter about a lot of them at the time, God forgive me, particularly the vigilante types, and I remarked to my own social worker that they'd probably come to make sure she was really dead. Or to drive a stake through her heart.

I'm not bitter any more, by the way. I can now see their point. I'd nearly join the Concerned Parents myself now if I thought James was in serious danger, and I totally agree that pushers' lives should be made as difficult as possible.

> **Devine, Rose Alice**, late of Dublin and Birr, Co. Offaly. After a short illness, bravely borne, in the loving care of the sisters and staff of Our Lady's Hospice. Sadly missed by her five sorrowing children, Angela, Francesca, Justine, Nicola and James, and a wide circle of friends. At Rest.

There's a lot of emotion in death notices, isn't there? Bravery, love, sadness, sorrow, all in a couple of lines. It was the head nun at the Hospice who suggested putting 'At Rest' at the end of Mammy's death notice, and I thought it was lovely. I still have the cutting. I keep it under 'D' in my *Concise Oxford Dictionary* because it's the book I use most and I like to be reminded of her.

None of the others wanted to but I insisted on going to the Hospice to see her before they put the lid on the coffin. I was glad I did. She did look 'At Rest'. They'd done her hair and put make-up and blusher on her so her cheeks looked quite healthy. And although she was terribly thin, the white shroud they put on her plumped her out a bit, even though you could see the bones at her hips. Up to then, I always 'saw' a shroud like a kind of flour bag. It's not, it's more like a loose dress. It was ladylike and I think that's why it suited her so well. Mammy'd always been a lady.

She'll be praying for you now, the nun held her hand.

She looks like an angel, doesn't she and that's how you'll think of her now.

I closed my eyes and tried to picture Mammy in heaven, smiling and laughing with joy and greeting all the other angels. I asked the nun could I be alone with her for a few minutes.

When the nun was gone I opened my eyes again and whispered Starlight Starbright into Mammy's ear, and then I kissed her on the forehead, the way she used to kiss me. She was cold and smooth but I really do think she was 'At Rest'. I could feel it from her.

I didn't see Patsy at the funeral until we were all outside and waiting for the hearse to move off. I hate that bit at funerals, no one seems to know what to say to the bereaved and they all talk to one another very loudly about the races and the weather or it won't be long until Christmas. Anything at all except what they're thinking about, like, thank God it's not me this time or, I wonder who's next. The forecourt of the church was absolutely enormous, like the tarmac in front of an airport where they park the planes, and it looked even bigger that day with the tiny little crowd in the middle of it clustered around the hearse. I got angry on Mammy's behalf. I didn't want people thinking that the death notice was a lie, that she didn't have a wide circle of friends.

Since she never practised her own religion I had decided that we wouldn't bother trying to get the Protestants interested in her at this stage and I had her brought to our local Catholic church. The Vincent and the social workers helped with this and I have to say that the priest who said the Mass that day was very nice. I wouldn't have any readings or anything like that, I don't like hypocrisy, but he asked me a few things about her so he could include them in his sermon.

Some of it worked, some of it didn't. I wasn't all that

keen on his enthusiasm about God showing that he loved Mammy very specially because he gave her so much suffering to bear, and how she was very lucky to be now enjoying her extra special reward. But he meant well. The best bit was him talking about her gentleness, and about how her children loved her. That was certainly the truest thing anyone ever said about anyone.

When I saw Patsy, I went over to her and shook her hand. I know it's usually the other way around but she was sort of hanging back and I suppose I was being a bit belligerent on Mammy's behalf. I was certainly not going to show anyone I was ashamed of the smallness of the crowd.

She had her mother with her and that was a bit of a shock. I remembered her as a dowdy little woman with a hairnet and here she was with streaks and a miniskirt and black opaque tights. Like a model, well, a small model. It was weird, I can tell you, when I thought of the way Mammy was just before she died because they had to have been within a few years of one another in age.

Although, as I told you, Mammy was only thirty-eight, she looked about sixty. It was the bad teeth, I suppose, and the way her hair had got so thin. She smoked a lot too and that gives you dreadful lines.

I thought you wouldn't know me, Patsy says.

She was older, of course, we all were, but I would have recognized those eyes and that hair anywhere. She still wore it long. She was already in fifth year in secondary school, just a year before the Leaving Cert. She was always brainy. But at least I was still as tall as her. That was something. And I wasn't ashamed of my clothes either. New everything. My social worker had come up trumps.

The hearse was moving off and we had to go. Sorry,

Patsy, I said to her, but thanks for coming, I really appreciate it. I did too. She promised to stay in touch but I thought to myself, That's the end of it. You know the way people just say these things.

But to my astonishment, Mammy wasn't gone three days when there was a knock on the door and there stood Patsy. I said I'd come, she goes, handing me a bunch of flowers.

Now this happens to be the first bunch of flowers I've ever got in my life. They're pink carnations, the kind you see everywhere nowadays outside newsagents' shops but, that time, you'd have had to go to a flower shop or to Moore Street.

I'm overwhelmed. Thanks a million, I say, come on in.

The place is a mess, because I'm in the middle of giving it a good cleaning. James is asleep for his nap so we have a bit of time.

There'd been nearly a problem with leaving just me and James in the flat, it was supposed to be for a much bigger family, but thank God they didn't insist on us moving out straight away. My social worker was able to argue that it would have been too disruptive for me and James to have to leave what had been our family home. And at that time she thought it was a good idea to have the access visits there. Big mistake. I'll tell you why later.

Sorry about the mess, I say to Patsy, as I pick up the scrubbing brush and the basin, don't fall, will you, it's very slippy . . .

We smile at each other and she sits down, and honest to God it was like we'd seen each other only yesterday. I place the flowers in a jug of water and make her a cup of tea and we sit down and have a right old natter. And that's the start of it. Friends again for ever. Or so I thought.

On the way up to the Maddens in Drumcondra, I think to myself that I will be able to tell Patsy about James. She'd be better hearing it from me, anyway, rather than from some other source, like the newspapers. It's just that I find it very hard to admit it to anyone at all.

→ Eight ←

They lived in a nice place, the Maddens. It was end-of-terrace, on a corner, with a lovely glassed-in balcony over the front door, probably coming out from the master bedroom. I love sun porches and balconies. All that light.

I was quaking and it took me ages to get up the courage to open the gate. If they'd been looking out, which they weren't, they'd have probably had me sussed as a suspicious character – although there was a bus stop in front of them and I'd spent ages pretending I was waiting for a bus while I spied out the territory, so to speak.

They had a side entrance, probably for the business. Their front door was shiny green, the brasses done to a T. The knocker was one of those fancy ones, like a lion's head, and the car in their driveway was a '94 Toyota Corolla with the plastic still on the seats even though we were nearly half-way through 1996. There wasn't a single daisy on their lawn. But a black mark was, she had put plastic flowers in the window of the sitting-room. They weren't even the good silk ones that you'd have to go really close to know. You could tell a mile away.

Plastic flowers get on my wick. I take after Mammy, she always thought they were common and I agree with her.

You get used to making judgements about people
when you're a professional cleaner and I instantly put the
Maddens down as the houseproud but fussy type. I'd
already pigeonholed Mrs Madden as maybe a bit timid,
judging by her hat she'd worn both times at the court, so
she probably wouldn't have been the one to decide about
the plastic flowers. He couldn't stand pollen and falling
petals and all the rest of it, so he laid down the law and
she wouldn't stand up to him. I could have been wrong
but why else would she put plastic flowers in the window
of such a nice, well-cared-for house?

I have to knock a second time. My hand is shaking, and
I hold the lion's head with only the tips of two fingers.
You'd be afraid to mark the shininess of it.

Oh Jesus oh God. She opens the door herself. The girl.
Rosemary.

It has to be her because she's the only daughter. I
know that from James.

Words fail me. E-excuse me, I blubber, but it comes
out really high, like a squeak, and then I come to a
complete stop. She's pretty, in a prim sort of way, short
dark hair in an elfin cut, good little figure, with a peachy-
coloured blouse belted inside her jeans. She wasn't
wearing any shoes and her toenails were freshly painted.
A nice pale colour.

Yes? she goes, half surprised, half impatient. Can I help
you?

I don't blame her for being brusque. Opening the door
to a complete stranger who's squealing like a stuck pig.
I'm – I'm sorry, I go, I was expecting someone else.

She stares at me, frowning. Who are you?

Nobody. I'm nobody. I back off. Sorry to bother you.
It's the wrong house.

She steps a bit out into the porch. They have these
little evergreen bushes stuck in tubs on either side of the

door. Phoney, too, although I have to admit that with these you'd have to be right up against them to know. Which I was, of course.

Who are you? she goes again. And she's staring at me now, really staring. Piercing.

I'm sorry, I go, and I flee down the driveway, just managing not to run. I don't dare to look back but I'm absolutely sure she's watching me. I bet she knows now exactly who I am. I've blown it.

What an idiot. What a complete and utter prat. I can't believe I've made such a fool of myself. I think I see everyone in the road, every single blessed person, busmen, milkmen, oul' ones walking their dogs, looking at me and jeering. I think I see a huge big finger pointing at me from the sky. Look, everyone, look at Angela Devine, the bloody eejit.

Talking about being an eejit, it was I broke off the engagement with Tom Bennett.

And I didn't even have to, that was the really stupid part. He was definitely in love with me, I can see that now. And he was a decent bloke, he really was.

For years I'd considered, on and off, looking him up, just out of curiosity, to find out what happened to him. Then, the minute I'd think of it, I'd lose heart. Where to start? Like, we had no mutual friends. I had no friends anyway, except Patsy, of course, and she was busy at the time with her Leaving Cert and then her job and her own fella, and when we met for a jar or something I didn't want any man tagging along. You can't talk properly when there are fellas there, can you?

Anyway, I hate that group thing or even couples thing. You know, let's all do this or that and aren't we having fun, when you're really gritting your teeth because you can't stand at least fifty per cent of the people you're supposed to be having fun with. Maybe I'm eccentric but

I really only enjoy people one at a time. How can you sincerely talk otherwise?

So during the whole time Tom Bennett and I saw each other, the guts of a year and a half, we were very private. He didn't seem to mind and we didn't seem to need anyone else.

I suppose I could trace his present whereabouts through his orphanage or through the Salvation Army. But he's probably married with a squad of kids. He always said he wanted kids. You can see why. Remember, we're talking here about someone who invented the Finglas Waltons. The last thing he'd need is someone from his past landing in on top of them all. Especially someone who'd jilted him.

What happened was he came home drunk. We weren't exactly living together – you couldn't, the welfare officers have eyes in the back of their heads and I wasn't going to jeopardize my entitlements. And of course there were those so-called good neighbours of ours who'd have been only too delighted to spill the beans. (Although, to be fair, some of them were very good during Mammy's last illness, I have to say that for them. That's Irish people for you. They're the best in the world when you're down. They love you then.)

He used to sneak in after dark and stay some of the night and then sneak out again. It was quite hard to do, it was at the time when the vigilante movements against the pushers were just beginning, nothing as organized as the Concerned Parents or COCAD but pretty effective all the same. They were watching the courtyard and the landings like hawks but luckily our place was at the end of a row, near the entrance to the whole complex. And instead of going down the steps into the yard, Tom Bennett was able to drop soundlessly over the balcony and scarper before anyone knew what was happening.

The first time he came in drunk I was shocked, completely shocked. He never drank much, or so I'd thought. I was nearly too shocked to give out to him but I did, naturally. I had to let him know it wasn't on.

And of course the next morning he couldn't remember a word of what I'd said so I might as well have saved my breath. He was dying, vomiting, the whole works. And naturally full of remorse. He told me what had happened. Apparently that Jason and that Sharon were getting married. (Shotgun, of course.) He'd been at Jason's stag.

Why didn't you tell me? I go. I'd have been prepared.

I didn't want you to worry and I didn't think it'd get out of hand the way it did, he's really humble, and as contrite as Peter after the Agony in the Garden. I keep silent, let him grovel. I mean, I've seen enough at this stage of my life to know what drink does to families. There is no way, *no way*, I'm going to let any fiancé of mine behave like that. And once you start down that slippery slope you're gone. It's only a short step to beatings.

He's sitting there with his head in his hands and he can't even touch the cup of tea in front of him and I'm looking at him, at the tousled top of his head – his hair had grown a lot and he had a pony tail now – and, of course, I start feeling sorry for him. I put my arms around him and he immediately snuggles in tight and says sorry, Ange, sorry, sorry, sorry. He'll never do it again. It's a once-off.

Not even at any other stags?

Definitely not.

Even your own?

Definitely. Definitely. It's finished. No more drink. Cidona from now on.

Strangely enough, we had sex then. It wasn't great, naturally – the smell off of him would knock down an elephant at twenty paces – but he was very tender and loving and I suppose it gave me a certain satisfaction to be forgiving.

That happened to be one of the access days. The five of us saw each other every fortnight. The social workers would collect the other three from their foster homes – Justine and Nicola were together in Darndale but Francesca was in Stillorgan on the southside. They couldn't get anyone on the northside to take her at the time they all went into care and she settled in well so they didn't want to move her when a place became available near the other two. Her foster parents were even considering adopting her.

It was a bit of a disaster, though, in one way, because she was going to a school in Stillorgan and she had this accent. In fact, there was no getting away from it, she was a snob and she was always fighting with the rest of us as though we weren't good enough for her. (Remember I told you about her kicking up stink when she was brought back to the flat? Well, that's why. We weren't good enough for her any more.)

The social workers were aware of the problem, I have to say that for them, but I could also see that they were on the horns of a dilemma. They were worried about how we were developing as a unit, with her being ashamed of us and being grudging about participating in the access visits, but although their priority is always to keep natural families together as much as possible they could see she was incredibly happy with her foster family and they didn't want to ruin that.

Anyway, we had to meet for access and she'd no option about it. I'd organize James and the whole five of us would do something with one of the social workers, like on a fine day go to Stephen's Green to feed the ducks and then we'd have chips afterwards. God love the social workers, they probably drew straws. We were some handful.

Wet days were miserable. We usually hung around in some place like the lobby of the Gresham Hotel or the Royal Dublin, trying to make our Cokes last until it was time for the chips. We'd very little to talk about, to tell you the truth, and Justine and Nicola were always ganging up on Francesca because of the snobby way she treated them, so the social worker and I spent half the time trying to keep the peace. James inevitably got bored and cranky. None of us wanted to talk about Mammy even though the social workers were always bringing up the subject to try and lead us into it.

A great time was had by all, I don't think.

After the sex that day, I left Tom Bennett in bed with his hangover while I got up to get James ready. He said he'd sleep it off and we'd go out to Howth or some place when I got back. It did occur to me that lately he seemed to have no qualms about missing work. This wasn't the first day he'd spent in our place when he was supposed to be at Cadbury's. But I reckoned I'd done enough giving out for one day and he was so miserable, even despite the sex, that I didn't want to kick him when he was down.

The third time he came in drunk, that was the end.

I forgave him the second time – that was someone at work's twenty-first, he said – but I told him that second time if he ever came in again like that it would be the end. (And that second time there was no sex, although he tried. I wouldn't have it.)

The odd thing is you'd think he would stay away, wouldn't you? I wouldn't have known anything about it then. It was like he *wanted* to be caught. So when the third time happened, I had to keep my word. I'd said it would be the end and it had to be. It was the hardest thing I'd ever had to do in my life up to then.

I had to think not only of myself but of James. He was still only a baby. I couldn't expose him to someone untrustworthy for all of his little life, he'd enough strikes against him as it was.

And once you're married, you're married. That's my philosophy. The divorce legislation that's going through now, I'm not so sure about it. I know all about personal freedom and civil rights but I voted no.

I'm half sorry now, though. If it was held again I'd probably vote yes. I can't stand it that I've cast my lot in with the kind of people who challenged the result of the referendum in the courts. All right, it was a terribly close result, but in my opinion the yes people won fair and square and I hate sore losers. I don't want anyone to think I'm one of them. The majority is the majority, even if it's only one person. That's democracy and if you don't like it you go and live in China.

It was certainly not for religious reasons that I voted no, I don't even go to Mass. I voted that way because I thought that William Binchy had a good argument about changing the nature of marriage – that if you get married in a 'divorce jurisdiction' you're not entering a permanent bond at all.

We had a lecture once at one of the missions in school from a Jesuit. (He was one of the reasons I wanted to send James to Belvedere because he was very impressive.) The lecture was about moral dilemmas now that we were approaching womanhood. One of the things he said always stuck in my mind. It was about mental reservations. According to the Church, you're entitled to say anything you like, even if it's not true, and provided you make a mental reservation at the time it's not a lie. Suppose you're apprehended in Dunne's and you're accused of shoplifting a pair of tights. You can look the dick straight in the eye and say, 'I didn't steal a pair of tights', even though the tights are sitting there right under your armpit in the sleeve of your coat. What you said is not a sin or a lie, provided that in your mind, silently, you add 'from you' 'or as far as you're concerned' to the statement. Or the phrase of your choice which tells the truth. That's how mental reservations work. (I don't use it much but I have done so from time to time.)

Getting married in a 'divorce jurisdiction' is like having a mental reservation. You're saying 'until death do us part' but with the blessing of the state you have a mental reservation where you're adding silently, 'or until I'm sick of you'. William Binchy kept hammering on about that on the television debates. I hate hypocrisy. You're either getting truly married or you're not.

For days after we broke up I was sick with grief. For the first week, day and night, I expected him to turn up. Every time, especially at night, when I'd hear anything out on the balcony, a cat or a dog or one of the vigilantes, I'd tense up and wait. We had a special knock for late at night, three followed by a gap followed by one. But he never came.

I went through the days like a zombie. It was the first and last time I ever took Valium. (For obvious reasons, I have a personal morality about drugs.) Patsy gave it to me, even in those days she seemed to have an unlimited supply.

Go on, for heaven's sake, she goes. They're not going to kill you, it's just for a short period.

They did help a bit, they certainly helped me sleep at night. But during the day it was sort of like wearing an angora cardigan around your brain. Fuzzy. And I hated the thick taste in my mouth.

I can't tell you the number of times I went to ring him at work but I always came home again without doing it. I suppose the Valium helped to make the hard decisions. I'd recommend it. But only short term. I've gone through the drawers in James's bedroom, I won't allow a single tablet in this place that I don't know what it is. So far so good with him.

I probably wouldn't have got through that period without Patsy. It brought us very close together, just like we were at school, and it was like the gap of all those years never existed.

Although she did have a fella, she hadn't yet met Martin, her husband, and she was working in town in the Revenue Commissioners so she was able to come and visit me in her lunch hours. They give great lunch hours in the civil service. She was a brick.

I'll definitely have to tell her about James soon.

I saw Tom Bennett just one more time after we broke up. It was by accident. I was in Henry Street on Christmas Eve, would you believe. James was being obstreperous in his buggy and, with the crowds shoving and pushing and all the hawkers roaring, I was really on a short fuse. He was flailing around so much he'd slid down on the crotch strap holding him in and his feet were dragging on the ground. I pulled into Roches' Stores doorway to get a bit of space to sort him out and when I straightened up I found myself looking into Tom Bennett's eyes.

My stomach did a back flip.

Hello, he goes, obviously as shocked as me. He's wearing clothes I recognize only too well. It's then I see he's with a girl. She's red-haired, like himself – their children will remind you of a bunch of carrots – but I'm glad to see she's very small. Scutty, even.

I have to admit, though, that she's nice-looking, with a figure she knows how to emphasize. She's wearing a pair of jeans so tight they're probably cutting her in two, and a sort of bomber jacket in black shiny pvc. Belted, to show her teeny tiny little waist.

My heart is jamming in my chest. How are you? I go, in this phoney voice that I can't stand but that always comes out of me when I'm nervous.

Grand, he says, and turns to her. This is so-and-so (to this day I can't remember her name) and he introduces the two of us.

There ensues the most stupid conversation I ever had before or since. We talk about how crowded it is, as if this is a surprise. Christmas Eve on Henry Street is legendary. And here we are saying, It's desperate, you can't move.

And the noise! (This is from your woman.) This is the last year we'll ever come in here on a Christmas Eve.

We all nod our heads like we're Methuselahs. We're all lying through our teeth and looking for an exit line and she's certainly sizing me up. I bet he never told her about me but she can certainly see by the way he's behaving that I'm something that crawled out of his past life.

Thank God for the day that's it, we can legitimately finish up with Happy Christmases all around and get away with none of us losing face. Very civilized. I don't feel civilized, I feel like murder.

It took me ages to calm down and poor James got short shrift, I can tell you, when he started bawling for a selection box from one of the hawkers – there were fellas selling selection boxes every five feet. I relented – my less than perfect love life wasn't the poor kid's fault – and I went back and spent some of my hard-got money on one of the damned things.

It's an odd thing the way hawkers hunt in packs, I've noticed it before. It stands to reason they'd all have sparklers around Hallowe'en but other times what they try to flog you seems to make no sense at all. In Henry Street, one week, they'll all have sports socks. Then the next week it'll be lighters or strips of Elastoplast or posters of Boyzone. I imagine this huge central warehouse where they have corporate meetings and all decide on the weekly strategy. That this week it'll be Mars bars or ten Kit-Kats for a pound but let's save the cotton socks for when there's a shortage. Maybe they even have a chief hawker to whom they all give a vote of thanks at the end. Once I saw them all with golf tees.

Wouldn't you know it, when I took a good look at James's selection box, it was a Cadbury's one.

Looking at the bright side, at least I never had a ring so I had no moral dilemma about whether or not to give it back to him. And at least I never got pregnant.

Can you imagine?

✦ Nine ✦

G uess what? Our luck changed!
Five hundred pounds!

I couldn't believe it. I bought the scratch card when I got the *Herald*. I try to limit myself to two a week, usually on either a Monday or a Tuesday and then again on a Thursday or Friday. For one thing it makes the week go by a bit faster, but for another I deliberately buy them on the days that there's no Lotto draw. I have a feeling that to buy them on the days of the draws would be greedy. Tempting fate.

And I wouldn't mind but I wasn't even thinking about fate or luck, because this Monday was the fourth remand – Patrice Murphy's told us it's going to be a long haul until the trial because of the book of evidence, the backlog, all that – and I was too worried about what I'd find when I opened the paper. (I can't understand how the papers haven't copped us yet. Or maybe it's one of those things where you think the entire world revolves around you, and what's happening is that your story is not half as important as you think. If that's the case, lucky us and thank God there's so much going on in the world and in the courts to distract them.) I still haven't got up the courage to tell Patsy.

I was thinking so much about all of this, I forgot to

scratch the card until after tea. Just think! It had been sitting there in my bag the whole time with its lovely secret message.

After I scratched – the third five hundred came out only on the very last panel – it was like when something is lost or stolen and you don't believe it. You keep going back and back to the empty space as though it'll be miraculously there again. Well, it was the same with that card. Every time I'd go back to the table where I'd left it I'd be half afraid to look in case I hadn't read it right – that one of the five hundreds was really a five thousand or a fifty, or that the whole card would be just plain gone. No. There it was every time.

I mean, with all my jobs, even if we had gigs every single Sunday plus a wedding on a Saturday, I wouldn't make that much in six weeks. More than a whole month's wages, a month and a half's wages, just for a pound.

The danger is, of course, that you'll go out again straight away and buy a hundred more.

Immediately, though, I began to see the downside. Typical.

Was that it, the apogee of it? Was that the best it was going to be, ever? So now I'd never get to spin the wheel for the quarter of a million on *Winning Streak*? Only a measly five hundred in the whole of a lifetime?

I couldn't believe how ridiculous I was being, looking a gift horse in the mouth like this. Five minutes ago I had a couple of quid in my purse. Now I have five hundred and I'm miserable? Get a grip, Ange . . .

That five hundred is only the first instalment. *Winning Streak*, here we come!

That win gave me shivers up my spine for another reason too. When I was a child, about seven or eight, I think – Francesca was already out in Stillorgan and

Mammy was pregnant with Justine – didn't she win five hundred pounds on the Golden Goose. That was a competition that you entered when you bought your groceries. It made hardly any difference to us as it happened, because one of the boyfriends, I can't remember which, took it off of her to 'mind it' for her. Mind it, my eye. All we got out of it was a new Hoover (when she was well she was a demon for cleaning) which, in due course, made the trip down to my uncle's in Marlborough Street. But she was so excited about it for the short while she had it. I still remember the evening the man from the Golden Goose shop came to tell us.

We could be a lucky family, you know . . . I don't think it's a coincidence that we both won *exactly* five hundred. There's more going on here than coincidence. Do you think it was an accident that I won five hundred when that was the *exact* amount I was in hock for? (Plus interest but that wouldn't be all that much since the stuff had been in only a few weeks.) I rest my case.

So the five hundred thing is serendipity in our family. That's a favourite word of Pat Kenny's on his radio show. I was delighted when I heard him use it the first time because it's one of my favourites, too. It has a wonderful fairy ring to it, you can almost see its little wings beating with delight. It was a word I originally learnt from Mammy. She didn't have a great vocabulary, now, not brilliant, but certainly streets ahead of the people in the flats. She encouraged me.

I associate the word serendipity with forget-me-nots, I'm not quite sure why, other than that the sounds are quite similar, light. Maybe it's because forget-me-nots were her favourite flowers, they're country flowers. She had a tablecloth, hand-embroidered with them, and she kept it until the very, very last. Maybe she explained serendipity to me when the tablecloth was on display and that's why I make the association but, unfortunately, I can't remember. With the exception of her jewellery and her christening spoon, it was the last of her good things to go and I think this was what finally broke her heart.

So was I to use the five hundred to get her stuff back out of hock or not? I couldn't make up my mind. On the one hand it was her precious jewellery and winning the exact money seemed like a message that I should. On the other hand, we could have done with a few little things around the house and I knew she would want me to have the place nice.

Or was I meant to use it to help James? Sort of a fighting fund, like all the unions have. I decided to sleep on it.

I didn't tell him although I was bursting to. It didn't seem right to be so joyful when he was in such awful trouble.

I couldn't keep it to myself, though, so I went out to ring Patsy to tell her but she was out. Her youngest, Darren, answered the phone. He's a bit of a pup, but I'd never say that to her. He never says hello on the telephone, just yes, or what do you want, or who's that. If we had a telephone, my fella'd know his telephone manners, I'm telling you.

At least I had an English class that night so I didn't have to sit in all night, hugging the great news to myself like a security blanket. My insides felt like a swelling air bubble that I was afraid would pop so I just had to tell someone. I told Mr Elliott while I was helping him distribute the sheets of notes. He's very good that way, he writes out commentaries and notes for us and makes enough copies to go round.

Congratulations, he goes, that's great. It seemed mechanical, though, like saying happy birthday to someone else's friend. So it kind of deflated me. Here was I thinking it was the best thing that ever happened to me, the first rung on the stairway to heaven, and all he can say is congratulations, that's great, in the same tone of voice as if I'd gone back to Unislim and had lost a couple of pounds.

I was determined, though, not to let the lovely feelings go. All through the class I sat there and daydreamed. Suppose I went for the option of keeping the money and not redeeming the jewellery . . . Another part of my brain would kick in then – *tut, tut!* I knew how Christ felt in the desert. Get thee behind me, Satan.

I've always wanted a decent hearthrug for in front the fireplace, Reddy's idea of good taste is a half-moon rug with a cat on it in that kind of fluffy synthetic bathroom-mat material.

A Black and Decker, definitely. Hammer action so you can drill through walls. It would give me a great feeling of independence. And maybe a little tumble drier. I hate hanging out washing, and a tumble drier would be just the height of luxury. Although I've heard they use an awful lot of electricity.

If I did keep it, I should give something to Concern, God love those poor people out in the Third World. Or to Sister Stan for the homeless. I like Trust too, I saw Alice Leahy once on a chat show, and she struck me as doing the most charitable work of all. I mean, could you do the things she does for those poor old men? Like cutting their toenails and treating their poor scabby scalps? Ugh!

I got a great insight into being homeless the night I had to sleep rough down at the Irish Life Centre. Please God neither of us will ever, *ever* have to go through that. I couldn't bear to think of James sleeping rough. It's hard to describe how you feel. Lonely, of course, that goes without saying, but it's a special kind of loneliness. Like you don't belong to anyone and no one belongs to you and you're floating away from the world into some terribly cold, disconnected place and no one would ever come to look for you. That's very scary.

Thank God I had to go through it only that one night. Despite being so worried about what was going on back at the flats, the most irrelevant pictures kept waltzing into my mind. Her special toothbrush that she got from the dental hospital so she wouldn't hurt her gums. The half tin of yellow paint she got from a neighbour to do up the door again where one of the boyfriends had kicked it.

It's funny what adds up to a home, isn't it?

Talking about lonely, I bet Lady Macbeth must have been one of the loneliest people on the planet. I know she was a bad egg but I still felt sorry for her. I mean, deep down, I'd say she only wanted the best for her man and it just all got out of control.

Mr Elliott is getting us to act out bits of both plays to make them come alive for us and to help us remember them. I'm always petrified he'll ask me. He never has, yet, so no doubt my number will be up soon. It must have been terrible for the poor children long ago who had to learn every single famous speech in the plays off by heart for the exams and then get slapped if they didn't know it. What am I talking about, sure didn't it happen to me when I was doing the Inter. I was an execrable pupil, I freely admit that. But I didn't deserve to be slapped. Nobody did.

Thank God the education system is a lot more enlightened now. James doesn't know what it's like to be afraid of a teacher. And if one of them had once lifted a finger to him I'd have been on top of him like a ton of bricks.

Mr Elliott keeps hammering into our heads that we should be able to quote verbatim a few key speeches but nowadays, he says, the examiners go for the sense and the context and the analysis more than the actual words of the play or the poem. All the others in the class ooh and aah over the big, grand speeches, but for entertainment I go for the offbeat bits, like in *Macbeth* when Ross comes in with the Old Man.

> *Threescore and ten I can remember well;*
> *Within the volume of which time I have seen*
> *Hours dreadful and things strange; but this sore night*
> *Hath trifled former knowings.*

Can't you just see them? Nothing's changed in four hundred years, has it? I hear them every day over there on the benches in Mountjoy Park across the road. Coats on and collars turned up even though the sun might be splitting the stones. Giving out the pay about the youth of today and the Government and the price of a pint. Keeping the footballs or the basketballs that roll over towards them from the playground, just out of badness. Falling over each other with horror stories. Everything's always dire, according to them, God love them, with their waddly, ancient Jack Russells on ratty-looking leads that must be as old as the flood. I wonder do they start with big dogs and then move downwards as they get older . . .

We've a mixed bag in our class, including a woman of seventy-four who has three great-grandchildren. There's a carpenter, Ken, who is very nice, I've struck up quite a friendship with him. A rock musician (at least, he says he's a rock musician, I have my doubts) and a couple of other men in cardigans who sit at the back looking furtive. I wouldn't blame them, it's nearly all women and the majority seem to be housewives. We're all doing it to better ourselves. Some of them even say they're going to go on for a degree.

I don't think I will. At least here we're all in the same
boat. We missed out first time round and we feel
sympathetic towards one another.

But maybe that's not strictly true. I think it's a bit of a
waiting and watching game so far and I think I can see the
beginnings of rivalry in a couple of the women. In my
experience, women are desperately competitive, far
more so than men. And very much so with each other.
Men seem to be invisible when women are competing for
whatever's going. It's like the Tour de France. The
women are the peloton always and they let the men off
in front while they watch each other. Amn't I very
knowledgeable, now, about the cycling? (You have to
admit that peloton sounds much better than 'the main
bunch'! Everyone in Ireland is able to toss off those
cycling terms since Stephen Roche's three great victories
in 1987. Not many little countries can boast the Tour de
France, the World Championship *and* the Giro d'Italia all
in the same year – eh?)

That was a great year. Will you ever forget Stephen
coming down the Champs Elysées with his hands in the
air and Charlie Haughey up there on the platform to
meet him. Leave it to Charlie. I like him. I think deep
down, all Dubs do think he was the best Taoiseach we
ever had. You wouldn't be ashamed of him, like, in
foreign company. He knows about wines and he can talk
about the French Revolution with the best of them.

So far there have been no As at all in the class. And, so
far at least, I didn't detect any change in any of them
towards me after my B. I suppose it was such a rare bird
– because I get mostly Cs and Ds – that no one felt
threatened. But I'm watching and waiting. In a university
it must be much worse. I think I'd feel like a fish out of
water. We'll see. Maybe I'll feel more positive about it

when (and if) I get the Leaving. Sometime in the next millennium!

At one stage I did have great hopes of James going to university. Wouldn't Mammy have been proud then, and it would certainly have been one in the eye for the folks down in Birr. Her revenge. I knew it was out of the question for him to be a vet, but maybe zoology or agriculture, something that would really interest him. I could just see him as a student. I see them streeling around town all the time, with their black clothes and their clumpy Docs. They're endearing, in a way, they always look as though they're going on a mission of deadly importance. I suppose at that age everything is important. I don't remember much of that myself, my entire energy was consumed by just looking after James and minding the two of us.

He's very down in himself at the moment. And, to tell you the truth, I can't think of a single thing to say to cheer him up. The solicitor's too busy for me to be bothering him but I must say I think free legal aid is a wonderful invention. I don't know what we'd do without it and I can't think what the poor people must have had to go through in the old days.

The day I went to Drumcondra, which would be a couple of weeks ago now, he questioned me when I got back to make sure I hadn't. I lied. I told him I'd changed my mind. I'd calmed down enough by the time I got home to able to make it convincing.

Her face haunts me.

I can't sleep that night after I've seen her, my imagination is running away with me. I keep seeing him and her together in the Furry Glen. Did she scream? Did he hit her? I can't stand it any longer.

It's about three o'clock in the morning and I hear him

still mooching about in the bedroom, even with all the staying in bed he's not a great sleeper at night, particularly recently.

I go in. Did she scream?

What are you talking about?

You know what I'm talking about. Did she scream?

Shut up. Get out of my room.

I won't get out of your room until you tell me what happened that night. You owe me that much, I'm in hock for you—

I didn't ask you to go in hock for me – all you think about is money—

Tell me what happened or I'll—

Or you'll what?

We glare at each other. He always gets me that way. He knows damn well I won't throw him out. Tough love, they call it. I'm not sure I could ever face tough love. I love him too much. And each other is all we have.

But this time I'm not going to go meekly. There's a lot at stake here, I have to try to understand. I sit down on his bed. I'm not going until you talk to me properly.

It's three o'clock in the bloody morning, he goes. Exactly, I say back to him. So you can see how serious I am.

We start a silence match. He sits down too, he has an old car seat he found in a skip somewhere up on the North Circular Road. One thing about these old houses that people like Reddy have converted, there's plenty of space for you to spread out. He puts on his Walkman and all I hear is the g-dhunk g-dhunk from the little earphones. He'll deafen himself but they all do it. I'm getting irritated although I'm not going to show him that. I'm trying to demonstrate that on this one I'm impervious. So I just sit there, like Mount Rushmore.

His walls are decorated with posters I wouldn't be

caught dead looking at, Black Grape and Oasis, his Kung
Fu stuff and Eddie Irvine. He's mad into racing cars. And
The Cure and Megadeth, although up to recently I
thought The Cure was yesterday's news. Apparently not.
Apparently they're making a comeback and they're even
coming to Dublin.

The silence match stretches on. He's not going to open
his mouth and I'm not going to leave this room until he
does.

I stare at those posters as though I'm in a museum.
They all come to Dublin now, from Springsteen to Take
That and Tina Turner. Even Pavarotti and Placido
Domingo and Barry Manilow. Dublin's huge on the
international circuit.

They all love coming here because of how warm we
are as an audience. I heard Garth Brooks couldn't *believe*
that everyone in the audience knew the words of every
one of his songs, even the new ones on his new album
that was only just being released. I've never been to see
any of them myself but I'll tell you one thing, if Barbra
Streisand ever comes I'll hock more than my possessions
to be in the front row. Although I believe I'll be killed in
the homosexual rush. I don't care who else likes her or
who doesn't, as far as I'm concerned she's fabulous. I
went to see *The Way We Were* three times. Cried buckets.
The Owl and the Pussycat twice. And don't talk to me about
Funny Girl. She can do anything, sing, act, direct, anything. (I didn't go to *Yentl* out of loyalty.)

The minutes tick by, as they say — although he has no
clock in his room.

I'm starting to shiver, because I've only my nightdress
on. He's grand, of course, because he sleeps in his
clothes. I hate that, I've tried to teach him to be hygienic
at all costs but since he was about sixteen, I've been
wasting my breath. If he's tired, he just gets into bed and

pulls the duvet up over his ears and that's the end of it. I
suppose I should be grateful he takes off his boots.

So you're not going to tell me? The shivering is getting
to me.

Of course he doesn't react. His head is bopping to the
g-dhunk g-dhunk, and he has his eyes closed like he was
receiving the stigmata. So I go over and lift one of the
earphones and I bawl at him, Turn that damn thing off.
He gets such a fright he actually does.

Right, I go. I'm too cold and tired now to pursue this
tonight but I'm warning you, I want to know what went
on and that's the end of it. So don't think you can weasel
out of it. I march out of the room.

When I'm back in the bed-settee the doubts start to
creep in. Am I just being a voyeur? But her face is there
every time I close my eyes. I won't lower myself to ask
did she lead him on. Sex is a very complicated matter.

→ Ten ←

Less than two weeks to the Leaving. Yet I'm glad PA System has that wedding on Sunday. I don't think I could stick hanging around the house. His mood becomes very black on Sundays, which, of course, is understandable since he has to face the remands on the Mondays.

I suppose you're surprised I can even *think* of something as ordinary as the Leaving or gigs. To tell the truth, I'm so uptight I've amazed myself that I'm able to concentrate on the books at all – but I am. The human mind never ceases to astonish me.

You can't be wound up to high doh all the time, can you? I don't think your brain would take it. (When I was a child I never associated high doh with singing, I always pictured it as *dough*. Bread dough. I could never understand why everyone thought 'being up to High Dough' was so awful.)

Weddings with us – it's a straight cash deal, nice and clean. We charge eighty quid for the church, forty each. Handy money for an hour's work. It's word-of-mouth and we have a fair reputation now. The only drawback about them, when you compare them to pub gigs, is that you have to dress as if you're a guest and that's a bit of a pain. But we're in the background – we don't do the afters because they usually want to dance and anyway

those afters get pretty messy with drink — so we don't
have to put on too much of the ritz.

Actually, it's as easy as pie, we have the songs down.
Pie Jesu. Panis Angelicus. From A Distance. Barcarolle
sometimes, if the priest doesn't object. And usually the
happy couple wants something that means something to
them. Once we were asked to do King Of The Road
because the groom was a truck driver but the priest drew
the line there.

The classroom that Thursday was hot, and I don't
mean just because of all the tension. It was real summer
heat — I started this summer thinking we were going to
have fabulous weather all season long.

I got a bit dreamy, to tell you the truth. I love the way
the setting sun lights up the top panes of the glass in these
windows so it doesn't even look like glass, more like
delicate polished copper. They're sash windows. Georgian. I think I've already told you that this is one
advantage we have, living in Dublin. Our Georgian
heritage. There is a Georgian Society in Dublin, very
active. They advise you how to go about restoring your
house. In different circumstances, if I owned our couple
of rooms, I'd certainly be a member, although I don't
know if they'd have me. You might have to own a whole
house. But there's a lovely plaster ceiling rose in James's
bedroom and some of the coving in the living room is
intact. It's carved in that classical shape, I think it might
be Greek, you know, sort of like continuous open
swastikas. It'd be nice to know what to do with it to stop
it flaking off on to your shoulders so anyone who spends
any time in our place looks like they have a bad case of
dandruff. I'd even paint it myself if I knew what were the
correct colours.

But with Reddy, you might as well be talking to the
wall. The fanlight over the front door has had two bits of

cardboard in it covering the broken glass since we moved in and that was nearly ten years ago. If he won't even fix that there wouldn't be much hope of him fiddling around with bits of plaster. There's new legislation now, which I think will force him to upgrade the place. He has to register as a landlord with the Government, I think, and they send inspectors. The sooner the better. I'll give them an earful, I will.

All the houses around our square are Georgian, even Discount Electrical. I don't know for sure but they probably have a preservation order on them so that's why Discount Electrical and DID can't put up huge horrible signs.

Proper order, too. To appreciate why, you'd need to see our square on a very early summer morning. Sometimes I try to go out there a few minutes before the minibus calls to collect me for work, just to look at it with all the litter cleaned away. The Corporation is good like that, they're up at the crack of dawn with their sweepers and their little pushcarts. I certainly appreciate them anyway, one professional to another!

Those mornings, you just wouldn't believe the peace and the beauty. Especially if it's a sunny day. No people, no cars. The blackbirds singing their hearts out, the dew on the trees glistening like marcasite. In those early summer mornings it's easy to imagine the people who lived in this square before us. I don't mean this century but years before, when the dresses were huge and made of fabric like cambric or sprigged muslin and everyone wore corsets and they had people handing them down from horse carriages at our front door. I'd have loved that (except for all the manure, of course, but then you'd have servants to clean up that). And strolling in the park with your gentleman friend. Totally safe. That was the time when there were no gurriers, only urchins.

This classroom we're sitting in was probably part of the drawing room in this place. It's an awful pity to see the plywood partitions cutting up all the lovely rooms and the folding doors permanently sealed up. But no blame for the partitions and so on to the people who run this school. They're just entrepreneurs, good entrepreneurs.

In my opinion it's well worth what they charge. I know you can do your Leaving Cert in the state VECs for half nothing but here they get terrific teachers who deserve every penny they make. I'm all for entrepreneurs being rewarded, provided they don't earn it by doing something hookey.

I'm not sure these people even own this building.

Oh, God, he's looking at me. Look away, Ange, don't catch his eye. Anyway, with only two weeks to go we should be concentrating on our notes, not still acting out the bloody thing.

Angela, did you hear me? Are you with us at all this evening?

Sorry, Mr Elliott.

Would you read Ophelia's speech for us. I don't know how you've escaped so far – Ken, you're Hamlet, Mrs B, you be the Gentlewoman. Yes, come on, stand up, the three of you. Start with you, Hamlet—

I go beetroot. *Beetroot*. But I have to stand up.

I'm quite taken aback when Ken starts. God, he's actually quite good. And I never noticed before that he has such a nice voice.

Your woman's useless, but! I wonder does Ken sing—

Angela?

Sorry, sorry, Mr Elliott, I'm nervous, I got a bit distracted.

Try to concentrate, Angela! Please?

Can we start from the beginning again?

No. Start where you come in.

I start. And do you know what? After I get over the initial embarrassment, I find I quite enjoy reading in public. Maybe I'm a secret exhibitionist! I can tell everyone's listening . . .

And Ken is looking over at me, quite surprised too. Bet he didn't think old mousy-boots had it in her . . .

That was very good, Angela, Mr Elliott says, when I come to the end of the speech — you were all very good. Now, ladies and gentlemen, who can tell me why Hamlet reacts the way he does to Ophelia — yes, Dwayne?

I don't listen to Dwayne, I bet Dwayne isn't his real name at all. Rock star, my foot!

I wish we could do it again, dammit, I'd certainly do it much better second time around. Now I'm quite sorry this is the last time we'll be formally acting out the play. *Hamlet* isn't nearly as good as *Macbeth*, though — it's like they're all behind a set of net curtains in that palace.

Poor old Lady Macbeth, what an end. I wonder if she really went to hell? I'm terrified of fire. Don't laugh but until I went to my first cremation I had this incredible vision of what it was. Hell had nothing on it and I was petrified at the thought of going up to Glasnevin to attend it. It was the mother of one of the women at work who was for the flames. I thought that you'd see the remains being taken out of the coffin and shovelled into the fire and the poor face being consumed, the hair on fire and so on. I couldn't sleep a wink the night before.

No hell any more, or so they say. Hell is other people now. I can relate to that, you'd want to walk down O'Connell Street sometimes late on a Saturday night and see what's going on there. It's like one of those intense films from South America you get late night on Channel Four. I wouldn't walk there at times like that, certainly not without James to accompany me. It's a whole other world. Menacing. Not something you could put your finger on, it's just to do with the way the gangs and crowds of young people hang around together and look at you. (And remember where I came from! If they make me afraid, what would it be like to be someone from the suburbs or the country.)

And the things you read these days about poor inoffensive shop assistants being terrorized with syringes full of HIV and gougers beating up old people in rural Ireland and throwing them down wells and shovelling a load of sand on top of them.

Still, I suppose it's not quite as bad as some other parts of the world, or so we're told anyway.

So was there a cut-off point at some stage where those who were infallibly sent to hell were just unfortunate to be born during the time that hell existed? I don't believe a word of Papal Infallibility. Never did. As soon as it was explained to me at school I knew it was a lie. Probably to stop people asking awkward questions. Put your hand down, Angela Devine, you just have to believe it, it's an article of faith. They always said that if you pursued them. Or, You're not supposed to understand it, it's a mystery. That was a great one.

Don't ask me how I knew about infallibility, I just knew. I mean, if the Pope is infallible he's God, isn't he? Isn't it only God who's perfect? (I know the old argument about them being only infallible when they're speaking *ex cathedra*, but it seems to me they insist on being infallible all the time if you challenge anything they say.)

The last time I prayed, really prayed, was the night I sent Tom Bennett packing. I don't know what I was praying for. I meant it when I banished him and I was certainly not going to renege but I was sick to my stomach. I didn't regret it exactly, it was more like, *what have you done?* It was the exact opposite of the giant air bubble feeling after I won the five hundred pounds on the scratch card. This was like my whole body was a crater as big as Australia.

I'm ashamed to say I prayed like a baby, to Saint Jude, would you believe, although up to then he never did anything for me. He's the patron of hopeless cases. I was a hopeless case, all right. I'd made the decision and I had to stick with it but you wouldn't know by my behaviour that night, blubbering and carrying on.

He's pretty far gone when he comes to the door, swaying on his feet and bouncing off the uprights when I open up to his knock. I take one look at him and order him out. What? His eyes are bleary. He's blinking very, very slowly.

You heard me, I go, out. And this is the end of it, we're finished. I warned you and I meant it.

What?

He can't understand words of one syllable. He's bobbing in the doorway there like he's in one of those baby bouncers. I'm so angry that at this stage there isn't a chance I'll weaken. Although he does look pretty pathetic with his mouth hanging open and drool running down his chin. His fly is open too. You'd never think by looking at him that he's usually a sharp dresser. I give him a little shove and he looks shocked. What? he goes again.

Have you a one-word vocabulary or what? I say. I want to shout, the noise is forcing its way up my throat, but I don't want to wake James. You and I are no longer engaged, I go as calmly as I can. It is over. Capeesh?

Well eff off, so, he says it quite quietly and he's still looking surprised. He backs off and I close the door and that's that.

It doesn't really dawn on me what's happened until

about twenty minutes later and that's when I begin to cry. And then the praying starts. Like I've been brainwashed from a baby. Cry – pray – cry – pray. Or like a spy, who has this 'pray' microchip buried in her which is only activated by tears.

Stupid. Because I don't believe people should pray for things in a fair-weather way. It's like being married, you're in it for better for worse, for richer for poorer, not just for worse or for poorer, which was the way I seemed to be acting. In the club or out of it. And I was out. I couldn't cherrypick just because I needed it.

Lately, though, I find myself envying people who can get comfort from religion. I see them hurrying into Gardiner Street church just down the road from here, that's a Jesuit place, and when they're going in, they look as though they feel, well, here's at least one place where we really belong.

On the other hand, if it was really a religion the way Jesus Christ founded it, wouldn't one of the local clergy have called around to James and me to ask if there was any way he could be of assistance? Isn't that what they're supposed to do – after all, we are parishioners even if we are lapsed. They're not supposed to make judgements, are they? They're supposed to rush to help souls in trouble, no matter how sinful.

And don't tell me they don't know. Of course they know. They bloody know everything. In the olden days how come they seemed to know girls were pregnant nearly before they knew it themselves.

The tension of this thing is obviously getting to me. The last thing James and I need at this moment in time is a Jesuit on the doorstep.

It's eating me up, the thought of him raping a girl in the Furry Glen. If it was really rape, of course.

I wish I'd already told Patsy, then I'd have someone to

discuss it with. I've tried to analyse why I haven't told her, she is my best friend after all and I see her regularly. Something's stopping me.

There's something on her mind too and I bet it's Martin. She rarely mentions him voluntarily these days. When I ask her how he is, or how he's doing, she becomes animated. Jaunty. Everything's always hunky-dory.

Too hunky-dory.

He's got the prize for selling the most cars for two months in a row, the partnership (he's in with another fella in a fast-food place somewhere on the South Circular Road) is going a bomb, he's had this great idea where he and another pal are going to start importing some bits of a computer which are terribly expensive in Ireland. They'll do it through the North, all above board and legal, pay all the import duties and they'll still make a fortune.

If it's true that he's doing so well, I sometimes wonder why she does the gigs and the weddings. Forty pounds, even into her hand, shouldn't make that much difference to her. I did ask her once but she dismissed it airily. It's her fun money, she says.

Somehow that doesn't wash with me. You just know by the way she's talking that there's something going on underneath. And then there's the constant moan about the children being at such an expensive stage.

Yet I don't want to pry into her business. If she wants to tell me, she'll tell me. Like me. If I really wanted to tell her I'd tell her.

In a funny way, I think what's holding me back is that I've been confiding all my troubles in her for years now and she's never confided any back. Not real ones. She appears to go tit-for-tat, telling me when her kids fail their Christmas exams or whatever.

But I know she has real troubles, she has to, everyone has. So we've become unequal. If I tell her about James, that will tip the balance. We'll be so unequal then as to be out of sight of one another. And I don't want to be unequal to anyone, even my best friend. It's a conundrum, I know, but it's what I feel. And the older I get the more I trust my feelings. She'll probably be hurt if she finds it out from the papers before I tell her but that's a bridge I'll have to cross when I come to it.

To give her her due, she was thrilled for me about the scratch card. Genuinely. And she's going, oh, Angela, you should take a holiday. We should both go, we'll go to Minorca, Martin has a contact in a travel agency, he'll get us a discount.

Of course, then I was up against another conundrum. I couldn't tell her about my problem as to whether to use the money to redeem Mammy's stuff because she'd want to know why I hocked it in the first place.

What about James, I say to her, I can't leave him. Pish tosh, she says back, what age is that boy? You're going to have to cut those apron strings sooner or later.

She hasn't a clue. It's all right for her, with her nice family with a mammy and a daddy and a real semi-detached house on the Navan Road.

I mumble something and she lets it be but she warns me it's only for now. She's going to insist that I knock some enjoyment out of my winnings because we'll all be dead long enough.

I hated not telling her the truth. We were losing intimacy.

Anyway, I didn't have the money yet. Would you believe, two weeks on and I still hadn't brought in the scratch card to the GPO to cash it in. I sort of felt that when I did that the die was cast. It's like cutting a round birthday cake with flawless royal icing as white as diamonds. As soon as you make the first cut with the knife it's ruined and you'll never get that perfection back. That scratch card with those three beautiful five hundreds was perfect the way it was. I loved it. If I was to give it over to get the money, it wouldn't be perfect any more, even if they gave me lovely new crisp notes.

Because then I'd be up against all the decisions. In a funny way, as long as that card was there, uncashed, I saw it as sort of protecting me from my problems. A talisman. Every time I looked at it, it grew into my chest like a warm ball of wool.

Crazy, really, when you think of it, because every week that went by the interest was mounting up at the pawnbroker's.

All right, I say to James, when I get home from the class, we still haven't got a trial date and you still haven't told me.

He goes to leave the room but I block his bedroom door. Please, James, I'm standing by you. You see I am. Why don't you trust me?

That does it. He bursts into tears.

Oh, God, when I think of it the tears come back into my own eyes. I mean, he acts so tough. And here he is, crying like he's four and the playground bully has just thumped him. He's heartbroken.

What can I do. I stand there. I want to throw my arms around him and squeeze all the tears out of him and take them into myself for him. But I can't. He's too big for that, he'd die. I'd give anything in the world, everything I owned, to make it all go away but I can't do that either. So I just wait. Don't cry, I go, don't cry, James. And I'm still having a desperate job trying to keep from crying myself. He's saying something through the crying, how did I get into this mess, but he's saying it with his mouth open wide, so it's hard to understand. How did I get into this mess, how, how, how.

It'll be all right, I go, it'll be right, James. Sit down and we'll talk about it, we'll talk about our strategy.

He's snivelling and naturally he doesn't have a tissue so I go to get some. Luckily I've just done the shopping so we have a whole box. I hand him a wad of them. Here you go, come on now, blow your nose. It's going to be all right.

He takes the tissues and blows and then there's another storm of crying and then it dies away.

Would you like a cup of tea? I go. And a chocolate Kimberley? I'd splashed out a bit that week, what with the five hundred snug in its hidey-hole down by the side of the bed-settee.

He nods miserably.

I go to make the tea and take a bit of time about it to let him compose himself and when I come back he's sitting just staring at the floor. But at least he's calm again. Because it's midsummer, there's still light in the sky even though it's well after half past ten. And our windows are so huge we haven't had to turn on the lights yet. He's sitting in shadow, with his face turned to the outside world, like a silhouette against the brightness. As you've probably gathered, the backs of their necks always gets to me. I don't know why. It always looks so tender and vulnerable on boys. Not exactly weak but naked. Like it's been made ready for the guillotine.

Which James's was in a way.

He hasn't had a haircut for a good while (thank God, because he favours the skinhead look, number-one blade) and a bit of his hair is flopping down over his forehead like a kid's. Hair grows a lot faster in summer.

He takes the tea and the Kimberley but he's afraid to

look up at me. I know him so well I can tell. I wait again while he unwraps the biscuit and takes the first bite. And then the first slug of tea.

Tell me about it now, I say.

→ Eleven ←

The following night, I went back to Patsy's house for a cup of coffee after one of the gigs. A huge twenty-first birthday bash. I was surprised when she told me about the booking. I wouldn't have thought our kind of music would have been suitable. But apparently the father had heard us during some Sunday-morning pub gig when he was in curing a hangover from the night before. Probably he was in the doghouse and we were handy. You know, sort of as a peace-offering to the wife – look, I do care, I've made these arrangements . . .

It turned out to be a very rich family from Castle-knock. And I needn't have worried about how our music was going to be received, they had *two* marquees, one for the birthday girl and her pals, one for themselves and the parents and their own friends. We were in theirs. Imagine! A garden big enough to take two marquees with enough space between them so the loudness of the disco didn't interfere with us. Caterers. Professional barmen, balloons, flowers, even special buses for after the party so people could drink themselves silly and not be caught driving by the Guards. All for a twenty-one-year-old!

And the presents! None of your travelling alarm clocks or your cheapo cassette tapes from O'Connell Bridge.

Real gold jewellery, vouchers for a hundred pounds from Brown Thomas, stuff for the girl's pony. There was a special table for the presents in the hallway of the house and I sneaked a look.

We don't know the half of the money in this country.

But they still only paid us the going rate. Ah well, that's how they keep it, I suppose.

When we let ourselves in Patsy's house was quiet and dark. I'm usually tired and looking for my bed on Friday nights after the week – and I had the Saturday job to think about – but you do get fired up after singing, so when she suggested going back to her place I agreed right away. Her mother was staying with her for a few days and I didn't want to run into her because the tension between her and Patsy is terrible. But I figured it was late enough for her to be in bed and I was right.

Would you prefer a drink? Patsy asks, as she switches on the lights in the kitchen. No thanks, I go, coffee will be fine. Then I ooh and aah over her new kitchen. They had it done by a designer from one of those places that specializes in kitchens and bathrooms and this is the first time I've seen it. It's gorgeous, all pine, with dark red tiles on the wall and a white tiled floor. Two sinks, all the appliances built in.

She has one of those new tumble driers where you don't have to put a hole in the wall, it condenses the steam and puts it in a bottle. It's been on the tip of my tongue for weeks to ask her about her old one – don't get me wrong, I'd buy it from her – but I don't want to put her under any obligation. She might have given it away to a charity and then she'd feel awful about not thinking of me. My plan is to find an excuse at some stage to go into their garage. It might be stored there – and then I could bring up the subject by-the-way. Do you really like the kitchen? she asks.

It's beautiful, I say, and I'm being sincere. It's like something out of a magazine.

She doesn't seem to care one way or the other what I think about the kitchen. She seems distracted as she measures coffee beans into a grinder and plugs in the coffeemaker. You'd think you were in a restaurant.

Neither of us says anything as we wait for the coffee to be ready. She stares at the machine and I'm so tired I just sit there at the table drinking in the peace. The sound of the percolator plunking away to itself is soothing.

We're sipping the stuff, still saying nothing, when suddenly, without warning, the tears start to slide down her face.

I'm absolutely poleaxed. I've never, ever seen Patsy crying before, at least not since we hooked up together again after Mammy's funeral. Of course I saw her crying as a child. We were both always crying when we were in Sister Concepta's class. She used to slap us with this leather belt that she kept around her waist with one long end hanging down. I often wondered later on what she thought about when she put it on every morning. I mean, she had to put it on for no other reason but to slap us, it certainly wasn't necessary for keeping up her habit! Was she saying her matins when she fastened it? Did she see us all out on the line and her going down it, slapping us one by one? Did she look forward to it? (I wonder is that the origin of the sayings 'give him a belt' or 'hit her a belt'. I never thought of that before.) She used to shove the tip of her tongue out through her lips as she concentrated on lining up our hands just right for maximum impact.

What's the matter? I go. Please, Patsy, what's the matter? I get up and go around the table and put my arms round her. (It's weird that I was able to do that with her and not with James.) She shakes her head, it seems she can't say anything.

Talk about feeling helpless.

There has to be something the matter, I'm nearly in tears myself, tell me, please. Go on, no matter how bad it is it can't be that bad. I'm thinking cancer. You know the way you do. But she looks fine.

Then I'm thinking, Martin's left her. Is it Martin? I say it very gently, I don't want to make things worse.

It seems I've hit the nail on the head. She has a box of tissues on the counter top near where we're sitting – she has this island unit in the middle of the new kitchen – and she takes a handful and blows her nose. She's nodding while she's blowing and the tears are really pouring now.

Oh, God, another woman, is it?

I think so, she goes, and you can barely hear her.

I wait. These days, I seem to spend half my life waiting. I'm half sorry I didn't accept her offer of a real drink although I've given up drink for the duration. Not that I drink much, hardly at all as a matter of fact, but at the moment it's a combination of wanting to keep a clear head and some sort of instinct that I have to make sacrifices if this thing with James is going to turn out all right. Superstition, I suppose. But it gives me a feeling that I'm doing *something* rather than just hanging around waiting for things to happen to us. One good thing – I'm losing weight. Patsy had remarked on it earlier that evening, looked keenly and then asked if I'd gone back to Unislim on the sly.

The whole thing comes spilling out. She found condoms in the pocket of one of his suits.

I stare at her. I'm on tricky ground here, I don't quite know what their marital arrangements are in that department. Women are funny about sex. They either tell you everything – you should hear some of the stuff that goes on after a few jars at our Christmas party at the cleaning job – or they go all coy. Patsy is somewhere in between. Over the years I've got hints that their sex is pretty volatile, great one time, useless the next, but I never initiate the conversations. I have nothing to offer in return, the Tom Bennett situation is such history now that it's antique and I wouldn't want the confidences to be a one-way street.

It turns out that those condoms are a dead giveaway because she had her tubes tied after Darren.

Now this is the first I've heard of this but I try not to show how surprised I am. She doesn't notice. She's looking into her cup of coffee. She's barely touched it yet. You remember I went off that time for a few days, she says, supposedly to a hotel in the country to learn to play bridge?

I remember, I say. Well, I didn't go to play bridge, she goes, I went to a clinic and had it done.

I see, I say. I'm trying to sound matter-of-fact. Patsy goes to Mass and even confession. Having your tubes tied is definitely out as far as the Catholic Church is concerned, but now is not the time to go into that.

I keep my voice quiet. I'd been wondering about that, I say, because you never seemed to want to play bridge again—

Well, that's when I had it done.

We both sit staring into our coffee.

So did you ask him about the condoms? This is awful. Nobody thanks you for interfering in a marriage. They might be going through just a temporary thing and then she'll be embarrassed that she told me.

She shakes her head.

Why not?

Because there'll be a huge row and he'll leave me. She bursts into tears again, real heavy sobbing.

Through the noise she manages to get a few things out. The main problem seems to be not just Martin leaving, but that if he does she thinks she'll be destitute. That if he skips she won't be able to find him. And as she's told me so often before, the three kids are just coming into the expensive stage. Darren is still only six but Maeve is due to start secondary school in September and Pauline has a Confirmation coming up next year.

I have to be sure. Is that what'd really bother you? I ask when I'm pretty sure she can hear me. The money? Not him leaving?

She puts her hands over her face. I don't know, I don't know.

I think as fast as I can. Now I see why she's doing the gigs. It wasn't just for fun money.

I try to disregard what James told me about seeing Martin in that club. Look, I go, just finding a handful of condoms doesn't mean a damn thing. Maybe he was minding them for a friend who's married and having an affair. Maybe it was for a stag and they were going to play a trick on the fella – had he any stags coming up?

She's just sitting there with her hands over her face and shaking her head and crying and saying, I don't know, all the time.

I have to let her cry. I realize I don't remember seeing his car in the driveway. He drives an Audi, she has a little Toyota Starlet. She was as proud as punch when he got it for her for their anniversary two years ago. (I know all about cars. You couldn't live with James Devine and not know about cars.)

I see another opportunity to get in. Where is he now? I ask.

I don't know, I don't know, she goes, wailing, and then she hushes up, afraid her mother will hear and come down to see what's up. She's beginning to sound like a stuck record.

I realize that's unkind and I try desperately to think of

some positive input. We wear a lot of make-up for the gigs and hers is now all over her face, mascara and kohl spreading black spiderwebs through her blusher. She looks her age too, whatever way the light is shining on her neck you can see those horrible crinkles, like unironed washing. I hated seeing her like that. She's usually so chic. The situation isn't helped by the fact that our working dresses are black — we copied them from the backing singers in *The Commitments*. Black is all right when you're on stage but it's dreadful under fluorescent light.

All right, I go with as much confidence as I can inject into my voice. Let's look at this clearly. What we have here is just a suspicion, isn't that right? This could be just a bad patch. You've no idea that he's playing around. Not really. What we have to decide is whether to face him with it or not. There are pluses and minuses in each way of doing things. You could scare him into sense or you could push him into running, it depends what he's feeling at the moment. He might want to be caught or he might want to be given an excuse to go. And don't forget there might be a perfectly innocent explanation.

But where is he now? she goes. It's two o'clock in the morning and he's not here—

That's a fair point, I have to admit that.

But, I go then, we have to decide what you want and what's the best course to take, taking the kids into account. And the principal thing, if we do find out he's messing, we have to decide how much you can put up with and what you really want deep down in your heart. It's your life, Patsy, you have to think of yourself. This is not a rehearsal.

I'm ashamed of this. This isn't me, it's Gay Byrne on the radio. I'm obviously listening to too much of him. The money factor is not to be discounted, I say quickly, and you know and I know what happens when marriages break up. It's the women and kids that have to take the drop.

Now I don't really believe that, not deep in my heart. What I really believe is that some women — most women actually — are far better at coping than they want men to think. But Patsy's in no condition to go into the niceties and I know that this is probably what she wants to hear.

For whatever reason, something clicks and she stops crying. She scrubs at her eyes: I must look a fright. She gives this pathetic little laugh.

This is breaking my heart, this is the woman who's always holding the reins. You do, I say like a teacher. Now go and wash your face and we'll talk this over rationally.

Thanks, Ange, she says, and goes to repair the damage. They have a downstairs loo.

I drink my coffee — cold as rainwater now — while I think things over. How I've missed the depths of poor Patsy's problem I can't imagine because it didn't just happen overnight. I'd had my little niggles, like I've told you before, but I never dreamt they were anything more than that. Thought I was just being cynical. I'm kicking myself now for not being more aware.

I suppose I've been so wrapped up in our own troubles. Where they're concerned by the way, I have to tell you that at least I know now exactly what we're dealing with there.

It turns out to be a very simple, very small, tawdry little story.

The whole episode had started the previous night. They were at a party in a house somewhere up in the Strawberry Beds, some friend of this Rosemary's. Another twenty-first — I seemed to be haunted by twenty-firsts, these days. Anyway, they were all drinking, cider, beer, vodka. And a few of them also had marijuana and E. James did *not* take the drugs. He swears he didn't and I believe him. Maybe I'm being gullible but I believe him.

I asked him where the parents were during all this. They were away, apparently, it was a free house.

Anyway, they're all drinking and dancing and having a good time and a few of them are availing themselves of the bedrooms. Rosemary and James are dancing and he gets the signal that she's giving him the come-on. They go outside into the garden but it's freezing that night and it's starting to rain. There and then they make a date to meet the following day. And she kisses him and she says, You bring the condoms.

He's telling me all of this and he can't look at me. I don't blame him.

Next day they meet as arranged and he's all excited. He can't sleep the night before, thinking about what's going to happen. He says he's never gone the full, whole way with anyone before. (And here we all are, thinking young people today are at it like rabbits from the age of twelve!) They go up to the Park and on the way they have a few little spats, he's going too fast on the bike, that sort of thing. In hindsight I can see that she was being very tense. And to be fair to her, maybe she was already regretting her invitation. But if she was, that was the time to say it, wasn't it?

So they get to the park and he stashes the bike in some bushes and they go down into the Furry Glen. Because it's a weekday and the weather is still a bit cold, there's nobody about, only two girls on horses who don't give them even a look.

There's a particular place down by the bridge over the little lake where the forest is very thick. She wants to stop to look at the baby ducks swimming about under the bridge and he's trying to drag at her to come in under the trees, come on, come on. She pulls her hand away, no, there's plenty of time. She thinks the little ducks are beautiful, wishes she'd brought bread to throw at them. He's kissing her everywhere he can and she's half responding, half not. Then she starts to give out to him. Tells him to have some patience.

Then some old lady comes along, dawdling, picking up bits of twigs and dead leaves and putting them in a bag she's carrying. James gets embarrassed, thinking she may have seen him kissing Rosemary, and then he looks closely at her and sees she's not paying a blind bit of attention. In fact, he thinks she's a bit of a head case. Come on, he drags at Rosemary again, I haven't got all day, I've got to get back to work. He tells me he's dying of frustration at this point, that he's like a kettle that can't boil.

Because she insists, they wait until the old lady passes and then they go into the forest and lie down. He's all set to do it straight away but she wants to take her time. It's her first time, too, to go all the way and she wants it to last. She doesn't want him to take off any of her clothes. She'll do it herself in her own good time. He's going mad now.

She puts her arms around him and starts kissing him and he takes that as the signal. He starts getting really excited and shaking and kissing her back wildly and she tells him to take it easy or the whole thing's cancelled. He tries, he tells me he really *tries* to stop himself, to take it easy like she said, but some demon takes hold of him and he starts pulling at her clothes. Her underclothes. He mumbles this as he's telling me, he obviously can't say the word knickers. I've brought him up better than that.

She slaps his hand away and when he sulks, she laughs. Now will you take it easy, she says. She kisses him some more. He's going mad now. He thinks he's going to burst. He rolls on top of her. First she lets him and keeps kissing him and stroking his back and then she stops. Stop it, she tells him, stop it . . . He admits she says that.

But, according to him, he can't stop it then, it's too late. And he rips off her knickers and goes into her. He can't remember the next couple of seconds but he hears her scream, not a loud scream into the sky, just a scream into his ear, where she calls him a terrible name. He won't say what it is in front of me. I can well imagine.

And now, according to him, he immediately stops and pulls out. He insists he did not have an orgasm. He now has a pain down there which is so bad it's worse than when he had to get his appendix out.

As proof he didn't go the whole way to orgasm, he tells me he had forgotten to put his condom on and she didn't get pregnant. It seems James's grasp of the facts of life and of virginity and conception is less than perfect. Well, I did my best.

They lie there, not exactly side by side, more with their backs to each other. The pain he has eases off a bit. He feels and hears her getting her clothes to rights again. She stands up and he does himself up and stands up too.

She tells him she's very annoyed at what he did to her knickers, the elastic at the waist has snapped and she can't wear them now. But he can tell by the way she stuffs them into the pocket of her anorak and won't look him straight in the face that she's ashamed about the whole thing. He is too, now. He's mortified, actually, feels like a right prat.

They go back to the bike and neither of them says a word. He takes her to Drumcondra and lets her off. She says goodbye to him and he thinks she's calmed down. But he hasn't the nerve to make another date. Not just yet.

Instead, he just says, See ya around. Yeah, she says, see ya.

Now this is his version and I accept it is one of the areas which is in dispute. According to her statement, I haven't seen it but the solicitor told me, she does not say see ya or anything like it. According to her statement, she's so traumatized and agitated about what happened earlier she runs away as fast as she can go to get away from him. Without saying anything at all.

He *insists* she said see ya and that she walked. And that, as far as he was concerned, they were both just a bit embarrassed.

I think this is crucial. I mean, if she did talk to him and say see ya — well, you can work it out for yourself. It opens up a host of possibilities. And she did take the lift home from him on the back of the bike. She would have had to hold on to him. Would she have accepted such intimate contact if she'd been so traumatized by a man who'd just raped her?

Whatever about who's in the right in that regard, he's very upset for the next couple of days, doesn't know quite what to do next and that's why he buys the Cadbury's Roses to bring up to her. Cadbury's Cadbury's Cadbury's . . .

I don't know what to make of the whole incident, to tell you the truth, I've told you as he told me and as honestly as I can. Is that rape or is it not?

Patsy comes back from the loo. She's taken off all her make-up and her face is red and greasy from the remover. You'd know she'd been crying, you couldn't miss it, you can hardly see her eyes. My heart goes out to her.

We bat the problem of Martin to and fro but we come to no conclusions. We decide to sleep on it and that she'll do nothing, say nothing, for the short term anyway. If he brings up the matter of his whereabouts tonight — and we think this is unlikely — she'll just pretend she came in and went to bed and she was so tired she didn't even notice he wasn't there.

It's so late now I decide not to embark on telling her about James, although with the balance between us redressed, I know I'm going to be able to tell her after all. It's not that I'm glad she's having problems too – far from it – but it does make me feel that James and I aren't alone.

→ Twelve ←

Another remand. The weeks are flying by. Half of me is dreading the awful day getting closer, the other half welcomes the way Mondays keep coming up so quickly. Because the sooner we get this trial over with and know the worst, or the best, the better.

He certainly didn't mean to rape her. I'll go to my grave believing that much.

I've tried to be fair and to look at it from her side. She definitely told him to stop. He definitely didn't stop.

On the other hand, she's there by appointment to do it. It was she who told him to bring the condoms. She willingly went in with him to that wood to do it. All right, she changed her mind and of course I accept that she had every right to change her mind.

At that stage, though, he was too far gone, he mightn't even have heard her telling him to stop at the beginning when there was still time for it to stop short of – you know . . . He certainly believes he didn't hear her.

Like, didn't he stop the minute she screamed into his ear? As soon as he understood she really meant it? Shouldn't that count on his side?

She just got scared is my interpretation of it. Probably it was only when it was really happening did she realize what she was getting into. Probably worried that her parents would find out. Who knows.

I remember in my own early days, long before I met Tom Bennett, there was an oul' fella in the flats, oul' Mooney, who used to flash at me and not only at me, at anything in a skirt. One day he caught me when I was taking a short-cut through the back alley between the street and the flats. He got me up against a wall – I must have been only about thirteen at the time – and shoved his manky dirty thing in under my skirt. Yuck. It felt like a horrible dry worm. I never reported him. I suppose I should have.

But it didn't blight my whole life.

Neither did the episode with the boy I met at one of the discos run by some outfit or other – I can't remember the name of it now – which was trying to provide amenities for young people in the inner city. I was fourteen and a half then. He was a nice-looking boy, tall, fair-haired, the kind I always go for. We danced a bit and at a certain stage, we sneaked out around the back. There were loads of couples hard at it up against the wall.

We started to snog and things began to get out of hand. I could feel him getting too excited for his own good. I started to say, No, stop it, no, and he wouldn't. He just kept on. He might have gone the whole way with me, he had my knickers half-down and his own fly open – he was much bigger and stronger than I was – if it hadn't been for the girl keeping nix on the corner who spotted the chaperone coming so we all had to scatter.

That episode didn't blight my life either but I suppose nowadays I could claim it did. If it happened now I could probably bring him to court for sexual assault. But it never occurred to you in those days, you just put it down to experience and got on with it. The statistics say that more than one in ten Irish children have suffered sexual assault. Well, I definitely did, with oul' Mooney, but I would definitely not count the time with the boy out the back at the disco because I was half to blame as far as I was concerned. God knows, we were warned enough about boys.

And as far as I'm aware, I'm not psychologically scarred. Or am I? If I went to a psychiatrist, would he find that I am?

And does Patsy's experience count? We did have a discussion about this once. The only time she could remember anything like that happening to her was the day she was on the top of a number 54 bus on the way out to visit her auntie in Terenure and an oul' fella (they're always oul' fellas) sat in beside her and slid his hand up under her skirt. We were always told just to get up straight away if that happened and tell the conductor. She did that and that was the end of it. She didn't even tell her auntie because loads of us knew people to whom it had happened. And she had thought no more about it until we were both racking our brains that day to find out did we fit into the statistics on child sexual abuse.

We decided we were both marginal, but I suppose nowadays not many of the experts in the field would agree. And if you were to ask me objectively, I'd say that if it had happened twenty years ago, James's episode with Rosemary would have been on the marginal side too. Unfortunately for us, it's not twenty years ago.

Do you know what I think? I think she got in a row at home about where she was that afternoon – maybe they started getting on her case about mitching from her bookkeeping course. Or the mother found grass stains on her – or even the torn knickers. Yes, that would have been it. She had no way to explain the state of those knickers without implicating herself. So to defend herself she cried rape.

It wouldn't be the first time that's happened.

It's nearly time for this morning's proceedings to start. He's fidgety this morning, and it took me ages to get him out of bed. I think he's still not sleeping.

I'm not looking at Mrs Madden, nor she at me. We're both sitting in the same places each time. At least she is, she must be first in the queue every Monday. The courtroom is so crowded at the beginning of the sessions that sometimes I can't find a seat but I tend to hang around in roughly the same area. It's a funny thing but familiarity always makes you feel a little less uncomfortable, doesn't it?

We're lucky so far that the girl from RTE, who's the only reporter I've recognized here from the beginning, is still showing no interest in us. Bigger fish to fry, I suppose, with the trial that's coming up after all us remands. I think it's about fraud. Money anyway, you'd know by the number of senior counsel. And today there are two other girls and a man I haven't see before on the press bench so there must be something big.

I hope to God one of them's not from the *Herald*. Rape is meat and drink to that paper and everyone I know reads it.

If I closed my eyes, I could draw this courtroom from memory now. We're all getting to know each other, especially the other groups of remand people. Some of the defendants are in custody, my heart goes out to them, the weather is gorgeous at the moment and they come up looking like E.T.

Actually, it's amazing how quickly you get acclimatized to who everyone is and what everyone does in a courtroom. If I wasn't so worried I'd be blasé about it, it's that familiarity again. For instance, I'm not all that pushed any more about people looking at us. We can look straight back at them — I mean, why are *they* here? What do *they* have to hide? And we're all innocent until proven guilty, aren't we? Solicitors seem to be the only ones in the whole system who look completely at ease and in control of things. In fact, most of the time they look quite bored.

And as for the barristers, God love some of them, they look as if they've just got out of nappies.

And now that I've settled in a bit, I can see details I missed the first few times like, I can't get over how shabby some of the older barristers look. I mean, they're supposed to be earning a fortune, you'd think they'd get their gowns cleaned, wouldn't you? At least brush the dandruff off the shoulders and get someone to sew on a few buttons. The young women are a bit better, I have to admit, but even they could smarten up a bit, shoe polish must be going out of fashion. And I have a thing about scuffed heels, nobody need have scuffed heels in this day and age, not with all the heel bars in this city. I insist that James is turned out as shiny as a soldier. I believe it will pay off in the long run.

I can still feel him shaking beside me. Familiarity is certainly not helping him much.

We haven't seen any juries yet because we're always gone before the jury is called for whatever case is on that day but the court clerk must be the most miserable-looking individual I have ever seen in my life. Talk about being unhappy in his work. He seems to have a tic.

Now that we're on barristers, ours is a bit too nonchalant about the whole thing for my liking. St John Markey (would you believe!) looks about thirteen. I exaggerate, he looks about seventeen. They don't have to wear the wigs any more but most of them still do, and St John's looks as though it's just come out of its tissue paper. I suppose it makes them feel more grown-up. The state side has a much older man. I wish we could get an older man, I think I'd feel more confident.

All rise.

I remember *Rowan and Martin's Laugh-in* when I was a little girl. 'Here comes the judge' was one of the catchphrases on it.

Oh, God, is it my imagination or did she nod down at us? She certainly looked down at us. Kind of speculatively. I definitely wasn't imagining that – there was a look on her face for an instant. What does that mean? Does it mean she's thinking about James's case? In her mind is James already guilty? Dammit, I wish we'd drawn a man judge . . .

I'm just being ridiculous. There's been no evidence yet. And they're required to be impartial.

Our solicitor Patrice Murphy thinks she'll be very straight with us. He has a small reservation, though, she's quite new and nobody knows yet what her track record is going to be. And nobody knows what she feels about rape, because when she was a barrister she was never involved in either prosecuting or defending one. Or, not any notorious one that anyone heard about.

I wonder; do women barristers try not to take on rape cases on grounds they might be prejudiced? It's a very emotive area.

Jesus, St John Markey has one foot up on the bench while he's talking to the judge. I bet she won't like that. Put your foot down, you eejit, you . . .

I often wonder how much of Mammy is in me. To be more accurate, I worry about it. It's one of the reasons I'm very strict with myself. Even when I have a whole day off, such as Sundays with no gigs, I get up and dress myself properly, ironed blouse, polished shoes, the lot. Some of the women at work come in in track suits and runners. I despise track suits and runners. I know they're comfortable – or so they say – but I think they're the lazy option. They say, Who cares, who'll see us at five o'clock in the morning, but that's not the point. We see ourselves, don't we? I'm meticulous about keeping my nails clean and although it costs a fair bit, I have my hair cut every six weeks and I go to the dentist at least once a year.

Maybe all of this make me a bit of an obsessive but I'd be afraid that if I let myself go at all I'd start down the slippery slope. You have to be careful of your genes.

I'll never know for sure but I'd say what happened to Mammy was that she'd had nobody to set her an example, even though, reading between the lines, her own mother seems to have been a bit of a tartar. (Her father was apparently more easygoing.)

Unfortunately I gather that even when those children were small, neither of their parents had much to do with them. They were in business in Birr and they were always, literally, minding the shop. Shops, plural – they had two, a hardware shop and a clothes shop. Their children were looked after by maids and housekeepers all the time but, from what Mammy said, the staff turnover was pretty high. They were always being fired for nicking, or on suspicion of nicking, or they couldn't take the sharp end of Mammy's mother's tongue and they left in high dudgeon.

Imagine, though! Our family once had servants!

Although her father's stock was probably Irish, Devine is quite an Irish name, my grandmother's maiden name was de Vere. That part of Ireland, Laois and Offaly, are the two counties which were the first to be planted by the English. One day, just out of the blue, the King of

England granted our land to some of his English pals and cleared us off them. In fact, Offaly was called King's County and Laois was Queen's County. (To the day she died Mammy referred to Portlaoise and Tullamore as Williamstown and Maryboro – they were named after King William and Queen Mary.) It was weird for me to be learning about this in history class in school and to know that my own family were probably planters. I kept quiet about it, of course.

You'd know, right up to the end, that she had blue blood in her. There was something about her, a sort of delicacy, and she had small, elegant hands which were very expressive, they reminded me of little cabbage moths. So you can see how ill-fitted she was for life in the flats. It's no wonder what happened to her actually did.

On her behalf it makes my blood boil when I read articles in the papers going on and on about single mothers with five or six children sponging off the state. What did they expect her to do? Put us all in the bin? I'm not saying she shouldn't have toed the line a bit more but she tried, she really did. She just had a fatal flaw and she couldn't manage in the real, cruel world. She had no training for it. Her mother apparently wouldn't let her open her mouth to her and the maids and housekeepers didn't give a damn. She had no role model.

Why don't they write their brilliant articles about those people who used her, used our place as a squat and a party venue and then dumped her and left her to fend for herself when the authorities intervened. Every time the going got a bit rough they bunked off and left her to try to pick up the pieces herself. Even Joey, the one I think was Francesca's father and whom, as you know, I liked.

I hate them.

If it hadn't been for my stubbornness (and, I must acknowledge again, the pretty enlightened social worker I had at the time) she'd have had nobody to look after her and she would probably have died a lot sooner than she did.

After that awful night when they took James from her and I ran away and slept rough and she'd vanished when I got home after the zoo the next day, I searched for her all over the city, all the hospitals. Although I hated doing it, I went down into the really rough places, derelict sites down by Jervis Street and down along the Quays, even the docks.

I went through quite a see-saw in feelings that couple of days, the awful low of the night living rough, followed by the surprising high of meeting Tom Bennett at the zoo, followed again by the trek around the dives and most awful secret places of Dublin while at the same time fighting for the right to mind James. I was wrecked at the end of it.

On one of my returns to the flats, I can't remember now which day it was, my social worker had put a note in our door to contact her.

It was she who told me they'd found Mammy and she was now in hospital. There'd been a disturbance at a squat on the Richmond Road and the police were called. That's how she was found.

She'd gone there with that filthy, horrible man, the last guy she was with, I can't remember his name, I'd pollute my brain. He was by far the worst, he was a dealer and a junkie and a drunk as well. Those days there were only a few of them around and the cops knew exactly who they were so this fella only came out after dark, like the rat he was. He took advantage of her sweetness. Mammy rarely drank, she didn't like the taste. I hope he's dead and rotting in hell.

The social worker warned me not to get a shock when I went up to see her. So I prepared myself, or so I thought.

I was devastated when they brought me in to her bedside. Her face was all purple. Half of it was bruising, half of it was just discoloration. She never came out of hospital again, only to go over to Harold's Cross to the Hospice. To die.

They were absolutely lovely to her there. They washed her properly every day and you could really feel their love. It's a great consolation to know she died peacefully and 'At Rest'. But every single day of my life I live with the guilt of not having been able to look after her.

So you can see why, although I'm a much tougher proposition, I still feel I have to watch myself. Her blood is my blood and you're always your mother's daughter, aren't you? Of course, there is my father to take into account too. I sincerely hope he was made of sterner stuff than she was. Because now and then, under the strain of all of this with James, I do feel myself wilting.

I suppose looking after James is my way of making it up to her. I would have done it anyway, it's just that I hope that, wherever she is, she knows I'm doing it.

Although as it turns out, of course, I obviously didn't look after him well enough.

He's getting worried about keeping up the pretence at work, says he's running out of excuses as to where he is every Monday morning. I can't keep saying I'm going to a clinic, he goes, they'll think I have Aids.

Well, let them fire you, I go back, as confidently as I can. We'll manage.

Speaking of managing, I eventually cashed my precious, beautiful scratch card. It nearly broke my heart to see it go, having all that money just wasn't the same. I've decided not to redeem Mammy's stuff just yet. He might lose his job and we'll need every penny we can get. I've tried to follow the consider the lilies in the field concept but it just doesn't wash with us, somehow.

One of Mammy's sisters was called Lily, the other was Adeline. The brother was called Jeremy. Is called Jeremy. They're probably still alive. James is their nephew. It would be lovely to be able to go and talk to my aunties and uncle and have a family around me at a time like this, but I could just see their reaction if I arrived in their lives and announced why I'd decided to contact them after all these years.

Excuse me, hello, are you the Devines? The de Vere Devines? How do you do, I'm your long-lost niece and this is your long-lost nephew, we're the ones belonging to the derelict. There are three more of us . . . And, by the way, he's being charged with rape at the moment. Any chance of a bit of solidarity?

Can you imagine?

The last time the whole five of us met for an access visit, Francesca left after ten minutes. She told the social worker that she'd had it and she didn't want anything more to do with any of us. There was a big argument, I was really annoyed with her and I could tell the social worker was too, no matter how valiantly she tried to be professional and hide it. But Francesca was coming up to sixteen and there was not much anyone could do. At sixteen she was free to live her own life.

Thinking about it, what was probably bothering her was that after all the promises, her foster family hadn't adopted her yet (and they never did). I've never been able to find out whether there was some technical hitch or whether they changed their minds. All of that kind of stuff is very confidential and you might as well be trying to break into the Vatican as winkling information out of the Eastern Health Board or the Adoption Board.

I suppose I didn't help the situation. I was just twenty-one and I was probably inclined to play the mammy a bit too much, lording it over the others. Well, I was feeling pretty much like a mammy, with some justification, it has to be said. James was five and I hadn't killed him yet.

We were in the lobby of the Gresham — all of us except James were fed up with the feeding-the-ducks lark. Anyway, the Gresham was handy, it's in O'Connell Street and easily accessible to us all. It was summer and the place was crammed with people having afternoon tea and drinks, a lot of them tourists. I don't know what they thought of our happy little group. (I don't think! They couldn't have missed what was going on.)

Our Cokes haven't even arrived yet when Francesca's on her feet, reacting to something Nicola said. A silly mimicking of how she pronounces her Os now that she's living on the Riviera. You see, it was the beginning of Dalkey being called the Irish Riviera because of all the rock stars et cetera who were moving in there. Nicola was being jealous, the family she and Justine were with were lovely but they were struggling a bit to make ends meet. Anyway, she was wrong. Francesca became part of the poppyseed rail syndrome long before she moved to Dalkey from Foxrock.

With my usual tact, I make the insult worse by laughing. My guard was a bit down that day.

This ribbing is all the excuse Francesca needs. She jumps up and starts to march out of the hotel. The social worker jumps up and runs after her and then I jump up and run after her. Like three of the bloody Marx Brothers.

The social worker and I are arguing with Francesca just in front of the swing doors, with the porter holding one of them open for us and looking at us like, are yiz going out or are yiz not. I'm holding on to Francesca's arm and she's tugging and tugging and the social worker is talking to her in a quiet, intense voice, asking her to reconsider.

She's adamant. She's going back to Dalkey and that's the end of it. And she's coming on no more access visits.

The social worker goes with her to see her to the bus – she's allowed to travel on her own at this stage – and I go back to the other three. They're just sitting there, staring. I arrive at the same time as the Coke and the buns. James immediately takes his up and forgets everything else. Go on, I say to the others, we'll see her next time, you know how she is, and we all tuck in while we wait for the social worker to come back.

But there was no next time.

It's funny how people can just slip out of your life. You'd think you'd have some clue. In a film you'd have all the music, telling you it was significant. It's always a humbling experience to know that something terrifically important to you is of no importance whatsoever to the world at large.

Like when I went down to cash my scratch card. I had to queue at the hatch. That was the first disillusionment, I'd thought I'd be the only one. Special.

Nevertheless, when my turn came, my heart was thumping as I pushed it under the bars protecting the clerk.

I don't know what I was expecting but I would have liked it marked in some way. Bells ringing? Hooters? Even something negative – if he was to challenge me to produce evidence that I hadn't stolen it, or look for proof of identity.

Something. Anything to say that this was not an ordinary transaction.

The guy was bored out of his trolley. He never even looked up at me. Not one word passed between us, not one. That'll teach me. Talk about Macbeth's hubris.

→ Thirteen ←

I answer the door on the Monday evening and it's Patsy. Now this is odd – for her to come to the flat unannounced. She usually calls only to pick me up in her car for a gig, or on the rare occasion we're going to the pictures. And she looks weird, her face is scrunched.

Come on in, I go, this is a surprise. I'm even more surprised because she knows the first English paper in the Leaving is coming up, and I should be studying. It'd be unlike her to cut across that.

The way she looks I'm immediately thinking of Martin. Is everything OK at home?

She doesn't answer, just comes in. The hallway in our place is a kip, holey lino on the floor, the original wallpaper painted over so many times it's flaking off so the skirting boards look like they're covered with shavings of mouldy chocolate.

Don't mind this place, it's getting worse by the day, I say, trying to be cheerful as we go up the stairs. These could be nice if he'd put a bit of carpet on them, or even lino. The banisters could be beautiful as a matter of fact, I've always loved how at the bottom they curl into themselves like a periwinkle's shell.

We go through the door of our flat. Thank God James

is not home from work yet — he usually goes for a pint with some of the lads — and the place is decent. When he's sprawled in front of the telly you can hardly see him for half-full cups and empty crisp bags. Cup of tea? I ask, going towards the kettle.

No, thanks. It's the first time she's said anything.

I leave the kettle. That bad? I say sympathetically. Sit down and tell me all about it.

Instead she comes across to me and holds out the cutting. A nineteen-year-old courier from Mountjoy Square in Dublin was remanded on continuing bail in the Dublin District Court today. He is accused of raping a twenty-year-old woman in the Phoenix Park.

One of those little stories in boxes down the side of a page. The exact words are engraved in my brain.

Wouldn't you know it, the one Monday I don't buy the *Herald*.

Patsy says nothing, she's obviously waiting for me. There's no point in protesting or telling fibs, she knows James is a courier. She knows he's nineteeen. She knows we live in Mountjoy Square. Doesn't take Remington Steele to figure it out.

It's a surreal moment. I'd been watching an Eddie Murphy film and it's still running. Patsy and I looking at one another, me holding the cutting, her as grim as death and Eddie Murphy going ha ha ha! in that manic way of his. I go over and I switch him off. I'm sorry I didn't tell you, I say to Patsy, I was going to but I couldn't get up the nerve.

She's still standing there. Still looking at me.

Did he do it? she asks in a peculiar voice.

That's what the trial is going to be about, I retort. He says it was consensual and I believe him. I'm looking straight into her eyes. I love Patsy but I'm not going to be intimidated by anyone on this. I can't get a handle on what she's thinking or why she's behaving like this, this is not a Patsy I've seen very often.

You've picked up the jargon very quickly, she says.

I don't know what to say next. Let's sit down, I go, are you sure you won't have a cup of tea or coffee?

No, thank you, she says very quietly.

I stare at her and she stares back. If we had a ticking clock it'd be ticking very loudly at this point. She's the one who breaks it. Look, she goes, I'm sure you're going through a terrible time and I'm very sorry for you but, you see, I have a couple of daughters . . .

I'm shattered. Her meaning is perfectly clear. My best friend is making judgements without even hearing the story.

It's out before I can stop it. Why did you come here, so, if you're so afraid you and your precious daughters might be contaminated by us?

She doesn't answer, just looks at me with an expression that I can only say borders on the pitying. I'm sorry, Patsy, I say humbly, I didn't mean that, you know I didn't—

I know you didn't, Ange, she goes. I just wanted to come and tell you that I've found out about it and to reassure you that, in case you're worried, it won't make any difference to our professional relationship. She's tight but sad.

I beg your pardon—

Looking back at it now, I think that at this point I must have sat down. It was still too new to take in.

Why would I be worried about our professional relationship? I was being genuine here, it had never occurred to me that James's unfortunate situation could have anything to do with PA System.

Before I can say anything else, she puts the cutting down on the coffee table in front of the bed-settee. I'll pick you up next Sunday morning, all right? She says this very gently. I'll be praying for you. Oh, and good luck on Wednesday in the exam, I'll send you a good-luck card. She tries to smile but you never saw a less successful smile in your life.

She turns and goes. Leaves me with my mouth hanging open. The whole scene had taken only about two minutes.

To this day I've never fully worked out why she came that evening – unless it was to rub my nose in it and I wouldn't want to believe that of her.

I guess she did me a favour. At least she showed me exactly what we were facing in the wider world. There ended my half-baked, no, *quarter*-baked, idea of going to the Rape Crisis Centre and looking for counselling or some kind of help for us.

It was a beautiful evening – no pathetic fallacy tonight – and the walls of the flat were suddenly very close to each other. I felt I couldn't breathe.

I should have gone back to the studying but instead I grabbed my keys and hightailed it out, across the road and into Mountjoy Park. In the summertime it doesn't close officially until half past eight.

It's full of people who seem to have no worries, groups of young ones with their buggies, the usual old jossers and their dogs who never seem to leave the place, kids playing football and basketball. Even a girl swaying around the place using a hula-hoop. Now there's a blast from the past. I manage to find a bench and make myself relax, letting the sunshine soothe the back of my neck and my shoulders.

I start to feel a bit better. A small blue butterfly flutters past my foot and lands on a wallflower in one of the beds nearby and then takes off again. I wouldn't have known this until recently, but did you know that butterflies can't

fly when there is no sunshine? One of the men in one of
the offices we clean was in early one morning, just after
seven. He dumped an *Irish Times* in a bin beside his desk
and on a whim, when I was doing the bins in his section,
I took it out and saved it. I learned about the butterflies
in it – that paper is full of this kind of information.
Apparently butterflies are solar-powered. They have to
have energy from the sun to be able to lift themselves.
On cloudy days, or even when clouds pass over on sunny
days, they immediately rest, clinging on to grass or a
bush or something.

At the risk of sounding like someone from the PR
department of Dublin Corporation, once again, I have to
give fair dues to the people who run the parks. They
won't be bested. They plant little baby trees in this park
and the gurriers come up and break them. They
immediately replace them and along come the gurriers
again. They plant them again. And so on and so on until
they wear the gurriers down. God knows how many
little trees it takes but so far this year the parks people
are winning and there are three new flowering cherries
here now that haven't been touched for at least a week
and which will maybe survive.

The last time I was in here I saw a young fella
systematically using a bicycle chain to swipe the head off
every tulip in the place, hundreds of them. Unfortunately, I didn't interfere. I'm sorry I didn't now, chain
or no chain. I'll tell you, if I catch any little thicko at
those little trees this evening, or anyone deliberately
trampling the flowerbeds, the way I'm feeling right now
I don't think I'd be responsible for my actions. This
evening I'd welcome an opportunity to have a go.

I find myself watching a man playing with a small dog
at the far side. It's an uplifting thing to watch a man and

a dog, if you throw a stick or a ball, the dog always behaves as though it's the first time you've ever done it. He's always thrilled skinny with you even if you've left him locked up for days. Dogs are the tsars of forgiveness in this world.

So, anyway, I'm sitting there and I'm half watching this man and his dog, and half watching the little sun-fuelled butterfly going about its business. But all the time I'm going over and over in my mind what happened between me and Patsy. It was bizarre. One paragraph. The word rape. That's it, that's enough, no more questions. She's my best friend and she doesn't give me a chance to present our side. Not even remotely interested.

But why? All I could see was that odd look in her eyes. Pity definitely, but there was something else. A sort of triumph? Glee? Surely not.

Well, tough. We've managed on our own before and we'll manage again. I believe in him. If I don't, who will?

There and then I make up my mind to go and have a proper talk with the solicitor, find out what the worst-case scenario is. I know we're only free legal aid but there's a lot at stake here and the state will pay him for his time.

I'm feeling much more optimistic already. I look away from the butterfly and across the park to the man and his dog again and find they're much closer. And what do you know, it's Ken, the guy from my class. He happens to be looking this way and I've waved before I knew what I was doing.

Why did I do that? What kind of a stupo am I? Now (a) he'll think I'm forward and (b) I don't want company, I'm not in the mood for chitchat.

Too late. He picks up the dog and come towards me, a

big smile all over his face. Hi, he goes. Isn't it a lovely evening? I couldn't look at those English notes for one more minute. Are you nervous about Wednesday?

Hi, I answer, yes, it is a lovely evening. And if we don't know the stuff now we never will. Do you live around here?

I'm in the Custom Hall complex down the road. The two of us are. He looks at the dog under his arm. And you?

Over there – I wave my arm vaguely in the direction of DID Electrical.

Well, you haven't far to go for your electrical appliances anyhow! He blushes. I see for the first time that he's quite shy, we haven't talked all that much in the classroom.

I look away from him to give him a chance to compose himself. You're sort of in the trade, aren't you? A carpenter? I didn't know you were allowed keep dogs in apartments?

You're dead right, he says, you're not allowed keep any pets. But we're very careful.

When I look back he's stroking the dog's head. This dog has no tail but his rear is crazy with wagging. He's panting, his tongue fluttering as fast as a bird's wing. Sure he's only small, Ken says, and I've trained him to be quiet. He's in the van with me all day and I smuggle him in and out of the block in my rucksack.

I never would have put this chap down as a dog lover. Don't know why – not that I gave it much thought! He's lovely, I go, what's his name?

Sam.

Sam. I reach up and stroke the dog's head myself and he gives me a lick. Obviously this is one of those dogs who love everyone. That's a nice name for a dog, I say, is he a purebred?

Ken takes this as an invitation to sit down beside me and does so. Not at all, he says, letting the dog jump out of his arms on to the ground, I got him in the pound. It'd break your heart to go up there, Angela, you'd want to take them all. I had to be choosy, though, I wouldn't have been able to keep a big dog in my place, it wouldn't have been fair. And anyway, I'd have been caught! He grins.

He has a lovely grin, something else I hadn't noticed before.

We chat a bit and he gets a bit easier with me. When he was looking for a dog, he had to go to the pound up beyond Finglas. Apparently the cats' and dogs' home, which used to be very handy, just off the Quays there, near where the gasometer was, has moved out to the sticks, Rathfarnham or some place.

The dog is lying across his shoes now. He bends down and strokes it again. Can you believe it, Angela, this fella was rescued off of a Hallowe'en bonfire. They'd tied his legs together so he couldn't run and they'd tied his tail to a tyre so he'd be sure to burn.

Who rescued him?

The Guards rescued him, he says. They always patrol the bonfires in certain parts of the city. They were just in time. His tail is gone, you can see that, and look . . . He picks the dog up again and shows me a place on the belly where there's no hair and the skin is like crazy paving. The dog licks him again. Gratitude never-ending.

Who'd do that to a dog, I go, I don't know what this country's coming to. That was good of the Guards, though.

Yeah, Ken agrees, the man who rescued him had to go to hospital to get dressings on the burns on his hands.

He lets the dog jump down again. How are things with you in general?

Uh-oh! I go to myself, wondering if there's anything behind this question. It's occurred to me this guy might have seen the *Herald*.

Grand, grand, I go. Cautiously.

We run out of conversation. But although the silence is a bit awkward, I realize it's normal-social-awkward, not embarrassed-awkward. It had been just an ordinary question.

You read very well the other night, he says then, looking across the park. You could probably be an actress if you put your mind to it.

Rubbish, I go, but I'm pleased. You're not bad yourself, I say then. You have a lovely voice. I sing a bit and I can tell you would be a singer too.

Not in the slightest, he goes. The bath. That's about the height of it. A singer, eh? I was always trying to guess what you did. He brings his eyes back from the far end of the park. You're really a singer? Professionally?

You could say that, I go.

Then I can't resist it. So when you were guessing, what did you think I might do?

I thought something in an office, maybe, a solicitor's office or a bank. He looks down at Sam who seems to have fallen asleep. Since you're only now doing the Leaving, I thought maybe you might be one of those yellow pack workers. An alarmed look across his face and he looks back at me. Sorry, I don't mean to insult you.

You're not insulting me, I say. I'm chuffed that he thinks I'm an office worker – even a yellow pack. I see nothing wrong with being a yellow pack, by the way, even though, according to the unions, they're being totally exploited, doing the same work as fully paid workers under the pretence of being trained. My attitude is, it's work, isn't it? Would they prefer the poor kids to leave school and have to go straight on the dole? Or emigrate? All right, it isn't great pay but it can lead to something. At the very least it's experience to put on your CV. If James had the opportunity I'd make him jump at it.

Suddenly it's important that this Ken thinks the best of me. Don't get me wrong, I'm not ashamed of being a cleaner and I don't want to fudge what I do, but something makes me leave it ambivalent. I'm not quite an office worker, I say, although my main work does involve visiting offices.

I hope I'm looking serious.

I knew, I knew you had something to do with an office, Ken goes. You always look so neat.

M-mmm, I go. Piling on the mystery. I hope he never attends an occasion where he sees me in a French maid's outfit! (I'd been thinking of giving up the kissogram business anyway. Maybe now's the time. Especially with that extra injection of cash.)

So where do you sing? he asks, maybe I could come to one of your shows sometime.

Maybe. I'll let you know if I'm doing one I'd consider suitable.

I can't believe it, I'm being flippant with this guy, it could almost be called flirting.

We smile again at each other. He picks up Sam, I'd better be getting back, this fella needs his beauty sleep. And anyway, I still have to do a bit of revision. Good luck with the work, see you in the salt mines.

I return the wish, he says goodbye and off he goes.

That was the holy all of it but it left me with a nice feeling. Which, of course, I instantly dismissed. I'd no right to be having any nice feelings about men. Not at this point in my life. Not until we get certain things sorted out one way or the other in my real life. And I've

managed perfectly well without a man since Tom
Bennett.

I look for the butterfly and it's gone, even though the
sun is still out. Probably heading to its roost. Do
butterflies roost?

At least I know he's not married. Who'd be married
and live in one of those piffling little apartments and have
to smuggle in a dog for company?

One of the girls, I think it was Justine, found a kitten
in the laneway behind the flats one day. The poor little
thing, it couldn't have been more than a couple of weeks
old, hardly any hair and no teeth to speak of. I fed it with
my finger, dipping it in milk and it latched on – it was a
very strange sensation. I couldn't give it enough that
way, though, and it died within twenty-four hours.
Justine couldn't have cared less. She'd forgotten about
it. She was only two and a half, something like that, I
know that because she was taken into care just before her
third birthday.

That was one of the times I was taken, too. They never
learned. I was back out in less than twenty-four hours.
Into care again, back out again, in, out, like a yo-yo. At
one stage they were going to commit me into Madonna
House – residential. There was no way I was having that.
Although they couldn't control me, they couldn't say I
was out of control or a danger to society or to myself.
Because all I was doing was coming back to my home.
And I was doing nothing illegal. Just illegal by their rules
for children at risk. In my opinion I was at risk of nothing
I couldn't handle. Mammy had to have someone respons-
ible with her.

By the way, I don't mean to imply, just because I keep
going on about our problems, and social workers, and
my siblings being put into foster homes, that I had a
completely rotten childhood. I emphatically did not. The

bad times were gruesome all right, but there were good times too. Take school. Apart from my being pretty much a dunce – because I didn't care about the lessons and never did my homework – school was good fun, especially after the monster Concepta skedaddled out of our lives.

Also, the social workers cared a lot and did the best they could for us. We had help from a lot of good people in the Vincent, and when Mammy was well, she was the sweetest, most gentle mother you could imagine.

It's probably a difficult concept for you to take in, that a woman who according to the authorities was unable to look after her children, who could never name the fathers of any of them and who was a substance abuser, could be the sweetest and most gentle of mothers and be really loved by us all. Well, all I can tell you is I loved her to bits and I wanted more than anything in the world to protect her.

It was hardly her fault she wasn't ready for the world when she came to Dublin and found herself in the flats, was it? I blame her parents. What about their responsibilities in the matter?

And I do have good times to look back on with her, very good times. For instance one day she and myself and Nicola, who was just a baby then, went to see Santa Claus in Clery's. It was a memorable Christmas, the best ever, because for once there were no boyfriends around and she was clean.

God knows where she got the money but off the three of us went, walking down to O'Connell Street as though we hadn't a care in the world. We moved slowly because she was quite frail but she was in great spirits. When she was up to it, Mammy was a chatter, about anything and everything. And very charitable about people who were not in the least charitable about her.

It's dry, not half as cold as it should be for December, and the streets are jammed with cheerfulness. The Christmas lights are on, it's half past three and already getting dark and I hold her arm tightly so we won't bump into people. We stop at RTV Rentals at the intersection of Talbot Street and North Earl Street and isn't *Sesame Street* on all the tellies in the window! My happiness is complete. Big Bird in full glorious colour – it's the first time I've seen that he's yellow. At home he's only in black and white. Colour is a complete novelty at this stage for most people.

She waits there with me while I watch through the glass – which has a big Santa drawn on it in artificial snow – all the way to the end of the segment. Everyone around is saying happy Christmas and hawking huge happy parcels and the woman with the barrow on Marlborough Street just around the corner is shouting five for two bob the Christmas tangerines. I'm leaning against Mammy, warm and quiet, and happiness spreads all through me like a virus.

I adore Christmas ever since that time. If it was up to me and I had unlimited resources, James and I would be up to our necks in artificial snow with Rudolf blow-ups in every corner of the flat and the ceiling invisible under the weight of paper chains. Every present would be in luxurious gift boxes, like they do them up in America, where people just lift the lids to see what's in the tissue paper inside. And I'd get a piano and we'd drink mulled claret and sing carols.

It's funny, I remember hardly anything about the actual Santa that day with Mammy and Nicola, but I remember every step of that walk, every second of the feel of her thin arm in mine.

I wish James could have known her like I did. It's a terrible gap in our relationship. I've tried to keep her memory alive for him but I haven't even a photograph to show him because we never had any.

I'm going to brave it down to Birr, I think, while I'm sitting on that bench in Mountjoy Park after Ken has gone home. I'll find her family and ask for a photograph, they must have something, her Confirmation or something — Protestants have Confirmations, don't they? We deserve at least that much.

I'm half afraid, though. Afraid that they will have exorcized her so completely that they'd have nothing at all. That would kill me. In my imagination I see her mother making a bonfire and throwing everything to do with Mammy on it after casting her out.

And to think that that woman is James's and my grandmother. Talk about the witches in *Macbeth*!

Fourteen

On the subject of genes, I wish we knew who James's father is. A boy needs a father at a time like this. But the chances of finding him are non-existent, the birth cert has a blank space under where the father's name should be and not one of us has a clue about his identity. Given the type they all were, there's a fair chance he'd be dead anyway.

I did my best to start the tracing during that court business a few years ago, I got in touch with my old social worker to ask for help. She'd given up the job, too stressful, but she had kindly left me her address in case I ever wanted to have a chat.

Unfortunately, even with all her experience, we had no luck. When she came back to me in the end, she explained that nineteen years ago, they would have kept records of boyfriends only if they were abusers. Or if they had acknowledged themselves as fathers at some point and someone was alleging serious neglect.

Even substance abuse wasn't all that a big deal then amongst the authorities, although I think probably there was a fair bit of it going on, not as much as now, obviously, but a fair bit nonetheless. (The difference is, now it's been discovered by the politicians and the whole country, and we're all 'concerned'.) I know for a fact that nowadays the social workers tally every spittle of everyone who comes within an ass's roar of one of the kids on their books. They have to be so careful now, situations can blow up so quickly into public uproar and then they're held responsible.

At least being illegitimate is not the stigma it used to be, I have to hand it to the Catholic Church, even they don't use the word any more. One of the women I work with got an annulment last year. She worried herself half to death about it. Like, if no marriage ever existed, ever, it meant her kids were illegitimate, didn't it? She was a religious kind of woman and she didn't want that.

Then one morning, at our tea-break, her eyes are out on stalks. Ah, no, they told her in a letter she got from them. Not any more. Nowadays the children stay legitimate.

When you think about it they're a howl, aren't they? I am the rock, my eye. More like, I am the quicksand. What about all the poor kids they made bastards of in the past thousands of years? Floating around in the now non-existent limbo I expect.

He's at home when I get back from Mountjoy Park. The best way to describe him is to say that he's stricken. He's sitting with his head in his hands. The telly isn't even on.

What's the matter? I ask him.

He doesn't tell me to eff off, he just jerks the top of his head towards the table where the cutting is lying as Patsy left it.

Oh, God, I say, I shouldn't have left it there for you to find like that, I'm sorry.

He mutters that it didn't make any difference. That he'd seen it already, they showed it to him.

Who showed it to you?

At work. He keeps his head in his hands.

There's nothing I can think of to say other than would you like a cup of something? Or if you like I'll go down to the chipper and get us each a one and one.

He shakes his head again.

I sit down. What did they say to you? How bad was it?

Apparently it was pretty bad, the word spread like wildfire amongst the lads and he got funny looks all morning. The boss called him in at dinner-time and asked him was it true. He had to admit it.

Now I get horrified and I yell at him how could he be so stupid. I hadn't meant to sound harsh, it just came out that way, like I'm his judge and jury too. I need a chastity belt for my tongue sometimes. But then I find out that he didn't admit the actual rape, just that he's been charged.

The holy all of it is, he's been put on suspension. He was told not to come back to work until it's all over. And if he's cleared in the trial his job is still open to him.

Big if.

That happened at dinner-time. Where was he until now?

At last he takes his hands down from his head and looks at me. I'm expecting him to eff and blind me, and tell me to mind my own effin' business, that it's his own affair where he effin' was. But no. Instead, he looks at me like he's one of those baby seals in the Arctic that they're just about to bludgeon to death. I was just riding around, he says.

That image is going to haunt me. James, big, macho James, in all his leathers and on his big thundering bike, just riding around. Maybe even with tears in his eyes. I think it must be worse with boys. Girls roar crying and let it out. Boys keep it all inside where it rumbles around and gets to volcano proportions. Or suicide proportions.

The number of young men who are committing suicide in Ireland is terrifying.

All the puff goes out of my sails. I wish he would have effed me.

But in a funny way, now that it had come out in the open, it was a relief. At least we could stop looking over our shoulders all the time, waiting for it.

I look at his bended head, wondering what I could do or say to make him feel better. I briefly consider bringing up the subject of the unfair dismissals legislation – like everyone at the cleaning, I would know every tittle-tattle of it – but I feel there's no point in raising his hopes at this stage. Anyhow, since he was suspended rather than fired he's still technically employed.

The bad news about *that*, of course, is that he's not entitled to unemployment benefit or assistance.

Thank God for scratch cards.

I'm not going to be able to give you any more money. He doesn't look at me when he says this.

The amount of money he gives me is pretty irrelevant as it happens. He smokes and he likes his pint and that doesn't leave very much out of his paltry wages. I'm sitting on one of the chairs at the table and I get up and go across to the bed-settee. We don't have to worry for the moment, I say. See this? Like Mandrake the Magician, I pull the scratch card winnings out from the side of the settee where it's hidden.

What? He's still not looking.

It's five hundred pounds. I won it on a scratch card.

That gets him. Five hundred pounds?

Yep. On a scratch card.

On a scratch card?

Are you a parrot or what? You heard me. I won it on a scratch card.

Jesus, you have five hundred quid and you never told me. He's getting angry now, indignant. Here's me sittin' here like a dork, worrying me bleedin' head off about not being able to give you money and you had five hundred effin' quid all the time.

I cheer up. This is more like it.

The next evening, after class, I go somewhere I've never been before in all my twist although all the time I was growing up in the flats it was less than half a mile away from me.

It's our last session before the exam and we're all wishing each other luck and so on, and Mr Elliott finishes up with a little pep talk, telling us all he's proud of us and he knows that we're all ready and we're to knock 'em dead. Funnily enough, I find I'm not a bit nervous any more. I've done as much as I can and I just want now to get the whole thing over and done with.

Ken, the electrician or carpenter – or whatever he is – comes up to me as we're all gathering up our books and notes for the last time. Would I like to go and get a breath of fresh air? He's blushing again.

Now, I don't want to go all gooey about this guy. But my clothes are stuck to me and my nose is all stuffed from the heat in the classroom. (Contrary to my earlier expectations, this summer has been hit and miss so far but today is very hot and humid.) Anyway, the idea is appealing, he seems like a nice chap. Sure, I go, why not. A breath of fresh air would be great.

Then I instantly start thinking. What's James doing? Does James need me? Is he upset? Is he sitting over there in the flat with his head in his hands?

Too late to change my mind now, this Ken's grinning. When Ken smiles, his whole face shines, did I mention that? You know the way that happens to some people? Terrific, he says. He suggests we go to the South Bull, and we spend the next five minutes, while we're walking to his van, marvelling that I've lived in this city all my life and I've never taken a walk along the South Bull.

Well, I have to tell you that the South Bull is a revelation.

It's very old, an old sea-wall which runs from the Pigeon House – it's a mystery to me why a power station is called a Pigeon House – all the way out to a lighthouse. This sea-wall is so old that the blocks of stone from which it's constructed are desperately uneven and have gaps as big as doorsteps between them. You have to walk very, very carefully, and of course the shoes I've on are totally unsuitable. Cuban heels. Sure to get jammed. I'll break my ankle and I'll fall and Ken will see my knickers and he'll have to carry me back to the van to take me to hospital.

Shut up, Angela.

It's such a fine clear evening, half of Dublin seems to be here, we even pass a pair of nuns. Who are wearing, would you believe, pristine Nike runners. Concepta, or to be fair the Concepta I knew – maybe she was different outside the school, hah! – would have kittens if she could see them.

The point of going on this walk is that you're actually walking down along the side of the Liffey where it's broadening out into the sea. It's amazing. Although I knew about Dublin Bay being a curve, I'd never seen the full of it before. The South Bull divides it with the southside on your right and the northside to your left and the inner city behind. Ken waves to the right, points out RTE and Vincent's hospital, Dun Laoghaire Harbour and even Dalkey, and then, to the left, Clontarf, Dollymount, Fairview, Sutton, et cetera. The poor old northside seems to be mostly as flat as a pancake, while the southside, wouldn't you know it, gets to have the lovely purple mountains.

Ah, yes, but we've got Howth, Ken says.

Howth rises from the edge of the northside and juts into the sea. From this angle, it'd remind you of the bowl of a very big spoon turned upside down. It's where Gay Byrne lives, as we all know. Ken points to where the house should be, if you could see it. He seems pretty sure. I can't see anything. All I can see is a bunch of little white dots which could be houses. Or sheep. Or light-coloured rocks. Maybe I need glasses.

I pretend to be able to see it. So how does he know which particular white dot it is?

Guess what, turns out a mate of his did a bit of work for the great man. Shelving.

Now here's a conversational gold mine. Who wouldn't like to be walking along the South Bull on a glorious evening like this, with someone who intimately knew about Gay Byrne and his house. So naturally I ask him did his mate tell him what Gaybo's really like. And what she's like too.

They're both ordinary, in the best sense. They have everyday snacks in their kitchen like the rest of us and they watch telly, although Ken's mate never told him what he saw them watching.

So the big news is that they're just like you and me, except they have this wonderful view where on clear days they can see as far as Wicklow, maybe even Wexford. Or they can watch the ships go into the port, or track the planes going into Dublin airport. They go for a lot of walks. (That's more like it. Poor people don't go for many walks.)

Yet I'm disappointed to find out they're so normal. I

would have liked to hear that they lived in a place like
South Fork. Else what's the point of being famous?

Ken hadn't worked for any of Ireland's celebrities and
the height of his mate's achievement was the Byrnes so
that's the end of that conversation. He points across the
water. That's the Bull Wall over there, he says, it's the
northside equivalent of where we're walking, and you
probably know Dollymount Beach behind it.

We're talking quite easily now. Sam's zigzagging from
side to side of the South Bull, giving me heart attacks.
There are no fences or barriers along the edges and I'm
terrified he'll fall in. I'm not the only one having
seizures, he's cutting in and out between all the other
walkers, nearly tripping them up.

I do, indeed, know Dollymount. A few times, one of
the social workers took us out there on fine access days
and to give her her due, she went the whole hog,
buckets, spades, even a beachball. I suppose she got
pretty fed up with all the fighting and the squabbling in
the hotel lobbies and in Stephen's Green when we were
supposed to be feeding the ducks. Maybe, God love her,
she thought the wide open spaces would help Francesca's
disposition. (Boy, was she wrong there . . .)

I wasn't all that pushed about the place, it's miles and
miles of sand and dunes with the sea so shallow you can't
even swim. And with the family dynamics the way they
were, it was never a successful outing. None of us
seemed able to find much to do. Sandcastles? Our family?
Give us a break.

Right now, though, it's hardly appropriate to launch
immediately into our dysfunctional history so I ask Ken
why is he doing the Leaving Cert, why does he need to
when he seems to have a nice little business going for
himself.

He's not quite sure why, it turns out. It was something to do in the evenings and he always feels a bit inadequate admitting to people that he never got it.

And you? He turns the tables.

The same. I smile and leave it at that. By this time we're at a half-way point on the South Bull where there's a bench seat in front of a little building marked 'Half Moon S.C. founded 1898'. It doesn't take a genius to work out what the S.C. stands for, because there are two men swimming just off it, not really swimming, puddling around, enjoying themselves and talking to each other. I wouldn't swim there if you paid me, Ken goes, looking at them and wrinkling up his nose.

Although I take his meaning, I don't get any bad smells at the moment. In fact the only smell I can detect right now is quite sweetish – seaweed maybe, or the day's heat coming back off the warm rocks. (I have to admit, though, that because of the sewage pumping station beside it, the smell up closer to the Pigeon House did leave a lot to be desired.)

The seat in front of the Half Moon S.C. is vacant and we sit down. Sam jumps up on Ken's lap and snuggles down like a cat. Now we're directly facing the city and God, is it a lovely sight . . .

See that big building with the red roof? Ken says after a bit, pointing towards Dollymount and an enormous house in the shape of a Swiss chalet. Its roof is more than plain red, it's like fire under the sinking sun. That's Royal Dublin golf club, he goes, I'm a member.

He says this as though it's the most natural thing in Ireland that a manual worker who doesn't have his Leaving Cert could be a member of a golf club.

I see, I say back. Then, what's your last name by the way?

Sheils.

Mine's Devine.

We go silent again. But because there isn't a breath of wind, we can make out individual words and sentences as other walkers chat to each other as they pass.

In the city you never really notice sunsets. Or even the sky, much. When you look up, even in a park, all you see is a square and not this quiet, infinite space that makes all the buildings of Dublin, plus the mountains on the southside, look like toys.

And it's hard to describe properly that huge setting sun in front of us, red as the inside of a volcano. *Huge.* A magnificent, spectacular rosy ball descending through fluffed-out jet trails and letting its colour seep out over the blackening spires and cranes and spiny docks. We can see that one of the ferries is getting ready to leave. There's wispy smoke coming from it, lifting straight upwards.

Soon we hear a sound like a deep drumming and another ship, this one stacked with containers, glides past us. The sea on either side of it is like satin smoothly rippling. And because of the sunset, the colours on these ripples are graduated from dark pink near the ship to a delicate dove grey by the time they reach our side of the water.

All this calm and beauty. I could be the *Starship Enterprise*, floating along.

The mood is broken when a brown mongrel-type dog comes up and sniffs at Sam and Sam puts the run on him sharpish. I start worrying again about James.

Ken picks up the shift. Are you ready to head back, or do you want to walk all the way out to the lighthouse?

I'd better not, I say, and I use the cuban heels as an excuse. They're murder on these big blocks, I tell him. I can't appreciate all this lovely scenery because I have to have my head down all the time watching out for the cracks.

He stands up, letting Sam jump off his lap. Here, let me help you, hold my arm, he says. I stand up and take his arm and we set off.

Immediately I feel very odd. He links me quite loosely, but a bit too loosely, if you know what I mean and we both become self-conscious about it. I know this is crazy but I haven't walked linked to a man for years and years and I've obviously lost the knack. I feel, and I'm sure he feels, that we have blinking signs all over us. Look At Us! We're An Item!

It's ludicrous, here we are, walking through the completest, most wonderful sunset, and all I can think of is trying to make sure the pressure along my arm is uniform and that I'm not transmitting any signal. The more I try to relax, the stiffer my arm gets and the stiffer his gets in return until – I'm sure he feels the exact same – our arms feel like two of those enormous cement drainage pipes welded together for all eternity. We're just a pair of walking arms.

It seems to take three hours to get back to the Pigeon House where he's parked the van. And when we separate to go to our respective doors, the feeling of release is so great that I feel shaky. He keeps his head down as he gets into the driver's seat.

We stop for chips at a place in Ringsend that he knows. He brings them out to the car and bit by bit, as we're eating, we start to be able to talk again. He tells me a little about himself. He's originally from Fairview, but when he was about fourteen, his parents, through one thing and another, found themselves thrown on to the Corporation's lists and they all had to move out to Ballymun, to one of the towers. I see him looking at me sort of sideways to see how I'll react. He's as much of a snob as me!

Ballymun? I go, I've loads of friends in Ballymun.

Which is a lie. But I see by him that it was the right thing
to say. I believe those flats are lovely inside, I start to
embroider. Don't they have free heat? And all the hot
water you can use? I believe it's boiling in the winter-
time?

Yeah, he says, the problem is not the flats, the problem
is some of the scumbags outside the flats.

I decide not to pursue the flats issue in case he asks me
my so-called friends' names. What happened that you all
had to move? I ask him. But tell me to mind my own
business if you like.

They had a shop that failed.

Closedown.

This is a man who obviously hasn't talked to anyone
for a long time. But in a little while he does thaw. He
tells me quite wistfully that until they moved to Ballymun
he was in Sutton Park school. No fault to Ballymun
Comprehensive, he goes, they did their best in pretty
tough circumstances, it was just that I wasn't tough
enough myself . . .

So after the Inter Cert, he decides to chuck it in. He'd
always been good with his hands and he starts work right
away, mowing people's lawns, clipping hedges, that kind
of thing.

And when I'd be mowing their lawns I'd see doors
about to come off their hinges – I'd offer to fix them.
Gradually it built up. Women recommended me to their
friends. He chats on, quite easy again, I suppose it helps
that we're both eating the chips.

The big news comes then. He's twenty-nine years old
and four years ago he separated from his wife, Diandra.
They'd no kids.

Is it Michael Douglas's wife who's called Diandra, I ask
him.

He looks across at me, surprised. I didn't know that,

he goes. I thought it was just one of those makey-uppey names. Come to think of it, he goes then, I've never seen her birth cert. I bet she couldn't have been christened that. How long has Michael Douglas been married?

I shouldn't have said anything about Michael Douglas.

I start to draw him out further about himself. It turns out he's neither a carpenter nor an electrician, not formally, he has no training. He just continued on with what he had started after the Inter Cert. I'm one of those people who are good with their hands, he says. He never has any problem getting work and makes quite a good living. He'll do anything that comes along, a bit of gardening, plumbing, building a wall, repairing a roof, anything. He also uses the van – to shift furniture for people who are moving or to carry stuff to one of the tip heads. There are apparently thousands of people in this city – and not just rich people – who can't be bothered to take the time even to mow their own lawns. Or who don't know how to change a washer in a tap and are not interested in learning. He shakes his head in wonderment. Imagine . . .

One woman got him out specially just to fix a Dustbuster to a wall.

Another one hired him to do a few bits and bobs, wallpaper a hall, cut a few trees, trim bushes, change plugs. He looks at me. Now you won't believe this. This woman had a husband and three sons.

I widen my eyes, marvelling. (I don't think! He hasn't met James Devine!)

And then there are all the elderly widows living on their own, Ken goes on. He always feels very sorry for them. He's done a deal with another mate of his who goes to the North every so often to bring back stuff. This guy brings him job lots of items like burglar alarms and security lights and window-locks. He gives the materials to the widows at cost, charges them only for the labour. This is the Climate of Fear we're all living in these days. He shakes his head again.

He's gone up several notches in my estimation. It's nice of him not to overcharge widows, myself having been on the receiving end of shysters who salivate when they see a woman on her own in need of someone to screw a shelf to a wall.

How does he get the work? I open my mouth and stuff in the last handful of chips — the ones from the bottom of the bag encrusted with salt, I love those.

Usually word-of-mouth, he tells me. He leaflets as well. Leafleting is huge in Dublin. You can't open the front door of our place without tripping over a mountain of them, everything from double glazing to undertakers to Toymasters, all offering deals of a lifetime.

A wasp flies into the car and it takes us ages to get rid of it.

Then Ken uses the H word. It's following me around. He advertises in the *Herald* Useful Services small ads column. Handyman available with van. Honest, reliable and hard-working. He puts the ad in when the word-of-mouth falls off a bit and always gets enough work out of it to tide him over. Again, it seems to be mostly women, he says. He's half apologetic — I'm not implying women are helpless, far from it.

I know you're not, I say. I've always meant to buy myself a Black and Decker. I just never had the spare cash — or when I did there was always something more urgent to spend it on.

You can borrow mine any time. He grins. Now, changing the subject, what about yourself? We've been talking about me all the time. Tell me about you. Where's your office?

I ball up the chip bag so it fits in the palm of my hand.

There doesn't seem to be a bin bag in the van and he's put his under his seat. I couldn't litter if you paid me, littering is one thing Mammy had great principles about, at least when she was well. I'll have slime in my hands from carrying an apple core all the way home if I can't find a bin.

We'll leave me for next time, I say, presumptuous enough. I should be getting back — I promised myself I'd do at least two hours of revision tonight. And I've an early start in the morning.

Right-oh, he goes and reaches for the key in the ignition. Before he turns it he darts a look at me. I enjoyed it, he says.

I smile at him. Me, too. Good luck tomorrow.

Good luck.

We move off.

Just my luck, of course. Separated. Nothing is ever simple in my life.

→ Fifteen ←

The two English papers traditionally take up the whole first day in the Leaving Cert and I should imagine this enrages the jumper brigade because Irish is supposed to be our official first language.

Although the exam room was spacious enough and all the windows were open, the place felt like the inside of an oven. Outside, the sun was raising the tar on the roads – it's always glorious weather during the weeks of the state exams, and I always feel sorry for the poor kids who are going to be cooped up inside for the whole two or three weeks it takes to do the whole panoply. Today, though, I feel sorry for myself. Talk about ask me sister, I'm sweatin'!

The butterflies in my tummy went wild (maybe it was all the sunshine, ha ha!) when I saw the pink Honours paper lying there in front of me. I tried to calm myself down by being chuffed that I was here at all. Who'd have thought. Angela Devine from the flats. Leaving Cert English. Honours.

We were taking the exam in a boys' school with a whole load of fellas, who were very well behaved, contrary to my expectations.

And then the moment came when the supervisor told us we could turn over the paper. Did you ever hear a shower of hailstones?

When I read it, I couldn't believe my eyes, I nearly cheered out loud. Someone up there loves me, I thought, because there were two of the essays I could have done standing on my head. A Farewell to Adolescence. A City of Dreams.

Here I'd been, dreading the choices would all be philosophical – they can be terribly abstract in the Leaving Cert – or something to do with the Peace Process or the EU, neither of which would be my strong point. But, A Farewell to Adolescence? A City of Dreams? And me a Dublin woman? And Guardian of the Adolescent of the Year?

I raced through the Unprescribed Prose section of the paper then pounced on A City of Dreams. I let my imagination run riot, threw caution to the winds regarding Mr Elliott's warnings about structures and what you have to start with in your opening paragraph and how you have to develop your themes and summarize at the end. Out the window. I've long thought, anyway, that the people who correct these exam papers must long for a bit of relief from that sort of stuff.

This was me and my city – the South Bull and its sunsets, a Dublin, I wrote, dressed in cloth of gold. You get the flavour . . .

I wrote until the last possible minute, but towards the end the heat was getting to me and I was finding it hard to keep a grip on the biro, my right hand was covered in ink and the plastic was so slippy with sweat it kept sliding. I find that Bics tend to crack under extreme pressure. Mind you, as Tom Bennett used to say, what do you expect for tuppence, Moby Dick?

But when the supervisor called time up, I felt it had all been worth it and I floated out of that exam hall on a high.

Mr Elliott was waiting for us when we got out. He

went through the prescribed passages with us — I hadn't
done too badly at all, I found — and then he asked us all
one by one which essay we had done. When my turn
came, he gave me a rather peculiar look when I told him.

What's the matter? I ask. He's frightening me now.

Nothing, nothing, he says, but you know you and your
essays, Angela, that imagination of yours and your big
words. I hope you kept your feet on the ground with this
one. Did you remember the structures I taught you?

I'm looking at him and I'm remembering the argument
one of the other women in the class had with him about
surely it's better to be creative. Him saying back to her
that we should keep the creativity for the writing classes
and groups he was sure we'd all belong to sooner or
later. That what they were looking for in the Leaving
Cert was structure and summary and intelligent, well-
ordered argument. That's definite, he'd said, trust me on
this one.

Now I feel about one inch tall. There I'd been thinking
C1 or even a B2 if I was lucky enough to get the right
fella marking me. (You have to be a genius to get an A in
English.) That old hubris again.

I reassure Mr Elliott that I had, of course, remembered
everything he'd taught me but I'm talking out of a burst
balloon. Far from a C1 or a B2, now I'm thinking, Ah,
well, all I want really is to pass the damned thing . . .

Ken is listening and he obviously sees that I'm upset
because when Mr Elliott turns away to the woman beside
me, he asks me if I'd like to go for a drink later, after the
second paper. We deserve it, he goes, especially if you
did as well as I think you did.

I'll be eternally grateful to him for that.

So I agree to go for a drink. With the adrenalin still
pumping I convince myself that I *deserve* a bit of an outing.
Anyhow, I just couldn't face the flat right now, not with

poor old James moping around and MTV blaring –
although I've learned to block it out. I can usually read
or study as if I'm in a forest glade.

It's only when I'm half-way through the poetry section
of the second paper that afternoon that I remember Patsy
didn't send me a good-luck card like she'd promised. I
try to shrug it off but I'm afraid that for a little while it
comes between me and my Patrick Kavanagh.

Our exam room is in one of those old-fashioned
assembly halls made from a bunch of classrooms between
which you can open a series of partition doors. Today,
these tall doors are folded back all along the wall, like
Beefeaters standing to attention. Even still, the atmosphere is stifling, worse than the morning. And the place
is so venerable that, no matter how much you clean it,
it'll always be dusty. Old plaster, old wood. (Trust me, I
know about these things!) The windows are set high – I
suppose to stop pupils daydreaming out of them – and
you can see this dust floating in the light slanting from
them. Motes. Millions of motes.

Not that I'm watching dances of dust. Even though it
might well be fairy dust. Because the good news is that,
to my absolute amazement, once again I have it cracked.
I could have answered nearly every single question in
every section of this English paper.

And would you believe that in the play section we've
been asked to 'consider the qualities of *Hamlet* which
account for its popularity as a play throughout the ages'.
Which gives yours truly a chance to compare the
inhuman pressures on the human mind of Hamlet versus
the even worse pressures on Macbeth and to discuss why
Hamlet is more popular. (Wrongly, in my opinion, as
you know.) This paper could have been set by yours
truly's guardian angel. What a doddle. Thank you, Mr
Elliott. Thank you, angel . . .

It's odd that I'm thinking pressure here, because wait till you hear what happened next.

For a short while all I can hear in the room is sighing and the odd rustle of paper or small scrape of a chair. I'm writing furiously — the old Bic slipping and sliding again in my hand — when from behind me I hear this sound, like a little scream, but not quite. I'm not the only one who heard something, everyone else did too. We all turn around.

There's a kid freaking out in the second last row. At first I think he might be having a fit or something, his head is back and his shoulders are shaking but then I see the tears pouring down his face and I realize he's having some sort of emotional breakdown.

The supervisor goes down to him and puts a hand on his shoulder to see what's the matter but it turns out to be the wrong thing to do because I'll never forget as long as I live what happened next. The kid shoots to his feet and overturns the desk — no, 'overturns' is too mild a word, he throws it over so violently that he catapults it into two other desks and chairs and the whole lot, boys and all, take a tumble. Desks, chairs, papers, pens, answer books, rulers, arms, legs, all flying.

Then he starts on a rampage around the room, flailing with his arms, kicking out at people. There's pandemonium. The rest of us are jumping up to get out of his way. More chairs get overturned. The supervisor is running around the room after him.

Now the kid picks up one of the chairs and flings it at a window, breaking the glass. We all duck. The glass comes back in and flies all over the room because there's a wire security grille on the outside. Now he's kicking, throwing over everything in his path.

One strange thing — you'd think he'd be roaring. No. All you can hear is the furniture and the glass and the rest

of us making little whimpery noises while we're scurry-
ing out of his way.

He picks up a second chair and the supervisor dashes
to the door and yells at the boy who's on duty outside to
go quick and get the head teacher and to tell him to fetch
the Guards and a doctor.

You might ask what are the rest of us doing. Absolutely
nothing is the answer. We're all like we're in shock.
Paralysed. All we're doing is looking. There's a sort of
exclusion zone around him.

The kid throws his second chair at the window just as
the head teacher comes running in the door. The head
teacher is yelling, Gary! Gary! but the kid completely
ignores him and throws a third chair, bang! What's left
of the glass shatters.

The head teacher rushes forward and something clicks
with the kid. He runs away from the window and into a
corner. He turns around to face the opposition. Now the
head teacher and the supervisor do a pincer movement,
coming at him from two sides. The head, fair dues to
him, is not making any jerky moves and has both of his
arms outstretched, hands open, like a gunfighter showing
the other dude that he's unarmed. Come on, Gary, he's
saying, come on, no one's going to hurt you. He's
talking like you'd talk to a wild animal. And that's
exactly how the kid is behaving now, he has his back
shoved tight into the corner with his legs splayed in front
of him and arms out on both sides against the walls as
though he's supporting the whole building. His head is
up and sort of sideways, like a stag who's going to be
shot in the neck.

As it happens, I'm one of the people nearest to him, so
near that I can see the veins, like little red threads, in his
eyes. My heart goes out to him. I've never seen a more

terrified expression on anyone. Even James when the cops came.

Now there's near silence in the room. After all the crashing and banging it's eerie to hear nothing except the head teacher going softly, Come on, Gary, come on outside. We're going to get someone to look after you, everything's going to be all right, you're not going to get into any trouble, come on, Gary . . .

The kid makes a strangled noise, high in his nose, 'mmmffff,' as though he's frightened to death, which for sure he is.

I step forward, hear myself saying to the head teacher, Excuse me, let me help, I have a fella at home, I can probably handle this. I don't wait for permission, instead, I walk up in front of the kid and look him straight in the eye. Look, I go, as quietly as I can speak, I give you my word that I won't let anyone do anything to you. Come on out with us. Don't worry about the damage to the bloody windows, it's only a bit of glass, it's easily cleaned up.

Isn't that right? I say, over my shoulder to the head teacher but without taking my eyes off Gary.

That's right, goes the head teacher.

There's this pause and then the kid peels his arms off the two walls he's plastered against.

The head teacher and I take him one arm each and the three of us walk out through the door. The face on the attendant boy outside is a study. He couldn't be more than sixteen, glasses, pimples, half of him thinks all his birthdays have come at once with all this drama, half of him is scared to death. He's probably thinking he'll be blamed for something.

Gary is broken. Apart from anything else, he'll fail English and if you've to have any hope of getting into third level, you can't really afford to fail English. He goes off with the head teacher towards his office because I have to get back inside to finish the exam.

And that's the end of it from my end. You might well ask why I'm going to the bother of telling you this, like, Gary is not my problem, is he? It's just that the incident brought it home to me – where it hurts – how vulnerable boys of that age are. I'm sure I don't have to spell it out for you any more than that.

Back inside the exam hall, the supervisor is standing wiping his forehead with a hanky – he's the jumper type, they always have real hankies – and when he sees me arrive back and now it's all over he galvanizes. It's only then I realize what I've done. 'I can handle this'? I can't even handle my own brother. But somehow it worked. It was quite a valuable lesson, if you act as though you're in charge, you probably are.

The supervisor springs up on to the dais at the top of the room and makes a little speech. This incident is unprecedented, *unprecedented* in all his experience. And the best thing to do now is to get all the desks and so forth to rights again and to continue. And we're all to calm down and he hopes we're not too upset to continue our examination.

One of the men in our group speaks up and asks if we can have a short recess to collect our thoughts.

Out of the question. The supervisor is recovering his status now and he tells us, sternly, that he hopes no one has taken advantage of the situation.

We all laugh, nervously, because we know what he's talking about – cogging – but we don't really know whether he means it as a joke or not.

He doesn't. Because he tells us that he's going to stay up there watching our every move until we put the room together again and all get back to work. He'll make

allowances for what happened. We can have an extra
fifteen minutes at the end of the time to make up for the
upset.

Big deal.

As it happened, it didn't take me all that long to get
back into discussing the pressures on Ophelia. I'm about
to compare them to the pressures of Lady Macbeth when
I decide not to go overboard. There's a difference
between displaying knowledge and showing off. I suppose knowing these differences is what being a mature
student is all about. So for what remains of the time I've
allocated to the play question, I concentrate on poor old
lily-faced Ophelia.

And eventually, when the man on the dais calls time
up, I'm happy enough. I'd put in the work, the questions
fell my way and I've done my best.

Ken and I decide to go the the Gravediggers, which is
a pub he knows at the back wall of Glasnevin cemetery.
It isn't too far away and it's very famous because of its
association with James Joyce and Bloomsday. We think it
might be appropriate for people who'd just finished
Leaving Cert English. But wouldn't you know it, as
we're just about to leave, we hear Mr Elliott suggesting
the same outing to others of the group.

Ken and I look at each other and then, without saying
anything, we know we want to be on our own. I find this
disturbing, for want of a better word.

Are you sure you won't come with us for a drink,
Angela? Mr Elliott is put out. I think he likes the feeling
of running the modern equivalent of a hedge school and
doesn't want to let any of us go. No thanks, I say, Ken
here has kindly offered me a lift. I hear my own voice
saying this too brightly, as though I've something to
conceal.

Get a grip, Angela Devine.

As we walk towards the van, Ken stares straight ahead and suggests another pub he knows, the Brian Boru, which is not all that far from the Gravediggers.

Anyway, he says as he starts the engine, it's much of a muchness, the Brian Boru is in *Ulysses* as well.

I'm impressed. You've read it then?

Have you?

We laugh.

The pub is one of those refurbished jobs, darke woode and olde worlde jugs and Gold Flake mirrors on the shelves in amongst the bottles. It's nice, though. Because this is now tea-time, the place is buzzy with office workers, mostly young.

We have three drinks in quick succession and I'm having a great time. In fact, by the time I'm finishing the third I'm quite giddy and I think he is too. But all of a sudden I'm thinking urgently of James, I'm probably spooked by the incident with the berserk kid.

I tell Ken I have to go. Now he looks off into the middle distance. Is this the end then? I mean, I'd like to see you again. He's beetroot and I realize I'm being offered a proper date. It's donkey's years since anyone asked me on a date.

Well, that's not strictly accurate. Men have asked me. To be precise it's donkey's years since I had either the time or the inclination to consider going on one.

The drink makes me reckless. Are you asking me out? I mean *out*?

If it was possible for him to go any redder he would have. What a good idea. He tries to laugh. Dismal failure. Yes, as a matter of fact. As a matter of fact I am. Asking you out.

Then the answer is yes.

When so? We could go to a film?

Sure. It's ages since I've been to a film.

We arrange to meet the following evening to go to see *Sense and Sensibility*. At my suggestion, we make it the six o'clock show rather than the night-time one. If there's any suggestion in his mind that we might become an item, I want to slide gradually towards it, see how it hangs with me. He agrees. He's so embarrassed I can see the pulse throbbing in his forehead. I don't know how this man ever got around to getting married.

It's quite late, well after tea-time, when I get home. Even before I open the door of the flat I can hear the cacophony of the rock music. I despise MTV. I tried and tried to be flexible and modern and understanding about the needs of the young and so forth but now I've decided that its co-called music is just noise. You can't hear the words of the songs and the singers are nearly always out of tune.

There are a few exceptions, I suppose. I definitely like Bono's voice, it has a haunting, lyrical quality to it and he does sing in tune. It makes me wince, though, because he's strained it with not minding it so now he's hoarse even when he talks in interviews on the radio. In my humble opinion, if he goes on the way he is he won't have any of it left by the time he's fifty. (Not that he needs my opinion, from what I hear he's enough fortunes made at this stage never to have to open his mouth again.)

Their backing has some discernible pattern to it too, The Edge's guitar work is quite exciting. In fact, I have to confess that if I had the money I'd go to a U2 concert. I believe they're brilliant live.

We're very proud of all our world-class singers and bands from Ireland, you know. For a small country, I think we're great, for instance who'd have thought only twenty-five years ago that we'd keep winning the Euro-vision Song Contest? Or Nobel Prizes? And, of course, in other fields — no pun intended — we have Ronnie Delaney

and Sonia O'Sullivan and Michelle Smith and Eamonn
Coughlan. Not to speak of Paul McGrath and George
Best and all the golfers and writers and cyclists.

When you consider that we have half the population of
Haiti. When is the last time you heard of a world
superstar from Haiti? Papa Doc and that's it.

I steel myself to open the door and go in. Hi, I say to
James. The music is so loud I see his lips saying, Hi, back
but I can't hear him. He's lolling on the bed-settee with
both legs over one of the armrests and he has three plates
— *three* — on the floor in front of him with two empty
glasses and two cups. Plus he's pouring crisps into his
mouth, using the bag like a funnel, and he has a can of
Coke in the other hand.

Something snaps in me — maybe I'm a bit reckless
because of the few gins I've had with Ken in the Brian
Boru. I march over to the telly and I turn it off.

I turn around. Get your great big spawgs down off the
arms of that settee and clean up this room.

He opens his mouth to say something back and then a
miracle happens. He closes it again without saying
anything, he takes the legs down and stands up. He
gathers together all the plates and cups and glasses and
takes them over to the sink. He runs the water. I'm left
with my mouth hanging open.

Then I go and ruin it. I start in on him about how hard
I work for the two of us and how I don't want to have to
come home to see chaos around me when all he has to do
is to put in a modicum of effort . . . That it's not fair . . .
I hear my own voice rasping on and on like a rusty needle
on a cracked record.

He throws one of the glasses at the back of the sink and
it breaks.

Eff off, he says. (Except he doesn't say 'eff'.) And he
storms out of the flat.

My instinct is to run after him but I don't. I could kill myself. Here he hands me a golden opportunity for progress in the relationship between us and I blow it.

All right, in one respect I have right on my side, he should have a bit more consideration and try to make more of an effort, domestically speaking, but in his defence, he has to be absolutely miserable. In turmoil. He was probably comfort eating. And it hasn't been easy for him, no siblings, no father or mother, just one much older sister. A pretty bossy sister at that. Now he has all of this rape stuff to contend with. And in all fairness to him, he has been indulged a great deal – I have to take some of the blame for his self-centredness.

I stand there in the silence. The flat seems desperately empty. I realize that this is probably what it's going to be like when he goes to gaol.

I mean if, of course . . .

I notice a dinge in the armrest of the settee where his legs were and I go over to smooth it out. It's still warm. I get upset. It's that bloody gin, no wonder they call it mother's ruin. Now who knows what'll happen. Talk about selfish.

❧ Sixteen ❧

Two pieces of good news.

I forgot the next day's hangover when I read the letter from Patrice Murphy. It was addressed to James, of course, and although normally I wouldn't dream of opening up his post – not that he gets much! – in this instance I felt justified.

Number one, James's boss had agreed to go into court as a character witness. Number two, even better, the psychiatric evaluation of him had come in and thank God it was quite favourably disposed. The psychiatrist was of the opinion that the incident with Rosemary Madden was most likely aberrant and was unlikely to reoccur.

I didn't get a chance to tell James until quite late that evening. He didn't come in until nearly half past ten.

When I did tell him I could see, although he was trying to hide it, that he was thunderstruck about his boss. After all, this guy was the same one who had suspended him.

Unfortunately, when he arrived in, I was on my way out the door, kissogramming, so I couldn't hang around to discuss the implications. With him bringing in no money I had to earn every penny I could so I had had to abandon (temporarily, I hope) my plans to give up those gigs. I'm sorry, I say to James, I have to go now but I won't be long.

Wha'? He looked at me as if I had two heads.

I didn't engage. I was having to force myself to go out to work that night and I didn't want any extra hassle. Apart from all the trauma that was going on in our lives, this particular night I was acutely aware of what a wally I looked in the outfit. It'd still be daylight up to eleven o'clock and you'd want to see the looks I get in the street!

I started this work about six years ago, up to then I couldn't go out much at night because babysitters cost too much and it didn't make economic sense. But when James came to be about thirteen, going on fourteen, I spotted the ad in one of those free newspapers they deliver through your door, and I figured he was old enough to be left alone a couple of nights a week. 'Top wages for suitable candidates. Sense of humour essential.'

How hard could it be? I'd always believed I've a sense of humour (although lately I'm not so sure!).

The interview went grand. I'd been afraid they'd ask me to strip in front of them but they didn't. Maybe it helped that I made sure I wore a short skirt that day. The chap interviewed me just as if it was for a real job although a lot more informal, of course. He asked me what my attitude would be to kissing fellas, or putting them across my knee and spanking them. I said, Whatever turns them on is fine by me, provided it's all play and it doesn't get out of hand. I could see him watching me carefully while I talked.

And how would I feel about going in a novelty costume, like a stripping banana or a wicked chicken.

No problem, I said, looking at a point on the wall behind his head so that I wouldn't burst out laughing. He gave me a gig on a trial basis for that very night.

It went OK – he obviously checked back with the client – so he gave me another one and put me on the books. So that was that.

The only difficulty was that I didn't have a telephone so I had to make sure to ring them to tell them when I was available. Just as well, as it turned out, because it left me more in control. If I didn't want to work, I just didn't ring in. And on our side, if we were short urgently – say, if the Hoover broke down or if we had to get a new kettle or a toaster – then I knew I had an avenue to raise instant cash for it.

Within a couple of months I was an old hand. Once you get the hang of it, you can be anything. It's just a matter of not being too inhibited and of focusing on the client. It's half acting, half yourself. All eyes are usually on the victim anyway, not on you. And if you concentrate on him – ninety-nine per cent it'll be a him – then it's actually quite easy.

When I got better acquainted with the boss he told me that he knows within two minutes of meeting a girl or a fella whether they're going to be able to do the job well. He says he finds that the work is an extension of a person's own personality. Well, whatever it says about me I started even to enjoy it. (For a while.) It seems I may have a genuine talent for entertaining people.

I definitely found that the more of the kissogram work I did the more confident I became. For instance it certainly helped with PA System. Patsy and I didn't start those gigs until I was well into my stride with the kissograms and I found that when I stood in front of an audience I wasn't half as nervous as I should have been. I was able to concentrate on their enjoyment rather than on what they were going to think of me. You start with an advantage in these circumstances, they're on your side, at least at the beginning. After all, they paid their money so they could have a good time, not to be critical.

At the beginning, I kept this side of my life very quiet

— they still don't know at the cleaning job, although the clock is ticking and very soon I'm sure I'll run into one of my cleaning colleagues at some gig or other. Dublin *is* a village, everyone who lives here says it all the time, you can't walk down O'Connell Street without meeting at least one person you know.

I didn't tell even Patsy until I'd been doing it for the best part of two years. I must say she took it well. But I often wonder what Mammy would think. She was such a lady, I doubt she would approve of all the innuendo. She certainly would have hated the pair work, like when two of us go as a priest and a nun.

The money was a godsend, of course, it was because of the extra cash that James and I were able to move out of the flats and into the private rented sector.

So anyway, this particular gig this night, I'm requested as a French maid. I tippy-tap into the pub, feathers and fur flying, so to speak.

The first person I see is St John Markey.

Talk about shock. I don't know which of us was the more taken aback. Yet why should I have been so surprised to see this baby barrister in a pub in Dorset Street? Somehow you don't associate Dorset Street with lawyers. They'd be more Grafton Street or the Shelbourne, southside anyway . . .

Whatever. I'm absolutely mortified. Of course I pretend I don't recognize him and I go and do my job. But I'm tickling the victim with my feather duster and I'm ooh-la-laahing and telling him he's a naughty boy and making a holy show of the poor guy but all the time all I can think of is St John Markey's eyes boring into the back of my head. Or into some other place on my anatomy. These French maid's outfits are pretty skimpy.

Would this go hard for James? I mean, when this kid is

arguing James's case in front of a judge will he be seeing me in my Wonderbra and my frilly knickers under my lace apron?

I was never more glad to get out of a place. And luckily that gig was the only one I'd accepted for that night, so I was true to my word about getting home early.

It turns out that this is a lucky break. Because James is in bits when I get in. I mean in *bits*. He's in his bedroom, face down on his bed. No telly on, no music, no lights. He's rigid.

What's the matter? I go, did something happen?

What did I think was the matter. He says it to the wall and he doesn't move a single muscle.

I say nothing more at that stage, I feel totally helpless. That's one of the worst aspects of this entire situation. There is nothing I can do about it. It's rolling towards us like an avalanche. We see it, we hear it, it's above us, but we've nowhere to go to get out of its path. We just have to stand there, staring up at it over our heads. Waiting for it to bury us.

Correction. Waiting for the main weight of it to bury us. It keeps dropping little mini-avalanches on us as warnings of what is to come.

I make two cups of tea and I bring them into his room. Listen, James, I say, here's a cup of tea for you. Drink it. Come on—

I don't want it. Still to the wall.

I know you don't want it but please. Drink it for me—

I don't effin' want it.

Sit up, then. I want to talk to you.

Eff off and leave me alone.

I stand my ground, it's my turn now. I won't eff off, I say quietly. I'm staying here until you sit up. I didn't get us into this problem but I'm staying with you. I'm not abandoning you.

Whether it was me swearing or what – he's certainly not used to that – he slowly sits up. I hold out his cup of tea and he takes it, still without looking at me.

We sit there, both of us sipping at the tea. I'm trying to tell myself that what I'm doing is just being there for him. I don't care if on the surface he seems not to want me. I'm the adult here. I have to trust what I believe is right for him.

There's some kind of disturbance out in the street, a couple of drunks probably, man and woman. Shouting and roaring. Lots of bad langauge. To me, it makes the two of us inside, in that quiet room, seem unreal. It's not real behaviour to be sitting here with the lights out, sipping tea and not saying anything.

You know how that happens? How you recede from where you're sitting and look down on yourself and at what you're doing as if you're watching yourself in a play? James and I are sitting on this bed, he's as hollow as a ghost and I'm in a French maid's outfit and we're barely visible amongst the heaps of his clothes all over the place.

We're not real people. We're the Macbeths.

It's funny that *Macbeth* should come into my mind at this point. It's the exchanges between the Doctor and Macbeth. She's completely mad now but he's still asking the doctor what's wrong with her. The doctor tells him that she's not physically sick at all but troubled with thick-coming fancies that keep her from her rest.

Exactly. The fancies and fears are always worse than the actuality. Shakespeare's brilliant. Even if I fail the bloody English exam, at least I'll have had the privilege of having read Shakespeare for once in my life.

One quibble I do have about the Shakespeare curriculum, though. Whereas I admit you need to be taught how to understand it because of the archaic language and so forth, I have a gut feeling that all the analysis and questioning and notes that you have to study ruins the actual play for you. I wonder if Shakespeare, when he wrote *Hamlet*, or any of the other plays, really meant people to be comparing and contrasting or discussing it? To go back to *Macbeth*. That's a gut-feeling play. You just know in your gut what's going on when you hear it acted out.

Mr Elliott told us that the people in the Globe Theatre used to munch their lunch while they were watching the plays and shout across to each other and heckle the actors. That sounds like they were having fun. I don't know how many Leaving Cert students would think Shakespeare was fun.

Do you think I'm a rapist? His voice is small and light and scared.

Of course not, I go.

I'm glad it's nearly dark.

I'm sure you'll appreciate that, in the circumstances, *Sense and Sensibility* was not exactly a barrel of laughs for me. I tried to put a good face on it on the way up to the Omniplex where the picture was playing. (That's another good thing about Dublin, by the way, I think we must have about a hundred cinemas at this stage and there are more promised.)

Ken Sheils and I speculate about the Leaving and what marks other people in the class might get. We exhaust this topic by Whitehall church.

Tell me a little bit about Diandra, I go then, do you see

her often? Immediately he looks across as me as though I've hit him.

I try to laugh it off. This is not a trick question, I say, I'm just making conversation but if you'd rather not—

No, no, he says quickly. Of course I don't mind talking about her.

He has to brake quickly, because he nearly forgot to turn off the dual carriageway into Santry, and Sam shoots forward against the dashboard. He has a habit of standing upright, with his hind legs on the floor of the van and his front ones on the base of the gear lever between the two front seats.

We sort Sam out then Ken starts to tell me about Diandra and him. She was only seventeen when they got married. Everyone was naturally dead set against it and wanted her to wait at least until she was eighteen. But then she broke down and admitted she was pregnant. There was murder, of course, but what could anyone do?

They got a flat in Ballymun, which is where her folks lived, and after they were safely married, she had this really quick miscarriage – which, according to Ken, didn't take a feather out of her. He says this without a hint of bitterness. According to him, at the beginning, he genuinely tried to make the best of it, but it wasn't long before they started having serious rows.

And no, he doesn't see much of her now. Hasn't seen her for about six months. She doesn't care as long as the cheques keep coming in the door. Now he's sounding a bit sour.

It turned out that Diandra was using him to get away from home. Her mother was living with some deadbeat – the father was long gone – and Diandra couldn't stick the guy. Hands all over the place, she told Ken. She had two brothers who couldn't stick the situation either and spent half their lives in Diandra and Ken's flat rather than in their own. Then they started bringing their friends in. It became like Father McVerry's hostel for the homeless.

I'm not sure I'm liking the sound of all of this, I mean, this was Ken's home too. Where was he while all this squatting and mayhem was going on in his house? Up in Mars?

I ask him why he didn't put his foot down. We're just turning into the car park of the Omniplex now. The place is hopping. These shopping centres with their cinemas are breeding – I don't know if Dublin can handle many more of them, but so far there seems to be no limit to the number of people who throng them, day and night.

I reckoned that she was very young and that things would get better, he says. Anyway, I was out working all the time. I had to. She liked going out, nice clothes.

I think about that for a minute or two. This Diandra is some tulip, as far as I can see, but then I wasn't there at the time, was I?

I know he has a father and a mother, both still *in situ*. And four siblings – two brothers, two sisters. They were all living at home, together, until recently when Ken got his own place at the Custom Hall and then, within months, one sister and one brother got married. How did his own folks feel about the way he was treated by Diandra and her family?

Sam has to brace himself between us now because Ken's swinging the van around the little roundabout in front of the cinemas. I can see he's using the manoeuvre to fob me off. He straightens up the car again and starts to travel down between the rows of parked cars. My folks? he says then. My folks didn't know.

He finds a space and puts the van into it. He turns off the engine and gives Sam a Bonio.

When we're getting out and he's locking the van, he

says casually, I never told them why we got separated.
I'm not close to my parents. The way he says it closes the
conversation. I'm beginning to see that, with this guy,
there's a complicated area down there he doesn't want
to open up.

This news about him and his folks and them not being
able to talk to each other comes as a real shock to me. To
me, up to now, Ken Shiels's early life had sounded like
The Little House on the Prairie – real mother and father and
sisters and brothers all living together.

What is it about me and families, do I jinx them just by
knowing them? Take Tom Bennett's so-called family, I
was over the moon about that one and look what
happened there. And now here's Ken's.

Or maybe I just don't know what goes on inside real
families because my own experience is so lacking. I'm
probably trying too hard to latch on. Seems to me like
I'm a homing pigeon who keeps bumping into walls.
Maybe all the ordinary families are only on the telly! (Or
down the country.)

I cried all the way through *Sense and Sensibility*. I didn't
look, but I have a feeling Ken wasn't too chirpy either.
It was exactly the wrong picture to go to if you come
from a dysfunctional background. All that hominess
and people being concerned about each other. All that
hugging.

So, as you can see, the evening was not a success
although we did make plans to meet again the following
Saturday night to go for a meal. Apart from my birthday
last year, when Patsy took me to a lovely little Italian
pizza place just off Chatham Street, I have been in a
restaurant approximately three times in ten years. You
probably don't believe me but it's the truth. When I told
Ken this, he perked up. Well, in that case I'll have to
take you to somewhere very special.

I tried to perk up too and nearly managed it. But not for long.

Because when I open the door to the flat, I find James is not alone. Patrice Murphy is there with him.

He stands up when I get in. Hello, Ms Devine, I hope you don't mind the intrusion. You have no telephone, you see, and I was passing here, I was working late. I thought I'd pop in rather than wait until I saw you on Monday. You got my letter, I see – he points to where it's lying on the table.

James is avoiding my eye.

No problem, I say, thanks. I was delighted to hear the news.

Neither James nor he looks even the remotest bit delighted.

What's up? I go, everything's going all right, isn't it?

The answer, when it eventually comes, is yes and no. Certainly no from my point of view.

Everything is proceeding, as they say, but Patrice Murphy is here to try to persuade James to plead guilty to sexual assault. He says that if James does this, the case will be likely to go well for him because sexual assault is a lesser offence than rape. From the state's point of view, it would help ease the backlog and save legal expenses and the cost of a jury trial. From our point of view, apart from pleading to a lesser charge, psychologically, it would also mean that we wouldn't have this awful prospect hanging over us for ever and ever. But, most importantly, the victim won't have to be put through the ordeal of giving evidence. Judges apparently like that and they take it into account when they're handing down sentences. And I think that any judge would see that James's remorse at what happened that day is genuine. That would be very helpful.

Patrice Murphy bounces – did I tell you he has this

habit of doing little bounces on the balls of his feet when he's concentrating? When I talk about a backlog, he says, the courts are completely bogged down. It's not unusual to have to wait a year or more for a jury trial. We could get character witnesses to bolster the psychiatrist's opinion that what James did that day was uncharacteristic and that he would be extremely unlikely to reoffend.

He's bouncing away, I'm standing there, looking between him and James, whose head is nearly on the floor by now. I'm dumbstruck.

But he's not guilty, I say, when I can get a word in edgeways. You know his side of the story as well as I do. That's not rape or sexual assault, is it? They were there to do it— Remorse – are you remorseful, James?

I take a couple of steps towards James. James, say something.

James looks at the floor.

I start in then and go on and on about the condoms and all the rest of it. Patrice Murphy listens patiently. When I wind down, he says again that his professional, legal advice, solicitor to client, is that James should plead guilty to sexual assault. His tone of voice is exactly the same as it was before I started. It's like I haven't said one thing.

I turn to James. I'm desperate. What do you think? I ask him, say something, for God's sake. It's your life. You're the one who has to decide. What do you want to do?

He mutters something to his toes.

What? I go, I can't hear you.

He looks at me full frontal. I want to get this over with, one way or the other, I'm sick to death of it.

I panic. You're going to plead guilty to something you didn't do just because you're sick to death of hanging around? Land yourself in gaol for sure? Where's your courage? I'm so het up I don't give a damn, normally I wouldn't dream of having a family row in front of a stranger.

I'm going to gaol anyway, James looks at his toes again. You know I am.

He's really annoying me now. I don't know anything of the sort, I say. Who says you're going to gaol? People are acquitted in courts as well as being convicted. Have you never heard of the word justice?

He looks up at me then. A pitying look. It stops me in my tracks because there's a world there in his eyes that I don't know. I recognize it, though. I'm bang up against a generation gap but also, much worse than that, I see what kids of his generation expect for themselves. Nothing. In James's eyes I see a life with no expectations.

This kills me. All his life I've tried to convince him to expect that miracles do happen. That if you pay your dues and are decent, that decent things will happen back. I can see in one instant that I've been wasting my time.

I sit down. You're going to plead guilty, aren't you?

The solicitor puts his oar back in now. Don't be too upset, Ms Devine.

Please don't call me Ms. I'm a Miss.

Petty, I know, but I had to show some spark of life. And I do hate Ms. And I don't care whether or not married men should change their titles. That's nothing to do with me. I'm not a married woman and that's the end of it. I'm a Miss.

Your man doesn't bat an eyelid. I'm sorry, Miss Devine, he says, you never know nowadays, do you? To get back to what we were talking about, the substantive issue, as it were, I've had the opportunity to review the case with St John Markey and he agrees with me. Our strong advice is that James here should plead guilty.

Now what's in my head is the look on St John Markey's face when he recognized the French maid who came into the pub in Dorset Street.

St John Markey's junior, isn't he? Not a senior? I'm

playing for time now because I have to think of some other arguments.

Patrice Murphy lowers his voice as though he's in a church. Yes, St John is a junior but in my opinion he's very fine. He'll certainly be a senior before long.

All right. Supposing, just supposing we agree. What sentence could James get?

He shrugs a little shrug. I can't guarantee anything, of course, but our strong guess is that when the judge hears all the facts in the case, the sentence will be minimal. He will ask for a victim impact report—

I interrupt him. What's minimal? How long?

Two years? Maybe eighteen months if we're lucky?

Eighteen months if we're lucky? Does this guy have any idea how long eighteen months in Mountjoy Gaol would seem to someone like James Devine?

Somehow I manage to keep my voice steady. And if we're not? Or if we don't take your advice and let it go to trial?

It's possible to get a life sentence for rape.

If you're found guilty.

If you're found guilty.

Which is a big if . . .

He doesn't answer.

What this guy's telling us is that one way or the other we're going to gaol. Our own solicitor. Even though he knows exactly what happened. So much for fair play and justice.

James is still just sitting there and I turn to speak. Speak for yourself, James.

He screws up his face like he used to do when he was a child and was going to cry. He's whispering, I can't stand it any more. I just want to get this over with.

✦ Seventeen ✦

Needless to remark, with the trial hanging over us, I couldn't think of going out for a meal with Ken Sheils that Saturday night so I put a note in through his letterbox cancelling it. He wasn't too hard to find, I was lucky, found his letterbox on only the second block I tried in his apartments complex. (I'd been worried that he mightn't be using his real name – some people don't put their real names on their letterboxes because of security or to keep former wives and girfriends away.) I was very apologetic in the note but I said something had come up in my personal life.

Coincidentally, that Saturday was my birthday. James hadn't remembered – he never does so I hadn't expected anything from him – but for the first year ever since we were kids, Patsy hadn't remembered either. Ah, well, I suppose oblivion comes to us all!

I couldn't have celebrated anyway, in the circumstances. For some reason, I kept thinking back to James as a baby, as though it was his birthday and not mine.

He was a gorgeous child, genuinely beautiful. I thought I was the bee's knees wheeling him up and down our street with oul' wans googling at him and admiring him. And you know, nowadays, even since all this trouble, I still don't see him as this surly leathered 'youth' with his earring and his big spawgs hanging over the arm of my bed-settee. I still see this little lad in his go-car, soother in his mouth and a battered denim baseball cap on his head with his curls peeping out from under it. Or him crying his heart out over a baby deer that's being eaten by a cheetah on one of his wildlife programmes.

He's very good-looking, you know. By far the best-looking of all five of us, I'd say — although since I haven't met them for so long I'm not quite sure how the other three are looking lately. His only drawback at present is his skin, which is a bit spotty — I assume from all the crisps. He's around six feet or six feet one and although he's thin, I'm sure when he fills out a bit he'll have a brilliant body. Also, when he gives his hair a chance to grow, like right now, it's real film-star hair, dark and crisp.

And considering all the pints and the smokes and the late nights, not to speak of his work taking him through the traffic fumes of Dublin, his eyes are pretty clear. Actually, I don't mind boasting for once, his eyes are amazing, large and pale grey with a paler, honey-coloured fleck through them. Those eyes kill you if he looks straight at you, as I know to my cost. It's probably one of the reasons he was able to get away with murder when he was small. Whoever his father was, he had to have been a stunner.

At first, when I took him out of Temple Street hospital that time, the social workers and public health nurses were all over me, checking up on whether I was looking after him properly or not. I can just imagine the case conferences! They rode me very tightly. The nurse went mad when she found out I'd flavour his milk with Ribena — what about his teeth? All that sugar. They were only his baby teeth, I said back to her. I promised her I'd go easy but I made a mental reservation. Like hell I'd stop giving him something that he really liked. Anyway, it was full of vitamin C. I hid the Ribena bottle when she was due to visit.

(Anyway, who's had the last laugh? James has fantastic teeth.)

I found early on that there's no mystery about caring for a baby. Feed him, change him, love him, feed him again. Their stomachs are perfectly designed. If you give them too much, or the wrong stuff, they'll sick it up again. If in doubt, feed, that was my motto.

Yet because for those first few weeks I was so desperately anxious about Mammy, I was probably not as good at being a mother to him as I should have been. I do worry about this, they say that the first few months of mothering are crucial to babies, to how their characters and personalities turn out. It could be all my fault that he's in this trouble now – but you'd drive yourself mad if you thought too deeply about everything you've done, or failed to do in your life, wouldn't you?

Once Mammy was put into hospital it was plain she was not going to survive, even though no one would come right out and say it. Apart from being malnourished and all the rest of it, she had pneumonia. And as I told you, now I reckon she could have been HIV. I must check sometime when exactly HIV came to Dublin. She could easily have been one of the first. Once again demonstrating the Devines' great good fortune.

The hospital was old and every crack in the paintwork on the wall of her ward is as clear to me today as it was that first visiting hour. When I walked in I immediately resented that she was in a bed surrounded by those of geriatrics. My mammy was *young* . . . These people were all on their last legs, coughing up phlegm and making disgusting noises. Some were obviously senile, roaring all the time for the nurses.

And the smell! Urine, of course, but another smell, too, which I can only describe as being like rotting fruit.

I definitely want to die young. I made up my mind that night and have never changed it.

When I calmed down a bit, I had to admit that in some respects she did look every bit as decrepit as the others. She'd cut her hair, or what was left of it, and there were bald patches showing through the clumps. As well as the purpling on her face, bruising and discoloration and so forth, she had her eyes closed and under the neon light, the sockets were so dark they were nearly black. She had a big cut on one of her cheekbones and a crusty cold sore on her lip. She was on two drips and she had an oxygen mask covering half her face. It gurgled.

It took me all my courage not to turn tail and rush out of there. I could have too, she was so out of it she'd never have known. Hello, Mammy, I said.

She opened her eyes and looked at me with this milky look. I realized she didn't know who I was. And then the strangest thing happened to me. I got so angry I wanted to kick her. Hard.

Can you believe that? Here's my mother, the person who means more to me than anyone else in the whole world. She's probably in desperate pain, probably dying, she's probably frightened and lonely, and here am I, furious with her. It's like I'm hit by a huge red wave of rage that scoops me up and throws me towards the ceiling. I want to hit and kick and roar. I want to overturn the bed and beat her around the place with my fists.

Yet at the same time I'm feeling all this, I'm also dying with sorrow.

Can you understand any of that? I didn't at the time. In fact, I remember I became so guilty about my reaction that it took me years to get over it.

Funnily enough, studying *Macbeth* brought it all back, not literally, of course, because it's all ancient history now, but I certainly identified with some of the blacker emotions unleashed by the witches in that play. It's something to do with control. You think you're in control but you're not. As a matter of fact, you're in control of nothing at all in this world, not even your own feelings. No wonder people have to believe in some sort of a god. Someone has to be in charge of this chaos.

Anyway, I did the best I could that night. I forced down the rage and I gave her the pathetic little bunch of flowers I'd brought in. Her eyes filled with tears, although she said nothing – she wouldn't have been able to anyway with the oxygen mask – and I could see she still thought I was some stranger. I didn't stay long. I couldn't.

That night, when I got back to the flat, I did something of which I remain so ashamed that I cannot possibly tell you what it is. Perhaps some other time. All I'll say now about that horrible wheeling merry-go-round period of my life is that the memory of what I did still frightens me.

To get back to James as a baby. He, of course, had no idea what big events were going on in his little life. All he cared about was his bottle and his soother and me. This was a bit of a boost for me. Despite everything else, I felt loved and important and necessary in someone's life.

The other three? Forget it. Francesca, as I've explained already, even at that age, wished us all off the planet so she could get on with her real life. For an eleven-year-old she was as poised as a model. Justine and Nicola, who were eight and six at the time, were doing all right in their foster homes. The fact that they had a big sister and a little brother didn't really impinge. They were happy to come to the access visits because of the Coke and the chips. They would have been just as happy to go to a circus or a pantomime. Probably happier.

No, the real family now was James and me.

When it was clear Mammy was not going to get any better, she was moved to the hospice in Harold's Cross. I cried buckets when they told me. It was so final. Everyone knew that once you went in there you would never leave it again except in a wooden box. Nowadays no one is afraid of the hospice – all our Irish stars are involved in fund-raising for it, I suppose it's sort of insurance for them, they know there's a good chance they'll need it themselves some day. Then, though, Dubliners *whispered* the word 'hospice' because it's full name was the Hospice for the Dying.

I shouldn't have cried because everything improved that day, including my ability to cope with what was happening. As soon as she was settled in, the entire world calmed down, so much so that I didn't dread going to see her any more. All that anger which had surged up in me each time I'd seen in her in the hospital? Gone.

Her whole appearance changed straight away, she sort of smoothed out, if you can imagine that. And although she lasted only six weeks longer and never did come to terms properly with who James and I were, every time I think back to Mammy's very last days on this earth, thanks to the hospice, I see her surrounded by light and warm golden air.

I have to say that Tom Bennett was a brick during this time. One of the things that kept me going was the laughs we were able to have despite everything. He put up with me when I was in the dumps, or inclined to feel sorry for myself, or when I cancelled one of our dates because James was poorly. He even used to come out to Harold's Cross with me during those last few weeks. He didn't accompany me into the building, just waited outside and minded James so I could be uninterrupted with Mammy. The more I think of it now, the more I admire him for all of that.

All ancient history now.

Getting back to the story, on the Sunday morning after Patrice Murphy's visit, I found it hard to act naturally with Patsy on the way to the PA gig. She, on the other hand, was all over me. (Still hadn't remembered my birthday, though!) She cracked jokes, told me this long, endless saga about a plumber who didn't come to put in a dishwasher for her, gave me all her plans about their holidays in August. They were going to Minorca. Why don't you come, Ange? she goes, spend that money you won, for God's sake, you deserve a break.

She doesn't look at me while she's saying this. She knows damn well I can't come. And she knows why. All the time she's prattling on, James's predicament lies between us like a big black slug. And I don't like to tell her that there's already quite a dent in that money. What's more I'm damned if I'm going to tell her he's pleading guilty.

How's Martin? I ask, when I can get a word in edgeways, I'm a bit surprised you're going on holidays with him after what happened.

This is mean of me, I know, but I can't stand what's going on between her and me. I don't think that fundamentally I'm a bitchy person but the minute I saw her that morning I started to resent her. I certainly can't behave as if there's *nothing* going on. How dare she behave like that about James?

Martin? she goes, like she's surprised. Oh, Martin's fine, busy as all get out. And then she's off again on a story about him and his partner meeting some suspicious characters in the bar of their hotel in Belfast when they were up there on business the day before last. According to her, she wouldn't be surprised if they were even Provos. I worry about him going up there all the time, she says, with the ceasefire so shaky and all, you never know what's going to happen . . .

This is the same Patsy who's been so upset recently about finding a condom in Martin's pocket. I give up on human nature.

The gig is in one of those huge pubs, as big as haybarns, which have about as much soul as boxing arenas. They serve Sunday lunch and live music and you sure are left in no doubt about which is the real attraction. We're on from two o'clock till three which in theory is supposed to mean they get their food out of the way first. In practice, it always means that we're performing to the backs of people's heads and trying to drown out the sound of kids whinging that they don't like what's on their plates.

This morning bears out my worst fears. I see immediately we walk in that we're in trouble.

The place is packed with a mixed bag of punters, men in twos and threes who probably have nowhere else to hide out from the wives going demented at home, families with squads of kids running riot and throwing stuff, gaggles of women who are already well on and shrieking even though the pub is open less than half an hour. It's so thick with smoke that my mascara starts to sting straight away.

Patsy throws her eyes to heaven and for that one quick moment, we're best friends and it's like nothing has happened. We roll up and roll on and give the punters what they've paid for and in the end they give us quite a decent round of applause. I defy anyone to notice anything awry in our behaviour towards each other during that show. This is where experience counts.

After the gig, on the way home, she's off again with the stories, bright and brittle as a new tack.

I can't stand it one minute longer. Look, I say, I want to talk about what we're not talking about. I'm cleaning off my make-up at the time, using the little mirror behind the passenger sun visor. I deliberately scrub and scrape so I won't have to look at her. I feel I should give her a chance.

Oh? she goes.

I stop with the cotton wool. Please, Patsy, I say, this is me, Angela. We both know what I mean.

She looks injured. I'm damned if I do—

James. I cut her off before she gets too far down that road.

That shuts her up.

James? I say again, can we talk about James?

Oh, that.

Yes, I go, that. It's the single biggest thing in my life at the moment, Patsy, and I need to talk to someone about it. Correction. I'd like to talk to you about it.

She's now gripping the steering wheel as though she's afraid it'll turn into a flying saucer and get away from her. Angela, it's none of my business.

I know that strictly speaking it's none of your business, I say as gently as I can, but you're my friend and I'm your friend and I'm in trouble here. James and I are in trouble, Patsy. Please. I could do with a bit of help. Support . . .

That last bit was quite a shock. You know me, I can't bear to ask anyone for anything. Talk about swallowing your pride.

It turned out to have been wasted effort.

As far as Patsy was concerned she was sympathetic towards me, fair enough, but as for James, he had got himself into this situation and he shouldn't expect anyone else but himself to get him out of it. She sounds so weird suddenly that I look hard at her. What's the problem, Patsy, I ask her, did someone you know get raped?

Of course not. Of *course* not. She's outraged. In fact, she's so over the top about this that I feel it would be prudent to let it go. I'm right, though, there is something more to it. Her face is white.

I say nothing for a while and we drive on. There's a tape on of Barbra Streisand playing at some live concert where she's linking the songs by talking about all the psychoanalysis she's had and how it made her into a truer, better person. We could do with a few shrinks in this car right now.

Patsy turns to me. Please, Ange, don't let this thing affect our relationship.

Of course not, I go.

The two of us are beginning to sound like parrots.

When she lets me out at my grotty front door, we don't part as enemies, but to say that the customary ease between us is diminished is an understatement.

When I got in James wasn't in the flat and there was nothing on the telly that interested me so, after I'd changed my clothes and cleaned myself up, I went for a walk to clear my head. (Ken Shiels has a lot to answer for. Another walk? This was becoming a habit!)

Although it did have a few little incidents, this walk won't count for much when the history of Great Walks is written. I came out of our place, turned right down Gardiner Street, walked as far as Tops in Pops. Didn't see the potato skins outside, skidded, nearly killed myself. I could have developed instant back trouble or whiplash, but he's a nice guy and James and I always get our spuds there. I picked myself up, no real damage except a ladder in my tights and a rip along the seam in the armhole of my anorak. Walked on, turned right into Parnell Street, then left into O'Connell Street. Got to

O'Connell Bridge, couldn't think where to go next so I just turned round for home. At least I took a different route, along the Quays. Thrill a minute, that's me.

Maybe it's because I live in the area but it doesn't cost me a thought to walk by myself along the roughest streets in Dublin. Like everyone else, I know what's going on, syringe robberies, muggings, handbag snatches, all the rest of it. (In fact Handbag Corner is only a hundred yards from our place. Nowadays it's not a quarter as bad as it used to be, and there's even another new block of yuppie apartments going up on that corner. But the inside lane of the roadway continues to be empty when the lights are red. Old fears die hard.) Is any other city any better?

Anyhow, here I am, Miss Streetwise 1996, strolling home along the Quays, when I feel this thump on my back and at the same time someone tugging at the strap of my shoulder bag.

Thank God my reflexes are good. I manage to hold on to the bag as I whirl around and here are these two young fellas behind me, couldn't have been more than nine or ten years old. I let this roar out of me and before I know it I'm laying into them with the bag like it's a weapon. I don't know what comes over me, suddenly I'm Don Quixote. I frighten the wits out of them and they scarper.

An old wino, who's been hanging over the Liffey getting sick, has seen the whole thing. He turns his head round to me, are you all right, missus?

I am, of course, but then the reaction sets in and I get a bit shaky. So I go and stand beside him looking into the Liffey until the shakiness passes.

Now the funny bit. He starts a conversation with me about how Dublin's going to the dogs lately. This is a wino. A derelict.

Here's me with a ladder in my tights, in my cheap Dunne's anorak, which has the armpit ripped. Here's him without a tooth in his head and his face invisible under a hundred layers of dirt and hair. We're both standing there, looking down at the greeny-brown skin of the Liffey with his sick still floating on it and we're talking like philosophers about lack of political will, poverty traps and gaps, misplaced resources, judges having always to moan that there's nowhere for them to send juvenile delinquents.

Goodbye so, I say eventually, when we run out of anything more to say, I'd better be getting home. I start to open my bag to give him a quid for his trouble.

He holds up his hand. Ah no, missus, he says, no, you wouldn't insult me now, would you?

He tips his forehead in a sort of military salute and then shuffles off up the Quays towards O'Connell Bridge. I'm so flabbergasted I can do nothing except stand there with my hand still stuck inside my bag and my eyes out on stalks looking after him. You think you know people and then something like this happens and you realize you haven't a bull's notion.

Maybe it's the wino, maybe it's the mood I'm in, but on the way home I review my life. It's not something I normally do, I'm too busy just getting by.

Now, though, whichever way I look at it, I can't come up with much to cheer about. Leaving poor James out of it altogether, I'm up to my neck in manure.

An abbreviated summary. I'm in my middle thirties and not getting any younger. Financially I'm in that no man's land between poverty and making do. I've no relatives, fewer friends and what friendship I've had – i.e. Patsy – is going down the tubes. Also, based on our performance at *Sense and Sensibility* (we hardly talked at all on the way home and I hadn't heard from him since

I'd cancelled our Saturday meal) my burgeoning relation-ship with Ken Shiels is unburgeoning fast. Most of my work is of the pits variety and being realistic, Leaving Cert qualifications notwithstanding, there's little pros-pect of the situation getting any better in that area.

Little prospect? *No* prospect, with the unemployment figures rising every month and five hundred young fellas with honours Leaving Certs and even degrees applying for jobs as messenger boys in one of the semi-state companies. Unprecedented response, the guy said to Marian Finucane on *Liveline* — I think he was the personnel manager of the company that advertised. Someone else rang in then and said he had a Ph.D in English and all he could get by way of employment was pumping petrol.

I think you will agree that at that point my lifestyle and future looked pretty. Not.

And the day after I'm drawing up that little list James is due to plead guilty to raping a girl and no doubt is going to go to gaol.

Eighteen

The trial. Without further ado.

I absolutely hate this part of the story so I'll be as factual and as clinical as I can. Considering the circumstances and what happened.

I didn't ask for the day off work, I just didn't show up that morning. I heard the minibus beeping outside but I pulled the covers over my head and tried to ignore it. It's the first time I've ever done that, but I knew if I was asked why I wanted time off — which I would have been — I'd start to stammer and stutter. And anyway, I thought it would be bad luck to lie. If I'm fired, I'm fired. So be it.

I didn't sleep that night and neither did James. He went to the bathroom about six times. Once or twice I felt him looking over at me but I pretended to be asleep. There was nothing of comfort I could think of to say.

He was ready to leave forty-five minutes before we'd said we'd go. When he emerged from his room, and I saw behind him that he'd made his bed—

Should I take a sheet? He tries to make a joke of it, tries to laugh. He's shaking.

I can't write any more of this section.

We got to the Four Courts early. We were to see St John Markey and Patrice Murphy at half past nine, we

were there at a quarter past. We knew our way around
by then so we waited for them in the circular entrance
area. This is massive, with a marble floor and a huge
dome above it, which I heard on a radio programme is a
hundred and fifty feet high – no wonder it's such an
intimidating place when you first see it. I suppose that's
the idea. You wouldn't want justice dispensed in a shed.
You're not supposed to feel comfortable.

It probably should have made us feel better to see so
many people in the same boat as us but it didn't at all.
There was a sort of collective fear in the air. You could
sense it buzzing. Within five minutes of us arriving, I
don't know who was shaking more, me or James.

By far the saddest people in that whole place were the
defendants, you could easily pick them out – their eyes
kept shifting around as if they didn't know where to
look. They shuffled cheap shoes and pulled at badly
knotted ties. On the other hand, it was a hard call who
looked worse, them or the relatives. The mothers and
fathers and wives. Trying to look brave and hopeful at
the same time, to be loyal to their defendant because
they loved him (it was nearly always a him) while at the
same time trying to show that of course they didn't
condone what he'd done. And all the time you could see
they were hoping no one they knew would see them in
this awful place and in this terrible situation. I recognized
the phenomenon. With feeling.

Those where the relatives who had bothered to turn
up. There were an unfortunate few defendants who had
no one with them. God. Can you imagine?

Patrice Murphy came up to us at about twenty-five to
ten and brought us to meet St John Markey in an
interview room. His wig was on crooked and he had to
do a lot of flittering through files to find our case. He got
more and more flustered, maybe he was embarrassed

that he couldn't find it straight off. Maybe he was remembering the Wonderbra.

Personally I didn't give a sugar what his problem was. I had more deadly business on my mind. Like if this guy was competent to handle such a delicate case. Patrice Murphy seemed calm enough, though, and seeing this made me feel a tiny bit better.

James wouldn't look any of us in the eye.

Mr Elliott always pointed out in our prose selections how the good writers always furnish the room, i.e. help the readers to visualise where the action is taking place.

Right.

The little interview room where we meet our lawyers is bare and functional. Table. Chairs. Windowpane streaked with dirt, sun pouring through. Too hot even at that hour of the morning. Lino on the floor. A creased copy of last night's *Herald* on one of the chairs. The dominant colour pale brown. Rumble, like the constant roar of the sea, of lorries and cars outside on the Quays.

Markey eventually finds our file but it's Patrice Murphy who takes us through what's going to happen. He reassures us that our character witness – James's employer – and our psychiatrist, the one who had written that this incident was aberrant, will definitely be there.

I had volunteered to go on the stand to vouch for James so I ask them about it, but neither of the lawyers think now that this will make much difference. We won't close it off as an option just yet, Patrice Murphy goes, but I think it's highly unlikely we'll call you.

I'm ashamed to say that I'm relieved. Very. Poor James.

Patrice Murphy wishes us luck and then he and St John Markey go on to their next clients. Markey has a very busy day today, he's told us. Much good that'll do us.

As soon as they leave, James gets another attack of diarrhoea and has to go to the cloakroom. That leaves me sitting there by myself. I'm not feeling so terrific while I'm waiting for him to come back. It isn't nausea, precisely, just that churning feeling at the base of your stomach where you feel it's full of water rather than your insides. Every time I look at my watch, this lake of water sloshes around.

The next bit I remember absolutely.

James comes back at a quarter to ten. I ask him if he's all right and he nods. His face is as white as a plate. He looks at me with those amazing eyes of his. She's out there, I saw her, he says.

He doesn't have to tell me who he means. I'm flabbergasted she's here. Because with James pleading guilty, there was no need for her to come. She's only a witness in this case in any event and now she won't be called.

She can be here for only one thing, to see her revenge being exacted. What does she want? Blood? No point in asking myself that question, I know the answer. Revenge is not a beneficial emotion.

James goes to the window and rubs at one of the streaks on it with the corner of his jacket. Don't, I go, automatically, you'll ruin it . . . Then I stop. In the scheme of things does it really matter if the sleeve of a defendant's jacket is a bit grubby when he gets sent to gaol?

When we get into that courtroom, try not to look at her, I say.

Easy for you, he whispers. Then he turns round from the window and stares at me again.

What? I go – what is it?

Look, he goes, whatever happens today, thanks for everything. He turns around to the window again.

I can't speak. I leave it to you to imagine what I feel.

Next thing, we're in. First, there are the remand cases to be dealt with.

Don't I just wish . . . Aren't human beings hilarious? There was I, bitching to myself all through James's remands, wishing we could just get to trial and get the bloody thing over with and now here I've been granted my fondest desire and I want to unwish it. My heart is tattering in my chest and I can't breathe properly.

I can't even begin to imagine what James is feeling.

It goes on and on.

We get to a few trials where people are pleading guilty.

Larceny, judge.

Wishes for fifty-seven other charges to be taken into account, judge.

Breach of the peace, judge.

The goods taken amounted to a total value of twenty-nine pounds forty-one pence, judge.

I want to run. How many more do we have to endure before we get to it?

Oh, God — it's happening. His name is being called. Jesus. It's not only the bottom of my stomach, everything inside my whole body is water, even my brain. Here's St John Markey saying his client has decided on a certain course of action . . .

The next hour? I find it virtually impossible to remember it in sequence. I know the way it *had* to have happened, the start of the case, James's barrister, character witnesses, the psychiatrist, judge, et cetera. But it's a series of impressions, expressions, sounds, feelings, physical sensations rather than a logical progression of events.

To start at the end, you wouldn't believe it. Just over

ninety minutes after his case started, James and I found ourselves shaking hands with Patrice Murphy on the footpath outside the Four Courts.

If anything, the lake in my insides was more wave-ridden, if there's such a word, than before. It's like I was pushed through a time machine. I, Angela Rose Devine, was ninety minutes advanced but what had happened in the rest of the world during that time hadn't caught up with me yet.

The huge bright fact. James was convicted and sentenced to five years, suspended for one year. If he's of good behaviour during that year, the judge will review the sentence. Which probably means, according to Patrice Murphy, that he won't go to gaol. Congratulations, he says.

As I'm telling you this, I'm rolling the words, the whole scene, around and around at the top of my brain but they still won't percolate down any further. The judge recommended counselling for James, she told him he could consider himself a fortunate young man, gave out to him a bit, said his remorse seemed genuine, spoke directly to Rosemary Madden in the body of the court, sympathized, hoped she could put this distressing event behind her as quickly as possible. Next case.

I'm standing out on those Quays. I don't remember how I got here. I'm looking stupidly from Patrice Murphy to James and back again. I can't believe it. He's out. He's not in a cell.

James can't believe it. He's sweating, even though the wind whipping off the Liffey would cut the socks off an alligator.

Rosemary Madden certainly couldn't believe it. She rushed out of the courtroom at the end of the judge's words. The tears were pouring down her face. The mother bombed out after her, but not before glaring daggers in our direction. As for the woman from the Rape Crisis Centre, I leave it to your imagination. Daggers? Scimitars. Slash hooks. *The Pit and the Pendulum.*

I have a feeling Patrice Murphy can't believe it either, despite all his assurances to us earlier. He has to rush back in – his next case is already in progress – and he just keeps saying to us that he wishes us well and that we'll be in touch in due course. He has to shout because of the articulated trucks that are revving in the line of traffic on the Quays. That was a good decision, he yells. I felt all along it was going to go in our favour.

My eye. He felt no such thing. Why was he talking eighteen months?

He claps James on the shoulder and James doesn't react, just looks back at him, dazed. Goodbye now, says Patrice Murphy. Now he shakes hands with me. His hands are sweaty.

I look around me. I don't know what to do next, to tell you the truth. The lorries inching past seem as unreal as everything else in this scene, like they belong to another planet or at least a part of someone else's life. I can't feel relieved, I can't feel anything at all. I'm free-drifting.

At this moment I can't even completely remember what I had been expecting that morning before we got here.

Now, some time later, I'm ashamed to reveal that when I'd got up that morning I'd packed a little goody bag for him. Comics and snack bars and crisps. What did that say about my faith in my brother? In my defence, I was terrified. Mountjoy Gaol is hell, especially for newcomers. They're always doing reports on it on the radio, young men and boys have hanged themselves there and it's so crowded they have to sleep on the floor sometimes when they're remanded in custody. It's also a hotbed of drug abuse.

I'm so moithered I can't remember much about what our side's psychiatrist said in that courtroom. He was impressive, that I do know. Quiet. Matter-of-fact. He seemed to think that James and I together constituted a stable background for him — which at first I thought was a laugh, considering the true circumstances.

But then, when you think about the definition of the word 'stable' maybe the guy had a point. All right, it wasn't ideal, but James has only lived in two places in his life and he has been living with the same person since he was two months old. In one way maybe that could be defined as stability.

Fair dues to him, James's courier boss came up trumps too. He wasn't exactly heaping praise on James but he did say he was conscientious and honest. And, best news of all, he told the judge that he would give James his job back.

As I say, this is all episodic in my mind, I was taking too much in all at once, dividing my attention between Rosemary Madden, the judge, and the witnesses.

Rosemary Madden's expression was so intense it was frightening. She was dressed like a widow or a nun. Severe. Black high-necked dress with a white Peter Pan collar, black tights, black shoes. No make-up. A thin gold cross and chain hanging from under the collar. Her hair gelled back behind her ears so that her eyes looked enormous in her face. I have to confess that while on one level I felt awful about her being in the situation she was in, on another I was enraged. If I ever saw anyone dressed to fulfil a role, she was that person.

On the other hand, fair's fair, I suppose. We were dressed to impress as well, James's hair was shiny, his shoes were polished, his tie was silk – I blew some of the scratch card money on it in Marks and Spencers – £19.99 for one tie! – and I'd kept the new suit well pressed and clean. He hadn't been allowed to wear it anywhere except in court.

He would have looked fantastic if it wasn't for the terrified expression on his face. Yet now I can see how this may well have worked to his advantage with the judge. I can imagine how she would not have dealt quite so kindly with someone who seemed cocky and impudent.

I can recollect more of what the judge said to Rosemary Madden than what she said to us. It was sort of like a public speech. Even though she was talking directly to the victim – she was quoting from the victim-impact report, obviously for the benefit of us all. And, from our point of view, it did sound pretty horrendous – it talked about psychological scarring. It also said that while the victim was a strong, brave young woman who, in the opinion of the psychologist who wrote the report, would make a good recovery over a period of time, the event had been extremely traumatic for her.

While the judge was still talking, I remember that I zeroed in on that psychological scarring. Why wasn't I psychologically scarred by oul' Mooney and the boy who'd tried it on with me?

But then I'm on the other side in this case so I would think like this, wouldn't I?

She told James to stand up and she started to talk to him. Scold him, really. Her voice sounded to me as though it was coming from the bottom of a well, I couldn't make out the words although I recognized the scolding tone. I did hear her say 'five years' and then she stopped. Then all I could see was the top of her head as she started to write.

I couldn't get enough breath. Five years. Far worse than what Patrice Murphy had said, five years was like getting a thump in the breastbone. So much for it going well for him if he pleaded guilty, thanks a whole heap, Patrice Murphy . . . Five years, in a way it was a relief to know the worst. Not really . . . And then I started trying to look on the bright side. Maybe we could appeal. And no matter what, he'd be out in a couple of years and the way prison releases are going now, because of the overcrowding, he might even serve a lot less.

This all raced through my mind in a tenth of a second, you know the way it does.

I composed my expression to look over at James.

Something was awry. James was looking stunned, no one was making a move to take James down, St John Markey was shuffling his papers.

I looked up at the judge. She was still writing.

Across the courtroom at the detectives. They were muttering to each other.

I heard Rosemary Madden's reaction and I looked around. The door to the courtroom was to one side and her path to it was quite long so I was able to see her face as she raced out. I caught the expressions of her mother and her counsellor.

I didn't understand.

James was now looking round towards me. St John Markey was still messing with files. James was coming towards me with Patrice Murphy. Patrice Murphy was smiling.

Smiling.

Then we were outside and he was explaining to me what had happened.

So now he's gone back inside and I'm still standing there on these Quays with all this noxious traffic, trying to make sense of everything. It's starting to rain. That's real. Cold drops on my face. My cheeks are so hot I'm expecting the drops to sizzle. I always go beetroot when I'm stressed. It's like I've been hypnotized by Paul Goldin or Tony Sadar and I think I'm a statue.

Are we going or what? James says. Or are we going to stand here all day? He's looking around, nervous.

Yeah, I go, come on.

I ask him if he's hungry. That's automatic. Safe. I'm still at it – if in doubt, feed. Neither of us was able to eat anything this morning and this is a boy who would have got out of the lifeboats and back on to the *Titanic* if he saw a cheese sandwich sliding down the deck.

We decide to go to McDonald's. We start to walk up towards O'Connell Street.

We hear James's name being called. We turn around. Rosemary Madden's mother and the woman from the Rape Crisis Centre are standing on the steps of the Four Courts.

It's the mother who comes forward. You . . . she says. That's all. It's enough. There's enough venom in that word to fill an encyclopaedia of insults. I cringe inside. Something comes out of my mouth. I'm sorry. My heart starts banging again and beside me I feel, rather than see, James getting frantic.

Naturally I'm not going to show them that we're intimidated. Come on, James, I go. I grab his arm and haul him away. We're walking fast up the Quays when Rosemary Madden herself catches up with us. She runs in front of us, blocking us so we can't pass her.

Her language is unprintable. Her face distorts. It's like I'm looking at a film and the camera moves in and all I can see is this big mouth saying these things. The two front teeth, I see, have something, maybe a sliver of a cornflake or something, stuck between them. It's horrible to hear this, see this . . .

Leave us alone, eff off, James says back, but his heart isn't in it. He's still pretty shook. We try to get around her but she's still mouthing off, blocking us. She's certainly belying her demure appearance. She's roaring like a fishwife.

By this time there's quite a little crowd gathered. The mother and a man — who I figure has to be the father — have caught up with her and they're standing beside her. Staring at us. Now they're joined by two others, obviously her brothers, one thickset, a bit like the father, the other just a teenager. They're all just staring, like they're trying to knock us down with their eyes. A few passers-by stop to see what's going on. You know the way people stand a little sideways with their arms folded, or clutching their shopping, just watching the entertainment. It's a big dreadful scene. I want to die. Come *on*, James says again, and he drags at me.

Somehow we manage to get past them all.

When we get to McDonald's, the breakfasts are finished so I settle just for an apple turnover and coffee. I expect James to go the whole hog, Big Mac meal, but all he wants is a small fries. That's how upset he is.

We both sit there and neither of us can think of anything to say. We just eat.

When will you go back to work? I ask him.

He looks at me as though I'm from another planet. I'll see you at home, he goes, getting up and leaving. I have barely enough money to pay.

Then a brilliant thought occurs to me. No need for the bail money any more. As soon as my new bonds arrive from the post office, I can apply straight away to have them turned back into cash. I can redeem Mammy's jewellery. And he can have his video back.

→ Nineteen ←

You would think that would be the end of it, or at least the beginning of the end. That James would have gone back to work and so would I and we would have started to put the whole thing behind us.

Unfortunately no.

The first couple of days were all right, considering. James did go back to work, no problem, or none that he would tell me anyway. All the newspapers published a fairly factual account of what had happened. It was not as bad as it could have been. There were no photographs.

And there wasn't really much trouble about me not showing up for work on the Monday. Old Furry Slippers made me pay for it on the Tuesday, of course, she was all pursed lips and well-don't-let-it-happen-again. Then she made me do the toilets. I didn't really mind. I was still half shocked from the events of the day before and I wanted to be by myself as much as possible.

Over the first few days, I did get a few sideways looks from some of the women in work but that didn't bother me in the slightest because it could have been so much worse. They could have been coming up sympathizing with me — and you know what kind of sympathy that would have been.

Four days passed and I was just beginning to settle

down, in that I was not mentally looking over my shoulder a hundred per cent of the time. I decided to get my act together. I rang up and asked for as many kissogram gigs as they could let me have. Was I punishing myself? – you know I want to give up those gigs – I don't know. Anyway, he gave me four gigs, one on the Wednesday, three on the Thursday night. I managed them well because I knew I was pretty safe – no one would look beyond the outfits.

Then the bombshell hit.

It was Friday. I was getting ready to go out for a drive with Ken Sheils. He had called up to the flat on the Wednesday evening about tea-time and had asked me if I'd like to go for a spin in the Dublin mountains that weekend. Saturday was out of the question because of the deli and shopping and so forth and PA System had an event in Navan on the Sunday so we settled on the Friday afternoon, he'd take it off.

Feck it, he goes, I'm self-employed. What's the use of being self-employed if you don't get to treat yourself to a day off now and then in the summer?

You obviously got my note?

Sure. He shrugs. No big deal.

I watch him carefully but he gives no sign at all that he knows something untoward has happened. Some people don't read papers, thank God. I'm also waiting for him to ask me how I'll be able to get the time off from the office but he doesn't. I guess he's not naturally a curious person.

At about twenty past two on the Friday, I was putting on a bit of make-up. I'd washed my hair, I had on a new pair of white cotton jeans and a nice navy T-shirt. The sun was shining and the weather forecast was good, James was at work – which was great because I wasn't quite ready yet to introduce him to Ken — and as far as possible, all was fair enough with my world.

The radio was on. *Liveline* with Marian Finucane, except it wasn't her, it's never her in the summer, they all get very long holidays out there in RTE. This was someone called Breege-óg. (I'm just taking a stab at how to spell the name, that's how it sounds.)

Liveline is a programme I like a lot, largely because of Marian. She's a warm person, who's sympathetic and fair to everyone. Mind you, I do switch it off occasionally when the whinging and whining gets too much for me. That's not Marian's fault, it's not her who's doing the giving out.

It's a howl, actually. We're always hearing from some quarters about the little people of Ireland having no voice and no one to represent them because of the media all being liberal and the anti-Catholic bias of the opinion-makers, et cetera. But in my opinion, if a Martian came to Ireland and wanted to know what the little people were thinking about, all he would have to do would be to switch on the radio or the television. The little people voiceless? You have to be kidding me.

So I'm listening to *Liveline* while I'm trying out a new blusher I bought in the pound shop in O'Connell Street to cheer myself up. Breege-óg says our next caller doesn't want to be identifed so we'll call her Paula. You're really upset and angry, Paula, she goes. Tell us what happened.

This Paula starts in and I'm transfixed. Immediately I know who it is. It's Rosemary Madden's mother.

She's on about how her daughter was denied justice in the courts. How she was brutally raped. How the rapist has walked free with the connivance of psychiatrists and do-gooders. How the judge was a disgrace . . .

Breege-óg cuts in there. Steady on, Paula, she says, we don't know all the factors the judge took into account in the case and the judge isn't here to defend himself—

Mrs Madden goes ballistic. The judge wasn't a him it was a her, that's what makes it so horrendous. She's screeching and roaring now, and Breege-óg can't get a word in edgeways although she does her best to soothe her and quieten her down. I know how you must be feeling, Paula, she says. Do you have anyone you can talk to?

Mrs Madden breaks down completely. There's one of those horrible, dreadful hiatuses where all you can hear is sobbing. It's so bad that Breege-óg seems upset and stuck for words. She asks Mrs Madden if she's all right.

More sobbing.

I'm sure everyone can really sympathize, Paula . . .

Click. Beep beep. Mrs Madden has hung up the phone.

Breege-óg says that these things happen on live radio and she's so sorry that Paula is so upset and that she hopes she can get some help. There is help out there for you, Paula, she says. If you get back on to us we can put you in touch with someone who can help you.

She changes her voice, goes on to the next caller, Marie, who wants to talk about her son who has Down's syndrome. Marie, she says, is at the end of her tether because her son can't get a proper education in the system we have. There aren't enough resources being put in. Tell us about your son, Marie . . .

That is what I wanted to talk about when I rang up, Breege-óg, this Marie says back, but I was holding on for a while there and after listening to that poor lady and what she's after going through . . . I can't tell you how angry I am. I'm enraged. I know if it was my daughter . . .

She's off. She's forgotten all about her Down's

syndrome son. There's now a rapist walking free in Dublin while Paula's poor daughter, and poor Paula herself and all her family, are the ones serving life sentences. While that rapist is probably going to rape again. Statistics prove this. Once a sex offender, Breege-óg, always a sex offender. It's a disgrace, Breege-óg. And the politicians don't care. Marie hopes Paula and her unfortunate daughter are going to appeal. There should be checks and balances on these judges. There should be a committee of citizens . . .

All this time I'm standing there with the blusher brush in my hand. It feels like a boulder of ice. I can't even make myself turn off the radio.

I know *Liveline*, it's one of the most popular programmes. I know what's going to happen now. This is going to run on to all the other programmes. All the papers. Even the English tabloids. Everyone in Ireland will be wanting to call in to every radio show with their own opinion. I relaxed too soon.

Somehow I reach out and manage to turn it off but, of course, it's still there. I can still hear all their voices. Marie's and Paula's and Breege-óg's and God knows who's on now. I'm terrified. They're going to get James, after all.

I sit down on the bed-settee. I've made the flat pristine because it will be the first time Ken Sheils sees it. But I don't see the bunch of carnations in the nice jug, the polished surfaces, the unnatural tidiness. I'm staring at an ashtray with 'A Present from Tramore' on it in the middle of the table. I can't take my eyes off it.

I don't know how long I sit there.

Our doorbell rings. I jump. Literally. It sounds like a fire alarm. I look at my watch, five to three, Ken Sheils is five minutes early. I try to stand up but I'm a jelly.

I get hold of myself and plaster what I hope is a bright

smile on my face as I go to open the door. Wouldn't you know it, on the landing I meet one of my neighbours. We all keep ourselves to ourselves in this house but obviously you can't avoid people completely and we all know a modicum about each other. This man is one of my least favourites. God forgive me, I've never liked him – but if I'm honest, I probably never gave him a chance. You know the way you just take against people without knowing why. Maybe it's because of the poor man's unfortunate appearance, all nose and chin. His name is Dwyer, he's a civil servant, something in the Department of Defence, I believe. He wears woolly cardis.

As we're both going towards the door there's no avoiding him so I nod hello to him and say something crappy about it being a lovely day.

It is indeed a lovely day, Miss Devine, he goes, and he looks at me. Sidelong.

Now there are looks and looks. Am I just being paranoid or is this look one of those meaningful ones? For instance, did he hear *Liveline* and did he read the papers on Tuesday and has he put two and two together?

What's he doing at home in the middle of a Friday afternoon, anyway? Shouldn't he be at work?

We get to the door together, and just as he reaches for the snib, our doorbell rings again. That's for me, I go – as if it's any of his business. That's what paranoia does to you. It makes you explain your next breath.

I open the door. It's not Ken Sheils, it's two men. One of them has a camera. I just have time to see this before the flash goes off in my face. At the same time I hear one of them shouting James's name. That's all I hear before I slam the door shut.

In the hall, Dwyer blinks. But he doesn't look all that surprised and I see now that I wasn't being paranoid. He does know exactly what has been going on and without a shadow of a doubt he had heard *Liveline*. The doorbell rings again.

I become calm. If you wouldn't mind, I say, I'm going back to our flat. I'd appreciate it if you wouldn't open the door until I'm well inside.

He nods. (Thinking about it now I suppose this was the most drama that ever happened in his whole life. I can imagine the subsequent tea breaks in the Department of Defence.) Thank you, I say, and with as much dignity as I can find, I go back to our flat. The doorbell rings again.

I sit down inside our place and I start to shake. What am I going to do? What are we going to do? We can't just stay here passively and let this happen to us.

The doorbell rings.

But we can't leave the jurisdiction either because James has to go through his counselling sessions. Although it wasn't made a condition of the suspension of the sentence, Patrice Murphy tells us that it would be in James's best interests to attend them religiously. So it will look good when the sentence comes up for review.

Still, who'd find us if we just went down to the North Wall or out to Dun Laoghaire and got on the boat. We buy the tickets at the ferry port and just walk on with the rest of the punters, walk off in Holyhead and that could be the end of us. We wouldn't be the first Irish people to vanish in England. They don't check identification and you don't need passports between here and the UK. And since we're both able-bodied we wouldn't be registering for any social-welfare payments or official help of any kind . . .

The more I think about it the better it all sounds.

Next thing, there's a knock on our own door. I can't believe it. That stupid so-and-so Dwyer let them in after all. Go away, I yell. Just go away.

There's silence for a few moments. Then Ken Sheils says, It's me, Angela. It's Ken. Is everything all right?

I'm so upset I've temporarily forgotten about him.

I open the door. What's going on? he says. What are those two thugs doing on the doorstep? They're looking for you, they tried to come in with me . . .

Again I get calm. I don't know what it is with me. I get calm in the most stressful situations and I turn to blancmange as soon as everything is all right. Come in, Ken, I say, I've something to tell you.

I'd like to say he was great about it. He was in a way but then again he wasn't. He didn't run out, or throw up his hands in horror. On the other hand he didn't come right out and say, I'm really sorry for your trouble and is there anything I can do. Which is, of course, what I wanted him to say.

Instead, he just kept saying, I see.

I left nothing out. I didn't spare James but I didn't spare your woman either. I told Ken exactly what had happened, how she'd wanted to have sex and then didn't but how it was too late for James to stop. How she was the one who initiated the whole thing by telling him to bring the condom. About *Liveline* and the papers and how we were now going to be crucified.

I see, he says.

Look, I go, I'll understand if you don't want anything to do with us.

I see.

But he's my brother and he's all I have and I'm all he has and that's the end of it. He has to come first. So I'll understand.

I see.

Christ, I'm thinking, if he says that one more time I'll kick him. This is the first time I've noticed this annoying habit of his. I'm all over the shop now, I'm trying to hold on to my temper. So do you? I ask him.

Do I what?

Do you want to let it go?

Do you mean do I want not to see you again?

That's what I mean, yes. I'll understand.

I see.

Has he gone on like this before? I don't remember. Now I have to wait for his decision. By this time I don't care. To be frank I'd just as soon he'd leave right now and take his van and his wretched little mongrel with him. I've never cared much about the Dublin mountains anyway. There's nothing much there and even if there is you can't see it because it's always cloudy and raining.

You can keep the Dublin mountains.

The doorbell rings again and Ken and I look at each other. Well, we can't stay here, he says. Let's go anyway, we can talk more about it.

This sounds ominous. I've told him everything already. What he means is he needs time to work out his own attitude. But I can't stay here, so I agree.

What about the two on the doorstep? I say then, I don't fancy having that camera shoved in my face again.

Ken asks if there's a back entrance.

There isn't, but there is a fire escape. To get to it you have to get out through the window of our facilities. I'm not even embarrassed telling him this. This is oul' Reddy's fault, not ours.

I scribble a note to James, telling him to be careful, that he might be ambushed either here or at work. Of course, he might be caught as he's coming in before he gets the note but there's not a lot I can do about that.

Then we leave the flat, feet first, through the window and on to the fire escape. I feel absolutely stupid. As I haul myself up on to the hand basin, dislodging hunks of powdery plaster, I'm thinking, This is the future, this is not the last time I'm going to have to do this, or James either.

Ken Sheils starts to sweep the plaster aside with his foot. Leave it, leave it, I go . . . On the positive side, I'm thanking my lucky stars I have jeans on. Can you imagine the indignity of doing this in a skirt?

Because it was a Friday, the traffic was terrible until we got as far as Dundrum and after that it was plain sailing. Ken was very quiet and I just left him to it. I felt fatalistic, to tell you the truth. The next move was not up to me. Thank God for car radios and thank God Ronan Collins was on. His music is pretty good and he has a very easy style. Undemanding, but he can be funny in a gentle sort of way. I couldn't have stood it, I think, if we'd had to listen to any of the pop stations. They're grand if you're feeling young and good about yourself. Which, at that moment, I certainly wasn't.

Do you know what, I have to revise my opinion of the Dublin mountains. Even I have to admit that the Sally Gap is spectacular, just spectacular. I don't say it out loud because Ken Sheils still hasn't opened his mouth.

On the other side of the Sally Gap we stop at the side of the road and get out. Ken stands with his head thrown back. Taste that air, he goes, taste that freshness. I feel a bit of a prat but I copy him anyway, closing my eyes and throwing back my head and taking several deep lungfuls, so deep that I get dizzy. He's got it wrong, I think. In my opinion it isn't the taste of the air, it's the absence of taste that gives you the sensation. Because there's nothing to smell, the air cuts right through the fug in your nose and your throat which, up to that moment, you didn't even know you'd had.

There's no wind at all, which Ken says is unusual for

up here but as a result you can hear this concert of buzzing and humming. Insects. Moths (butterflies?), a lot of bees. There are a couple of little streams nearby, you can hear them running. And the birds! And the little clouds! I'd had no idea it could be like this. James and radio programmes and all our troubles could be a million miles away.

I turn my head and find him looking at me. When I catch his eye he reddens a bit. I took the liberty of bringing a picnic, he says, I hope you don't mind.

Mind? I'm now so hungry I'd eat a rasher off a sore leg. I haven't had anything to eat since our tea-break at work this morning at about quarter past seven. It's now nearly four o'clock.

He takes the picnic out of the back of his van – he's made three different kinds of sandwiches, salad, egg, and ham, and he has tea in a flask with two cups. He's even brought the sugar separately, and a Madeira cake. I'm bowled over. No man has ever made me a picnic before. I'm beginning to feel like I'm in an English novel.

We spread out his anorak on a flat, grassy place a little way in off the road and we sit together on it side by side. We're baking, I'm beginning to wish I'd worn a skirt instead of the jeans. The grass we're sitting on is spongy and he says that's because we're in the heart of a bog. It's hard to imagine that underneath us are thousands, millions of years' worth of squashed trees. The colours all around us are quiet, browns and golds and soft greens. And the contours of the mountains – Ken says they're not real mountains, just hills – are quiet too, curved rather than peaky.

Not one single car.

Now here comes the only human being we've seen since we've sat down. A cyclist. German. (No, I'm not that clever, he has a little German flag flying from the top of his backpack.) He nods 'hello' to us as he comes abreast, then he freewheels down the hill away from us, shiny black bum in the air, like two olives in a jar. I cycle a bit myself, Ken goes shyly. I smile at him. Ice now thoroughly broken.

You can see the city, or most of it, from where we sit. It wears a sort of grey haze. That's the pollution, Ken says, but then tells me it used to be much worse. Some days from here you couldn't even *see* the city, just this huge ball of grey. Especially in winter, before Mary Harney's smokey-coal ban a few years ago. If the Government did nothing else it did that, he says.

I'm surprised he mentions Mary Harney. I wouldn't have put you down as one of her lot, I say to him.

What would you say I am? He grins at me.

I'm on tricky ground here. In this country lifelong feuds can start with simple political discussions. Remember the row with Tom Bennett all those years ago about Patrick Pearse and the Easter Rising?

I do admire Mary Harney, she has great integrity, to me the Progressive Democrats would be mainly southsiders. Ken is not only a northsider, he's a manual worker — definitely not standard PeeDee. That's your own business, I say cautiously.

I'm nothing at all, he says. I'm sick of the lot of them. I don't vote.

There's no answer to that, is there? I grin back at him and take another sandwich.

I look back out over the city while I'm chewing. I feel quite proud. This is my city and it's lovely, curving all the way along the sparkling rim of the sea. I pick out landmarks. The Ballymun towers. The RTE mast. I can follow the course of the Liffey, cutting right through to what I know now is the South Bull — and of course, those are the Pigeon House chimneys, I say, although I shouldn't get a medal for recognizing them, they're the biggest things in the whole city.

Where's the airport? I ask him.

Ken points out a little glint of silver, the sun shining on an aeroplane taking off. He looks away then and I try to figure out what he's thinking. Which is difficult. I don't really know the guy at all. Cycles a bit. Doesn't vote although he seems to like Mary Harney, they're the new items of information. I'm surprised he hasn't mentioned the James situation. Definitely lacking in the curiosity department.

I'm certainly not going to bring it up. Whatever else, I'm not a masochist.

Now that I think of it, here we are, on our third time out, two mature adults. Who haven't even held hands, much less kissed each other. It suits me but I wonder about him. Gay, maybe? But then there's Diandra . . . Although he wouldn't be the first, would he?

That must be Dun Laoghaire Habour, I go, to cover over the awkwardness. And this brings me back full circle to my predicament. Less than two hours ago I was thinking about the boat.

It is, yes, he says back, and look, the new high-speed ferry is coming in, do you see it?

I see it. Teenchy. Minute.

Even though we seem on the surface to be getting along just fine, the James situation is hanging between us, the exact same way it did between Patsy and me.

✦ Twenty ✦

Next I must report to you on a trip to Birr.
I had asked Ken would he take me, that day we were having the picnic in the Dublin mountains – I suppose I felt I had nothing to lose. I was prepared for him to refuse, given the circumstances, but to my amazement he said yes. I explained that I had an inner demon that would never be satisfied until I went down there.

I start to tell him why – about Mammy and all – but I get stuck straight away. Somehow, no matter what I was going to say about her, it wasn't going to come out right. I wasn't going to be able to explain to someone who never knew her what she was really like. That she wasn't just this social problem or that social worker's case. So I clam up. Sorry, I say, it's something I can't really talk about. I just need to go to Birr, that's all. It's to do with my roots.

He gives me a funny look. You don't have to give me your reasons, Angela, he goes, I'd be happy to take you. We could both do with a day away from Dublin. (Reading between the lines that day, from some of the things he said about Diandra, she was pushing him a bit. Looking for money, for instance. I didn't ask for the details because, to tell you the truth, I didn't want to know. I had enough to worry about.) He hesitates, then, Will you be able to take more time off work?

Oh, yes, I say, there'll be no problem about that.

I still wasn't ready to go into my complicated work life. I'd tell him sometime but not now. And he had no idea how right he was when he said I could do with a day away from Dublin.

It doesn't take a genius to guess why the need to go to Birr suddenly became so urgent. I felt that if I could get down to where Mammy's origins were, maybe it would help James and me. Make things sort of solid. Best-case scenario was finding her relatives and having them talk to me, brilliant-case scenario would be if they came onside and said they'd be our family again. I had this stupid vision where the two of us could nestle into a cat's cradle of relatives.

But even the worst-case scenario — just seeing the place and the family business and her house and all the rest of it — wasn't at all bad. Those places were always going to be there. Immemorial. We'd know at least where I came from and that's important

She had planted certain things in my mind about Birr. The Manchester Martyrs, for instance, Allen, Larkin and O'Brien, who died for Ireland sometime in the last century. Two of them were from around Birr and there was a monument to them in the town. If I could see where she lived, even the monument to the Manchester Martyrs, at least I'd have some framework to picture around her in my mind every time I thought about her. I hated picturing her only in the environment of the flats. Or dying in her hospice bed. In my mind, when I thought of her as a *person*, as opposed to the woman she was forced to be, she was surrounded by soft fabrics and daisies.

I also felt she was prompting me to go. Is that too weird?

We set off for Birr on the Wednesday after our Dublin mountains excursion. He picked me up at one o'clock – I went down to the front door when he rang because James hadn't gone to work that day. In fact he hadn't been to work for three days. (He said this was OK by his bosses, and that he had some holiday time due. I didn't know whether to believe him or not but there wasn't much I could do about it. I couldn't physically drag him down there, now, could I?)

Anyway, that Wednesday I didn't want to complicate matters by having James and Ken Meet. That's how it was looming in my head at the time, a Meeting, with a capital letter. If I was being honest with myself, I was already beginning to see the situation between Ken and me as something more than friendship.

He wasn't making it easy for me, however, there were very few hints from his side about how he felt. For instance, after he left me home from the Dublin mountains that day, he squeezed my hand when he said goodbye. Pretty straightforward, you might say, eh? Yet when I got to remembering it later I couldn't make up my mind whether it was a romantic squeeze or the kind of squeeze you give without thinking – like pucking your friend in the arm when you see something interesting and want her to see it too before it disappears.

I suppose that we were making progress of a sort. Although we hadn't discussed the Problem With James any further during that Friday picnic, at least now he knew about it and I could feel him thinking about it on and off during that whole afternoon. It has to be significant that he hadn't headed for the hills, hasn't it?

I won't go into the precise contents of the Sunday papers. I got all of them, even though I knew what had to be facing us. After *Liveline*, it was inevitable that they'd all have a field day, but I was like a rabbit faced with a snake. A posse of snakes.

I had this glacier in the pit of my stomach when I left the house to go to the newsagent's and it seemed to grow bigger and bigger with every step. I nearly forgot to buy my scratch card, so that will tell you how upset I was.

Don't things happen at the most inappropriate times? Wouldn't you know it, for the very first time I get three stars to enter for the TV game show (with twenty-five million others, of course!). As I'm scribbling my name and address on the back of the card, those newspapers are like fire under my arm and the newsagent's voice is like a grinder. Mike Murphy is gone for the summer, Marty Whelan's the main man now and it's not *Winning Streak* any more, it's *Fame and Fortune*—

Hey, he goes, when I'm scooting out, you forgot your envelope.

Thanks. I rush back. I grab the envelope and run.

I'm not able to wait until I get back home to learn the worst – anyway, I want to protect James. So I divert into the park, sit down on a bench and start to read. The birds are singing. That's a travesty.

The front page of the *Sunday World* has a huge, blurry picture of James leaving the courthouse. They've put a small black rectangle across his eyes. Like a little coffin. Quite appropriate. Anyone who sees that picture and who knows him will be able to recognize him at a hundred yards.

I don't read the article ('Inside, Pages 2, 3, 6 and 7') Instead I look at the *Sunday Independent*. It isn't front-page news, thank God for that, but it's bad enough. Worse than bad. It's one of those little coloured boxes at the top. In this box they've put the same picture of James that the *Sunday World* used, including the little coffin.

And beside it they've advertised what all their biggest writers have to say on the subject.

Eamon Dunphy included.

When I see this I know we're sunk. Eamon Dunphy was a footballer at some stage in his life, with a club in England, but he's now the *Sunday Independent*'s star writer and when he decides to take a scunner against someone he really goes all out. He's absolutely passionate about despising people. Judging by what he writes, he seems to live in a permanent state of apoplexy about other people's opinions and shortcomings.

I'm not sure how many people take him seriously, but for me that doesn't count today. Everyone reads him. The women at work. They all say, 'Isn't he desperate?' but they read him every Sunday for entertainment value, to see who he's having a go at. Ireland's like that. We'll sympathize to your face when someone says something nasty about you. And we'll be rubbing our hands in glee behind your back. We love to see someone pulled down a peg.

I'm no better than anyone else, I read Eamon Dunphy's column, and while from time to time I've felt sorry for the people he's having a go at, I'm ashamed to say never sorry enough to stop me reading the article. It doesn't matter that it was thoughtlessness on my part, I'm disgusted at myself now that I see only too well what the object of his derision must have been going through, not to speak of that person's family. Do those people who write so glibly in those newspapers have any idea about the hurt and damage they cause? If they do, they've a lot to answer for.

I'll be more careful about what I read or believe in future, I'll tell you, because now I realize they couldn't know a lot of the facts behind what they're writing about. For instance, I'd be amazed if any journalist knows *why* James's judge suspended his sentence. She had 'background' reports they wouldn't have seen. Or that they shouldn't have seen. Stuff about the actual incident in the Furry Glen that day that wasn't openly talked about in court. Rosemary Madden's part in all of this is crucial, I believe.

I'm so upset by the thought of what Eamon Dunphy has probably written that I can't look at the front pages of the other newspapers. Instead, I take the whole bundle, leave the park, cross the road, and go round the back of the house where Reddy's left out a few ancient dustbins for his residents' use. I stuff all of those papers as far down inside one of those bins as I can. I'd burn them but that would draw attention to myself. Thank God James isn't up yet.

I leave you to imagine what the atmosphere between Patsy and myself was like on the way to our gig a couple of hours later. Listen, she said immediately, as I got into the car, I've seen the papers and I think that we really shouldn't discuss the situation. Not at all – all right?

All right, I said.

She made conversation, of course, all about Martin and some pal of his who had invited him to go to London. They were at Wimbledon yesterday, Ange, she says gaily.

As though I gave a damn.

Turns out she's always wanted to go to Wimbledon for the tennis. This was news to me.

And they're going to try to get tickets for the European Cup Final this evening, she says, all chirpy. Martin's friend has contacts over there . . .

I'd had to sit through the Germany–England semi-final with James so at least I knew who was in the final. Oh? I go. Germany and Czechoslovakia? Sounds like a thrill a minute to me. (I know it's the Czech Republic now but I keep forgetting. I don't even know where Bosnia is any more. All that part of Europe is as unreliable as the Shifting Whispering Sands.) She looks sharpish at me. Are you being sarcastic?

I put on my innocent look. (Well, I can't be St Teresa of the Roses all the time, can I?)

Thank God none of the customers at the deli knows me except by my first name, because of the badge I wear. Even if I did have the second name on there I doubt they'd twig. I hate the way they say Angela too deiberately. And too much, that's the dead giveaway. You're the hired help and they know it and you know it but they want to show how liberal they are. It's called equality, I don't think. Even the regulars wouldn't recognize me if I met them in some other part of the shopping area. I've served them ten minutes ago, I've been serving them every Saturday for years, yet take the pinny and the name badge off and they've never seen me before.

The day before that Sunday, which was my first appearance at the deli after the court case, I was on full alert during my whole shift but as far as I could detect, they were all just being their ordinary airy selves. I'd had to come clean with the owner – she was going to know everything anyway from the reports of James's trial – but I have to say she was marvellous about it. She isn't a friend of mine but she behaved more like a friend than Patsy is currently doing. If there's anything I can do, she said, and I could tell she meant it.

To get back to the trip to Birr. Ken seemed quite cheerful and ordinary when he came to the door punctually at one minute to one on the Wednesday. I watched him very closely for any signs of conflict but I saw none. So I reckoned (a) he hadn't read the papers,

(b) he'd read them and decided to ignore them, or (c) he was holding fire for a while.

I admire punctuality, I really do.

It must be great to be your own boss, I remark, as we cross the road to where the van is parked.

Sometimes, he says back, sometimes. Like now, when I want to take off for somewhere and I can just go without asking leave of anyone. King of the Road, that's me! He smiles and he looks quite jolly so I reckon the choice is now narrowed down to (a) or (b).

Sam licks me when I get in. I think he believes I'm now part of the fixtures and fittings. I give him a pat but, for myself, I'm nervous about what was facing me. I hadn't slept all that well for obvious reasons and when old Furry Slippers made me redo a long corridor with the polisher that morning I was so tense I snapped at her.

She couldn't believe it. I think that up to then she'd thought I was Miss Meek 1996 or the aforementioned Teresa. The last thing I needed was a row, however, so I buttoned my lip, apologized for being rude, made the excuse that I was very tired, and then pushed that damn polisher away from her like it was a howitzer gun and I was using it to kill enemies lurking in the pattern on the lino.

How are you, Ken goes, as we're heading through the traffic and out of town. You look very pale.

I'm grand, I say, grand. A bit dozy – early mornings, you know how it is.

So far so good, I think, as he chats on about what we can expect to see in Birr. An enormous telescope, apparently. World famous, owned by some lord. And before we go any further, he says then, I'm glad your brother's case turned out well for you. Let's forget about all our troubles today and concentrate on having a good time. I've never been to Birr. It's one of those towns you have to have a reason to go to because it's not on the way from anywhere to anywhere else.

In one way I was delighted with this neat wrapping up of James's case like that. In another, though, I wasn't so sure. Pfft! gone. Just like that. James is a *person*, a human being with feelings. I said nothing, though, I was being done a favour here. Quite a big one. I know what you mean about Birr, I said. That was a fib. I didn't know diddly squat about Birr, as I told you, even though I'd looked it up on a map.

It was a fine day, sort of. One of those days where it's warm all the time but the sun can never quite make it through the clouds. The air in the van was stuffy and I hadn't been lying when I said I was dozy. Even still, my mind was churning.

I'd tried to rehearse what I was going to say if and when I successfully met Mammy's relations, but no matter from what angle I had tried to see it, some other argument they might come up with would instantly occur to me. I was starting in on this circle again, driving myself mad, so I decided to let it go and to enjoy the drive. Just to wait until I got there and to let things happen.

Big mistake.

The omens were not good for that day. The first thing we see as we're leaving the city is this commotion at a big crossroads just beyond the beginning of the Naas dual carriageway. An island of Guards and squad cars, dozens of them, around the traffic lights, lorries and cars backed up in all four directions, being diverted away. The lights were going green, red, orange, green, red, orange, all to themselves with nothing moving around them. There were loads of other cars parked along the grass partition down the middle of the road, drivers and passengers all out on the verges. All staring in the same direction. At a red car.

One of the Guards directed us to keep moving along the shoulder of the road, and as we passed the lights, I saw that the front of the red car, which was pointing in the Dublin direction, was covered in a blanket. That meant there was a body or bodies. I was puzzled, though, because I couldn't see what the red car had hit. No other cars dented or smashed up.

Maybe a heart attack at the wheel? This was Ken, who kept straining over his shoulder to look back at the scene, so much so that, talk about heart attacks, I was afraid *we'd* have an accident!

Maybe, I said back.

Whatever had happened, it had been a long time since I'd seen so much Gárda activity. The nearest was a huge hugger-mugger in the flats between two of the criminal families who were always having wars with each other. That one went on for hours, in the courtyard and the entryways, and by the end there were so many blue lights flashing on the roofs of the squad cars you could read your evening paper by them.

As it turned out, it had been no accident or heart attack that day but very bloody murder. There was indeed a body in that red car. Two thugs had come up on a motorcycle and had shot a reporter whose mission was exposing the crime underworld in Dublin. She had been just sitting there, waiting for the lights to change when bam!

It was a huge thing for days in the city and in the rest of the country. I suppose the reason everyone was going ballistic was that she was a reporter and not just a Joe Soap. I always have mixed feelings about this kind of thing, where the death of a politician or a famous person seems to be presented as far more tragic than the death of someone ordinary. I didn't know this reporter's work, because largely I try to avoid as many horrible stories in the newspapers as I can – I have enough of them at home, ha ha! – but according to everyone I talked to and everything I read, she was very brave. She'd been shot before, in the leg, and had also been sent death threats, but none of it had stopped her writing her stuff and I suppose this accounted for all the hoo-ha.

I have to admit that maybe this bravery is the other side of the coin when you talk about journalists and newspapers. I still wish, though, that the rest of them would take a leaf out of this girl's book and go after the real stories in Ireland and leave people like us alone. We all see events from our own point of view, don't we.

Mind you, the only thing that surprised me when I found out the true story was that people were surprised in the first place. All the politicians were on the telly saying it was a descent into chaos and an attack on the foundations of the state and all the rest of it, but sure do they not know there are fellas being stabbed and shot on a daily basis all over the city? And didn't the same thing happen a couple of weeks previously down the country when a detective was shot the same way as that poor girl!

None of them seem to have the first clue about what it's really like to live day to day in places like the flats where I grew up. Even where I live now. I don't count many politicians or other toffs amongst my neighbours. They should all be forced to live in the inner city for a few weeks. A few days, even – anyone round where I live could bend their ears about what's going on in the real world.

Imagine, though, dinner-time on a summer day. Five bullets. She was a mother too, Lord rest her.

But since we didn't know the story, Ken Sheils and I just blessed ourselves, made cluck clucking noises like you do, isn't it terrible, Lord have mercy on their souls, and carried on down the Naas dual carriageway.

I have to say that even along here, and then a bit later on both sides of the motorway, even though it was so close to the city the countryside was gorgeous. Like a magic carpet. Splurges of bright red poppies, cows up to their armpits in green and yellow fields, hedges and trees drenched with creamy-coloured flowers. Ken said this was hawthorn, and that this year was a great year for it because of the brilliant summer we had in 1995.

We hit our next problem when we turned off the main road and found that the way to Birr was covered in rough stone chips called, apparently, loose chippings. Ken says this is how they do the roads in the country – they just throw down lorry-loads of this stuff and let the passing cars do the work of squashing them into the tar on the surface. He hates it, they do it every single summer, according to him, and it's brutal on the paintwork of your car. Little pieces of the stone fly up from under your tyres and the tyres of everything that passes you, particularly going in the opposite direction. Not to speak of potentially shattering your windows.

He shows me what everyone does – you put one of your fingers up high on the windscreen as if you're pointing out, and this is supposed to stop the glass breaking if it does get hit. He didn't know the principle behind how this works but everyone does it.

It wasn't long before I saw an unexpected side of Ken Shiels.

☀ Twenty-One ☀

The incident started quietly enough. I was admiring the lovely gardens, full of flowers, in the bungalows by the side of the road. It must be lovely to have a garden. We have the park, I know, but it's not the same.

We pass one particularly nice one and I point it out to Ken but he's so afraid of the loose chippings that he's slowed down to the point where we're crawling at about ten miles an hour and he won't look. M-mmm, he goes, m-mmm . . .

At this point, a big lorry comes up behind us. Because the road is narrow he can't pass and he has to crawl behind us. The driver starts leaning on his horn.

The first time he does it, it's so loud, like a ship's siren, I nearly jump out of my skin but Ken just flushes up and white-knuckles the steering wheel. Feck him, he says, who does he think he is?

Pa-a-arp! the horn goes again. The guy is right up behind us, right on our tail. He's so close I look behind and I can see the edges of the tomatoes in his sandwich on the dashboard.

Ken grips the steering wheel even tighter, if that's possible. I'm not going to be bullied, he goes — and would you believe he slows down even more. Now he's going so slowly the needle on the speedometer isn't even moving. The guy behind goes crazy. Pa-a-arp, pa-a-a-aarp, pa-a-a-a-a-a-a-a-rp! He's playing a symphony.

Next thing he pulls out and tries to pass us. Ken speeds up and moves out a little, just enough to frustrate the guy because now there's a tractor coming in the other direction. By this time, I'm gripping the sides of my seat. I know no good is going to come of this, I can feel it in my bones. I can also feel waves of heat coming from Ken Shiels. I swear.

The lorry driver waits until the tractor goes past then he pulls out suddenly and attempts to pass us again. Ken speeds up, moves out a little.

Pa-a-a-a-rp! Now the lorry's lights are going as well as the horn. I can see them flashing in the mirror but I'm afraid to look back. I'm also afraid to say anything to Ken – after all, I don't know him that well and I'm a guest in this van.

We come to a bend in the road and on the other side of it we find we're coming towards a bunch of travellers' caravans parked on a wide verge. They have horses pegged out at intervals all along. One of the traveller boys, about twelve or thirteen, is pulling one of these horses on the end of a rope from one side of the road to the other. The horse is pulling and dancing a bit. There's no danger, because we're going so slowly, but Ken jams on the brakes and – you've guessed it.

The lorry runs into the back of us. Not hard but enough to jolt us about a bit. And the sound of the crash! Have you ever been inside a hollow van when it's been hit?

Sam goes crazy, barking up a storm.

Ken turns on the flashers and so does your man and the two of them jump out. I'm afraid to – anyway, it's none of my business – so I just sit tight. I stare straight ahead. I literally don't know where to look because now the travellers, men, women, kids, have started to pour out of their caravans to watch the fun.

I can see the altercation in the side mirror of the van if I turn my eyes a tiny bit to the right. The driver is small and stocky with a beer belly as wide as a door. He has this belly stuck up against Ken and except for it being in the way the two of them are nose to nose. I can hear them with no effort at all but I can't make out what they're saying. They're both roaring so loudly that all the words are swallowed up in the general mayhem. There is quite a lot of effing, that much I can make out.

A traveller woman comes up to me and knocks on my window. I wind it down. Would you like a cup of tea, missus? she asks me. She has a kid on her hip who has the dirtiest nose I've ever seen. Two green waterfalls are rolling into that kid's open mouth and neither the kid nor its mother makes any effort to staunch the flow. You can hear its poor chest rattling.

No thank you, I go. I try to smile.

It's no trouble, missus, the woman says, I've the kettle on. She goes to pull at the handle of the door. She smiles at me, she has terrible teeth.

Until that moment, I never knew I was prejudiced against travellers. But now I panic. I immediately think everything in this van is going to be stolen if I leave it unattended. All Ken's tools and stuff. Sam obviously has the same idea. He's hurling himself against the door across my lap. He thinks he's a Rottweiler.

I grab him and try to hold on to him but it's like grappling with a whirlwind. No, really, thank you, it's all right, I have to shout to make myself heard above the dog, I had tea not half an hour ago at home.

I'm sickening myself with this. The poor woman is only trying to help. I suppose I'm conditioned to believe the worst about people at the moment. Where did these feelings come from? A bigot, me?

Next thing some man comes around and pulls the woman away from the door. He's not gentle about it either. He grunts something at her and she leaves.

Sam gives one last bark. A sort of triumphant 'r-rrufff!' – that's seen *them* off – then he jumps into the back and settles down again on his blanket.

Meantime, all this bedlam is still going on behind me. Now there must be at least thirty people standing back enjoying the show and I can see why they think this is the height of entertainment. I remember Mammy telling us not to act like tinkers. Now here were the tinkers being given an excuse to roar at their children not to be acting like settled people!

There's also a traffic jam, two tractors, one car with a foreign registration plate and another van. Not to speak of the boy and his horse, who are still in the middle of the road.

I continue to look straight ahead. Cows. Low hills. Huge fields. Beautiful colours in the fields and in the garden of a house in the distance – you can see why the Americans think Ireland is so green. I wish I was a cow. I wish I was anything except Angela Devine here in this van, embarrassed out of my brains. Anyone but companion to this man who's going purple in the face and who's roaring and shouting and cursing like a sailor. I sincerely hope these travellers don't think he's my husband. Or even my boyfriend.

There's a lull and Ken comes back to the driver's side of the van to get his insurance papers out of the glove compartment. Now the purple's gone from his face – it's as white as paper. I daren't say anything.

When he goes back to the lorry driver, they scrutinize

each other's documents. Some of the traveller men are wiping the bumpers of the two vehicles with their hands as though they're assessing them, talking amongst themselves. The driver of the foreign-registered car is getting out. He's enormous. About six foot eight. How he fits into a Volkswagen Golf I don't know. He wanders over to the verge and takes a picture of the traveller camp. They don't like it but he seems not to notice. Three teenage boys are standing alongside our van, quite close, staring in at me.

I get twice as paranoid.

What's the matter with you, Angela? You're the one who *beats up* gurriers. *Dublin* gurriers, for God's sake. These boys, they're perfectly respectful, they're just inquisitive, that's all. *Get a grip . . .*

Sorry about that, Ken says, a few minutes after we're finally creeping along again over the loose chippings. He bangs the heel of his hand off the steering wheel. I couldn't let him away with it.

I don't answer, I'm still shook at my own reaction to the travellers. I *know* travellers in Dublin. I have a regular woman who comes in every so often for a chat and a cup of tea. But back there I was like a fish out of water, had no idea of how to behave. This trip is very educational.

Is there much damage to the van?

Just one of the brake lights, Ken says back, but it wasn't that, it was the arrogance of the man. I won't be bullied. Nobody bullies Kenneth Shiels.

That's a bit of a jolt, it's the first time it's occurred to me that he's a Kenneth. But I can see he's getting het up again so I don't say anything more. He glances across at me. I hope it hasn't spoiled your outing for you.

For obvious reasons we arrive at Birr in a quiet mood.

I suppose we might as well buy a guide book, he says,

as we drive into a wide square which seems to be used as the town's main car park. My stomach is fluttering so all I can do is nod.

While he's in the shop, I get out of the van and lean on the warm bonnet. Look around, get my bearings. The real tourist. First thing I see is Dooly's Hotel on the far side of the square. Now my stomach really flips its bananas. This is it, this is really it. Mammy talked about Dooly's. It's where her parents used to go.

Ken comes back. All I could get was this. He shows me a little booklet with flowers on the cover and a picture of two houses. The man behind the counter told me that Birr has the only branch of the Georgian Society outside Dublin, is that any use to you?

I can't speak, I don't give a sugar about Georgian societies, I'm still seeing Mammy's mother and father having their night out in Dooly's. Cups of tea? Sherry? What?

Great, thanks, I go, taking the booklet from him.

She wouldn't give me up for adoption or put me into an orphanage, that's what I reckon. That's probably why she had to flee to Dublin. It must have been so dreadful for her. I've a lot to be grateful for.

Ken and I go for a walk down what seems to be the main street, O'Connell Street. Just like Dublin. I wonder how many O'Connell Streets there are in Ireland. I hate Daniel O'Connell. He was bloody oul' Concepta's favourite patriot. She beat him into us.

It's still warm, still cloudy, but with the sun still struggling to shine. I suppose I'm hypersensitive now but I think I feel her everywhere. Did she go into this drapery shop with the knickers in the window? It certainly looks as though it hasn't changed much. What about that hardware shop across the street? There are people gossiping here and there, all along the street, who would have been about her age if she was still alive. Did they know her?

When I tune in as Ken and I pass them, I hear they're all talking about the reporter murdered on the Naas dual carriageway and this is when Ken and I put two and two together. It's was a very shivery feeling. That poor girl, Lord have mercy on her, was alive and whistling just a few minutes before we came up to her car.

We come to the end of the street and another, smaller square. Here's the famous monument to the Manchester Martyrs. Dear God, one of them, the one from Cork, was only nineteen. James's age. Executed. By gun? Hanged? I can imagine the feeling in his stomach that morning when he woke up. If he slept at all. I hope he didn't write to his mother. It would have killed her if he did. I know if James wrote to me on the eve of his execution I wouldn't be able to read it. I'd probably want to kill myself rather than read it.

What am I thinking about? That drapery shop and that hardware shop could be the very business that belonged to Mammy's family. Neither of them had Devine on them but that didn't matter. Maybe they never had Devine on them. In Dublin, Clery's is still Clery's although as far as I know there hasn't been a Clery for yonks.

That must be the castle – the one with the telescope—

What? Ken's voice has sounded like thunder.

That must be the castle down there. He's pointing to the end of a street where there's a high grey wall and a massive stone building flying a flag.

I couldn't care less about any castle. She mentioned it, I think, but not so it made much of an impression on me. She certainly never mentioned any telescope – I'd have remembered that. (Now that I think about it, it was surprising she didn't talk about the castle, since the

family was Protestant.) Yes, it must, I say, and I turn
away immediately to walk back up O'Connell Street
towards the van. I want him to stop yakking.

Do you not want to see it? He catches up with me.

I want to shout at him. I want him to go away. He's
behaving as though I'm a normal visitor to this town, as
though I just want to see the sights.

I grit my teeth. Remind myself he's the one doing the
favours here. How could he know when I haven't told
him? I try to smile. You must let me buy you some
petrol.

He looks at me as though I have two heads. It's diesel,
he says, very slowly. I must seem demented to him.
Well, I am.

Look, I go, I hope you don't mind or you won't be
insulted or anything, but this is proving to be more
difficult for me than I thought it would.

He frowns and I realize he thinks I mean being here
with him. It's not you, I say quickly. What I mean is, just
being here for the first time is the problem, I'll explain it
all to you some day. Would you mind awfully if we split
up for half an hour or so, so I can wander around by
myself? Would you mind going for a drink – or a cup of
coffee even? I'd spotted a nice coffee-shop-cum-deli
across the road.

Sure, he goes, of course. See you in half an hour then
– back at the van? He walks off and goes into the coffee
shop. Through the window I can see him pointing at a
cake under the glass-topped counter. Professionally,
even from the outside, I would rate this as a pretty good
deli.

I'm still standing on the other side of the street,
pretending to be reading *Birr: Heritage Town* – the little
guide book. Now what do I do? My lack of a definite plan
is glaring. I can hardly go up to some stranger and say,

Did you know Rose Devine and where could I find any of her family, please? I'm beside the drapery shop so I turn and look in the windows. Quite nice stuff. Through the doorway I can see there are no customers, only three people who look as if they own the place or at least work there. I stand there, trying to get up the nerve.

Maybe the hardware shop across the road? It's very busy – everyone would hear the questions, look at me . . .

I walk back slowly towards the van and it's when I get to it I have this brainwave. The Gárda station is right in front of where we parked. The Guards know everything, they'd help. I should ask for the Devines and say I was a long-lost cousin. I consider putting on an American accent and then decide this would be stupid.

As you can imagine, in my present circumstances, Gárda stations are inclined to give me the heebie-jeebies so it takes all my courage to go in.

A lot of toing and froing in there and telephones ringing – and the first setback is that the young Guard at the front desk doesn't know from Adam who the Devines might be. He's a recent transfer into the town. He goes off to consult a senior colleague, who comes back with him. This individual is exactly one of those Guards you see in old black and white films on the telly, the ones made in Ireland with Abbey actors. He's roundy, with a grizzled head and a kind, shrewd face. Good afternoon, he says, who's asking for the Devines?

I'm a relative from Dublin, I say, I just happen to be passing through and I thought I'd look them up.

And what's your name?

Angela, I go. Angela Devine.

The slow look the Guard gives me leads me to believe he knows exactly who I am and my heart starts to thump. But he couldn't possibly know. He couldn't possibly. I try to keep my face as blank as I can.

And what branch of the family would you be now? He's still looking . . .

There's nothing for it. I'm Rose's daughter, I say as formally as I can.

Ahh, he goes. I see.

Is this the first year I've noticed or does the whole of Ireland say 'I see' at every available opportunity?

The Guard, who I reckon would be about the same age as Mammy would be now, leans on the counter as though he's haggling for a horse. He shakes his head, puts on a sad expression. Very sad, very sad, he goes. There's only one of them left in the town now, Adeline. You know what happened, of course? His eyes are boring into me. The younger Guard is pretending to be sorting through the entries in a big ledger at a desk. He's all ears. I lower my voice a bit but then he just happens to have to come nearer where I'm standing to search for something on a set of shelves. This gets on my wick but there's nothing I can do about it.

I admit to the older Guard I don't know anything of what occurred and that I've never met any of my relatives.

He makes a clucking sound, shakes his head again, I should probably let Adeline fill you in.

Could you direct me to where Adeline lives?

He leans on the counter again to give me the directions. My aunt Adeline apparently lives about half a mile outside the town on a little byroad – we passed the turnoff to it coming in. You can't miss the house, he goes, she has an old Morris Minor she parks outside it, right into the hedge. He puts his hands on his big hips. Not that she drives it any more. Don't be expecting too much now. She keeps herself to herself a lot. He sticks out his hand. You're welcome to Birr. And I have to say you have the look of your mother. But she was dark.

I'm back outside. No wonder poor Mammy had to flee to Dublin, it's quite clear you can't sneeze here but everyone gets a cold. I look around the square for Ken Sheils. Then I remember it was I who insisted he go for coffee. I have to cool my heels for a bit. Just as well. Steady me up – but now that I'm so near—

Did they have a chauffeur, I wonder.

I saw a picture of Mammy's parents once. That was some lady that was, straight as a pole, formidable chest, dress buttoned right up under her chin. She wasn't someone you'd mess with in her shop, I'd imagine.

He was quite fat and smaller than her, with one of those handlebar moustaches. Maybe it was the moustache, maybe it was Mammy's mother's severe expression and that dress, but they looked more old-fashioned than they should have because they couldn't have been more than their middle thirties in the picture. Early forties at the most. And that had to have been a maximum of only forty years ago. The fifties, for God's sake, not the Middle Ages. Yet somehow those people – my grandparents! – looked Victorian or Edwardian.

I don't know where that snap is now. As I told you before I have practically nothing of my heritage.

Maybe Adeline will have more pictures, better ones. She was the youngest, so she would be only around fifty now. That's young in 1996 so maybe she won't hold a grudge. Maybe she'll welcome me with open arms. At last maybe I'll have a family. I've often wondered do I have cousins. I should have asked that Guard if Adeline is married . . . Suppose Adeline knows who my father is? Was. Is? Oh, my God—

Whoa, whoa. You're going too fast. One thing at a time. You're here to look for your *family*. Mammy's family. Take it easy . . .

Twenty-Two

We see the Morris Minor when we come around a bend. It's ancient, all right, one of those estate ones with a square wood frame along the back. Paint flaking off, you could see it had once been navy blue. Sweat starts to trickle down between my shoulder blades and it isn't just because the sun has come out at last.

Ken turns off the engine. We get out. The quietness! Nothing but fields and grass and hedges for miles around. Flies buzzing like helicopters all over the dry cow dirt on the tarmac, a car on the main road a half mile away as loud as if it's right beside you. The air here is much heavier than it was on my last country trip, the day we went up the Dublin mountains. That was lofty, this is thick like syrup. You have to wade through it.

We walk towards Adeline's house, which is a concrete cottage – a bungalow, really – set back off the road behind a high hedge that badly needs cutting. No flowers in the garden, just untidy grass full of dandelions. Hens and ducks grubbing around.

Hey! Ken says. What about those! Look at those, aren't they extraordinary? He's pointing at a pair of stone lions, big ones, set on both sides of the front door. They look terribly out of place, they're three-quarters the height of the door. Who are we visiting anyway? He looks at me.

I still haven't got around to giving him my complex family history. This woman should be my aunt, my mother's sister, I say to him. I've never met her before. She must have brought those stone lions from her old home, they were well off in their day. This sounds terrible. Prissy. So I add quickly that I'll tell him everything in the very near future. To give him his due, he doesn't bat an eyelid.

The gate gives a groan when we push it open. As for the front door behind those lions, Ken knows by looking at it that it had probably not been opened since the turn of the century. Never mind painted. Not a shred of paint left. Neither is there a knocker or a bell.

Maybe there's no one in. Ken looks up at the roof and this irritates me. Who the hell does he think he's going to see up there? Maybe the flying nun?

I'm being totally unfair. She's in, all right, I say, that's her car outside the hedge.

Will we go round the back? he goes, she probably uses the back door, most people do in the country— Then he notices me hanging back. Do you want me to wait in the van? I don't mind, really . . .

No. I'd like you to come round with me, will you?

Sure, he says, come on so. He puts his arm around my shoulders. Don't worry, he goes, she's not going to take a bite out of us, is she? She'll probably be delighted to meet her long-lost niece. He squeezes the shoulder under his hand.

We see her the minute we come around the side of the house. Wellington boots, man's trousers, an old raincoat and a man's pork-pie hat. The back garden is twice as untidy as the front and she's digging stuff which has to be manure into a vegetable plot. I call to her but she doesn't miss a dig. It's only when I get up close to her that I see she's wearing a Walkman. Two little earphones coming down from under the hat.

I walk around her into her line of vision and she looks up at me as though strangers are only to be expected in this vegetable patch on Wednesday afternoons in June. Yes? pulling one of the earphones a little bit away from her ears.

Hello, I say, are you Adeline Devine?

Hold on a second, she says, and plonks the earphone back into her ear. She listens for a few seconds and then makes a sort of grunting sound as though she's fed up. She lifts the hat and pulls off the headset, settles it around her neck. Her hair, as grey as a badger's, looks as though it's been cut with a lawnmower. She puts the hat back. Gazes at me. And who might you be?

I tell her.

I'd like to be able to report that she did something significant, like they do on such occasions in films or in books. Like, she should have let out a long, low whistle or stuck her spade dramatically into the manure. Anything.

Instead, she starts hauling spadefuls of the manure towards her. So? she goes, what do you want? If it's your inheritance, there's nothing, you're wasting your time. I don't own this house. She has a peculiar accent. Not Anglo, exactly, but not Irish either – her Ts are soft, that's Irish, but she doesn't pronounce her Rs and that's Anglo. Her voice is deep and fruity. The stink from the manure is terrible.

She's continuing to dig as though I'm not there. I don't know what to say or to do next. I'd just like to talk, I say to her, I promise you I'm not looking for anything. I just came to visit you—

Now she does shove the spade into the earth. I don't

get visitors. I don't ask for them and they don't come. I can't imagine why you'd want to visit me. That business is all finished. We look at each other and it's touch and go. Out of the blue, I'm not a bit nervous any more. 'That business' is the one involving my mother, Rose. Well, I'm not going to have it. Not from her or from anyone. My friend and I drove all the way down here just to meet you, I say, as though I'm the Queen of England. He took time off work. It wouldn't kill you to be civil.

Behind me, I hear Ken give a little cough. I'm sure he can't believe what he's hearing.

Well, well, well, Adeline goes, taking off her hat again and fanning her face with it. You certainly don't take after your mother. Wouldn't say boo to a goose. Who's your friend, then? She peers around me towards Ken.

I introduce him.

We'd better go inside, she says, but supplies are low. She makes no move and the three of us are left standing there looking at each other.

As matter of fact we do have a flask and a few sandwiches. This is Ken, calm as you please. I'll go and get it.

My aunt Adeline and I wait for him to come back. We say nothing at all to each other. She seems not put out in the least so I'm determined not to be put out either. She's my aunt and I'm her niece and I've every right to be standing here. We listen to flies. A *lot* of flies.

Ken comes back and the three of us go into the house. The kitchen to be precise. More hens. Hens' droppings. Piles of English newspapers, the ones at the bottom as yellow as bananas. Bottled gas cooker and a Super Ser, and the sink is one of those huge porcelain ones that stand on trestles. No electricity, as far as I can see. Looks like the only modern thing in the whole place is the

Walkman now hanging from the belt of Adeline's trousers.

To take you out of your suspense, the story of my relatives after my mother left for Dublin is a short one.

And no, I didn't ask who my father was – or is. Not yet. Somehow it didn't seem appropriate. My aunt Adeline gave me no opening, either. To tell you the truth, her attitude was a puzzle. I mean, how would *you* react if your sister's daughter, whom you've never seen or imagined, arrived on your doorstep? Wouldn't you be at least a *tiny* bit interested?

Neither does it take a feather out of her when I tell her Mammy is dead. Doesn't surprise me, she says. Don't tell me any of the gory details, all water under the bridge now. Poor Rose. Never very bright. But wouldn't listen to anyone, would she?

The story is that after my mother left, my grandfather and grandmother and their three remaining children continued to live in their nice house in the town. My grandparents ran their shops. Eventually Jeremy married a wealthy South African and went to live in Cape Town. Lily married an English captain she met at a hunt ball in Galway and moved with him to Derbyshire.

One night in 1968, when Adeline was out, her parents' house caught fire. My grandfather died in the flames, my grandmother died two days later in hospital. There was no insurance and when the businesses were looked at, it turned out they were in such debt they would have gone under in any case, even without the fire. Creditors had been holding off, apparently out of respect for what the family represented in the town.

Wouldn't happen today, my aunt Adeline says in her strange accent as she's lorrying into Ken's sandwiches and drinking his tea. No respect for tradition these days, any of 'em. (Nevertheless, she's already told us that this house belongs to someone in her church who doesn't ask her for any rent.) She now lives on unemployment assistance. I would have thought this would be humiliating for a person of her background, but not a bit of it. She tells us without a trace of irony that she deserves every penny of it after all she and her family did for this wretched country. As a matter of fact, it should be more.

She knows a bit about horses – I'm quite good on horses, someone should employ me to give tips. And I have my own vegetables and eggs. Here, chuck, chuck, chuck, now she's shaking the crumbs of Ken's sandwiches off her trousers onto the floor. She sells the surplus – free-range eggs are all the rage now, even in Birr. She says Birr like it sticks in her throat.

She was twenty-one at the time of the fire, which would make her now only about forty-nine years old. She looks way over sixty. She hasn't seen either Lily or Jeremy since the funeral of their parents, and as far as she knows from Christmas cards, which is the only communication between them, neither of them had any children. So any hope I had of cousins was out the window. On my mother's side at least.

She tells us all of this in a single burst, like she wants to get it over with as soon as possible. As if maybe she won't get rid of us until she gives us value for our trip.

But at least now I knew who I was and where I came from.

Naturally it didn't sink in properly until much, much later. But a couple of really good things came out of that day. For a start, I now knew it was no insult that none of them came to Mammy's funeral. My grandparents were well dead at the time, Lily and Jeremy were far away and Adeline seemed to read only English newspapers so she wouldn't have seen the death notices.

And she did have some photographs, which she gave me – Keep them, keep them, waving her arms at me as though I'm a plague of locusts, I don't want them, they just clutter up the place.

When we go back to Dublin the events of that day weren't over, not by a long chalk. I was dog-tired, and after Ken dropped me off, I could barely put one foot in front of the other climbing the stairs to the flat. I could already feel the kick of the cup of tea, the smoothness of the pillowcase against my cheek . . .

But when I pushed open the door, I saw a note on the floor. It had been shoved under.

James was in hospital. He'd had an accident.

Please contact such and such a number at the Mater hospital because James has had an accident, that's all it said. I didn't recognize the handwriting and I've never found out who put it in. Dwyer, probably.

Thank God it was the Mater, because it's only up the road from us. I flew. I think I've told you I hate hospitals, and that's true, but my own feelings were furthest from my mind as you can imagine.

He's still in Casualty when I get there. They let me in to see him only on sufferance, because they didn't want visitors getting in the way, they're too busy. But when I explain that I'd just got the message, they give me five minutes.

I hardly recognize him in the cubicle. He's asleep but even if he hadn't been I can't see how he could have opened his eyes. His entire face is bloody, and so swollen on one side that he looks like a man I once saw on TV who'd had a lot of chemotherapy. His lips are split and like two half-collapsed balloons, he's on a drip and one of his arms is strapped into a sort of cradle.

The nurse who comes in with me explains that they'd had to cut off his leather jacket – the remains of it are draped over the end of the bed – because the arm in the cradle is broken and he also has several broken ribs. I'll leave you with him for a minute, she goes, don't be upset by what he looks like, I've had much worse coming through here. He'll be fine after a bit of TLC. We're admitting him as soon as we can get a bed.

I have to warn you, though, she says, we're actually looking for eighteen people to be admitted at the moment and we might have to send him somewhere else. She sees my expression. Don't worry, she goes, we'll send him in a taxi and a nurse will go with him. She looks down at him, tweaks the pillow. He'll be groggy. We've given him something for the pain.

What happened? Did he fall off his bike?

I'd have to go and look at his chart. He's been here a while and the shift has changed. I do know that the ambulance crew picked him up somewhere quite near here.

She reacts to a call from outside. Sorry, she says quickly, five minutes now—

She bustles out. It's then I remember that his bike was parked outside the flat, locked to the railings as usual. In fact, Ken had remarked on it as he left me off. Said it was in very good condition for such an old one.

There's an unexpected atmosphere in this place. It's too quiet, cubicle curtains gently swishing forwards and backwards, low voices from the doctors and nurses, a quiet moan, except it's not really a moan, more a sigh. Pain and suffering changed down to low gear. I'd been in Casualty before, of course, but not for years, so I suppose that subconsciously I was now thinking it would be like *ER* with all that yelling and clacking and racket.

This semi-silence is a bit unnerving. And there's an awful smell — disinfectant, well, you'd expect that, but it's mixed in with another, very strong odour, like fabric Elastoplast. I presume it's the smell of hospital bandages. Or it might be plaster of paris.

I study James. He's lucky to be in a cubicle, there are poor unfortunates out there on trolleys. His head is turned away from me.

It occurs to me I should ring up to say I won't be showing up for the kissogram job tonight. Then I think the hell with it. Let them fire me. Big talk for someone who has only four hundred and thirty odd left of the scratch-card money.

Don't ask.

James, I go in a low voice, James . . .

His head turns and he looks at me. At least, he tries to. It's pathetic. I can barely see any eyes. Two small, roaring red openings in the mass of damage. He tries to say something but nothing comes out.

He tries again. This time I understand him. He didn't have the tenner to give to the office when he was brought in. Would I pay it to them? Imagine! In his condition and all he can think about is a lousy tenner. It's some sort of tax you have to pay to the Government.

Of course I'll pay it, I go. Then, You were in a fight, weren't you?

He doesn't have to answer. I can see by the way he reacts that I'm only too right.

I won't go on about what he said or what I said next as I'm sure that once again you're way ahead of me. The summary of what happened is that he was jumped by four men. In a little laneway off Dorset Street, near the pub he drinks in with his pals. He was on the way to the pub when these guys grabbed him and dragged him down this lane, where they got him up against a wall and beat him senseless with a golf club and baseball bats. And he thinks a hammer.

He didn't recognize the guys. The last thing he remembers when he was lying on the ground in his own blood is that one of them said to him he should make sure to remember them. That they were citizens concerned with justice. And that justice was not being done.

And that he should, for his own safety, get out of Dublin.

He's lucky to be alive. A hammer.

If I tell you I was shocked but not surprised, I hope that doesn't sound too confusing. I suppose now is as good a time as any to give you some flavour of what was happening with the media.

I'm afraid that putting those Sunday papers in the bin didn't make the storm go away. Monday and Tuesday were even worse than Sunday.

It was because Rosemary Madden had allowed herself to be interviewed. She came into the *The Gay Byrne Show* for the Monday morning, two days before my trip to Birr.

It was actually Joe Duffy that day, not Gay, and he interviewed her in that special hushed way they all have for when something really sensational has happened. I was sitting listening to it as though I was somebody else, not me. There was no stir from James's bedroom, although he does have his ghetto-blaster in there with him and for all I know he could have been listening too. (He wouldn't get up that morning when I called him after I got home from work.)

I turned down the radio and sat really close to it. I felt paralysed. I couldn't believe the way she was talking about James. She called him a beast. Her life was over, she said. All in the quiet murmur on the turned-low radio.

Her photograph was on the front page of the *Herald* on the Monday evening, Alongside the usual one of James with the coffin over his eyes.

Tuesday morning, front page, *all* the papers. And inside. (This time I read them.) And all that day she was being interviewed again on radio.

The gist of all these interviews and articles was the same. Rosemary's home was inundated with messages of support, people were sending her bouquets of flowers and cuddly toys. People were inviting her to their houses in the country to have a holiday. One travel agent offered her two weeks in Majorca. Politicians and prominent people were ringing up to express their concern. All the reports described her as 'tearful but determined'. She hadn't decided yet, they said, whether or not to appeal the leniency of the sentence.

The interviews got bigger. Women's groups were outraged. Everyone was queuing to be interviewed to say how sickened they were. People were asking for the resignation of the Minister for Justice, saying that judges had to be brought under some kind of control.

The message was clear. James would have to pay.

Sprinkled here and there were snippets with one or two people saying we had to be careful about civil rights and that we shouldn't be overreacting to a single judgement but I was so upset that to me those people's views didn't count. I'd never heard of any of them and they were drowned in the tidal wave of general opinion.

The morning of the day Ken and I went to Birr, the *Irish Times* ran a section in the letters page under the heading Rape Sentencing. In it, one woman wrote that she would be willing to start a public collection so that

Rosemary could get the best lawyers in the country to appeal the sentence all the way to Europe. Another argued that because of her courage in going public, Rosemary Madden should be given the freedom of the city.

The letter that got to me most said James should be castrated. The man who wrote that one said he would be willing to perform the operation himself.

Twenty-Three

Listen, James, I say to him in his bed in Casualty, don't let them get you down. Rest now and get some sleep. I'll check to see where you end up and I'll come in and see you first thing tomorrow morning no matter where you are. I don't care about visiting hours, they'll let me in. I'm going to get us some help, some real help. Whoever did this can't get away with it, I won't let them.

I had no idea what I was talking about but I knew I had to do something.

Don't, he goes, don't, just leave it, you'll only make things worse.

I stand up. Nothing more's going to happen to you, I say, I promise you that. Now try and get some sleep.

I lean over and kiss him on the forehead. I haven't done that since he was about seven but he doesn't pull away. I turn quickly and leave the place. I'm too far gone for tears.

There's a public telephone under one of those hood affairs outside the doors to the Casualty room, but wouldn't you know it, there's a woman talking on it. I wait. My brain is racing. I'm putrid with anger. James and I have paid for what he has done, over and over again. We've paid for it in spades. Look at us, we're basket cases. Look at his ruined face.

I'm a completely different person from the one who thought, up there in the Dublin mountains – was it only four or five days ago? – that we might take the boat to England. The hell we will. We're going to fight this.

The woman on the phone is making complex arrangements to be picked up. The person she's talking to apparently hasn't a clue where the Mater hospital is, let alone the Casualty entrance. She's making a dog's dinner of giving the directions . . . No . . . let me see . . . After you cross O'Connell Bridge and come up O'Connell Street, the best way to come would be up the North Circular Road . . . No . . . Wait a minute . . . It might be better to come at it from Eccles Street . . . do you know Eccles Street? . . . Well, do you know Dorset Street . . . Do you know where the Plaza Cinerama used to be? It's now the Wax Museum . . .

I feel like kicking the crutch from under her.

At last she hangs up and I dial Patrice Murphy's number. Needless to remark, I know it off by heart at this stage.

I get an answering machine. I've forgotten what time it is, of course, everyone's left his office by now. I briefly consider ringing him at home but decide against it. I leave a message that I'll ring again first thing in the morning. That it's very urgent.

I go to pay the bloody tenner into the office. Find I only have seven pounds and a few odd bits of change. They're nice about it. Sort of. Take it or leave it, says the new Angela Devine. I stalk off.

When I let myself in, the flat is more empty than I've ever known it – the note about James is still where I left it on the little table beside the door. I remember once listening to Gay when some woman was on giving out about her children's untidiness and he says back to her that some day you'll tidy up and it's going to stay tidy, missus, because they'll all be gone. Make the most of them while you have them, missus. For the first time, I know what he means, really know. I want James to be there, with his big spawgs over the arm of my settee and his crisp bags. I even wish MTV was on. And that I'm swimming in cigarette smoke.

I walk around the flat, which doesn't take long. I strip James's bed. Might as well take advantage of his absence to bring his bedclothes to the launderette. When the room is as neat as I can make it, without getting myself into trouble for disturbing some of his precious rubbish, I go back out into the living room. Adeline's folder of snaps is still where I left it too, on top of the telly.

I pick them up, look at them again. Still nothing, no emotion. Just like the first time I went through them. I'd expected to go all teary. Maybe they're not affecting me because they're such standard fare – Mammy and her sisters and brother as children on holiday in Bangor, Co. Down. Mammy riding a seaside donkey. Mammy and Adeline in their Sunday school clothes. It was lovely to have them but it's hard to see your mother in a child's face. This is what history is, dead and gone.

I did ask Adeline had she no more up-to-date photographs but we were standing at the back door at this stage and it was clear she couldn't wait for us to go. She was dangling the earphones of the Walkman, swinging them to and fro, dying to put them back where they belonged, in her ears.

No, she shook her head, that's the lot. Mother threw everything else concerned with Rose on the compost heap after she left.

I got such a shock, and it wasn't only because it

confirmed my own vision of her throwing things on a bonfire. It was largely because that kind of action is so *unmotherly*. Even if she'd burned stuff, you could put it down to a passionate fit of anger at how her daughter betrayed their principles. But a compost heap, where everything would take months to rot. That was some coldness. Adeline looked closely at me, shrugged. You really don't know much about Rose, do you?

I know a lot about her from the time I was born, I said back to her, tartly enough, I lived with her for the guts of seventeen years, after all. I waited. To see if she showed any curiosity.

Not a bit of it. She looked at her watch, put one of the earphones to her ear.

It's extraordinary, isn't it? Could you imagine wiping your own sister completely off your slate? As for the way she was treating me, I've never been so thoroughly dismissed in my life. We weren't on the same planet, Adeline was now living in whatever was coming through her ear. She was muttering. Come on, come on . . . Obviously some horse-race.

Ken gave me a quick little grin and took my arm. And that's how we left. I don't think my new-found auntie even noticed us going. I looked back before we went around the corner of the house and she was marching back towards the vegetable plot. That grizzly-haired Guard was right to warn me not to have high expectations. To be charitable about it, maybe she was so used to living on her own she'd become a bit eccentric.

A *bit*?

The Guard. It's as we were walking back past the stone lions it occurred to me he's the one I could ask about my father. He knew my mother, didn't he? He seemed to know everything about the others in the

Devine family – chances were he knew everything that breathed within ten miles of Birr over the past three or four decades.

I didn't want to ask Ken to drive me back to the station right then, though, some tasks are too private. Anyway I had trespassed enough on his generosity for one day. So I filed the Guard away for the future. (I have to admit I got a bit excited. It was the first time I felt I had a genuine chance. A teeny one, but real . . .)

I have to say that Ken Sheils was brilliant throughout this whole episode. He didn't open his mouth except to say how do you do when I introduced him to Adeline. But all the time we were there he kept this expression on his face, interested but detached, if you can get the picture. Like someone who doesn't want to be impolite but doesn't want to intrude either. He smiled when either Adeline or I smiled, nodded and looked interested if one of us looked at him. He even had the manners not to make any comment about her when we finally got away and were alone again in the van.

I don't know what I feel about this man. I've so much on my mind and in my heart at the moment that I suppose I haven't had much time to decide.

When we pull up outside my flat a couple of hours later we sit in the van for a little while. Sam jumps into my lap, turns around once, flops down and goes to sleep. It's flattering when a cat or a dog does that, isn't it? It means that it's accepted you as its friend. Or, at the very least, that you're no threat to its master. Makes you feel very peaceful.

I'd ask you in for a cup of coffee, I say to Ken, but I'm dropping on my feet.

Next time? He gives that grin of his.

For sure. Look, I say then, it's about time for you to

know all about me and my circumstances, *all* about me. I'm sure you're dying to know after today — I owe you an explanation.

Not at all, he goes, not at all. You'll tell me in your own good time.

I stroke Sam's ears, they feel like chenille. It's not a pretty story, I say quietly.

You mean James? Now he's stroking Sam's ears too. We're being very careful that our hands don't touch. We take an ear each. As for Sam — if Sam was a cat he'd be purring.

Not only James, I say. You know nothing about our background. Or even where I work—

No hurry. He stops stroking Sam, who looks hurt, leans over, gives him a little lick. We've plenty of time, Angela, he goes softly. Haven't we?

Whether it's the tiredness or the continual emotional up-and-down I don't know but I experience a genuine feeling of happiness. Small, but real. Right in the middle of everything that was going on. We have, Ken, I say.

There's another one of those moments, a pause where anything could happen. And before he does it I know exactly what's going to happen next. He's going to lean over and kiss me.

He does. It's the slightest of kisses, just a peck on the cheek. But it's nice. Our first.

Call down to me if you need anything, he says, now you know which apartment I'm in.

I will, I say, thanks. I peck him back. Thanks for everything, today and everything.

You're very welcome, he goes. We smile at each other. He takes Sam off my lap and I get out. He's still watching me when I get to the door, so I turn and wave before letting myself in.

And then, of course, I find the note about James, and have to rush to the Mater.

After I've tidied the tidy flat until I'm ready to scream, I can't stay in it another minute. I have to get out. And I'm not tired any more, at least not so that I'd go asleep.

Then as soon as I'm out on the street I remember I've nowhere really to go. I remember the kissogram gig and decide that, despite my bolshie attitude earlier, in all fairness I should ring them, even at this late stage. Let them fire me, as I said, but I have to give them the opportunity to get in a replacement for tonight – what's happening in my life isn't the poor client's fault, after all.

So I ring. The boss isn't there. I leave a message with one of the other girls. Cowardly, but I don't care. After I hang up I'm standing indecisively in the phone box. Now what? I haven't been to a film by myself for a million years and I don't want to start now. I could go for one of my famous walks but the way I'm feeling I'd probably do some criminal damage to something on the way.

I ring the Mater, find that James has been admitted to a ward there and hadn't been taxied anywhere else. That's good news, he could have been sent up to Beaumont or even across to St James's and there you're talking hours on the bus. Before I know what I'm doing I find myself ringing Patsy.

Hello? It's Martin who answers.

Hello, this is Angela, is Patsy there?

Hold on a minute – he sounds teed off. But that's nothing new, Martin always sounds teed off so I don't take it personally.

Hi, Ange, Patsy's on the line, she doesn't sound great either, they must be having a row. However, there's no point in beating around the bush. I need to talk to you, Patsy, could we meet?

Instantly the blinds come down, I can actually hear them, gdhunk! Ohh-hhh? Long drawn out. When?

Right now. Immediately. Can we, please? I don't care if I sound as though I'm desperate. I am desperate.

It's a bit difficult at the moment, she goes. There's a pause. Then, Maeve and Pauline have to be picked up from gymnastics in twenty minutes and I have to help Darren with his homework. Would it do tomorrow?

I have the feeling that she's just making this up, that she just doesn't want to come out, but I go for broke. Patsy, you're my friend. You're my only real friend in the world. I need you, I really do.

Pause.

I see . . . Cautiously.

I'm sorry to do this to you. Could Martin pick up the girls?

Pause. Then, Well, if it's that important, hang on till I ask him. The sound goes muffled, she's obviously put her hand over the receiver. I can't hear what she's saying.

A motorbike roars along the street outside the phone box, one not unlike James's. If only it were James's. When he gets better, when we come through this somehow, I'll never give out about motorbikes again. I'll never again give out about anything—

Patsy comes back on the line. All right, she goes, I'll come straight away. Where are you? Do you want me to come to the flat?

I couldn't stand the thought of going back into that clean, empty flat. No, I say, could we meet somewhere? A café or something? She agrees, and we make arrangements to meet in twenty minutes' time in a fast-food place on Dorset Street. Thank you, Patsy, I go, I really appreciate it.

See you soon, she says.

I try to kill time on the way to the café, but it's only a

few hundred yards from the flat and no matter how much I dawdle I'm there early.

An immediate blast of heat from the grill when I go in. That lovely smell, hot fat, frying onions, salt-and-vinegar. I know I shouldn't admit this, but I've always liked the atmosphere in fast-food joints. No one's better than anyone else when you're in there, particularly late at night when a lot of the customers have a few pints on board. Greasy chips are the common denominator of Irish people. I'm a kissogram girl and a cleaner but when I'm in Some Like It Hot or the Nite Bite or any of the others I'm every bit as good or bad as the solicitor or the wino or the bookie or even the higher civil servant sitting beside me. Could even be a judge.

Don't mention judges.

This particular evening is quiet. A woman, probably homeless – she has one of those drag-along shopping trolleys packed with plastic bags. A couple in their late teens or early twenties who've obviously had a row, they're staring in opposite directions. A taxi driver studying racing form in the *Daily Mirror* – I recognize him, I'd been in his cab a couple of times, we nod to each other. A young fella with a fancy collarless shirt, a waistcoat, a linen jacket and a mobile phone. Drug dealer, probably. He has that sort of plump, alert look. Gelled hair.

I take a seat facing out so I can watch the street. I don't want to think. I've been thinking too much for my own good. Yet I can't avoid it. The overwhelming thought is that, after all my hopes and dreams for us, how come we've ended up like this? I feel hunted. As far as I can see I've done nothing wrong and yet here I am feeling like a criminal.

I realize I'm just acting sorry for myself. Fat lot of use that's going to be to James, or to myself either.

I pick up the menu, one of those plasticized jobs. I pay close attention to it, like it's Holy Writ. Bunburger and Chips, Beans and Chips, Egg and Chips, Sausages and Chips, Deep Fried Plaice and Chips. I wouldn't touch a bunburger these days, not with Mad Cow Disease.

That self-pity stuff keeps pressing in in front of the print. BEVERAGES. Tea, Coffee, Milk, Coca-Cola, Fanta.

To my horror I feel tears coming into my eyes. Stop it, Angela, stop it this instant. Concentrate. SIDE ORDERS. Chips, Mushrooms, Beans, Garlic Bread — I hate garlic bread, I just hate it . . .

> For thou art with me here upon the banks
> Of this fair river; thou my dearest Friend,
> My dear, dear Friend; and in thy voice I catch
> The language of my former heart, and read
> My former pleasures in the shooting lights
> Of thy wild eyes.

Now where did that come from all of a sudden? 'Tintern Abbey', we did it *ad nauseam* because Mr Elliott tipped it to come up in the English paper. It did, too, and when it did I surprised myself with how much of it I knew off by heart.

Probably the reason it came into my mind right now is because it's Wordsworth talking about his sister Dorothy. It's exactly James and me. That had never occurred to me before. (It's odd I don't like poetry, I should like it because I certainly don't have a tin ear — I am a singer, after all.)

I see Patsy passing by the window of the café — she's driving very slowly, obviously looking for a place to park. I haven't thought out what I'm going to say. I haven't even thought what approach I'll take with her. All I know is I need to talk to someone. To my friend.

Hello. Patsy arrives with her breath in her fist. Sorry, are you here long?

Not long. What do you want? This is on me.

She wants nothing, only a cup of coffee.

Are you sure?

Sure. She looks terribly uneasy. The waitress comes over and we order. I've eaten nothing at all since lunch time so I order sausages and chips and tea for myself.

Before you start, Patsy says as the waitress goes off, I've something to tell you too. As a matter of fact, I'm delighted you rang. I have to talk to someone, we were in the middle of a row – you might have noticed he sounded a bit peculiar on the telephone?

It takes me a second to jerk myself out of my own misery. I did notice, I go, yes?

Do you remember the condom episode with Martin? she says back. Well, I confronted him with it.

She's off. What can I say? We'll get around to me in due course, I suppose.

Immediately I feel like a heel for entertaining such a thought. Patsy is jigging around in her seat, she's obviously as upset about her problems as I am about mine. And although we're at a table with a notice which says thank you for not smoking, she's lit up and is dragging on her cigarette as though her life depends on it. It doesn't matter all that much here, I suspect. It's not the kind of place where people are going to be sniffy about no-smoking areas.

➔ Twenty-Four ←

It turns out that this particular row between Patsy and Martin was the mother and father of all rows. She still hasn't got to the bottom of the situation but she is now convinced, absolutely convinced, that he's having an affair. And not just a one-night stand either, she goes.

At last I can get a word in – How do you know?

It's the *way* he's denying it. It's too important to him. If it was just a one-night stand or a fling, he'd have admitted it once I showed him the condom. Instead he acted all offended as though it was all my fault. He says I'm making the whole thing up and that I planted the damn thing just looking for a row. He asked me if I was suffering from PMT, if you don't mind. Then he asked me if I was going through the change.

She's nearly weeping now. I can see that the hand holding the cigarette is trembling. I feel desperately sorry for her – she looks shrivelled up. A lot older. She shuts up when the waitress comes back with our order.

I give her a bit of time to compose herself while I shake vinegar over my chips. The salt is all congealed in the shaker so I have to take the top off to dig it out. I can't wait for her to finish so I can tell her my own horrendous situation. Duelling problems!

I do my best to talk the thing through with her. Or,

rather, I let her talk and smoke while I work my way through my meal. The sausages aren't great — after a couple of bites I push them aside. The chips are grand. When you're in trouble yourself it's almost soothing, I suppose, eating chips and listening to someone else's troubles.

There were Signs, apparently, and she's kicking herself that she didn't cop on a lot earlier. It wasn't only the old cliché about the late nights when he was 'meeting clients'. He alternated between bringing her lavish presents one day and the next day being irritated if she just said hello to him. She noticed he was standing on the bathroom scales a lot, talking about joining a gym, leaving his tie off even when he was wearing a suit, pulling his belly in every time they were out shopping together and passing a plate-glass window. He asked her to buy muesli.

I can't offer any solutions, I can see that very clearly. I have to admit that I was never very comfortable with Martin. He always seemed a bit dodgy to me. I wouldn't dream of saying it, though, even now when Patsy's spilling her guts out about how awful he is. You never know, they could be billing and cooing next week and I'd be the worst in the world then.

I know I talked to you about this before, Ange, she goes, stubbing out her butt in her saucer. But having suspicions about someone and finding out you were right are two different things. Very different. You always think you'll be better off if you know . . . That's before you know . . .

She bends her head. Lights up another cigarette. I signal the waitress that I need more salt.

Ironclad confirmation that all the time I thought Patsy was using the dough from the PA System gigs as fluff money or to buy fancy gadgets for her new kitchen, she was doing nothing of the sort. Like me, she was stashing it away in the post office. That's how jittery she was about him.

Now, of course, all's changed. She's going to take him for every penny he has. Pauperize him. He's not going to get away with it.

She's through the second cigarette and she's stopped being so miserable. She's bulling. Enough about that bastard, she goes, sorry for going on about it but you're one of the few people I can talk to. I'm not asking you for advice, Ange, this is something I have to decide for myself. She takes a tissue out of her handbag, blows her nose. I'm sorry you got me tonight right in the middle of it. I bet you're sorry you rang, eh?

M-mmm, I go through a mouthful of chips. Then I say, Of course I'm not sorry I rang. I'm not sure whether I'm being absolutely truthful here. It doesn't seem to matter, because her question was rhetorical. She pulls her saucer close to her and stubs out the second cigarette in it as viciously as though it's Martin's face. I don't know how you can eat all that grease, she says.

She folds her arms, sits back against the leatherette seat. Then, So what did you want to talk to me about? I suppose it's about James? Has something happened? Something else, I mean?

She listens quietly while I tell her. But she's wearing that peculiar, closed-in expression I'd been half expecting but hoping wouldn't be there. I rattle on, however — it does feel good to get it off my chest.

She waits until I've run out of steam. How long will he be in hospital?

When I tell her I don't know she lights her third cigarette. Thinking. Then she launches into a long list of things I should do. Have I been to the police yet, I should go first thing tomorrow morning, actually, I should go right now, the minute I leave this restaurant. What I should tell them when I go. How I should get someone to advise me on security for the flat . . .

How James has a definite case against whomever assaulted him, who I should get as a solicitor, a paid one, not one from free legal aid – I could easily do a deal with one on a no foal no fee basis so it wouldn't cost me anything in the long run. The free legal aid people are very good but they're rushed off their feet.

All of her suggestions are good, helpful, practical, there is nothing I can fault. And yet all the time I have this nagging suspicion that it's all too pat, *too* helpful.

Too much on the surface. She might as well be talking about two people in a show she saw on the television.

Can you tell me what's really going on, Patsy? I say, interrupting her when she's talking about electronic door alarms. I can get all this stuff from brochures or from the police. I want to talk to you as my friend.

She looks at me. Exaggerated surprise. I'm just trying to be helpful.

I know you are. And everything you said is indeed very helpful. Brilliant. But I haven't heard one word of sympathy for either me or James. Just answer me one question. Do you think he deserved that hiding he got? Is that it?

Talk about a pause. This one feels as long as the Shannon. You know when your whole body goes still, inside. It's like your blood stops. Well, that's what this pause does to me. I'm in space, everything's slowed down. The fellow who's doing the cooking behind the counter throws a couple of hamburger patties on the grill and the hissing and spitting seems as loud as Hurricane Charlie.

I just can't, Patsy goes at last. Please don't ask me to go against what I really feel. I can't pretend. But I am your friend, I truly am. I'll do anything I can to help you,

anything. I'll lend you — I'll *give* you money, you must be
hurting by now, all those extra expenses and with James
not working any more—

I stand up. If I had a million years I couldn't explain
how bad I feel at this moment. It's like I'm standing by
myself on a rock in the middle of the sea and I can't see
anything in any direction except miles and miles of grey
water. There's nothing more to be said, Patsy, I go, but I
appreciate your advice and your offer. Thanks.

I take a fiver out of my bag and leave it on the table.
I'm really sorry for your trouble with Martin, I really
am. I hope everything works out for you.

She looks as upset as I feel. What's wrong? she says,
don't go, let's talk about it—

I leave the caff. I can't say anything more.

I walk towards home. I genuinely understand how she
feels, that's always my problem, I can always see the
other person's point of view. She thinks James is a rapist
and that's it. Black and white.

How can I blame her? Rape is a terrible crime, no
doubt about it. Her feelings are her feelings and I can't
ask her to go against them. And she is, no doubt, reacting
exactly like everyone else in Ireland. Certainly judging
by the letters' pages and the phone-in programmes. As I
told you, I don't count the handful of people who are
going on the programmes saying that we should all step
back and be cautious about asking for draconian changes
in the law or in the judiciary. They're just acting out of
their text books.

Real people all feel exactly like Patsy.

I find I can't go into the flat. I pass it without even
hesitating. Next thing I find myself ringing Ken Shiels's
doorbell.

Sam is delighted to see me. It's nice to have someone
loving me, even if it's only a mongrel. Ken's surprised,

but in a nice way, he was just about to go to bed, but of
course I should come in—

Then he sees my face. What's happened?

I can't answer, my throat seizes up. He takes my hand.
Come in, love, come in . . .

The apartment is neat but with hardly any furniture. A
bit like a monk's cell. Or what I've imagined a monk's
cell must be like. A modern monk. White walls. No
pictures. Beige carpet, one beige easy chair, a table and
two dining-room chairs. A telephone table with only a
telephone and a little stack of his leaflets, squared off. A
stand with a telly. The only splashes of colour in the
room are from the cover of the *RTE Guide* and from the
red blanket in Sam's basket in a corner of the room.

I'm surprised, with him being a carpenter and a
handyman. I suppose I'd been expecting lots of nice
shelves, coffee tables, lovely pine kitchen units that
he'd made himself. His units are white, completely
anonymous.

Would you like a drop of brandy? he goes, after he sits
me down in the easy chair.

No thanks, I say, but a cup of coffee, if you're making
it . . .

All I was looking for, or so I thought, was a bit of
company. But to make a long story short, we went to
bed together. I suppose you'll find that hard to believe,
given the circumstances. I would myself. Particularly
since you're talking about someone who hadn't been to
bed with anyone since Tom Bennett.

It happened as easily as one two three. When he came
in with the coffee, he gave me a cuddle. You poor old
thing, he said.

That did it. In one long swoop I told him about finding
the note and about James, about Patsy's attitude. Then I
told him I wasn't an office worker, that I was a cleaner.

I told him I had been a kissogram girl but I'd given that up. I told him about the deli on Saturday mornings. I haven't exactly mis-led you about letting you go on thinking I work in an office, I said at the end, but I wouldn't blame you if you don't want anything to do with me.

Drink your coffee, he said gently. Are you sure you don't want a real drink?

I felt that if I took a drink right then I would probably not be able to stop drinking, I'd probably drink for the rest of my life. I'd probably become a complete alky.

He came over and put his arms around me. It was a bit awkward for him because I was sitting and he had to kneel on the floor. I mean it, Ken, I said, I wouldn't blame you in the slightest.

He pulled my head down to him and kissed me. Properly this time. It made me feel as though I'd been holding my breath for days and I was allowed to let it out.

When the kiss finished he gave me another hug and said I was a silly moo to worry about what anyone thought about me being a cleaner. You do a helluva lot more useful work in offices than most of the people there. He kissed me again. It was lovely.

At least he had a four foot six bed, but the bedroom was as bare as the rest of the apartment. Except for his bicycle against the wall. A surprising bright blue. He must take it up in the lift with him.

I was behaving in a really odd manner – odd for me, that is. I wasn't thinking of what he might think of me, or whether he was thinking I was a tart for presenting myself to him on a plate like this. Or even if he thought I was fat. I wasn't thinking of a single consequence, I didn't care what he thought, actually, I was for once saying what was on my mind, doing what was in my desire.

As we were getting into the bed I told him how long it had been for me and that I was nervous. All he said in response was, Oh, goody, you've a lot of time to make up, then, haven't you?

Sex was different with Ken, much slower, more tender. More definite, too, if you understand what I mean. Maybe it was because he was married and was used to it. He had a nice body, as good as Tom Bennett's (older, of course) but it was smooth and hard, with terrific muscles. I suppose it's all the physical work he does.

He wanted me to stay the rest of the night in his apartment but I felt I needed to be in the flat. In some way I couldn't explain right then, I felt I would be betraying James if I stayed the whole night with a lover and anyway, I had no right to be out on the tiles when there was a chance I could be needed at home. (Although even as the thought occurred to me, I knew it was absurd, James couldn't possibly need me, he was no doubt fast asleep. But there you are. Your instincts are your instincts.)

Ken accepted this and walked me home. It was nice, I felt like I was part of the real world, where normal people in normal situations do normal things. Like get kissed goodnight at their front doors while gurriers whistle and jeer and shout obscenities as they pass by. I loved it.

After I kissed him back, he started telling me to lock my door and not to open it to anyone. He'd call around first thing in the morning to see me to make sure I was all right.

But I get up very early, I say, I told you I'm a—

He puts a finger on my lips to shut me up. I know, he goes, but you're not the only one in the world with an early start. I get up early too and I'll see you at about five. I'll ring the doorbell four times so you'll know it's me.

Him talking to me like this gives me the weirdest sensation, I'd never had a feeling like it before. Yes, Ken, I say humbly, thank you . . . I twig. He's minding me! It's like he's my daddy. This must be what it's like.

Be sure you get some proper sleep now, he goes, and kisses me again.

Once I get into bed, I can't sleep. I'm wrecked physically and mentally, but at the same time I'm exhilarated. That had to be the sex, I think for a while, but then I start wondering if it isn't more the novelty of someone fussing over me. Like I belong somewhere.

I certainly like it. For the moment at least.

The next thing I'm picturing my daddy like I used to when I was a child. I'd never indulged in it that much because it always felt to me as though I was being disloyal to Mammy. Even now, even with her dead so long, I still feel slightly guilty about it.

How old is he now? Does he still have his fair, Viking hair? Does he live around Birr? (If Birr is where he came from. He could have been a traveling salesman or an itinerant actor or a casual farm labourer. I have to root him somewhere, though, don't I?)

Is he a farmer? Does he have a degree from university? Is he rich? Famous, even? Could he be something really terrific like a brain surgeon, who'd given up a great career to go to the Third World or Bosnia? Or is he a quiet married man with six kids in a Corporation house in Finglas whom his family adore? So much so they're saving up to give him and their mother the trip of a lifetime to Australia.

Does he ever think about me? Does he even know about me?

I suppose it was the sex that did it but that night

brought down an avalanche of the most amazing feelings. And memories.

Tom Bennett. Poor Tom, I wonder where he is now. It's very odd how you can be so close to someone for so long, how you can be nearly married to him, how you see two heads in front of the sunset at the end of your life – and then something happens and it's as though you never met him. He disappears so completely out of your world that sometimes you have to work really hard to remember even what his touch felt like.

If you remember, way, way back I told you about the night I first saw Mammy in hospital. About doing something of which I was so ashamed that I could never bear to think about it, much less tell anyone. What triggered it was the stew of rage and sorrow I was in after seeing Mammy in the hospital with her discoloured face encrusted with scabs and her wretched, hacked hair. I think it was the first time reality hit me. For the first time I saw that there was no hope. This was the end of the road for us. She was going to die. I was slap bang up against those words. Die. Death. Dead.

And this made me really furious with her. How dare she leave us when we hadn't even got started? I know that when you look at it now this sounds really stupid. But honest to God, deep down, even through the worst days, when she was black and blue or comatose, or worst of all, when she brought home some new guttersnipe, I believed that, somehow, everything was going to turn out all right. Sometime.

In some future rainbow.

That if only we could get over this bad patch or that bad patch, if I was strong enough, or loving enough, or good enough, everything would get better and she'd settle down with us. That because we deserved it, somehow it'd happen. Something to do with justice.

Having seen her that night, though, all my hopes and long-term plans for us lay in smithereens. And for the first time I could see it wasn't anything to do with fate. The rage bubbled up when I started blaming her. Why couldn't she just stand up to them, all those people who used her? No, who *abused* her. How could she be so *weak*?

At the same time I was devastated at the loss that was going to happen to us.

All this preamble is not by way of excuse – there can be no excuse for what I did. It's only by way of explanation.

When I got back from seeing her and picked up the baby from the neighbour who was minding him, I let us into our flat. I walked round and round with him in my arms but the rage wouldn't settle. 'Walking' doesn't cover it, I was behaving like a madwoman. Every time I came to a clear space on a wall, I'd bang my back against it. Hard. I probably would have been smashing my head if I hadn't been holding James. But then he would have got hit too.

At first he thought it was a game we were playing – at least, I think he did because he didn't show that he was upset in any way. He just looked surprised every time he got the jolt. But then he started to whinge.

That nearly finished me altogether. I felt I was going to explode.

He got louder and louder and more upset, and wouldn't stop, no matter how much I shushed or rocked him. As you know by now I'm not a violent person but after a few minutes of this, I didn't trust myself not to hit him just to shut him up. Or to do something much worse. Like throwing him out through the window. So I dumped him in his cot and left him there. Screaming his head off.

Still I couldn't stick the noise so I went out onto our

balcony to get as far away from it as I could. It wasn't even the noise, it was what it represented. Need. Total dependence. Total demand. Me, me, *me*. I want, I need, *you owe*.

I didn't want this. From the bottom of my heart I didn't want it. I was still a teenager. Never mind that I asked for it, fought for it, went the full distance with the Eastern Health Board to get it.

I shut the front door. I could still hear him. Screaming.

I'm lying there on my bed-settee after coming home from Ken Sheils's apartment, and I'm in this bizarre state where I can't sleep but I don't feel in the least bit tired. My body's prickling from the sex but my mind is humming with guilt, round and round like a car on a Scalextric track.

I ran out of the flats. I left James there. On his own. Hysterical. A little baby.

While I went looking for Tom Bennett.

→ Twenty-Five ←

I find Tom Bennett in a pub on the Quays. He's surprised to see me, naturally. He's not looking the best. The copper hair I admire so much is greasy and all over the place, he hasn't shaved for maybe a couple of days and the stubble is horrible. Gingery.

What gives? he goes when I walk up to him and ask him to buy me a drink.

Nothing gives, I go back, I've just had it, that's all.

Oh, is that all, he goes. Welcome to the club. He buys me a Bacardi and Coke and we find a place to sit down.

I tell him Mammy's going to die.

That's terrible, just terrible, he says. Are you sure?

I'm sure.

Drink up, he says, I'll get you another.

I protest, feebly, but the first drink is already hitting the spot. It doesn't take much to persuade me to have the second one. Bacardi and Coke goes down very easily, especially for someone who's not used to spirits at all. It's like Coke on its own, really, only sweeter. It's only when I'm finished the second one and I'm feeling no pain, that he tells me it was a double. I'm too far gone to argue.

James's screaming is filling up my head.

Tom Bennett is very sweet to me. He doesn't get

embarrassed when I start to cry and when people around us start to stare. Instead he puts an arm around me, scowls at them, yells, Eff off, you've little to think about . . . This works, they put their eyes back in their sockets.

Let's get out of here, he says.

We leave and when the fresh air hits me I feel sick. I want to vomit, but somewhere in my mind I realize that would be the last straw for Tom and I manage to control it. Let me take you home, he says.

All I'm thinking about now is that James is dead in the cot. And it's all my fault. And even if he's not dead, someone in the flats will have been only too delighted to ring the Guards or the Eastern Health Board and get him taken away from me for neglect. It serves me right. I'm going to be prosecuted one way or the other. How am I going to tell Mammy?

Suddenly I have to get back there as quickly as possible. On my own. I don't want Tom Bennett to see what I've done.

I make up some cock-and-bull story about endangering my guardianship of James (in my condition I can just imagine the way my tongue got around that one!) if I brought a man anywhere near the flat that night. Tom seems to accept that although, to tell you the truth, everything from this moment to the time I get back home is more than a little fuzzy.

He comes with me as far as the entryway and then leaves me. Like a perfect gentleman.

If only Tom Bennett hadn't been a drinker the way he was shaping up to be, James could even have had a father. But I still think I made the right decision in the end. To be married to an alcoholic must be the real pits. I've seen enough of it in my time — you should hear some of the women at work.

Anyway, I insist Tom goes away and leaves me alone.

There's the usual messing and commotion going on in the entryway and in the courtyard but our flat is just overhead, and if James was still screaming, I should have been able to hear him.

I don't.

I'm afraid to go up. He's either dead or the Eastern Health Board has already taken him away. I'm as sober as Matt Talbot now. I'm in one of those states where my mind is clicking as cleanly as ice in a glass.

He's definitely dead. Because if the Eastern Health Board had been here there'd be plenty of people around to give me the bad news.

Well, I'm sure you've guessed by now that he wasn't dead.

He was lying in the cot with his blankets all twisted around his little legs. Asleep but hiccuping silently. You know the way they do when they've cried themselves to sleep and they're disconsolate.

I'm sure you can see how I find this very difficult to tell you. Talk about guilt! But maybe now that I've admitted it, the guilt will ease off a little. It's never left me since the night it happened. It's one of those episodes that wakes you up at four o'clock in the morning and you sweat and curl your toes and then put your head under the pillow so no one will hear you groan.

I picked him up and changed his clothes, they were all damp from perspiration and tears. I kissed him and kissed him. I gave him his bottle and concentrated really hard on telling him I loved him. Which I did. I love you, James. I love you. He kept gazing at me over the bottle with those enormous, beautiful eyes of his. Such trust. They're so forgiving, aren't they? It makes you feel even worse.

I didn't put him back in his cot, I took him into bed with me. I sang to him, all the songs I remembered from

Mammy's days with us. Rockaby Baby and We're Poor Little Lambs, and All In The April Evening. Then I whispered nursery rhymes, Ding Dong Dell, and Round And Round The Garden and Jack and Jill. And of course, Starbright, counting it out on his fingers. He loved it. I was concentrating so hard that I'm absolutely sure he understood how sorry I was and how much I adored him. I kept loving him until he fell asleep.

I swore that night as I looked at his little face that I'd never, ever leave him alone again, even for a minute. In a way, now that I think about it, the need to go home after sex with Ken Sheils in his apartment could well be linked, subconsciously, with that promise I made James that night after I'd left him. Because this really is his hour of need.

It occurs to me that he and I have never talked about anything that really matters. Is this what people mean by the generation gap? Like, we live together, so why is it we can't talk to one another person to person, like I do with Patsy – or like I assume he does with his pals?

Or maybe not. Do young fellas talk to each other? Does any woman know?

I've looked at him of an evening, when he's absorbed in something on the telly. He's so lovely, and so vulnerable. And sometimes seems so lonely I've wanted to throw my arms around him and say, Listen, whatever it is, don't worry about it. I'm here and you're all right with me. I love you no matter what.

Something always stops me, though. It's not just that I know he'd push me away – he'd certainly do that – it's something more. Like every word we speak to each other has a history of grievance. Each syllable reeking. As a result, being careful is second nature to me now, how's he going to react to this, what's the best way to say that to him . . . On his side, he's clammed up, not going to risk any response at all. Down to self-protective grunts and monosyllables. There's a word wall between us.

If I'm being truthful, I have to admit it's probably of my doing, each wordbrick formed from shoulds and shouldn'ts – why did you do this, James, you should have done that. You should get up earlier, you shouldn't drink so much, you shouldn't watch so much telly. You shouldn't talk to me like that, you should pull your socks up, look what's happened now, I told you should have done X . . .

I can see, too late probably, that I was trying to live up to some notion about what was 'good' for him. Discipline. Work ethic. Politeness. Work ethic again. Oh, I was a great one for the work ethic. I forgot about the lilies in the field. (All right, it's a theory that's hard to take when you're out working and he's in lazing. On the other hand, why do you think nature ordained some bees to be queens and some to be drones?)

From the time he could think for himself, James quite understandably resisted all my nagging, and after a while it became automatic for him to oppose everything I said or asked, good or bad. If it came from me it was to be fought at all costs. Now that I understand this a little, I don't blame him. I'd like to see the way I'd react if someone was permanently telling me what I should and must do. I find it hard enough to take instructions from Furry Slippers and she's responsible for my bread and butter.

It was so much easier when he was a baby, all I had to do was to hold him and rock him and make baby noises at him. Love him. I look at his school snaps and his eyes are full of bright, merry light. Up to about age eight or nine maybe. Then it died. Since then we've locked together in a war neither of us understands but that we can't get out of. I think it would be a great relief to both of us if we could start again as strangers. If we could get to know each other from the outside in.

Sadly, it's unlikely to happen now, unless I can find a way where both of us can gain free access to the enormous reservoir of love, the one hidden behind the wall of grievance wordbricks we've erected.

Correction again, the wall *I've* erected. Babies don't come supplied with bricks.

Well, it was up to me to do the work. At some stage, during what was left of that long, fraught night, I came to another decision. I firmly made up my mind that I was going to find a father for us. His or mine, either would be great.

On balance, going by the events so far in Birr, I recognized that finding mine was going to be the easier option since I had somewhere to start. If that old Guard couldn't help I would go back to Adeline, and I wouldn't care how iffy she'd be about it. Or to the local teacher, or to the clergy – Protestant, Catholic, whichever. The clergy are hard on the heels of the Guards when it comes to knowing what's what in their catchment areas.

It was hard to predict how my father would react. After all, he would be only a distant blood relative to James (I'd tried to work it out – half-half-son?). I didn't care, fundamentally, because he owed *me*. Therefore, if I asked him, he'd be *obliged* to help James, wouldn't he? Out of guilt, if for no other reason. I had no qualms about putting this kind of pressure on him, none whatsoever.

What's more, in the dead of that night I didn't give a sugar if my father turned out to be one of those people who believed that James should be castrated or put to gaol for the rest of his life or flogged until he couldn't stand. Tough. His beliefs were irrelevant here. We needed him and that was that. (Anyway, he might hold those views initially but we were going to change his mind.)

I managed to doze for a couple of hours but by the time Ken's four rings came to the door, I'd been dressed and waiting for the guts of half an hour. He's shaved and shining, wearing a pressed denim shirt and jeans. He could be in an ad for Old Spice. Good morning, he says, keeping his voice low.

Come in, I whisper back to him.

Talk about Old Spice – he comes in on a gust of aftershave, which one I don't know. James's Lynx is the only one I can recognize instantly. He sits down on the bed-settee, as easy in himself as King Farouk.

I have to rush him a bit, we don't have all that much time before the minibus comes for me. I'd the kettle already boiled and toast made. I've something to ask you, I say to him, when I'm pouring water on the coffee.

Fire ahead, he goes. But before you say anything, he says in a rush, that was wonderful last night. I hope it's the first of many such nights. It's obviously a little speech he's prepared.

I enjoyed it too, I say. I hand him the coffee and toast. It's time for my own speech.

I know it's a bit early in the morning, I start off, and I'm sorry to be serious, but I have to get one thing straight. I've told you about James, I haven't held anything back, but at this point I need to know what you really feel about the situation. About him.

I sit down, take a bite out of my own toast and wait.

He sips his coffee and he looks at me over the top of the cup. I've no opinion one way or the other, he goes, I just want to help you as much as I can.

I keep looking at him, continue to wait.

He gets it. Very quietly, he puts down his cup. But that's not enough, is it?

I'm afraid no.

Well, if you want me to be completely honest—

That's the general idea.

I can see him choosing his words. He's studying the faded pattern on the upholstery of the bed-settee. I hate rape, he says. I can't stand the thought of it. He hesitates again, still picking words. But the way you describe what happened, I would feel quite sympathetic.

I take a mouthful of my coffee. Don't taste anything.

The only thing is, Ken says, I'm sorry, but you've asked me to be honest, the only thing is, I haven't heard the other side of the story. He's now looking at the floor. I'm sorry, Angela, he goes again, but that's the way I feel. Until I would know what the girl's side is, I can't be objective. Or say what I really feel.

It's a quarter past five in the morning. It's a great day, sunny, the birds are having a jamboree over there in the park, there's hardly any traffic so the street outside is as quiet as Adeline's. I had sex last night for the first time in nearly twenty years and I'm sitting on my own bed-settee with the man who had sex with me. And what he's just said is killing me.

He's looking at me at last but he's terribly uncomfortable. Is that OK? Do you understand?

He's asking my permission to reject us. *He*'s asking *me* do *I* understand! Angela, he goes, leaning forward and taking my hand, Angela, don't let this come between us. I look at my hand and his together. They don't fit.

I manage to get something out. So long as we know where we stand—

Angela, please, he goes. After what happened last night, after the way we were—

Don't worry about it, I go. I take my hand out of his and stand up. It's no big deal. Honestly! I bring my cup over to the sink although it's still full of coffee. I throw the coffee down the drain and turn on the tap.

He comes over behind me. Please, Angela. I thought we were—

Of course we are, I say, as cheerfully as I can. Give us your cup there, are you finished?

I run water into his cup and rinse it as though my life depends on it.

He puts his arms around me from behind. Angela—

Oops! I go, I think I hear the minibus outside. I turn off the tap and wipe my hands, rush towards where I've put my bag on top of the telly, Sorry, I'm not throwing you out or anything but they don't wait long. I've got to dash—

Will you kiss me goodbye?

Of course I will. (Who is this person with the bright, cheery, *false* voice?)

I kiss him, he kisses me back. His is passionate. I can tell he feels he's off the hook. Whoa, I go, it's a bit early in the morning, isn't it? I kiss him once more. Peck. I feel like Judas. But at present I haven't the energy to tell Ken Sheils I don't want to see him again.

I have to save all my energy. No Ken. No Patsy. Just us.

Work was the pits that morning as you might expect. I screwed up, forgot to do one of the stalls in the men's toilets.

Furry Slippers was delighted at the chance to have a real go at me. The peaked-cap syndrome. When you give people who are only one jump up from you a bit of authority, it goes to their heads completely. I have to say she was a queen in this area. Peaked cap? Tiara! She called me aside, making sure as many people as possible saw this, and put on her sad-but-sorrowful face. You seem distracted lately, Angela. Now I know you've had your family troubles, and we've been tolerant of that, but when it gets to the stage where your colleagues have to be carrying you—

I let her at it. I'd read that the way these drug barons and tough guys, who are the bosses of organized crime in Dublin, deal with police interrogations is by picking a small spot on the wall and concentrating on it. That's what I did. There was a little screw hole in the door just behind her head and I watched it as though it was a microdot. My task was to decode it with my X-ray eyes – *your work has not been up to scratch lately, Angela, I'm sure even you can see that* – I imagined little woodworms wriggling in and out of the screwhole, generations of them. Too gross.

So I imagined that this hole was Stargate, like in the movie. A doorway to another dimension in time. I'd make myself small with a magic machine and I'd slip through it into the future. Or the past. Or anywhere better than here where she was still droning.

You don't seem to be *listening*, Angela, I don't seem to be getting *through* to you . . .

Sorry, I'm a bit tired this morning.

She sighs. She's Vanessa Redgrave. You're tired every morning, Angela, but I'm going to give you another chance, *yet* another chance, mark you, so please go back into that toilet and clean it properly. *All* of it. Right?

By the time I get to the Mater, thank God I've been able to scour my brain clean of toilets, Furry Slippers, everything to do with that bloody job. Oh, God, if only I could win the Lotto. (I wonder how many people are saying the exact same thing at this moment. The dignity of work, my eye . . .)

I march straight past the porter in the front hall as

though I'm bringing in something vital to someone very high up. I've hidden the grapes I'm bringing to James in my handbag. By the way, why does everyone bring grapes into a hospital? They used to be exotic, a great treat, but not now. I suppose it's a tradition, like Lucozade. The hospital smell this morning isn't totally bandages and disinfectant, it's mixed in with rashers.

I can tell he was watching for me because the instant I arrive at the door of the ward he hooshes himself up on the pillow, as much as he can with all the strapping and bandaging and so forth.

The consultants are doing their rounds and in a public ward they're supreme. In my mood, do I care? Pope John Paul could be doing his rounds or the Shah of Iran. I'm never intimidated by these guys in any case. They put their trousers on, one leg at a time, just like the rest of us. If I sound bitchy this morning it's because I'm feeling bitchy.

James had already been seen in any case – the Great Man with his entourage was already two beds down the row from him. Hello, I say, how are you feeling this morning?

Not the Mae, he says back.

I'm not surprised, I say, as I put the grapes on his locker. You don't look the Mae. You look the exact opposite of the Mae, as a matter of fact, you look terrible.

The bruising was not only black and blue this morning, but yellow and green as well.

Well, thanks a whole lot, he says. That makes me feel really much better, that does. He tries to glower at me but the effect is spoiled by the fact that both his eyes are still mostly shut.

I look down at him. Actually I regard him. After the sleepless night I've just had, not to speak of the situation with Ken Sheils and the row with Furry Slippers, I'm not inclined to put up with any lip from James Devine.

Then I remember that this was the old Angela. What about the darkest part of last night and my internal discussions about the relationship between him and me, brick walls and so forth? I take a deep breath and exhale slowly through my nose like you're supposed to do in yoga. I went to a yoga class once but the more I tried to relax my muscles one at a time, twenty others got rigid to compensate, but this time something works and I calm down a bit. I pull up a chair and sit. James, I say, could we talk?

What? He goes on full alert, looks as though I've threatened him with a machete. We are talking, he says.

I mean really talk. Without either of us having an attitude.

What do you mean, attitude? I don't have any attitude.

I wait. I can see he doesn't know what's got into me. He shifts around in the bed, then he winces. Is it very bad? I go, with as much sympathy as I can inject into my voice. I'm not acting, I'm digging deep into my real feelings. In normal circumstances I'd be giving out yards to him for getting us into this pickle. What kind of night did you have? I ask.

Immediately I understand something else — I have to stop asking him questions. When was the last time you had a conversation with a friend which was solely a question and answer session, with one party asking all the questions? You wouldn't remain friends for long, would you? I only ask, I correct myself quickly, because I had a terrible night myself. I couldn't sleep.

He's looking at me sideways. He doesn't know what the hell is going on. I slept all right, he mutters, they gave me a tablet.

Did it knock you ou— er, I mean that's what they

usually do in hospitals. Those pills are great for knocking you out. I remember Patsy gave me a couple of hers once when I was nervous about something. I forget what it was now. I think I slept solidly for three days – I missed work. God, I'll never forget it – did I tell you I've started walking? It's great exercise. And the fresh air! I went out to the South Bull the other night. Oh, James, it was gorgeous . . .

I'm chattering like a budgie. The expression on his poor bashed face would make a cat laugh, it's like he was expecting *The Sound of Music* and here I am with *The Texas Chainsaw Massacre*. Or vice versa, given his point of view on films.

I carry on. I'm on to my visit to the town of Birr and the Manchester Martyrs—

He pulls himself up and interrupts me. What's going on? Lookit, I don't give a fiddler's about the South Bull or whoever it is from Manchester— He makes a face and lies down again. He's done something to himself that has hurt him.

You must be in agony, I chirrup. Listen, I'm not staying long, I just came in to see how you're doing, this isn't my real visit. I've to make a few telephone calls, to the solicitor and so on. I'll come in again at the proper visiting time.

Before he could stop me, I'd stood up and leaned over and kissed him on the forehead. 'Bye, I say.

I leave. I don't look back. I consider it a personal triumph that I didn't even ask him what he might want me to bring in for him.

Twenty-Six

Patrice Murphy was in to take my call. Slow down, Angela, he says, slow down. I'm taking notes as you talk. Have you been to the Gárdaí?

I don't recall asking him to call me Angela but I let it pass. When I tell him I haven't gone to the Guards, he says I should go immediately and report the assault. He asks if there were any witnesses and when I tell him not so far as I know, he starts in on am I sure? Can James remember much of what was going on? Would he recognize these men?

All these questions. It's like now I've recognized what I've been doing to James, God's decided to have a go back at me!

Fitzgibbon Street must be one of the most rundown police stations in Dublin. Don't get me wrong, the Guard I speak to couldn't have been nicer. He's from the country – Kerry, maybe, or Cork. God love him, coming from those lovely airy places into what he faces in the inner city. He remains friendly even when I tell him who James is and why we think he's been beaten up. Don't worry, missus, he says. No matter what the lad's done or not done, he still has rights. Just one thing, he didn't provoke this by any chance?

No, I told you what happened, he was jumped.

Don't upset yourself, mam, I have to ask these things.
Come in here.

He brings me inside the counter and sits me down,
takes down all the details I know and says they'll be going
up to the Mater to interview James. He'll have to file a
complaint, he says.

I can't see it myself. If I know James, he'll want to take
his hiding and then have nothing to do with it any more.
The problem is, this Guard tells me, if he doesn't stand
up to these bullies now there'll probably be more of the
same in store for him.

I'm rightly depressed when I get out of there.

I know we've hardly any groceries in the house and
that I should do a bit of shopping but I'm abruptly so
tired that I have to go straight home. I don't even have
the energy to pull out the bed-settee, so I lie down on
the seat of it without even taking off my shoes. I barely
have enough energy to reset the alarm clock for lunch-
time.

But, wouldn't you know it, immediately I lie down,
my brain revs up again, not least because I can see the
two coffee cups on the draining board, the ones Ken and
I used this morning.

At present I'm amazed to find I don't feel anything
about Ken and me breaking up. I suppose that'll come
later. I'm not looking forward to telling him. Mind you
it was hardly *Romeo and Juliet*, now, was it? Our so-called
romance hadn't got off the ground.

I'm probably immune to love at this stage. All the
stores have been used up on James.

Thank God I didn't see the beating because I've seen
enough of them in my time. When they're talking on the
radio about women getting hammered by their husbands
or boyfriends and I hear them asking, Why doesn't she
just leave? it's clear to me they've never been in the

situation. It's too close to home, at any rate. Where was our Mammy to go? And that was only her. What about the rest of us?

It used to kill me, though, it really used to. Seeing her cover her head as best she could while she took it used to make me so angry with her.

Having got a few cracks myself when I tried to intervene, I learned early on there was no point in trying to protect her. A lot of the time she'd be doped up and wouldn't co-operate anyway, so for me the best thing to do was just to get out of there as fast as possible. On more than one occasion, I walked the streets for hours, trying to keep out of sight of any of the authorities, until I reckoned she and whoever it was had passed out. It was easier in the day-time but I developed great coping skills even for after dark.

It became a lot more difficult after James was born because I had to take him with me, but thank God that dilemma occurred in a serous way only once or twice during the couple of months he and Mammy were on this earth together. The crunch on those occasions came when we were sneaking back in and I was terrified he'd make a noise. He was a great little baby, though, as I've told you, hardly ever cried.

My strategy spilled over into the next day. To keep the nosy-parkers at bay I'd make sure that I – and for those couple of occasions during the last months, James and I – would be seen parading around, him well dressed, washed and brushed, both of us cheerful and happy and normal.

Pathetic, I suppose, but it worked.

When I finally nodded off that morning after visiting that hospital, my sleep was boiling with scary snatches of dreams. Incredibly vivid. Giant woodworms with heads like gargoyles slithering towards me. Or I was on a bus and fellas carrying hammers were stalking the aisle, looking for me. Then I was on *Winning Streak*, spinning the wheel, everyone was cheering, but the wheel suddenly turned into a gallows. Then, thank God, the alarm went off, as loud as the Last Day trumpet and I shot up into a sitting position, not having the faintest clue where I was, heart thumping like a kango hammer. For the first few seconds, Mike Murphy was still standing in front of me with his eyes twinkling at me through his dirty hangman's hood . . .

Never did oul' Reddy's wallpaper look so lovely.

I hauled myself to my feet, washed, then changed my clothes and dosed myself with the strongest coffee I could stomach before I set off again for the hospital. I didn't know what I was going to tell James. I'd promised him I was going to sort things out. Hadn't got very far, had I? Only drawn the cops on him. For which he would not thank me. My calf muscles felt like anchors as I dragged myself up Eccles Street.

When I got as far as the steps up to the front door of the Mater, I still had my head down, concentrating on coming up with something positive to say to James. Visiting hour was still five minutes away, so there were a lot of people milling around.

Hello, Angela!

This is so unexpected, I jump. I look up – and who's standing there right in front of me only Ken Sheils. He's carrying a bunch of flowers. Real florist's ones, an arrangement. They're for you, he says, I reckon you could do with a bit of cheering up. Everyone's looking, he has this silly grin on his face, and I feel myself starting to go beetroot. Talk about reversing roles.

How am I supposed to react? My brain won't work. Thanks, I go, taking the flowers. Thanks a lot, that was very good of you. Then, challenging, Are you coming in to see James with me?

Of course. If you want me to, that is.

I can see that in his own mind he's being very brave, very open-minded. Or am I being a cow? I'm too tired to care so I take it at face value. That'd be nice, I go, it'll give James someone different to talk to.

They open the door then and everybody rushes in. Like we're racing each other for the best seats at a concert or something – maybe they don't have enough chairs for visitors in the Mater hospital. Ken and I wait until the rush dies down. I feel calm anyhow, that's a blessing. I'm wavering . . . The flowers are gorgeous.

It crosses my mind that when I get home, maybe I should do Love Like Hate Adore Kiss Court Marry with our names. Childish but so is throwing apple peel over your shoulder. So is hopping three times on one leg around the Metal Man in Tramore. (Mammy did that umpteen times to know a husband within the year. Hah!) We all perform these little rituals.

The way he acts after the introductions, it seems James couldn't care less who Ken is, but I know differently and in my new mood of honesty I'm not letting him away with it. You've never met any of my friends before, James, have you? Except Patsy, of course.

No, he mutters. He glances at the flowers I'm carrying. Ken gave me these, I go, aren't they lovely? I didn't bring you in anything, I didn't know what you wanted.

Actually I had brought something, the photographs of Mammy that Adeline gave me, but even though Ken was in on this I didn't think it would be appropriate now for James and me to be looking at them together. It's all right, James says, I don't need anything. I'll be out of this kip in a day or two, anyway.

I ignore this. Ken's in business for himself, I say. Then

I turn to Ken. And of course, Ken, you already know that James is a courier.

I sit back and let them at it.

I must say, considering the circumstances, Ken is pretty good. He launches into the subject of motorbikes and James perks up immediately. I'm temporarily superfluous to requirements.

The ward is big — sixteen beds, three enormous windows at one end, south-facing. They'd opened the blinds and curtains fully so the sunshine is streaming in. With all the men's flowers and plants lined up on the windowsills — their lockers aren't big enough — the effect is bright and colourful. Thank God times have changed to the extent that you can now bring flowers in to men. I remember when no man would be caught dead near so much as a daisy.

I half tune in to the hum of talk from all the visitors. He said it was the size of a small grapefruit . . . Six injections, *six* . . . But sure it's all over now, thanks be to God . . . Twenty-seven stitches . . . It's hard to kill a bad thing . . . They gave it to me in a jar . . .

Et cetera.

It's so artifical, isn't it, all that? The patient trying to bridge the gap between being self-pitying and giving his visitors just enough of his pain and suffering to *earn* their sympathy. As for the poor old visitors, earnestly listening while trying desperately to think of what next to say that'll sound neutral enough not to draw on themselves yet another saga of blood or pus but that won't be taken as callous.

It's very warm and this, added to the low talk, is almost hypnotic, I find myself fighting drowsiness. To keep myself awake, I try to pay attention to the motorbike chat beside me. Greek to me, of course, but I sit up straighter, concentrate. Engine ccs. Carburettors.

Differentials. It strikes me then that what's happening here is a bit like don't mention the war.

I wait for a pause. Have the Guards been in? I've reported the assault and I've also been on to the solicitor.

Do you want me to leave? Ken half stands to go. I'm sure you'd like to discuss this in private.

It's up to you, I say. I don't mind if you stay. I turn to James. Ken knows all about everything. I've told him the lot.

I can see neither of them is happy with this but frankly, my dear, I don't give a damn.

What's going to happen? James asks uneasily.

They'll come in to interview you, I say, and then it's up to them.

Silence. Ken gives a little cough. Then, Did you ever see one of those Honda Gold Wings, James, he goes, I wouldn't call them motorbikes at all, they're just armchairs with wheels.

So be it, I think, and I tune out.

A little bit later, Ken does leave. I walk him down to the door of the ward. In the corridor outside, I enrol him to drive me again to Birr. No point in beating around the bush, I tell him baldly the reason why and he agrees immediately. James was to be released from hospital on the Monday, provided the results of one last blood test were OK, so Ken and I make an arrangement to go down to Birr on the afternoon of the Saturday beforehand. That way, neither of us would miss work.

Now you might think I was being ruthless, considering this was the guy who only this morning I was never going to see again. Well, you'd be dead right. I was being ruthless. Wouldn't you be? I would have used my granny if I had one.

Anyway, I'm thinking, maybe I shouldn't be too hasty about breaking up – it was quite possible he'd thought things over and had decided his attitude that morning had been unfair. It's highly likely that's why he came to the hospital – at least I should give him the benefit of the doubt. And as I told you, out there on those steps, I started to go soft . . .

By Friday James looked to be well on the mend. Physically, at least, even though the bruising on his face was still as bright as a rainbow.

He seemed down in himself, though, more than I'd seen him since the day he was first brought in. Everything in the hospital was now poxy. The food, the nurses, his fellow patients. The telly, which was mounted too high on the wall at the end of the ward and was turned at the wrong angle to him. Poxy. All of it.

Had I brought the Jaffa cakes? He loves Jaffa cakes, it was all he'd asked for all week.

I give the new packet to him. He tears it open immediately and lays into them. You'll get spots, I go, all that chocolate isn't good for you.

Who effin' cares? He stuffs another one into his mouth.

I sit down. What's new? I ask him, not that I expected any answer – conversation with James is still like pulling hens' teeth. And you may well ask about my good intentions in the matter of instituting a new era of open communication between us. I haven't quite lost sight of that, I'll get back to it soon. It's just too tiring at the moment.

I learn why everything is so poxy all of a sudden. He stops eating long enough to tell me. The Guards have been back in to him with photographs of people they want to eliminate from their inquiries about assaulting him. He hadn't recognized any of them. Worse than that, he's received an anonymous letter.

Show it to me, I say. He looks around the ward before opening his locker.

The letter is on lined blue notepaper, the small size.

Dear Scumbag, That's only a taste you got, you little shit. Get the hell out of this country, and take that lily-livered judge with you, the one who freed you to walk on the earth with decent people. Get out now or it'll be the worse for you and your sister. And next time it won't be just a beating. And don't even think of bringing the police into this. We'll know if you do.

Handwriting slanted heavily backwards. I know that trick, that's to disguise it. It's unsigned, of course.

Did you show this to the police? I ask James. He shakes his head. He's into the Jaffa cakes again but I can see by his eyes that he's terrified. To give me time to think, I pretend to be examining the envelope. This letter has been addressed to him in the correct ward.

They say they'll know if I tell the Guards, and now they'll think I showed it to them, he says. I got that letter before they came in.

As if I haven't made the connection myself. If he is being watched, certain assumptions will have been made. They won't think anything of the sort, I go, but I'm not as confident as I hope I sound. You can't let them get to you like this. Did you agree to file a complaint about the assault?

Yeah, I did – they said I can come to the station when I get out of here. But I can't now – what about that letter? He's so distressed, crumbs from the Jaffa cake he's holding are raining all over the bed.

All right, all right, calm down. I look around the ward. Who could possibly be watching him? Most of the men in the other beds are elderly, no one is looking over at us, they all seem normally preoccupied with their own families and friends.

It's hardly the staff of the hospital. Someone's visitor?

I make myself sound authoritative: The first thing you do is give this to the police, I'll give it to them if you won't.

Don't, don't, he goes, he looks so frightened that my heart goes out to him. All right, I say, but I'm keeping it.

I put the letter in my handbag. These things are poison, James, they're sent to frighten people. You're to put it out of your mind. You're perfectly safe here. You don't think they're going to come in here to your hospital bed, do you?

How did they know which ward I was in?

I wish he hadn't asked that question. I don't know, James, I say. But you're definitely safe here. And by Monday you'll be home and we'll have sorted something out. Patrice Murphy will help. Someone will help, I promise you.

That's when he starts to spew.

I, Angela, don't have the first idea about what it's like out there, I'm so naïve, I still think that most people are all right, and that might be true for people of my generation, but James and his friends really know the score. Out on the streets, you only have to look at someone in the wrong way, or he can think you look at him the wrong way, just one wrong look and you get a dunt and maybe you end up with a black eye . . . And then he gets his friends and comes back after you, and you and your friends find yourselves in a major fight that you never asked for. Sometimes they come at you with knives . . .

He's leaning over towards me now, unloading right into my face, so worked up I believe that if he didn't have a plaster on his arm he'd probably have grabbed my throat. I, Angela, don't have the first clue what's going on, what it's really like. I'm still living in a dream world,

I still think Dublin's all right because no one attacks women for no reason. Like they attack fellas for no reason.

I try to say something but he won't be stopped.

Shut up, shut up, you don't know. It's like effin' Beirut out there. You can't walk down a street any more with any of your friends, you can't have a drink in a pub, and it's not only at night, it can be in the middle of the day, you don't have to do anything to them, you only have to be minding your own business. It's all right for women, they don't get the hassle—

I stand up. James, James, I go, stop, please. Stop this . . . I keep my voice low but I can see that we're beginning to attract curious glances from some of the other patients and their visitors.

He falls back on his pillows and the tears start to roll out of his eyes. That's the problem, he goes. You don't believe me, nobody believes me, nobody knows what it's like. But ask any of my friends, ask any fella at all, they know . . .

He cops himself on, looks around in case anyone's noticed. He catches a couple of looks and puts his good arm over his eyes. He is a person in despair.

It's all right, James, I whisper. Nobody really heard anything.

Yeah, yeah, right, he goes, and he turns his head away from me. You just don't have a bleedin' clue.

How can I answer him? Give him some reassurance? He's wrong to think I don't know what goes on on the streets, I do. But he's shocked me, to tell you the truth. In my ignorance, I'd thought kids like him were street-wise – that what goes on in Dublin was no problem to them. I'd bought the toughie line they all peddled.

I'd worried about him every time he went out, of course – you're seeing the knife going in, or their teeth being knocked out, you can hear the sound of steel-tips breaking cheekbones.

But it's not possible to live with the octane of that a hundred per cent of the time – you'd go mad – so you soften it up and spread it out until the worry becomes flat and vague, with no specific highlights. It's like a permanent smell. You tell yourself you can't be at their sides twenty-four hours a day and anyway they're of age, they're adults, and you can't keep them inside as though they're still babies. So you hope, guiltily, that if it has to happen, it'll happen to someone else's and not to yours and after a time you get used to the slightly fearful way we all live now.

The problem is that the serious fear constantly regenerates itself. You're always only a moment, a telephone call away from bad news. (A note pushed under your door!) Every time it happens to any of them, he's yours. I see a newspaper photograph of some kid's bashed-in face in a hospital bed and my imagination instantly substitutes James's.

I'd managed to calm him down before I left but I was still in two minds whether or not to go to the police about that letter. I was certainly going to show it to Patrice Murphy and get his advice. Although the sum total of his advice in this matter so far – go to the police – hadn't achieved anything great, had it? Except to put even more wind up poor James.

And on that score, it was a bit of a worry to me that he hadn't been able to recognize anyone in the photographs they had brought in to him. That meant that the lowlifes who beat him up were not any of the usual crowd of bully boys the police would know. Amateurs are probably far more dangerous.

Twenty-Seven

Do you remember when Jane Eyre says, 'Reader, I married him'? That's not exactly what I have to tell you but it's just as dramatic.

Reader, I found him. My father.

Talk about lucky. I couldn't believe how easy it was in the end – maybe I should have done it years ago. (But then again maybe not. I wasn't ready, probably. Anyway, I didn't need him as urgently.)

But wait until you hear!

With the prospect of the trip you can imagine how difficult I found it to keep my patience with the Samanthas and the balsamic-vinegar brigade that Saturday morning. Although I say so myself, I was brilliant – mind you, I had to be, with all the problems facing us I certainly didn't want to lose *that* job.

And then I had to rush across the city to see James. He was morose enough but at least he was calmer and I could see he was pleased I'd come, although perish the thought he should say so.

He wasn't having very many visitors. To put it bluntly he wasn't having any visitors except me and one of his pals, Ferdia, the boy who works for his father's computer business and who has a car. He came in once.

One for the books. Here was I thinking this chap was

to be avoided because of loose morals – you'll remember he was the one who lent his car to James and Rosemary Madden so they could mess in it outside the club that first night they clicked – and here was he the one who comes up trumps when James needed a pal.

To make things more obvious, as though to underline how everyone else had headed for the hills, Ferdia had signed the plaster cast. The slagging you write on casts is meant to be cheery and jokey but that lonely name, one boat in an empty sea, nearly made me cry. I had thought of offering to sign it myself too, to take the bare look off it, but then realized this might be rubbing it in too much.

James needed cheering up. So I adopt my most businesslike-yet-optimistic voice. I tell him why I'm in such a rush and can't stay long.

He's indifferent, of course, couldn't care less if I'm going to Timbuktu.

Would it not be nice if we had a father in our lives? Not to live with or anything, just in the background.

I couldn't be arsed.

I ignore the vulgarity. Well, I'd like it, I say, wish me luck.

Good luck.

Like I told you. Conversation with him isn't easy.

It was cloudy, threatening rain, when Ken and I set off for Birr that afternoon. Right up to the time we hit the Naas dual carriageway I was continuing to toy with the idea of going straight to Adeline to ask her what she knew of my father. By the time we were passing Rathcoole, though, I'd decided to hold her in reserve. I wanted this to be as hassle-free as possible. (I guess I was pussyfooting a bit – not sure quite how much I could take. Adeline is nothing if not blunt.)

The Guard's name turned out to be Mick Flanagan. He wasn't at the station when we got there but I described him and we were directed by one of the other Guards out to his house. We were told to look out for a dormer bungalow with a field of cabbages to one side of it about three miles outside the town on the main Tullamore Road.

When we get there, I'm nervous, naturally, but he couldn't have been nicer. He comes to the door himself, what can I do for you? Then he recognizes me. Well, hello again.

I tell him immediately why we're here, no point in beating around the bush.

Well, well, well, he goes. Then, unexpectedly, he laughs. He's not wearing a jacket, only a stripy blue and white shirt, frayed around the buttonholes – and when he laughs heartily like this, he wheezes like a heavy smoker. It occurs to me that at his age he should be a sergeant at least. Maybe he's just too easy-going.

Come in for a cup of tea, he goes, wiping his eyes and shaking his head as if he's just heard some secret joke. I'm all by myself, Saturdays are very busy around here, the missus and the daughters are off on the fast track as usual, leaving me to fend for myself. Come in.

I'm reluctant, you know how it is, but I don't want to be rude. So we go in. It's a nice, snug house, I'd love it for James and me. Plenty of windows too, all looking out at the garden which wraps around the whole outside. I'd have to change the décor, though, too many patterns in the wallpapers and carpets and so forth. I like plain.

We follow him into the kitchen. More patterns – on the tiles, lino, cushions and antimacassars, on the millions of gewgaws on every surface. The wife seems to be into patchwork. There are two patchwork tea-cosies on one of the windowsills and a patchwork cloth on the table.

You know, I'm not surprised to see you, I was half expecting you back, Flanagan says as he's plugging in the kettle. I did warn you that Adeline wouldn't have been all that helpful. Would I be right now?

I don't want to let Adeline down – after all, she is my relation. She was grand, I go, she wasn't expecting us, she was out in the garden and I think we caught her on the hop.

His belly rolls jiggle as he laughs again. Oh dear, he goes. He moves a tea towel off the rail of the solid fuel cooker and settles his big behind against it. He folds his arms across his chest. Don't get me wrong now, he goes, we're all fond of her. We're thin on the ground for gentry around here – except for the castle, of course.

Can you help me? I say. I don't want this to take up too much time, although he seems to have centuries of it at his disposal.

He gets serious. I can help you all right, but I'm not sure it would be right just to give you a name straight off. Aren't there procedures that have to be gone through in cases like this?

Yes, I go. And I wouldn't expect you to do anything illegal. But there'd be no law against you telling me what you remember about my dead mother, surely? And that could include who she hung around with before she left here for Dublin. Her pals.

I was handing it to him on a plate. I'd thought it out very carefully because I knew only too well about the formal procedures that you have to go through to trace your parents in, like, adoption situations, where they have to agree to be traced. But this wasn't an adoption situation.

M-mmm, he goes. He doesn't know what he's in for, does he? Then he laughs again at that secret joke.

This laughing is beginning to worry me. What's so funny? Before I can ask, Mick Flanagan has turned towards Ken. Is this your husband?

No, I say quickly, before Ken gets embarrassed. This is Ken Sheils, he's a friend.

And so, Ken, what do you think of this? Flanagan settles himself, crosses his arms over his chest again. Do you not think that sometimes it might be better to let sleeping dogs lie?

I believe Angela knows what's best for her, Ken says quietly.

Your man drops the laughing policeman personality and gives me one of those looks I recognized at our first meeting. He may be jolly but he's nobody's fool.

Just then the kettle boils and he occupies himself making the pot of tea. How come you haven't been down here before, Miss Devine? he asks. His back is to me but I get the weird feeling he can still see me.

That's a question I can't answer, I say truthfully. I did dicky with the idea but I just never got around to it.

I hesitate, he isn't moving. His back is listening hard. I feel he needs me to say more. So I say, Maybe I was afraid of what I'd find out.

He turns quickly to face Ken and me, he's stirring the tea in the pot, round and round, round and round. And how sure are you that your father comes from these parts? The Devines had money, they were a family who went away on their holidays every year. Your mother could have hooked up with a Connemara man, or even a Dub.

I stare at him. Is he going to help me or not? She could have, I say as steadily as I can, and of course I don't know for sure he's from here. I'm starting from here, that's all, it seems to me to be the logical place to begin looking.

Whatever I've said, it seems to be the correct response. He relaxes, brings the teapot over to the table, where there are already cups — patterned, of course —

hanging from a mug tree. His tone changes, he's formal now. If I tell you where to go, he says, I'd appreciate it if you wouldn't say where you got the information. He sits down, looks off into space. It wouldn't be long before he'd find out who sent you anyway, he says, almost to himself. Then, looking me straight in the eye, But so long as you don't confirm it and I don't confirm it, there'll be no real harm done. All right?

Ken and I look at one another. I agree to keep my mouth shut. The Guard pours the tea into three mugs.

I get a cold shiver – as kids we used to say this meant someone has just walked over your grave. I don't think until that moment I had fully realized what I was doing. I had come to Birr instinctively, like a lemming. Now here I was on the very edge of the cliff. Who was it said, don't wish for something you don't really want? Suppose my father turned out to be a criminal? Was that why the Guard found this so amusing?

The palaver with the tea is taking centuries. Pouring milk from a carton into a milk jug, lifting the lid off the sugar bowl to see if there's enough in it. I'm ready to scream.

Right, he says eventually, heaping sugar into his own mug. Derrybride, he goes, it's just beyond Tullamore, you can't miss it. And you're looking for the only detached house in the village. If he's not there, his office is in the next village, he sometimes works on Saturdays, you can't miss that either. It's on the main street. Big place, double-fronted.

And the name? My heart is thumping a Lambeg tattoo.

His eyes sharpen up. Pius Crawford, he says.

Pause.

Then, The name means nothing to you?

I shake my head. I find it an odd question.

Ken puts a hand on my arm. Are you all right, Angela?

I don't blame him. I must look like a corpse. Pius Crawford. My name should be Angela Crawford. I swallow hard. Why would the name mean something to me? I ask this Guard.

Mr Crawford's well known around the midlands, he goes. He's — you're sure you haven't come across the name?

I shake my head. Well, he goes, shall we say Mr Crawford's a bit of a — what do you call it? A zealot, that's it. He's full of zeal when it comes to certain things.

Like what things?

You're familiar, I suppose, with organizations such as No Divorce?

Yes.

Mr Crawford and his wife are founder members of an organization called Catholic Rights. It's a small group, but its views would be broadly similar to those espoused by No Divorce, Youth Defence, groups of that nature. Only more so. In fact, I've heard it said that compared to Catholic Rights, all of those other groups look like Rastafarians.

It's now clear why he had been laughing. I'm not laughing.

Apparently, Pius Crawford, who is an auctioneer by profession and who has seven children, leads rosary rallies outside cinemas where they're showing anything with any sex in it. And as for the Irish Big Three, contraception, divorce, abortion, Pius and his mates, mostly women, have been known to chain themselves to the railings of churches to make their point. He also organizes petitions against everything from the Stay Safe Programme for school kids, to altar girls to women's shelters.

Women's shelters? I'm beginning to get my voice back.

Mick Flanagan raises an eyebrow. They believe these

shelters are anti-family. He's watching me hard. I'm surprised you haven't heard of him, even up in Dublin.

Look, he says carefully, now that you know what you're up against . . . He hesitates. And, to be fair, what poor old Pius'd be up against if you brought this out into the open. Maybe it would be simpler to forget about approaching him. If you change your mind, I promise I won't breathe a word to anyone about your visit.

This kills me. The hell with Pius Crawford's problems. What about our problems? I wasn't going to be diverted. I could see the irony, enigma, difficulty, all the rest of it, I simply wasn't going to be diverted. I had to keep my mind focused. James needs help. Plain as that.

I stare at Guard Flanagan. How do you know it's him?

He sits back in his chair as much as his bulk allows. The whole town knew it at the time, he says quietly. In fact the whole town was agog, I hope you won't take offence at this, Miss Devine, but around here the story was better than *Dallas*. The Crawfords were, are, big farmers and they and your grandparents were the local nobs. Friendly with each other too, in kind of a distant way. This was before ecumenism – he says this gently, without a hint of sarcasm.

Her family kicked her out because he was a Catholic, is that it? I was ready to fire up on her behalf.

Your grandparents weren't the worst, he says. They were upset, of course, very upset.

He leans forward again. Here, he goes, you haven't touched your tea. Have a hot drop. He pours – the sound in the still kitchen is as loud as Niagara Falls – then sits back again. Sure God love them, all this happened more than thirty years ago—

Thirty-six.

If you say so. More sugar? Milk? Would you like a biscuit or a scone?

Ken and I both refuse anything to eat. I'm having difficulty raising the tea to my mouth, the cup knocks against my teeth. Ken notices. Reacts.

I put down my cup. Why was the whole town agog?

Not to put a tooth in it, the Guard says, looking at me with those clever eyes, it wasn't only the situation itself. Your poor mother didn't seem to care who knew or what anyone thought.

He fills us in on what happened, as clearly as he can remember. Even more than my grandparents, Crawford's family went into a complete tailspin when they heard the big news. If I tell you, he says, that Pius Crawford has two brothers named Bonaventure and Canice and a sister named Annunciata you might get the picture. Pius was a second son and as you know, second sons in farming families were usually destined for the seminary. So when this happened, no seminary. And in a family like that . . .

He shrugs.

The Crawfords wanted the whole thing hushed up, they wanted my mother to be sent away to England where she could have the child — me! — secretly adopted.

Even if you were to leave me out of this altogether, I'd be finding this story extraordinary — we were talking the seventies here. I'd thought those kinds of attitudes went out with the Eucharistic Congress.

Mammy wouldn't be sent away, however. Both families and the clergy on both sides tried to persuade her but she believed that Pius Crawford and she truly loved one another. She became hysterical — the Guard picks his words delicately here but it's not difficult to read between the lines — and although her own parents tried everything they could think of to restrain her, she haunted the Crawfords' house for weeks on end at all hours of the day and night, calling out and screaming that she'd kill herself if Pius didn't come out to her. (Inside the house, the Crawfords, presumably, were beating him with rosary beads . . .) He never came out.

Flanagan is fuzzy about how she left Birr. All I know about that, he goes, is that one morning it was all over the town that Rose Devine had vanished. There were rumours, of course, that she'd gone to the States, to England, she'd jumped into the river. Well, I knew she'd jumped into no river, a colleague of mine who'd known her here but who had been transferred to Portlaoise definitely saw her getting a lift from a car going towards Dublin just outside Abbeyleix. God love the Devines, he shakes his big head, but it wasn't long before the next nine days' wonder came along and the town switched its attention away from poor Rose.

I know he's watching for my reaction. I feel not in the least emotional. As cold as the Arctic Ocean – isn't that odd?

Don't think badly of her, he says slowly. She was very young. I'd often wondered what happened to her afterwards, but when I saw your picture and your name in the paper . . .

What picture? What paper?

It was in one of the tabloids, the *Star*, maybe, or the *Irish Sun*. You didn't see it?

I shake my head. Then I remember the day I opened the door and the flash went off in my face. I hadn't looked at any of those papers. Now I understand how word had got around so fast right at the very beginning. It wasn't only those reports in the *Herald*.

For a couple of minutes, we're all three of us sitting there like the three blind mice. It had been almost too easy. An anticlimax, if you can believe that.

You see, deep in my heart I hadn't expected to get the name first go. Maybe it's because I'm a city woman, and hadn't fully realized how closely people live in each other's pockets in the rest of Ireland.

This is balderdash. I'm making excuses for myself. How many times have I been astounded at the extent to which Dublin itself is a village?

It's as clear as morning that if I'd come here ten years ago, fifteen years ago when I should have, I would have saved myself years of wishing and wondering. So why didn't I come here before? Because I knew, probably subconsciously, that I'd be afraid.

I was dead right. I am afraid. My phantom dad was grand and now here I've ruined him.

I have to face the fact that this sudden drive to find my father was just that, a *drive* to find him because I was feeling helpless. Unable properly to help James.

Even on the way down here I'd been seeing this Guard saying something like, Oh, yes, we never saw him after he went off that time to join the RAF. Broken-hearted he was. (For the RAF substitute the Foreign Legion. Or the Missions.) And then Ken would drive me to Adeline, and she'd rack her brains and give me a bit more information. Yes, we always wondered, he never came back, you know, not even for a visit . . .

I could continue then on my safe quest, writing to the Ministry of War, or the French Foreign Office or whoever I had to write to. And at the end of it, somewhere Out There in the woolly future, my dad, all square-jawed and clean-cut, was going to be waiting for his little girl, Kenneth More in *Reach for the Sky*. Rueful about his single indiscretion but delighted now to be offered this golden opportunity to make amends.

Well, the joke was surely on me – in more ways than one. I wanted clean-cut? I sure got clean-cut. And now I had to go to confront it.

I can't get over how much you're the image of your mother, the Guard says into the silence.

I stand up suddenly. Thanks, Guard, I say, I really appreciate it.

Take your time about this, he lumbers to his feet. Crawford's not going to go away, he'll still be here tomorrow and next week – next year. Think carefully about what you're at. He drops his eyes, almost shyly. Remember, he goes, he probably loved her as much as she loved him. Things were handled differently, those days.

This guy's likeable, But I don't want to hear any more. Not just now.

We leave and get into the van. Sam, who normally gives me a lick when he meets me, even after a short absence, stays well away. Dogs have a sixth sense, or so they say.

Drive quickly, I say to Ken.

He obeys without argument. Derrybride? he asks. I tell him yes and he starts the van and heads it in the Tullamore direction. I think in some ways he's as stunned as me.

Although he couldn't be. No one could be. From the beginning of the universe, no one ever has been as stunned as me. And still, for some reason I can't explain, I have to face it. Even if my father is Genghis Khan.

So much for driving quickly. Once again we hit the dreaded loose chippings and we're crawling at about ten miles an hour. I'm so tense I think I'm going to go into orbit. I'm drumming. All we need now is a lorry to come along and start beeping at us. You'll see some Angela Devine then so you will . . .

Why did you think that Guard never got promotion? I ask Ken, when we're a few minutes into the journey. He looks sideways at me. What do you mean?

Don't you find that irritating? When someone says, What do you mean?, when you've just said what you mean. I hold on to my temper. He sounds and acts too intelligent to be only a Guard, I say. At his age he should be at least a sergeant.

Who knows? says Ken, nodding his head like a wise old man. Maybe he stepped on the wrong toes. This is a small town.

At least I think that's what he said. I wasn't listening. I couldn't care less about Mick Flanagan and whether he made commissioner.

What am I going to say to this Pius Crawford?

✦ Twenty-Eight ✦

I hope you don't mind my asking, Ken breaks the silence between us as we're driving along, but are you and James all right for money?

That brings me up short, I can tell you. I hope I'm not giving off poverty vibes. We're grand, I go, thanks.

We weren't grand at all. By this time, you see, not only was my poor scratch-card hoard disappearing fast, but our budget was beginning to miss the few bob from the kissogram gigs. We'd be all right in the short term but it was the long term that worried me. The pay in the cleaning job was miserable, plus, my future in PA System was looking iffy to say the least. With Patsy preoccupied elsewhere – and she's the one who organizes the business side of our engagements – not to speak of her recent attitude to me, I wasn't all that hopeful we'd survive. We had no gig the following morning. As a matter of fact, I hadn't heard from her at all since that disastrous scene in the café.

Added to which, because of his injuries, James was going to be off work for the foreseeable future so he was not going to be able to take care of his monthly loan payment on his bike.

You might well ask why I didn't break into the money I had saved in the post office. After all, there was nearly three thousand there.

I don't know if you'll understand this but I felt if I broke up the wholeness of that money we'd be lost. In a way, I didn't see the total sum represented by those bonds and certs as real money, not like the pounds and coins you'd have in your purse. When I thought about it I saw the stash as a tight little ball, a perfect entity in itself. Sacred. Don't laugh now, but the nearest analogy I can give you is that this is the way I used to see the Holy Trinity when I was a child, the Three Persons all wound in together in a ball, so tightly packed you didn't know which Person's Arms and Legs and Feet fitted which Head.

The money was just as indivisible. It was an all or nothing wholeness – to be used for a house or a major operation. Or bail. But not for rent or bread.

We really will be fine, I say again.

You'd ask if you needed a dig-out?

(Never in a million years.)

You're very good, I go.

Right at this moment, anyway, I couldn't give a sugar about money. I'm like a hen on a hot griddle. We're still crawling. How much further, do you think? I try not to sound like a harpy.

We should be there in less than five minutes, Ken says.

I knew a Pius in the flats when I was young, and a bigger creep you never met. A flasher by the age of fourteen. (Could have given oul' Mooney, King of the Flashers, a run for his money.) I have this theory that if you've hated someone when you were a child, everyone you meet with the same name afterwards is automatically suspect. They really have to be honeys to get over the handicap of the name. I sure hope this particular Pius is the one who's going to disprove my thesis. I am *not* hopeful.

Ken slows down even more as we meet a tractor coming the other way on the road. It's another brilliant day, really hot and bright, and the dust this tractor is throwing up along with the loose chippings is quite a cloud. After we get past safely, Ken looks over at me, his lips are twisted in a grin against himself. Bet you thought I was going to hit him, didn't you?

I smile back. It breaks the tension a bit, but not much.

I can see you're very nervous, Ken goes, are you sure you want to go through with this? We can come back another day – I don't mind driving you, I really don't. You've a terrible lot on your plate at the moment.

I hadn't even told him about the letter.

We're here now, I say back. We might as well get it over with. I just want to see him, I'm not looking for any great confrontation.

Have you planned out how you're going to introduce yourself? he goes.

I hadn't. I tell him now that I'm just going to play it by ear. But don't worry, I say to him, you can drop me off, you needn't be involved in the slightest. I'm thinking to myself, I hope to God he's here, I couldn't bear another drive to his office. Then I'm thinking in the same second, Please, God, don't let him be here, don't let him be anywhere!

I want to be involved, Ken goes, please, Angela, I want to be. He puts his hand on my knee.

Just in time, I stop myself from jumping away. That wouldn't be fair. But I don't want his hand there, it feels enormous. Oppressive. The best I can manage without shoving it off is to put my own hand over it and to give it a squeeze. Thanks, I go. You're very good.

I hate myself for this. What a hypocrite. Only a few days ago I enjoyed the feeling of that hand. But now there's a sort of presumption about it I can't stand. Like, we've done it so we're intimates.

But I can't take my hand away without making it seem like a big deal. The crux is that I think he's the hypocrite. He wants to be involved in this – in me – and yet he can't really bring himself fully to be on James's side. Flowers and hospital visits can't paper over those cracks.

I guess I'm not a passionate person. Maybe where sex is concerned it's just that I haven't had the practice – a twenty-year gap is quite a gap.

On the other hand, my reaction mightn't have anything to do with sex or passion. It's more likely to be one of my character flaws rearing its ugly head again. I don't know what it is about me, any time anyone expects me to do something or to be something, I instantly want to do and be the exact opposite.

Oh, stop with the psychoanalysis again, Angela! Do something.

Both our hands are still lying there on my leg, like a pair of heavy puddings. I cross my legs so he's forced to take his away, but not before I squeeze his a second time to take the harm out of it.

We come to Derrybride – petrol pump, Marian shrine, pub and six terraced cottages, festooned with hanging baskets, a grassy triangle edged with flowers on one side of the crossroads. A big rock with lettering on it, Tidy Towns Special Commendation. One big house, detached.

We find we can't pull up directly outside the detached house because there are too many cars parked along the kerb so we pass it and park in the first space we can find, thirty or forty yards further on, past the crossroads.

I roll down the van window, look back at my father's house. It's long and low, a ranch-style bungalow set well back on a large site bounded by a low hedge, which is tidy to within an inch of its life. Rosebeds all along the short driveway, kid's mountain bike lying in the middle of the lawn beside — wouldn't you know it — a small grotto made of real rocks. I think this one is Our Lady of Lourdes, but I've forgotten which of the Our Ladys has her hands held out and which has them folded. Six arches running all along the front of the house, two cars parked in a tarmacadamed area to the side. The front door is open.

When Ken turns off the engine I can hear laughing and talk. It's coming from the back garden of the house. They must be having a party.

It's then I get the first inkling of how to do this. My father is an auctioneer. That's going to be the key — no pun intended, ha, ha! — to how I can manage to approach him so his family won't get suspicious. I'm thinking of the seven children here, I wouldn't want to upset them.

I go very calm. There's never a happy medium with me, is there? It's either panic or ice.

Still time to leave, Ken says quietly. They seem to have visitors.

There'll never be a perfect time, I say back to him. Anyway, we're here.

Are you sure you don't want me to come in with you?

No thanks, I go, this is something I have to do by myself. I give his hand a squeeze, a heartfelt one this time because he is genuinely being an all-round good egg. I get out.

As I walk towards the house, the laughing and the buzz of conversation gets louder. It seems to be quite a party. I see a young child, maybe three years old, run through the open front doorway and out into the garden. The child is gorgeous, blondie curls, dressed in a lovely pair of bright pink dungarees. Benetton? Before she can get too far, a woman in a yellow summer dress appears, catches her up in both her arms, and carries her back inside. On the way back in she nuzzles the child's tummy and says something which makes the child giggle. Like wind chimes. I can just imagine what she said – C'mere to me, you little rascal. Something like that. They look like a pair of happy squirrels.

I'm just at the gates now – wrought iron, wide open – and I hesitate. Was that my father's wife? If it is, she looks nice. The poor woman doesn't know what's going to hit her. My feet itch to run but I've come this far.

I go in and walk up the driveway.

It's cool along the front of the house, under the arches, the ground beneath them is flagged with stone. Niches on both sides of the front door – God almighty, I've only noticed now, two more shrines, statues of the Sacred Heart and St Martin of Porres! Through the doorway, I can see two women gossiping in a kitchen at the end of the hall. They're side by side with their backs leaned up against a kitchen counter, they've wine glasses in their hands.

One of them sees me and comes out – Hello? She's friendly, looks about fifty or so.

Could I have a word with Mr Crawford? He's the auctioneer? My voice sounds steady enough except I'm conscious of my Dublin accent. The woman doesn't act in the least surprised. Sure, she goes, come through. They're all in the back garden.

I wouldn't like to interrupt the party.

Not at all, she says back. You obviously don't know Pius! Saturday's normally a working day for him in any case but our Pius wouldn't be the one to turn away business on any day of the week, or at any time, day or night. She laughs.

In different circumstances I'd like this woman to be my friend. She has uncomplicated written all over her.

I hope *she*'s not the wife.

I've no choice but to follow her through the house. I

suppose it's because I know who Pius Crawford is and what he stands for that I can see nothing but religion everywhere. Mind you, you couldn't miss it, more pictures of Our Lady and the Sacred Heart, two Papal Blessings, another statue of St Joseph.

Isn't it funny but here I am under this incredible strain and I still have time to notice this kind of thing? I must be in a state of heightened awareness. I even register the kitchen. It's gorgeous. Like something you'd seen in *Hello!* where the owners have dedicated their lives to making a home for themselves and their lovely children. Peachy-coloured walls, a shiny red range, built-in units, honey pine presses, black and white tiles on the floor in a chequerboard pattern. A woman is rinsing dishes at the double sink while another is taking them from her and loading them into a large open dishwasher. Both these women, plus my guide's companion, smile at me as I pass through.

We go out through a set of French doors on to a patio. The garden is beyond.

It's a First Communion party. A little girl is racing around, veil flying out behind her. Like a lively seagull. She's playing football with two men. Her ankle-length crinolined dress is swaying like a bell, her tiny satin handbag dangles from her wrist, she hasn't taken off her lace gloves. But she has removed her shoes, her ankle socks are green with grass stains. In another part of the garden, a little boy, his white Communion suit already beyond redemption, is one of a swarm of children hanging upside down from a climbing frame.

Aren't they dotes? says the friendly woman, stopping for a moment on the patio and fondly indicating both children. The two of them are cousins and the two families combined for the celebration. Pius has by far the biggest garden of anyone in the family. Naturally. She laughs again. Ah, sure I shouldn't be giving out about him, he's not the worst.

I feel like Attila the Hun.

Please let me wait here by the door, I say, I don't want to disturb everyone.

All right, she says, I'll go and get him. What name shall I say?

Sheils, I go immediately.

I hadn't known I was going to say that.

She goes off towards the far side of the garden. Immaculate grass, not a weed in sight. A large glasshouse and a shed at one side, the play equipment – climbing frame, swings, sandpit – at the other, and at the far end, facing where I'm standing, a little summerhouse with a canvas awning, in the shade of which sits a group of six or seven elderly people, most of them wearing sun hats. A little table near them under a white beach umbrella supports two tiered cakes with white icing, nearly as big as wedding cakes.

The main tables have been set in a long row all along one side of the grass. Salmon, turkey, beef, salads, tarts, pies and about ten bowls of desserts. The meal is over, but people are still picking away at the remains. That was some spread – and as for the drink! The bar is as well stocked as a pub – there's even a steel barrel with a tap, beer or stout.

If I tell you there must have been forty or forty-five adults at this party, and maybe as many children, all scattered in loose little groups with loads of space in between, it might give you some idea of how big this garden is. I suppose space isn't at a premium in the country.

I watch my guide walk across the lawn and towards a group of adults who are sitting on deck chairs about twenty feet from the old people's summerhouse. She leans down and speaks to one of the men who has his back to me. He turns round and looks in my direction.

He's still too far away for me to see his features clearly. But I do see he has fair hair.

I'm so sensitized that, despite what the woman said, I can see he's pissed off at being interrupted at his party. His shoulders sort of slump in an irritated way. But he gets up, takes his jacket off where it's been hanging on the rail of his deck chair, comes towards me. A couple of people in his group who had turned round to look towards me too, turn back. My woman guide joins them.

Pius Crawford is shrugging on the jacket of his suit, he's refastening his tie as he starts towards me. He's quite big, about six feet. The hair, I see now, is receding a bit. He has freckles. I wasn't prepared for freckles. Freckles are friendly. I've always gone for freckles in men, as I think I've told you. Maybe this is why.

He's actually quite nice-looking – oh, God, I don't know how I feel about that. This man doesn't seem to be the whited sepulchre or creeping Jesus I was expecting. This man has 'Dad' written all over him. *Little House on the Prairie* dad. It'd be easier for me to be brave if he was repulsive. Or would it? He's arranging his face into a smile. He's holding out his hand. Good afternoon, Mrs Sheils, he says. What can I do for you? His hand is big, warm.

Could we talk somewhere? I say.

Sure, he goes. Come on into the house. We'll be able to find somewhere out of the mayhem, I hope.

He hasn't a clue. All he's seen is a prospective client.

We go in through the kitchen – the women smile at me again – and then into a little den place off the hall. Wood panelling on the walls, a real healthy Busy Lizzie blooming from a china bowl on the windowsill, family

pictures, including two wedding pictures and a graduation picture of a lovely-looking girl with long straight
blonde hair. An older couple – who could be my
grandparents! – yet another Papal Blessing. And on top
of his computer terminal is a statue of St Francis of Assisi.
I know this saint for sure because of the robes and the
little bird he has on his hand.

Pius Crawford closes the door. I work from here as
well as from the office, he says, we can be private here.
He points to a chair. Sit down, Mrs Sheils.

I sit. He does, too. He opens a big hardbound
notebook and turns the pages until he finds a blank one.
Now, he goes, taking a pen from a glass stand beside the
computer, then swivelling his chair to face me. You have
a property you want to sell, maybe? You're looking to
buy in our area?

No, I say. Look, Mr Crawford, this is nothing to do
with property.

Oh?

I've something to tell you that's not going to be easy
for either of us.

Now he sort of straightens in his chair. Oh? he goes
again. Still he hasn't copped.

My name isn't Sheils, I go, it's Devine. I know I'm fair
like you but people say I'm very like my mother.

Twenty-Nine

H e cops.
    The freckles on his face and on the places where
his hair had receded seem to get darker as the skin
underneath goes white. I'd feel sorry for him if I didn't
feel so peculiar myself. Kind of dizzy, as though there's
an electric wheel buzzing in my blood. Weirdly disappointed, too – what had I been expecting, us to fall into
each other's arms?

What's your first name? He's hoarse. Whispering. As
if I'm his worst nightmare, which I probably am.

Angela.

This seems to kill him altogether. He looks at the door
as if we're in some kind of hostage siege and he wants
someone to come and break it down to rescue him. Then
he looks back at me. It can't be, he says, I already have a
daughter called Angela. He glances at the girl in the
graduation picture.

I'm so uptight, I nearly laugh – you know, the way
you do at the most awkward times – but the situation is
too serious and I manage to control myself. Is that her? I
look at the picture too. He nods. His eyes are as huge as
those you see on those little desert creatures – what are
they? Meerkats? The ones that stand up straight on their

little hind legs, peering around for danger, that send sentries to the tops of tall trees?

What are the odds? (Although Angela isn't all that uncommon a name.) Well, you've two now, I say. You can call us Angela One and Angela Two.

He stares at me. Blinks. Stares at me again. Next thing I lose it and start to jabber, I hear myself rabbiting on like a madwoman. I'm sorry to disturb his Communion party, I'm not here to disrupt his life, yakkity yak . . .

I manage to roll to a halt by telling him why I needed to intrude on him just at the moment. Because we're in a bit of trouble at the moment, I go, James and I.

Silence from his side.

I'm beginning to feel a bit more in control. I really *don't* want to cause trouble, I say again—

James? Who's James? he's whispering.

James is not your problem, I tell him, he's my problem, but as I told you, we need help. I came here because you're my last resort. I've no other relatives. Well, none in Ireland anyway. Except Mammy's sister, Adeline. I met her last week. But I don't think she could help. Anyway, she's only an aunt.

His colour is beginning to come back. I see, he says slowly. He looks out through his window at his normality. I knew something like this would happen some day, he says, to no one in particular. Now that you're here, it's almost a relief, do you know that – er – Angela?

He doesn't look like it's a relief. He looks like he's standing on the parapet of a bridge and I'm behind him with a gun.

I say nothing, I've said enough. He glances outside, then around the room, like a forest animal who's smelt guns. He gets up, crosses the room and locks the door. Just in case, he says. But don't worry, we won't be disturbed, no one comes in here when I'm working or with a client.

This increases my confidence. I'm not worried about being disturbed. He is.

He comes and sits down again in front of me. I've been praying for your mother for so many years.

Fat lot of good that did poor Mammy, I'm thinking.

His eyes fix on me. How did you find me?

I remember my promise to Mick Flanagan. Your affair with my mother was very public knowledge in Birr, I say firmly. Once I came to the town and started asking questions, finding you was easy.

He starts to bluster. So it was Birr, at least we've now established that much. Thank you. Who in Birr? *Who* in Birr gave you my name? I have a right to know—

It's an old tactic, divert down a side road to buy time, but I'm wise to it, James does it all the time. It could be any number of people I talked to, I say to him. For instance, wasn't my aunt Adeline around at the time it was all happening?

He stops dead. Recovers a little. Was it she who told you?

I told you I'm not saying.

Well, here's another thing — why now, may I ask? It's a bit peculiar, isn't it — after all this time?

Mr Crawford, we both have a lot of explaining to do, we can talk about this again — I know you're anxious to get back to your party. Believe me, if I'd tried to find you ten, even twenty years ago, I can assure you I would have found you just as easily. I just didn't try, that's all. The timing wasn't right, I wasn't ready, I was too busy with more crucial things, I didn't *need* to find you *enough* until now . . . All kind of reasons, I guess.

Anyway, I return his gaze, can you know why you

yourself did or didn't do everything, every moment of your life?

His eyes hunt the room then come back to me. How many other people know about this?

The person who told me, as far as I'm concerned – no two. I'd temporarily forgotten Ken Sheils, out there in the van. Privately I'm remembering what Mick Flanagan said, that it was the talk of the town at the time. Poor Pius, leave him his delusions.

Who are these people? Are they local?

Look, Mr Crawford, I gave my word that I wouldn't tell anyone who gave me your name. The second person who knows about me and you isn't going to open his mouth. He's a friend of mine, drove me here. He's out there now waiting for me – he's from Dublin, so it's unlikely—

How much do you need?

It takes a second. Then I'm furious. How dare he think I'm a gold-digger? We're not looking for money, I say haughtily.

Then what? I'm sorry, he goes, what kind of help? This James, he's your son?

Although the implication is clear and I should probably take further offence (like mother, like daughter!) I don't. He's made me slightly uncertain. He's not playing the script I wrote for him on the way over here after talking to Mick Flanagan.

And although he hasn't exactly rolled out the welcome wagon, the oddest emotions are billowing around inside me. I'm having to fight not to like him. On the contrary, despite his bombast, I discover I very much *want* to like him. I'd been prepared for a super-Catholic version of Uriah Heep, who would fight me or throw boiling oil all over me, or try to repel me with a silver crucifix. To be fair to him, I'd say this man is only reacting normally to an abnormal demand.

James is not my son, I go, he's my brother. He's Rose's son. Sorry, he's actually my *half*-brother. (In case he starts to think that maybe Mammy had twins!) I've looked after him since he was a baby. He's in a little trouble with the law.

I can see his brain is working overtime.

By the way, I go, in case you think it's his father I should be looking for, you're probably right. The problem is, I have no idea where to start looking. Unfortunately for you – I manage a smile which I hope will break a bit of ice between us – you're the first in the firing line. I can hear my voice going lame.

All this time he's had his big notebook open in front of him on the desk and his pen in his hand. It's a fountain pen and he's gripping it so tightly there's ink leaking down his fingers. He puts it down very slowly and then closes the book.

Tell me about Rose.

He said this with such softness in his voice – this wasn't in the script either – that it really gets to me. Now I start worrying about the way he's feeling. About his emotions. Typical. I storm in here full of determination and courage and now I'm probably going to start behaving like his counsellor.

I try to harden up again. She's dead, I say firmly.

He makes the Sign of the Cross, Lord have mercy on her. How did she die? How long ago?

Stupid twit that I am, I decide to spare him the more sordid side of Mammy's life in Dublin. I tell him that she fell into poor circumstances when she first left Birr and she found it difficult to manage. Then I skip to the end. She died peacefully, I tell him. In the hospice. Nearly twenty years ago.

How difficult in Dublin? Was she poor?

Yes. Very poor. We were very poor.

He looks off towards the wall behind my head. Was it cancer? he goes. Did she go to the hospice because she was dying of cancer?

I stare at him. If Flanagan was even half-way correct about him, this man probably wouldn't have the remotest clue about a quarter of the problems which afflicted poor Mammy towards the end. We think it was, I say.

He peels his gaze off the wall. And did she get married in Dublin? Or is your half-brother illegitimate too?

Talk about insulted. I think of that happy little girl wheeling around in her beautiful, expensive Communion frock. Of the manicured lawns and the roses and the beautiful kitchen and all those warm, secure women who can smile at strangers. Yes, he is illegitimate, I say. I shoot at him with my eyes. And so are Francesca and Justine and Nicola.

Rose had *five* children? The horror in his face could even be comical.

Yep. By five different fathers.

Shattered, he gazes back at me. Probably there was he thinking all his life that his Rose went celibate through the rest of hers because she was still broken-hearted about him.

I've inflicted such damage that I'm finding it hard to hang tough. I don't know, do I, what pressures his own family put on him not to come out to see her when she was calling hysterically from under his window? Flanagan said he was so young——

Up and down, up and down, this has to be near the top of the see-saw conversation league. Stop it, Angela, you have to keep your mind on why you're here.

Through the open window, the sounds from the party

outside, the high-pitched voices of children, a woman calling to one of them in cross tones, seem to be coming from another universe. To help me stay strong, I conjure up a picture of James's battered face. I keep this picture in my mind while I sit there in the quiet, giving my father (my *father*!) a chance to digest this walking catastrophe sitting in front of him.

A quick wail from a child, and a man holding out his arms is crossing from right to left across the slice of garden I can see from where I'm sitting. The old people at the summerhouse are hardly talking to each other, just enjoying being there, like old people do. It occurs to me that a few of those old people could be related to me. Grand-aunts or grand-uncles. Even my paternal grand-parents. And which of those shiny people out there are my aunts and uncles by blood and marriage? I remember one of the names now – Bonaventure. I have an uncle Bonaventure. I wonder would he let me call him Bono, ha, ha!

You might think I'm treating this whole thing facetiously. Definitely not, it's just the way my mind works. I'm having to keep tight rein on myself, I'm afraid I'll start jabbering again and blow it. Let him off the hook.

The silence continues. I can feel his presence now. It's very strong, very male. I'm glad my father isn't some awful puny person. I think that, given other circum-stances, I could definitely like him.

He's fiddling with a paperweight on the desk beside him. It has a bunch of forget-me-nots inside it. His colour has improved. You say you've raised James, he's still living with you?

Yes.

If Rose is gone twenty years he must be—

I said nearly twenty. James was two months old when she died. He's still nineteen.

Where are they, the other three?

I tell him the truth – including the fact that we don't communicate much – and when I've finished, his demeanour is almost back to what it was when we first shook hands. Poor Rose. He shakes his head.

Then he blows it. But we're taught, aren't we, that repentance can take place between the saddle and the ground?

Repentance! For what? For her being her? He's making it easy for me. Prayers won't help her now, I go, she's dead.

He shafts me a look.

I'll pray for her, Angela, he goes. As I told you, hardly a day goes by since she disappeared that I haven't.

Piffle, I think to myself. His prayers were really a terrific help when she was having her skull split by some junkie. But facing an enemy he can recognize, i.e. an unbeliever, has put spunk into him. He folds his arms. Now, Angela, level with me. Tell me, what do you really want?

My mind goes strange. I don't quite know what I want. To see him? To touch him? To have him embrace us into his family? To have him fall on his knees and beg forgiveness?

He's watching me carefully. If it's not money, what is it? Could you be specific?

Before I can answer, there's a rat-tat on the window. It's the little girl in the Communion dress. Her veil is falling down on the side of her head and she's trying to straighten it with one hand while rat-tatting on the window with the other. Are you coming *out*, Daddy? We're going to cut the *cakes* . . .

A woman appears behind the little girl and takes her hand. She's tall, tanned and bottle blonde – the expensive, ashy kind – slim as bamboo, wearing a straight white dress with a red belt. Sorry, Daddy, she calls through the window, don't mind her, she'll have to learn a bit of patience. Take your time. She smiles at me.

Your wife? I say when both have vanished from view.

Yes. He glances over his shoulder towards the garden. Dorothy. She's English. She converted so we could get married.

Bully for her, I go, and instantly regret it. She's nice, I say. Really. (It does cut a bit, though, to think Mammy could have become this lovely, polished person.)

Are you going to ruin all this for me, Angela? He says it very, very softly.

I engage his eyes, dredging up my strongest reserves. I've no desire to ruin anyone's life, I say just as softly. I'm not going to blackmail you, if that's what you mean. I've rarely asked anyone for anything, it's a point of principle with me not to be obligated to anyone, ever. You can take it that I'm asking you now to help me and my brother only because you're a last resort. And I'm sorry to say this so bluntly, but it's my opinion that you owe us.

He goes very still.

I sit up as straight as I can, like I'm Queen Nefertiti or someone. Are you going to help us or not?

He seems to cave in. It's extraordinary, his chest actually becomes concave. You still haven't told me how can I help.

I remember I read somewhere that Tony O'Reilly from Heinz once said he hates people to pussyfoot when they have bad news. That facts are friendly.

So I don't put a tooth in it. I tell Pius Crawford about

my brother's trial and conviction — erroneous conviction — but that my opinion doesn't count. That he's out on a suspended sentence. That because of this he's been beaten up and threatened with worse. That he's getting anonymous letters in his hospital bed. That the papers are in full cry after him—

Then I wing it. We need somewhere safe to live outside Dublin, I say as solidly as I can. A place where we'll attract no attention. And it has to be arranged quickly. Like early next week, the earlier the better. I thought with you being an auctioneer . . .

He seems to catch my mood and to see there's no point in arguing. Nowhere near Tullamore or Birr, he goes, all right? He sits up, he's brisk, we're in barter mode. I can see that this is what this man's good at. You can hear the confidence returning with every syllable.

For the time being, I ignore the bit about staying as far away from him as possible. As well as helping us find a place, maybe you could help us get jobs — auctioneers know a lot of people, right? Business people? We'd be all right for money at least for a while. I've saved a couple of thousand towards a place of our own and now is clearly the time to use it.

I'm getting warmed up, now I'm seeing a cottage with roses around the door and me growing turnips in the back, like Adeline. A whole new life, straight out of Thomas Hardy. (I stop short at the picture of James as an honest labourer.) We might even be able to buy a place if the price was right, I go, as if I've thought this out, which I haven't, but with house prices shooting up every week the way they are maybe what I have wouldn't cover deposits and legal fees and all the rest of it. Could you go guarantor for us?

I'm impressing myself with my jargon.

As soon as we're settled and we're earning, I continue, if it has cost you anything to help us, we'd pay back every single penny it cost. Even if it takes years.

Now I know I'm getting carried away so again I stop. I'd been about to promise that if he helped us, in return we wouldn't bother him or his family. I'm not going to let us down that far. Let him think what he likes about us. We're people, human beings. He can't wish us away, and while we're not going to go out of our way to make trouble for him and his nice family, now that we're out in the open, we're not going back underground. I remind myself that this is quite reasonable. That he owes us.

His chair, one of those high-backed executive leather jobs, is a bit higher than mine and he's looking down at me like he's a judge. If I understand it correctly, you want me to help someone who's *raped* a girl?

He's my brother. And it's a matter of opinion whether he raped that girl or not. He's not in gaol, is he? He's free. And it wasn't rape he was convicted of, it was sexual assault—

He interrupts. That doesn't take away from the fact that he was convicted—

He's also a blood relative of yours, by the way.

What?

Yep. Through me. Think about it.

I never saw anyone before of whom it could truly be said that his jaw dropped. Well, I see someone on this occasion. His mouth hangs open and you'd think his face had just fallen into a mincer. I couldn't care less, I'm fighting for James's life here.

He looks out towards the window. An older boy is playing Donkey with the Communion girl and two other little girls. The old people are still sitting in their same positions, like in a painting. Angela, my father says eventually, without looking around at me, will you give me a little time? My whole world—

He shrugs.

We don't have time, Mr Crawford, I say quietly. We really don't. You're our only hope. Since Mammy – Rose – is not here to look after James, I have to. He comes first.

You're asking me to help a *rapist*, Angela. Look out there at Esther – he gives this helpless little wave towards the outside – just *look* at her.

Esther's your little girl who made her First Communion?

Yes, he whispers.

The child is racing after the ball with which they've been playing Donkey. She's holding on to her veil with one hand. Mr Crawford, I say, maybe you'll understand this. I'm asking you to be a Christian. Forgiveness. Charity. I promise you, if you let me tell you James's side of the story—

Please! He holds up his hand. I couldn't bear it.

Well, it's not only James, then, is it? It's me. I'm asking you to help me. That anonymous letter – I told you I'm warned in that too. I'm your daughter, Mr Crawford. If you like, we'll do blood tests.

There's no need. I believe you. At last he looks away from the window. You've no need to prove to me you're Rose's daughter. I have eyes, don't I? He spreads his hands and examines the nails. They're big and square with not a scintilla of dirt under them. I've never forgotten her, you know, he says. Not for one day.

Why didn't you come out and see her when she was crying for you? Despite my best intentions, my voice is rising. She was *pregnant*, you owed her—

Don't you think I know she was pregnant? He looks

away again. It's a long story. It's too dreary. You wouldn't want to hear it.

There's something so private in the way he says this that it would take a person with a really black heart to insist on intruding. I file it away, though. I'll be bringing it up again. Through the window, we see Esther stop playing and look towards us. She puts her hands on her hips and her head to one side, frowning in at us like an irritated little housewife.

Her father reacts instinctively. With pleasure. Then he remembers my presence and checks himself.

I know you have to go, I say. I stand up. Look, Mr Crawford, I'm sorry for the shock I've given you but, as I hope I've impressed on you, the problems we have are very urgent.

You shouldn't have to call me Mr Crawford, should you? He stands up too.

It doesn't matter what we call each other, I say. I can hardly rush up to you and start calling you Daddy.

He frowns. Can you at least give me one day to think about this? To get used to it?

Yes. Of course.

Give me your telephone number?

When I tell him we don't have one, it seems to throw him almost as much as finding out I was his daughter. We make arrangements for me to telephone him at his office first thing on Monday morning. I give him my address. And then, as an afterthought, I give him the only telephone number at which I can be contacted. It's for emergencies only, I said, and it's on Saturday mornings. (Not that I could see for a second what emergency could arise – but in this day and age you have to have some sort of telephone number, don't you?)

Now we're both left standing, not knowing from Adam how to get out of this room. There's this terrible moment when we both take a step forward at exactly the same time and nearly bump into one another. Then we stop and have to take a step back again. He makes this gesture with one arm towards the door. I'm to go first, like he's the host and I'm the honoured guest.

We're standing very close so I'm very conscious of how tall he is. And there's a faint smell of fresh sweat off him, and grass. It's nice.

Before I go, I ask him suddenly if he really says rosaries outside cinemas.

He blinks. Does this matter to you?

It does, I go.

He looks down at his feet. I believe this earth is sinful, he says softly, we're all sinners. The evidence of my own sinfulness is standing right in front of me at this moment. He hesitates. I wanted to be a priest when I was a boy. He sounds sincere and convinced but to me there's something not quite right about the sound of this. It doesn't match somehow . . . And now that I think of it, I didn't altogether go along with his commitment to the between-the-saddle-and-the-ground stuff either. (This was something I well remembered from school. The notion that even Stalin and Hitler could be in heaven always sounded a bit off to me. Stalin and Hitler could go to heaven but the poor unbaptized babies had to go to limbo?)

It'll be a while, though, before I can work out why Pius Crawford is saying one thing and my instincts are telling me another, but I've done enough here for one day.

I'll get out of your hair now, I say.

You're sure only the two people know? Can you vouch for both of them that they won't spread this around?

I'm about to get angry again, say that I'm a human being, not merely a Problem but then I think, what's the point? I can vouch for one of them, I tell him. And if it will put your mind at rest, given who the other person is, I doubt if – if the other person will be shouting it from the rooftops.

I'd nearly said 'he'.

He shows me out as far as the front door. He can't get rid of me fast enough. I can feel the panic in him in case someone from his lovely family at his lovely party sees us. I can feel him already out in that lovely back garden, making up stories, shrugging about having to get business wherever and whenever he can find it. Always on duty, that's me, smiling, grabbing his little girl and throwing her up in the air. Maybe even hugging her. Calling to his other Angela – she's probably out there too, isn't she?

The poor guy. As it turns out, I'm glad Mick Flanagan prepared me for worse because in my opinion Pius Crawford's not *too* bad. Although it's too early to say what his character is really like, at least he's manly looking and at his age a lot of his inner character has to be already written on his face – you know the way that happens.

He could have been a weed.

Thirty

By chance, I met one of my kissogram colleagues on the Sunday morning. I was on my way to Bewley's in Westmoreland Street to treat myself to a proper cup of coffee and I met her in Marlborough Street, just as I was passing Carthy's the pawnbrokers. It was desperate to think of Mammy's jewellery lying abandoned in there behind the steel shutters. I should have used the scratch-card money to get it back straight away. The minute those bonds came in the post I was going to cash them and redeem everything. I'd have to come up with an extra hundred or so if I was going to get the video as well – I suppose I owed that to James.

Hello there! She tips me on the shoulder from behind.

I spin around. Oh, hello! I'd never liked this particular girl, she always behaved as if the work was beneath her. On the other hand she could afford to be like that. For a start she was young. And gorgeous, with a little face that would remind you of Demi Moore – come to think of it, her looks weren't a million miles away from Rosemary Madden's. And like Rosemary Madden, she was from somewhere nice, like Drumcondra or Glasnevin. Passing through the lower orders while she waited for something better to come along or, more probably, for Mr Right.

She was coming from Mass in the Pro-cathedral. After

we shoot the breeze about it being a lovely morning, she tells me the boss went mad when I didn't turn up that first night – and continued not to turn up. If any of them saw me, this girl says, they were under orders to tell me not to show my face around his office again.

Well, you've told me now, I say, thanks. I make a move to go.

How's your brother? she asks, in a neutral sort of voice but I'm on permanent guard and I've no intention of falling into any traps.

Brilliant, never better, I say, as sweetly as I can. Well, I must be off. Tell our mutual friend you gave me his message and that I miss him too, ha, ha! I walk off. Devil-may-care, that's me.

I continued on to Bewley's as planned, but I didn't enjoy it. I couldn't settle. All that normal noise, clattering crockery, chat. All those normal people, boys and girls with contact rashes on their faces, who'd obviously spent the night together and who couldn't bear to let go of one another's hands across the table, men with the Sunday papers, tourists with maps and bum bags and little purses from which they carefully counted out their coins. Not one of these folk, as far as I could see, had a care in the world. Even the young waiters and waitresses, who frequently look stressed in Bewley's, seemed cheerful to me this morning.

It seemed so long since the situation had been anywhere near normal for me, I'd forgotten what it felt like. On the other hand, I guess I had become so used to this churning, knife-edge feeling I live with now, maybe I'd find it difficult to recognize any more what normal felt like.

Poor Ken Sheils had got the brunt of this edginess on the way home from Tullamore the evening before. (He certainly hadn't known what he was taking on when he met me!) As you can imagine, I was in no mood for confiding, or even for talking. I felt I owed it to him to say something, however.

Look, I say when I get into the van after I leave my father, before you ask, the past half-hour was difficult, as you can imagine, very, very difficult, although he's quite a nice man, much nicer than that Guard led us to believe. But I can't tell you what's going to happen next or what any of us is going to do. Because I don't know. Everything's up in the air. Do you mind if we don't talk about it any more than that? Is that enough to tell you?

He looks wounded. You don't have to tell me anything at all, Angela, I didn't ask—

I know you didn't and I appreciate it. But I feel I owe you an explanation. I'm not being awkward, it's just I can't say any more than I've just said. Do you understand?

The poor guy's game, I have to admit that. He doesn't push, doesn't argue. And the only thing he says during the whole journey home comes when we're passing the spot beyond Newlands Cross where the journalist was murdered. There are little mounds of flowers there now, browned by the heat and sun and the dust of passing traffic. And a plain wooden cross with her name on it.

Scumbags, is all he says.

I apologize to him for my mood as he drops me outside our door but he tells me there's no need to. When this is all sorted out, he says, you can buy me a pint.

I'll buy you more than a pint, I say, and I give him a puck in the shoulder. When I win the Lotto I'll buy you a Rolls-Royce so you can get rid of this old banger.

He laughs and cuffs me back.

As I'm looking around at all this normality in Bewley's, I remember that, in all the excitement, I never posted my three-star scratch card. I don't even know where it is now. I'm also thinking that maybe I should have called for Ken and offered to buy him a cup of coffee. But would it be fair to ruin his day? No matter how hard I'd try, I know I wouldn't be able to talk to him about anything even half-way everyday. James. My father. James again.

What an obsessive bore I've become. Some day, I vow to myself, we will have a cup of coffee here – and we'll be normal too. This from the woman who not four days ago decided she never wanted to see this man again. Irrational or what?

As it turned out it was just as well I was on my own this morning because my father was everywhere, through all my thoughts. No matter how hard I tried I couldn't shake him off. Everywhere I saw a man with a build even vaguely like his, I'd compare them. I'd look into my coffee. Did he like coffee or tea? I'd see a man reading the *Sunday Tribune*. Did he buy the *Sunday Tribune* or the *Sunday Independent?* Maybe both. Was he searching all the papers this morning for articles about his half-half-son? When he was making pillow-talk last night with his convert wife, did she ask him, just in idle conversation, who I was and what I wanted – and how did he get out of that one?

An American girl near me was wittering on about her star sign. She was a Pisces. For what it's worth, I'm a Cancer, on the cusp of Gemini. I haven't a clue what goes best with either, but at least with two sun signs to choose from, Pius Crawford and I have two chances to be compatible.

There's something nagging away at me underneath the more obvious stuff. I bring it up and examine it.

It's the religiosity. There's definitely something odd about it. Even making allowances for my own prejudices, in the short time I was talking to him, Pius Crawford's holiness didn't altogether wash with me. All right, so he does his rosary crusades and he writes outraged letters and all the rest of it but, in the flesh, the holy things he said did not seem to strike quite the right note. Like a bell that has a crack in it.

I got back to the flat at about twelve. It was as hot as a launderette even though I'd waited until the last minute before I went out to close the windows. For the previous few days, we'd seemed to be going through a mini-heatwave, although according to the weather forecast, this was supposed to break today.

In general, the weather isn't great this year. We'd all been hoping for another Mediterranean summer like we'd had in 1995 – I'd even heard a few dingbats saying that the fantastic weather we had last year was a reward from God because of the ceasefires in the North! If that's the case, maybe we're being punished this year because of the Canary Wharf bombing in London.

Actually, I was shocked about that bombing. Everyone was. We'd got used to peace and to just ordinary giving out about the politicians – they're all a shower, what Peace Process! et cetera. Before that bombing some of the customers in the deli even confided that they were going to try out the North for their holidays this year. (Shop assistants are like hairdressers. Holidays are *the* hot topic of conversation.)

They say that Canary Wharf is going to be the equivalent for Irish people of where-were-you-when-President-Kennedy-was-shot. We'll all remember exactly where we were when we heard about it – and typically, I was probably the last person in the country to hear about it. I hadn't seen the news the night before – James had been at home in charge of the remote control as usual – so I didn't hear until the next day, when it was the sole topic of conversation amongst the women in the minibus.

Tick-tock.

There are still nearly two hours to go before I leave for the hospital.

There isn't much to see out through the open window of the flat. The square is peaceful. I notice that all the yuppies in the new 'Georgian' apartments at the far side have their windows open like me. People are strolling alongside the railings around the square, pushing baby buggies and carrying newspapers under their oxters. I seem to remember reading somewhere that each city has a different heartbeat and every resident and visitor subconsciously responds to it. Like if you're in Manhattan or Tokyo you'll automatically walk faster than you would, say, in Thurles or Sligo. Dublin's Sunday beat is completely different from the rest of the week. Even the cars are driven more slowly. Maybe it's because a lot of them have grannies in the back, out for a Sunday drive.

Wouldn't that be blissful? To have a granny to take for a Sunday drive . . .

Before I know it, I've started fantasizing again. Me, my new father, James, one of our uncles or our auntie driving us all, including our aged relatives, out to the seaside for a breath of fresh air.

Stop it, Ange. I look at my alarm clock by the bed-settee. Only a few minutes gone. The whole place is as clean as a mortuary so it's pointless looking for something to polish. I've nothing to read – you might think I have a lot of books but I've already read every single one of them, many of them twice – and because I couldn't bear to read any more articles about James I hadn't bought a paper. I'm not hungry, Bewley's milky coffee has filled me up.

This must be what real loneliness is about. Forget the Old Woman of the Roads and her little house and stool and all. Loneliness is not only having no one to talk to, it's having nothing to do on a bright Sunday morning when everyone else has.

I get up and turn on the radio. Big mistake. There's a barney going on, people shouting at each other and Andy O'Mahony, who's the presenter of this programme, going, 'One voice, please, one voice.' They're squabbling about James. Two or three women, as far as I could make out.

I'm stuck to the floor, staring at our transistor radio. Annoyed women on the radio lose it. Their voices go up towards a screech.

Or maybe it's just the subject matter that's making me so critical. I should turn it off but I can't. Part of me wants to hear just how bad this is going to be.

Andy O'Mahony succeeds in intervening, gives one woman the floor. She's so furious, her voice is wobbling. At least she's lowered it. Listen, she goes, you have a male-dominated society and a male-dominated judiciary – well-educated, middle-class judges all out of the same mould. Private schools, golf clubs, Fitzwilliam Tennis Club, the Royal George Yacht Club, all the rest of it. Mighty massed ranks against the courage of one little girl—

Hold on a minute, hold on a minute, a man, not Andy O'Mahony, interrupts.

Andy says the name but I don't recognize it. The woman tries to shout him down but Andy shushes her, tells the man to go ahead. This judge wasn't part of the male establishment, this man says. Correct me if I'm wrong but this was a woman judge, wasn't it?

Same difference, says the woman in a disgusted tone of voice. It's the ethos I'm talking about, the environment in which our whole judicial system operates. Do you think, does anyone here think, that little Rosemary Madden will ever get over what she's been through? Does any woman ever get over an outrageous attack like this? This girl is a modern-day Joan of Arc. It's because of her bravery in coming forward, in being identified—

I turn it off.

The silence roars back at me. Rosemary Madden, Rosemary Madden.

I lie down on the bed-settee. I try to force my imagination into Rosemary Madden's mind. I have to. I can't go through the rest of my life not seeing the other side of this story.

But my imagination won't do it right off. It keeps sliding away, to my father, to money, to Mammy, to what time it is, to the washing I promised myself I'd do later, to Patsy and Martin and their problems, to what's happening outside in the square. Even poor old Tom Bennett gets a look-in. But I lead my brain back and back and back. Eventually it gives in and concentrates. The outline of Rosemary's story I know from James, the detail of it I fill in.

My name is Rosemary, I am a young woman of twenty. I have everything going for me. I'm pretty and I have a good family, a great address. My mother is very quiet but she makes our house nice for us. In an old-fashioned way. The family printing business is doing OK although I don't have much to do with it. My older brother works with my dad, in a set of prefabs at the back of our house, and one or both of them come in for their dinner in the middle of the day when they're not out calling on clients. My other brother, two years younger than me, has just done his Leaving Cert. He's a pain in the you-know-what but all teenage boys are and he's not the worst, really. We fight but not seriously. I

like clothes, especially ones which show off my body. I'd
like to be a bit taller, like Claudia Schiffer, but I'm still
proud of my body. I paint my toenails pink. I'm thinking
of putting a blonde streak in the front of my hair. Maybe
magenta.

I'm not a genius but I'm not stupid either. I might
even have gone on to Third Level – not university, of
course, but I did scrape enough points in the Leaving to
be offered a course in Waterford RTC. I wasn't all that
pushed about leaving home, however, and I'd had
enough of school. My parents didn't object when I didn't
take the offer.

But then I found it quite hard to get work I liked. I
wasn't going to work in McDonald's, no way. Daddy
offered to find something for me to do in his own
business. A telephonist or receptionist or something. No
fear of that either. You wouldn't meet many people in
the prefabs at the back of our house. Working with your
family is not my idea of independence. I want to spread
my wings.

It got a bit tense after a year or so – my dad was
getting a bit irritated at having to hand out money all the
time – and I had to do something.

So now I'm on a Youth Employment Scheme, which at
first I thought was going to be a disaster because a lot of
people think these schemes are all a con job to keep
people off the official dole. But to tell you the truth,
secretly I have to admit that what was really bothering
me is that I knew there would be kids on the scheme
with whom I wouldn't normally dream of associating.
And indeed there are. They have dreadfully common
accents and they're all named after people in Coronation
Street or the Pope. If I'm honest I was a bit afraid of
them. That I'd be attacked or ripped off or robbed. I
found out, would you believe, that they were as afraid of

me as I was of them. We sorted it out after a while and now we have quite good fun.

The work turned out to be OK. Under a Community Initiative Scheme, we're helping to set up a computer database to link together a set of small businesses in an unemployment blackspot in the North City. That's what they tell us anyway. Actually, though, it's quite interesting with very little really hard work involved. We're bookkeeping and they're letting me loose on the computer side of it. I'm quite good at computers.

I was at a club in town one night where I met a motorcycle courier, a really good-looking guy with amazing eyes, although his skin could do with a bit of Clearasil. But he's a massive dancer and I really fancied him right from the word go. He fancied me, too. In fact, I was sure he couldn't believe his luck – only scrubbers would normally be interested in motorcycle couriers from the inner city. (To me Mountjoy Square is the inner city.) But he has a great body. Great kisser, too.

This is where I, Angela, started having difficulty. It was hard for me to keep myself in Rosemary Madden's eyes as soon as I got near the physical stuff. I suppose most mother figures have difficulty picturing their boys kissing and so on. This isn't to say you don't accept it, you do. You can see it out there, but the actions involved are sort of gauzy. It's when you come right close up, to see the lips, that the problem arises.

I skirt away from it but when you come right down to it, I can't, can I? It's the nub of this whole problem.

I don't make myself go all through the dating and the parties and so forth. I make myself skip to the nitty-gritty. The afternoon in question and the Furry Glen. Like most Dubliners, I know the Furry Glen in a vague sort of way. The Phoenix Park is the biggest park in Europe, blah blah, and we're all very proud of it. But the

Furry Glen is at the far side from me. There's no bus service straight through, and most times I've ever been to that park it was to the zoo side because that's where the 10 bus terminus is. I remember the Furry Glen for the trees and the lake and the very steep hills. But the night James told me about the rape, I could see the scene vividly, even the little bridge and the ducks. So I must have been there more often that I'd thought.

I force myself to walk down that path with James and Rosemary. I see the sun coming through the trees (although he didn't tell me whether or not it was a sunny day), I hear birds singing. I see the horse riders he told me about and the old lady they were afraid would see them vanish into the bushes.

I see the two of them going in under the trees.

I'm Rosemary Madden again. It's dark in here, well, more gloomy than dark. And it's colder than I expected. The ground is damp. I'm afraid my clothes will get ruined, stained.

But I lie down and James lies down too. He's panting, all over me. His kisses are very hard. I'm getting frightened. What will I tell my parents about my clothes? I'm sure they're getting stained – we're lying on earth and pine needles and grass. And will they guess I've lost my virginity? Can you tell by a person's face?

But I'm the one who brought him here. The condoms are burning a hole towards me through his pocket. I can't feel them physically, of course, but I can in another way. I want to get out of it now but I don't know how.

Stop it, James, stop it—

He pulls away. What's wrong with you? You wanted this as much as I did. Are you just a tease or something?

Of course I want it.

I let him kiss me again. I want it and I don't want it all at the same time. It's going too fast for me, my knickers are tearing, he's too rough, I'm getting scared now – I can feel him——

I, Angela, jump up from the bed-settee. I can't do any more of this. It would drive me into Grangegorman. I can't split myself.

Anyway I don't want to. I don't *have* to because we have justice on our side. I'm gone way over the top, way beyond what James told me happened. Even way beyond what she said happened and the feelings she said she had in her statement. Me and my imagination – Mr Elliott always said it would get me into trouble.

I'm sweating and it's not from the heat of the day.

James and I have to find somewhere safe and quiet until the ruckus dies down. My father will help us. I'm James's sister and I'm on his side and that's that. No ifs, ands or buts. I'm James's *sister*. I'm standing by him. I believe James's side of the story. She asked him to bring the condoms. No way was it all one-sided. The judge is on our side. The judge judged everything. She thought he was worth giving a chance to. So do I. I'm sorry for Rosemary Madden's problems – or I would have been if she hadn't blown it. She's Joan of Arc now. To herself. To all her supporters.

Well, to me she's not. To me she's just a girl scared of her parents and of what she's done. So she has to cover up and blame James. She told her parents a story and she's sticking with it because she can't back down now. And now she doesn't have to because she's a heroine.

Joan of Arc?

Not.

Not to me. I have to believe Rosemary Madden's just a girl who's in love with all the attention. If I couldn't convince myself of that, I'd probably have to give up.

Thirty-One

D addy, she called him. That's what clicks it for me.
   The penny drops while I'm sitting in Mountjoy
Park, killing time until I had to walk up to the hospital.
For the second time in less than four hours, I wasn't able
to stay in that silent flat a minute longer. I've now to add
another worry to the list. How am I going to handle
telling James about Pius Crawford?

At least the weather's holding, it's like a real summer's
day, the kind you used to see in the illustrations in your
school primer – you know, with the blue sky and the one
little fluffy cloud and Máire agus Seán in their summer T-
shirts bouncing their striped liathróid. (That reminds me – I
have to make a decision fairly soon about whether I'm going
to register for Irish for the next year's Leaving. Ugh!)

The wife calling him Daddy was the key to what rang
wrongly about my father's religious zeal. Don't ask me to
explain why I think the two things are connected, they
just are. Call it instinct. I couldn't be sure, but I'd have
been prepared to bet that it was she who was running the
show. He was playing along with her, it wasn't coming
from inside himself.

You see she's a convert and they're always the most
fervent and scrupulous when it comes to their adopted
religion – you just watch the behaviour from now on of

the Duchess of Whatever across the water who came over to us recently. Converts are far more strait-laced than the people who are born into it. We take it for granted. We know it's always there for us if and when we decide to flop back after taking a walk on the wild side, but they're so fervent they won't put a toe out of line. It's all so new and exciting for them they take it terribly seriously.

I hope, by the way, you don't think I'm totally anti-religion. I'm not. It's just not for me, that's all. I'm the first to admit that there are some terrific priests – Father McVerry with his homeless boys, for instance, or the Franciscans on Merchants Quay with their Aids patients. All those other quiet men who work out of the public eye and who genuinely see their God in the poor and the destitute and the prisoners. My beef is with the rest of them who are always watching out for someone else's sin and trying to protect the whole of Ireland from it.

The clincher for me in my father's case comes when you add Dorothy's conversion to the way he was brought up by the kind of people who'd call a kid Bonaventure. (In the matter of his own family, though, I have to say that Esther isn't at all bad – and, of course, neither is Angela. I wonder what the rest of their children are called. One huge plus in this whole affair – it's only now it's dawning on me. *Seven* half-siblings. An entire tribe all at one go! If I ever get to meet them . . .)

Look at it this way – even if you didn't *want* to be standing outside cinemas waving rosary beads you'd have found it very difficult to stand up to them all, wouldn't you? Especially if you were someone with a guilty con-science, like him.

Or am I just making excuses for him? Is this just another of my stupid fantasies?

It was a good idea to come outside – I can feel myself calming down. Mountjoy Park is a hive of slow Sunday activity. The usual knot of geezers watching the world. The breeze waving through the leaves on the trees, kids tumbling, parents reading the papers. A knot of backpackers unrolling everything out of enormous rucksacks on to the grass as if they're setting up house. Therc's a youth hostel in the square and we get a lot of foreign kids around here. God love them, they haven't a clue that they're taking their lives in their hands walking down Gardiner Street. They're so sweet and blond and vulnerable, with their little padlocks which swing and bob around on the straps of their packs like neon invitations flashing, me, me, mug me! Sure they're not even a challenge to the gurriers around here.

One of them, a kid of about seventeen or eighteen, maybe, would remind you of Tom Bennett from the back. The same coppery hair colour.

You know, I've never lost a yen to find out whatever happened to him afterwards — I suppose you always feel that about your first love. Whatever, I'm dying for this backpacker to turn around so I can see if it's only the hair. I'm sitting there and I'm willing him to turn and then I cop myself on. Here I go, slithering back to the past again. Is this some sort of protective thing? That when the present gets unbearable you slip away to things you can control in your imagination? No wonder there are so many happy people in lunatic asylums.

Out of the blue, I start to daydream about one fantastic evening Tom Bennett and I spent together just before the end.

It was the time we went to the airport.

Now, on the surface that might not appear to be a very romantic date, but wait until you hear.

He'd warned me to wear my best clothes, so I put on one of Mammy's linen dresses, the cream one, and a black velvet bolero the babysitter lent me for the occasion.

That was one thing about the flats. We all mucked in, any of us who were on friendly terms. She'd agreed to babysit James for the whole evening, from tea-time on. She was the eldest in the flat next door so there was no problem about her walking home. We didn't have to be back until midnight.

When he turns up to collect me, I see he wasn't joking about us wearing good gear. He has on the famous crocodile jacket and the tight black jeans. And again his contacts in instead of his glasses.

Where are we going? I ask him, as we walk through the entryway.

Just wait and see, he goes, with this mysterious smile.

This dream date didn't begin very well. For a start, we had to wait nearly forty-five minutes for the 41 out to the airport, and even when it came, the journey took for ever. By the time we got out there, I can tell you I was pretty cranky. I just couldn't see the point, I kept telling him, of getting dressed up just to go out and look at a lot of aeroplanes. And having to spend half the evening on a bus, to boot!

He didn't lose his good humour for a single minute, though, and when we eventually got there, even though I was still grumbling — for God's sake, why can't we just go to the pictures like normal people, that kind of thing — he whisked me up the escalator.

Then he turns me and steers me into the restaurant. Not the self-service, the real one, the Silver Lining, with white tablecloths and cloth serviettes and a thick carpet on the floor.

But that isn't the end of the surprise. The second we arrive, we're welcomed like we're royalty and led over to a table by the window where we could look out at the planes. There's a bottle of wine in a silver bucket (on legs) already cooling beside that table, and at the place where

I'm put sitting, a little posy of flowers tied up in a white ribbon.

I'm struck dumb. Especially since I'd given him such a hard time about the whole thing. I've never been in a restaurant like this in all my life. The nearest I'd come to it was the lobby of the Gresham.

It's so peaceful. After the mayhem outside in the airport proper, in here is sort of an expensive hush. A murmur. You can barely hear even the engines of the aeroplanes you could see outside the wall of glass windows, which run all along one side. Is this all right for you, madam, sir? The man – small, dicky bow, dress suit – who's shown us to our table has this delighted smile on his face, like he's in on some great secret. He is, too. Turns out one of the fellows Tom Bennett plays football with is a trainee chef in this restaurant and the whole thing has been arranged in advance.

We sit down. Luckily I know how to behave – the benefit of listening to Mammy's stories again. I know about letting the waiter put my serviette on my lap and about using cutlery from the outside in and crumbling your bread instead of cutting it and so forth, although this is the first time I'd ever had to do it. Tom Bennett is watching me and learning from me. I always knew you were a lady, deep down, he whispers. His eyes are shining. Do you like it?

Like it? I go – I love it! It's brilliant.

We deserve a bit of a treat. Stick with me, kid, he goes, the sky's the limit. No pun intended!

The whole thing is almost too good – you know the way that can sometimes happen? How you can get overwhelmed so you can't react properly and it's only the next day or even the next week that you realize what's really happened.

The food is great. He lets me order, although to tell

you the truth I'm taking a wild stab at some things. Like
paté, for instance — a first. Then lovely thick soup — the
soup spoons are *enormous* — then fresh salmon, another
first, with some kind of sauce. We finish with ice cream
and then coffee out of tiny cups. Espresso. I have to
pretend I like it although I feel it's like licking tarmaca-
dam. The wine was difficult for me too, those days, I was
a Bacardi and Coke person.

After the meal he takes me into the bar. *Hopping!* The
counter is like a river, because the barmen are so rushed
off their feet they have barely time to fill out pints never
mind clean off the slops. Within minutes, my eyes are
sore from the smoke — people apparently smoke like
crazy before they get on planes. We have to shout to be
heard but it's a great buzz.

We can't find seats or a table so he puts me in a position
by the wall near the bank of windows where we can watch
all the action. Then he goes off to order — a small brandy
each.

He comes back with the drinks and we sip them and
I'm smelling the flowers in my posy and I'm feeling
terribly sophisticated and happy. I'm on such a high —
thrilled skinny that Tom Bennett would go to all this
trouble for me. He puts an arm around my shoulders.
Enjoying yourself?

Fantastic, I go.

He puts on an accent, like W. C. Fields. I brought you
here, m'dear, because some day all of this will be yours.
Then, right into my ear, Next time we're in here
together, we won't be in here just looking. We'll maybe
be going on our honeymoon, what?

You can imagine what that did to my equilibrium. It
was certainly one of the happiest evenings of my life.

And then, of course, not too long after, I give him

his walking papers. Ah, well, some things are just not to be.

The backpacker with the coppery hair has lain down on the grass now and put an open book over his face as though he's going to have a snooze. So I won't get to see if he does or does not resemble Tom Bennett. I'd still love to meet him again, just for a natter, see how he turned out.

There's still some time to kill so I decide to start walking up to the hospital. I take the long way around, Dorset Street, Whitworth Road and Phibsboro Road. It's hotter than I reckoned, though, and by the time I get to the Mater, I'm in a lather. It's not only the heat. I still haven't figured out the correct approach in telling James about Father Pius.

But James pre-empts me. He's sitting on the side of bed, waiting. He's dressed. He's being released.

This is not entirely a welcome development. For a start, I haven't a thing in the house to feed him with. Oh, I go, how come? What about that last test?

He's been told Casualty's jammed, the nurses are under strength, they need the bed. He's to contact his family doctor about the test. It's not essential that he be here for the results. Anyone who's able to put two feet under him is being sent home today.

Right, I go. Now I'm thinking, We'll have to take a taxi – more money! – because he isn't well enough to walk. And those poor old photographs of Mammy are taking another trip home unseen. I'll show them to him when we get home, it'll be something for us to do.

No chance – because when the taxi pulls up in front of the flat, who's sitting on the steps?

Patsy.

Her hair is stringy, her Goldie Hawn face is scrunched

up and woebegone like a monkey's. Ominously, she has a big black rubbish bag with her, it's bulging full but she's clutching the top of it as though she's afraid it'll blow away.

I'm astonished at the rush of savagery I feel looking at her. Normally I'd be barging over to console her, to ask her what's wrong, but the minute I see her I develop this hard ball of angry air in the middle of my chest that's puffing up and wants to explode. I'm *delighted* she's going to be confronted with the sight of James.

I help James out of the taxi – he's still wearing the splint and the sling on his arm and he's finding it difficult to move the rest of his body with the pain in his ribs. But then, of course, with her sitting there, he won't let me help him up the steps.

Hello, Patsy, I say, as civilly as I can when we get up next to her, what brings you here?

She doesn't answer me. Instead she bursts into tears. Not ordinary crying, big crying. Sobbing. As if she doesn't care a hoot who sees her making a show of herself. God, I hate scenes. Come in, I say quickly, come on in.

We all go up the stairs – the stink of cats' urine is particularly bad today, or maybe I'm just noticing it more. James is pulling himself up with his good arm via the banisters, Patsy is still wailing. You get the picture. I can't wait to get into the flat and close the door behind us, I can hear the neighbours listening. As if we weren't notorious enough! I discover I'm not being paranoid about this because as I reach our flat, I hear a small click. I look just in time to see the handle on Dwyer's door coming back to its normal position.

I get us all in. Patsy collapses on to the bed-settee, buries her head, storms away. James looks as though he wants to run back to the hospital as fast as he can. I don't think he's ever before seen a grown person go on like this. She'll be all right, I say to him above the hullabaloo, you go on into your room, I'll bring you in something to drink in a few minutes. Lie down and take a rest, all right?

He looks at her again, then goes into the room and closes the door after him. Patsy hears the slam and glances up. Her face is covered in bright red blotches. She looks terrible. At least she's trying to control herself now. I'm soh-ho-horry, she goes, hiccuping, I'm re-he-heally so-ho— I

I sit down at the table and look at her, as though she's an interesting species. Seeing someone upset like this, I'd usually be in bits weeping along with them but I don't feel a thing.

I'm a bit shocked, this new me is as hard as concrete. I know exactly how I should be behaving. I should be asking her gently to tell me what's wrong, even putting my arms around her. I think about doing that, I even see myself doing it, but I don't move from my chair. It wouldn't be honest.

Because right now I feel no friendship towards her at all. If anything, as well as this huge anger in the middle of my chest, I'm more than a little irritated that she's turned up like this when I've so much on my plate already. It hits me that I have something in common with Rosemary Madden after all, this hard, hot sensation is what revenge must feel like.

At last Patsy twigs something's unusual and that she's not getting the reception she obviously expected. Stops crying. Gazes at me with bloodshot, streaming eyes.

I know I shouldn't have turned up without warning like this—

Don't worry about it, I say.

She sits back on the settee and looks at her two hands in her lap. I've left him, she says, I've left the bastard.

Is that your luggage? I go, looking at the black plastic

bag. And what about the children? Does Martin know you've come here?

I'll sort all that out when I get fixed up. She looks at me sort of sideways. Are you all right? You seem a bit peculiar.

Tell me about Martin, I say back. I have no intention of getting into any personal discussions with her about myself. I stand up. Will I make you a cup of tea? I'm afraid we're out of biscuits.

She blows her nose. I'm sorry, Ange, I'm putting you out – and I know my timing couldn't be worse.

Not at all. Tea?

Yes, please, tea would be nice. Her voice is all quavery.

She sits staring through the window while I go through the motions. It would be in my nature to fill this silence, to chatter and yammer and try to cover up for any embarrassment there might be between us. But this new hard Angela does no such thing. I rinse out the teapot with hot water and get great satisfaction out of every little ping and clang. I don't say one word. I don't even look over my shoulder to see how she is now. I don't give a sugar actually. In a way it's a lovely clean feeling, very uncomplicated. Like a clear blue flame. And very calming.

I'm thinking the two of them deserve each other, her and Martin.

Are you very angry with me? Is that it?

Damn. I start to weaken. It's the smallness of the voice that does it. Patsy's usual voice would get on your nerves half the time, it's so cheerful and bubbly. This voice is like an orphan's.

After all, she was a good friend all these years. And she turned up to Mammy's funeral when she didn't have to. And she gave me flowers afterwards and came to see me in her lunch hours, to help me get through the grief. And it was her got all the gigs for PA System – she didn't have to have me on board, since singing talent is ten a penny in this city, she could have taken on someone much more dynamic. She took me because of our friendship.

Like hell I'm going to cave in completely, though. I turn towards her, swishing the hot water round and round in the teapot while behind me the noise of the kettle starts that roaring it gives off prior to boiling. You're right, Patsy, I say, I'm very angry with you. And I think you know why. I'm sorry for your present trouble but make no mistake about it, I'm very angry.

She looks back at me. If you could imagine one of those tiny dogs. The kind you can fit into a teacup — a chihuaha, is it? All eyes and scrawny faces.

It's James. Are you angry with me about James?

I swish the water out of the teapot into the sink. Bingo, I say. Right first time.

There's something you don't know, she says.

Try me. I put a spoonful of tea into the hot teapot.

She tells me then that an uncle of hers sexually assaulted her when she was eleven. Wouldn't you think she would have told me that before? When we were racking our brains about sexual assault statistics? So much for us being best friends! I look back at her. I'm imagining a little eleven-year-old body, real straight, without breasts, with lovely smooth skin. And a big hairy man.

But nothing happens. Instead, I receive an image of James and his Technicolored face and his poor battered body.

The kettle snaps off.

That's terrible, Patsy, I say. That's really terrible, an awful thing to have happened. I can imagine how you must have suffered. But it has nothing to do with James and me. I pour the boiling water onto the tea-leaves in the teapot.

→ Thirty-Two ←

Naturally I said she could stay.

Funny, I stopped being angry as soon as I started to lay down the ground rules. Yes, I was sorry that she'd been sexually assaulted, but it could have no bearing on what I was worrying about right now. My opinion on James was clear and just as she didn't want to discuss that situation, I didn't want to discuss hers of twenty-five years ago. I'd discuss her and Martin, of course, if that was her wish.

And this was James's home. It's not a castle, Patsy, I said, but it's the only home he has. He's not to be made feel uncomfortable in it.

Then, when I saw the way she looked after all this, I couldn't continue. Here was Patsy, my leader, meekly saying, Yes, Ange, and No, Ange, like I was the mother superior and she the new postulant. To stay angry at this beaten person would have been like taking a pickaxe to Bambi.

Why did you come here? I ask her, when we've settled down to have our cups of tea. Why didn't you go to your ma's house? Patsy's mother lives only a mile or so away from her, in Old Cabra.

I couldn't face her, Patsy says back. Anyway, she wouldn't be interested.

She's still snuffling a bit. She blows her nose hard.

Sorry, she goes, I'm whining, aren't I. She blows her nose a second time and then her voice comes back on with some of its usual zip. We'd get on each other's nerves after two minutes, she says. Oh, Ma'd love the drama of it all but she wouldn't be interested in the problem as such. She wouldn't be interested in me myself personally and how I felt.

As always, I find this kind of thing hard to believe, the woman was a mother, wasn't she? But I know of old that the relationship between these two is not brilliant. Privately, I've always believed the fault was more Patsy's than the ma's.

Patsy seems to resent that her mother doesn't want to play the little old granny. Remember I told you about the miniskirt and the dyed hair at Mammy's funeral? Well, the skirts are a bit longer now but the hair is still dyed and the face is still thick with make-up. According to Patsy, her mother spends most of her time playing golf or going to race meetings with her pals. It drives Patsy mad. She thinks her mother's get-up and lifestyle are completely inappropriate for a woman of her age and although she's never come right out with it, I believe that she wants her ma to be baking scones and planting herbaceous borders. We've had millions of arguments about it. It's illogical to me that while she herself always wanted the freedom to do her own thing – the gigs and driving her own car and having continental holidays and all the rest of it – she resents the older woman having the same desires. Or, more specifically, fulfilling those desires. Shove over, Patsy seems to be saying to her mother, it's my turn now.

But maybe I think that only because I would be so grateful at present to have any kind of a mother. Anyhow, it's between the two of them and I'm not going to help by interfering.

Whoever said that hot tea was the best drink for cooling you down was suffering from delusions, because drinking this one is making me feel hotter than ever. It's become so stifling in the flat that even the bluebottle crashing about against the windowpane is half-hearted about it. It wouldn't surprise me if we were about to have a thunderstorm. The sky outside the window is that dirty chrome colour, which is always ominous.

If you're staying, I say, you'll have to sleep with me, unless one of us sleeps on the floor.

Lucky the settee's a double, so, isn't it? She tries to smile but it doesn't work.

It occurs to me then that in all the years we'd known one another Patsy and I had never spent a night together. Kids nowadays have sleepovers and pyjama parties but who do you think I could have invited to the flats? To see what was going on in our place?

In other circumstances, for her to stay the night might have even been fun for Patsy and me. You know, sitting up all night, giggling and doing each other's hair and nails. That's what I hear from the women at work that their daughters do.

So tell me, I say.

The story is pretty pathetic. The row they were having on the night she came down to meet me in the fast-food place continued to rumble on until in the end it seems they weren't even sure what they were fighting about. Then, today, Martin tells Patsy he's going for a drink in the pub at lunch-time. She tells him he's to be home for his dinner at one. He says he won't, that he'll be back at closing time. She says if he isn't home at one o'clock she won't be here when he does come home . . .

Et cetera.

I hope I'm not making too little of the trauma she's

going through but I'm starting to feel impatient again. In some ways, bad and all as he is, James inside there in the bedroom is more mature than these two. As I'm listening to the saga (and then he said . . . and then I said . . .), I feel like yelling that the pair of them should just grow up. So who cares if you have your dinner at one o'clock or two o'clock or ten o'clock at night. I know infidelity's awful, I know it is. But, from what she tells me, with Martin it's only sex he's after with the others. Marriage is more than sex, isn't it? But then I curb myself. Who am I to talk about marriage? I'm the hurler on the ditch.

She has to get it out of her system, I know – but as I listen on and on, as she goes through every little detail of every awful thing he's ever done to her, my attention starts to wander . . .

I think I told you I never liked Martin, didn't I? I probably didn't tell you one of the main reasons for it, though, because up to now I wouldn't have wanted to let Patsy down.

The so-and-so once tried to grope me. Imagine! At their Christmas drinks party. In Patsy's own house. With Patsy herself inside in the sitting room.

I was in the kitchen breaking ice out of the ice trays to put into this joke ice bucket they have in the shape of a top hat. It's a devil of a job getting ice out, isn't it? I was effing and blinding under my breath – I don't swear out loud but when I'm giving out to myself it's a different matter – because I'd just broken off two of the false nails Patsy had given me as a present.

I've half of it out when your man comes up behind me. I don't hear him until I feel these arms going around me from behind and these hands nuzzling my breasts. Oh, Angela, he whispers into my ear, you've got the most gorgeous knockers, I've always wanted to do this—

He didn't get a chance to do any more because I back-kicked him in the shins. Little get. No, I never liked Martin.

It was nice of Patsy to invite me to go to Minorca with them but, to tell you the truth, my idea of hell would be to be cooped up with Martin. Anyway, they'll hardly be going to Minorca now . . . I'm lucky in some ways that James is the central relationship of my life and that I don't have a husband to worry about. How would you divide your loyalties? It must be very stressful to have more than one person to put first.

Patsy's still talking, I try to tune in. She's now beginning to worry about how Pauline and Maeve and Darren are getting on. About time she thought about her children, but I'm really wondering if it will ever be the same between us. I'm cast in the role of constantly listening to her and her problems – and boy, have I listened! – but now, when I need help with the biggest problem I've ever had, she can't hack it.

I know friendship is not about tit-for-tat, and I don't want it to be, but a bit of two-way would be nice occasionally.

She stops talking. Abruptly. Glances sideways at me. I know what you're thinking, she says. You're still thinking I haven't been sympathetic enough about yours and James's predicament.

Each time this happens, when she picks up what I'm thinking, it does give me a land. As a matter of fact, yes, I say, I was thinking something along those lines.

I'm very sorry, she goes. My attitude was probably wrong. Can you forgive me?

I stare back at her. I think of the innocent days, all the long years of innocence we had together. Of course I forgive you, I say. Slowly. Trying to sound as warm and sincere as I should be about this. Because there's no point in continuing this resentment against her, she just wouldn't understand.

It was that 'probably' that did it. She thinks she was 'probably' wrong. I know for certain now that we'll never get back to where we were. It's a real tragedy.

Patsy sees what she wants to see. Great, she says. Old friends are best, eh, Ange? I'm really grateful to you for all you're doing for me. I know it's hard for you to understand how hurt you can get within a marriage.

Patronising or *what*?

She's off and all I have to do again is nod and look grave. But she has triggered something. Old friends? What old friends? She's the only old friend I have. Actually the only friend I ever had. I was so busy with James and with just plain surviving that I never had time to develop friendships. Or (might as well be honest) I'd kept such a tight wall around myself and James that I'd kept any possible friends out. Maybe lack of friends runs in our family, I don't remember Mammy having any friends, besides the 'friends' that she brought home to the flat. And as for James's so-called friends, they aren't so hot in the loyalty and support department, are they?

I realize Patsy's looking at me, waiting for an answer to some question. What? I go, sorry, Patsy, I wasn't paying attention.

She sighs. She's coming back a little towards the old bossy Patsy. I was asking you what are the cops doing about the assault?

I don't know. I shrug. Probably what they do about all assaults. Very little. James didn't recognize any of the photographs they showed him. But since you ask . . .

Might as well go the whole hog, I think, as I get up and go over to my handbag, extract the Dear Scumbag letter from it. What do you think I should do with this?

She glances down at it, reads it, but it doesn't seem to

have the effect on her that it had on me. It's horrible, of course, she says, but I wouldn't get too upset about it. It's just par for the course. Look, she says then, do you mind if I say something?

Depends what it is, I say. (Uh-oh! I don't think I want to hear this—)

It's about James.

What about James? I tense up.

She gets all earnest. Despite what you think, she says, I do understand how you feel. You're probably not going to like what I'm going to say next but I've honestly been wanting to say it to you for a long time.

Go ahead, I say. But I don't want her to go ahead. Not now or in the future. This is not going to be helpful.

She doesn't notice anything in my tone of voice or if she does she ignores it. There comes a time, she says, when kids have to own up to their own failures. He got into trouble with a girl and the law, he should be punished for it. It's only right. It'll make a man of him, Angela.

I'm transfixed. Cold feet are marching up and down my spine. I can't identify yet whether it's from anger, outrage, panic, shame – what . . .

It's something to do with that word punish. The humiliation, the submission of it. I can't stand it. It's a word I *hate*. Along with retribution. I could never cope with reading anything in the papers or books about something as cold-blooded as official retribution. I've never been able to understand how Nazi-hunters can keep that flame burning for fifty years and for one second I can't contemplate the death penalty, even arguments about it. It's far too cold-blooded. I dream frequently about being hanged, I may have told you. It's my recurring nightmare.

I'm the type who could be mugged and then when I'd

see the guy who's mugged me in court, I'd immediately drop the charges. I'd see how nervous he is, I'd start thinking about what's facing him in gaol, his sorrow and loneliness, the pain of his mother, and that'd be me gone. I guess that makes me a very weak person. I'm certainly aware there's no logic to the way I think, particularly when I'm the person who so recently liked the taste of what I perceived as revenge. As human beings go, I'm quite a conundrum to myself. But, quite definitely, where James is concerned I'd rather die than see him 'punished'. I find it difficult even to say the word.

For once, Patsy doesn't pick up what's going through my head. She's looking at me but not seeing me, she's off on a crusade to convince me. James is a big boy now – what age is he? Nineteen? You'll have to let go, Ange, let him make his mistakes and pay for them himself. If dreadful things happen to him, well, they happen to us all and we all have to fend for ourselves eventually.

She stops as though she's waiting for an answer. I can't give one.

Amn't I right? Patsy says. You do too much for that boy. What'd he do if you were hit by a bus in the morning?

You're absolutely right, I say. But what I'm thinking is, what do you know? It's easy for you, I'm thinking, you smug little bitch, with your two point ten children and their ballet and swimming lessons and gymnastics and horse-riding and car pools. And your husband with his contacts and his cash economy. And your family holidays to Minorca and your terrific kitchen and your 'doing things as a family' and your bloody top-hat ice bucket. Bad and all as Martin is, he's your children's father and he does love them. That much I do know. There's two of you sharing the burden. Doesn't he bring them to football matches? Even the girls? Doesn't he help with the car pools when he's at home?

You're absolutely right, I say again.

It gives me no pleasure saying this, she shakes her head sorrowfully, and I'm not going to preach to you. I've said my say and, of course, it's up to you what you do.

She stands up. Look, I'm going to go outside to the phone box to ring home. You're right, I'm being selfish. The kids'll be worrying.

I hadn't heard myself saying anything about her being selfish.

Now she's shaking her head again, vigorously this time. But I'm not going home. Hell'll freeze over before I go back to that bastard. She leaves the flat.

She'll go home. Probably the minute she comes back in.

She hasn't left the flat ten seconds when *crack!* a huge clap of thunder rocks the place. It's followed by an instant deluge, so loud it drowns out the sound of the bus engine which has been revving outside at the traffic lights. Good. She'll be soaked. Good enough for her.

I rush over to the window to close it. It's already too late, the curtains are wet. I don't care, the wetter the better. How dare she? How dare she invade the private relationship between James and me?

But then I have to admit that it's not entirely Patsy's fault. At some very deep level I'm furious because something I've been maybe thinking about in tiny little dribs and drabs has been brought out in the open like this. What she said has impinged and it's shame-making.

Before I know it, I'm in James's room. The rain is just as loud in here, even though his window is shut tight. The air is so humid, you'd feel you'd nearly need windscreen wipers to see through it.

Did the cops ever get back to you about that assault? Have you done anything about it yourself?

He's lying on his bed with his hands behind his head. He has his Walkman on. He sees me come in and takes off the headset. Is she gone?

Temporarily, I say. Answer the question. Did they come back to you?

Did who come back to me?

The cops. Did they come back to you about the assault?

No. He turns away from me and lies with his face to the wall. Look, leave me alone. I don't care whether they come back to me or not. I don't care about any of it.

I look at his thin back. I notice that the cast on his arm is getting grubby. I'm testing out what Patsy said to me. I'm trying to be objective and to see this person as a young man who has to take care of his own problems. I'm trying not to see him as James. Trying very hard.

I hear myself saying, All right, James, I will leave you alone.

Good, he goes.

In a minute, after we've talked—

I don't feel like talking.

I can feel my top teeth grinding into my bottom ones. I insist, I say. I'm not leaving until you turn around. Please turn around and look at me.

Go away.

How many times do I have to tell you? I won't go away. Turn around.

All right! *What?* He spins in the bed and glares at me. But for once he isn't intimidating me. I just want to talk, I say as calmly as I can, that's all.

Well, go ahead, talk. Hurry up. What do you want to talk about?

This isn't easy, James. Please don't make it harder. What have I ever done to you that you should be as hostile as this to me?

For Christ's sake, he says, if you've something to say to me, say it. Why is everything always about *you*?

Now it comes pouring out. That's just it, I say. This is about me and it's about time I talked about me. Your days of hanging out of me are numbered, James. I'm a person. I'm a human being. I'm not just an anonymous robot who's here to support you and to pick up the pieces after you mess up. It's time you stood on your own two feet. You're nineteen and I'm tired of supporting you. I'm not your mother, you know, I'm only your sister − and I'm a woman. I'm tired of being taken for granted, I want my own life.

This is a jolt to my system. I didn't know I felt like this. But I find I mean it. Saying it has made me discover that I mean it.

Most of it, anyhow. What about the bit about not being his mother? I suppose, technically speaking, I mean that too, but it's sort of splitting hairs, isn't it? He didn't come out of my womb and that does give you an extra special bond. Maybe it's because I wasn't ever a mother that I can't imagine how a mother could feel any more love for a son than I feel for James. (Being a mother of a criminal must be torture.)

Someone in the street lets out a scream. They must be getting caught in the rain, which seems to be lashing down louder and louder.

Looking at James's expression, I'm in danger of starting to feel sorry for him as usual. I've never spoken to him this way in my life. I've lashed out, yelled, said things I didn't mean, called him names. But this is different, this has the ring of absolute truth. He knows it. The shock on his face is genuine.

Before I can weaken, I carry on. You've had a raw deal in your life, I know that, I say firmly. I'm sorry about it, but I've done the best I can. I'm exhausted, James.

His bruised eyes are wide. I know you're not my mother, Angela, he says. He hardly ever uses my name.

I read somewhere about the best way to deal with situations like this. When you have an advantage, don't use it.

Right, I say, I think I've made my point. Would you like a cup of tea or something?

Yeah, he whispers. He's still looking at me.

I go out into the kitchen. I start to shake as I'm filling the kettle. And I still have to tell him about Pius.

Damn Patsy.

➔ Thirty-Three ←

M onday morning. Still haven't told James, but my
father has come up with a plan. When I hear it I'm
in two minds about it. To put it mildly.

At first I rejected it outright. It seemed so outlandish.
I'll give him this much, he's nothing if not a lateral
thinker!

I ring him from a phone box outside an office block
I've just helped to clean. This booth is along the Grand
Canal, near Mount Street Bridge. The rain is bashing hell
out of the metal roof — we've had nearly eighteen hours
of it at this stage — and the road is clogged with rush-hour
traffic. He's whispering at his end, but even if he'd been
shouting I'd be finding it hard to hear him.

After due consideration, he's saying, his best advice
would be that James should go down to the monks in the
abbey at Mount Melleray. That he would arrange it. It
would give you and James breathing space, he says. It'd
take him out of the fray for a while until things calm
down a bit.

I'm sorry, Mr Crawford, I say, it's very noisy here,
you'll have to speak up a bit. Did I hear you right? Did
you say something about monks?

Instead of speaking louder he slows down. I . . . know
. . . the . . . Abbot, I . . . know . . . him . . . personally

. . . and . . . I've . . . taken . . . him . . . into . . . my
. . . confidence . . .

Monks? Abbots?

Can I think about it? I say.

Take all the time in the world, he says back. His voice
has got stronger – I can hear the relief. I haven't hit the
roof. I'm going to agree to us being nicely packaged away
from his nice life. James will wear sackcloth and ashes in
a monastery until all the publicity blows over. And, of
course, the main beauty of this great plan is that the two
of us, particularly me, can be safely kept away from
Tullamore. You have my office number now, he says. All
it'll take is a telephone call and we're all set.

Mr Crawford, I say quickly, I'm not sure about—

A motorcyclist – it'd have to be a courier, of course –
zooms past the line of traffic on the inside. Right through
the lake which extends six feet out from the kerb where
I'm standing. I'm soaked up to the chest.

Sorry, I say. Look, can I ring you back? There's too
much noise here—

I can hear he's put the receiver very close to his mouth
now. Would it be possible, Angela, that we could keep
this between the three of us? For the time being, that is.

If it wasn't James and me involved here it would be
almost endearing. I don't find it endearing. Does
Dorothy know? I ask him. Up to this summer I'd had no
idea I could be so bitchy.

Bull's-eye.

Dorothy? he goes, and I can hear the fright. Er –
not yet. Then, in a rush, But of course I'm going to tell
her.

Of course, I say. I'll telephone you back sometime
later on today. I smash down the telephone. Lucky for
me this phone is one of the vandal-proof ones.

A monastery – the very idea!

I call into the Fitzgibbon Street Guards on my way home. No developments in the assault case.

I wasn't really expecting any, was I? When what they're looking for is someone, or a group of someones, giving just deserts to a rapist. I'm getting bitter now? So be it.

It occurs to me to ask this Guard I'm talking to if there would be any difficulty about James going to a monastery – not that I'm agreeing he should go to any monastery, far from it, but just in case . . .

Could it go hard on him next year with the judge if we started cancelling his counselling sessions? (From the little he's said about the first one, I'd be afraid his counsellor will just cement his prejudices about women having it every way, these days. Reading between the lines, she struck me as a feminist first and a counsellor second, more interested in making sure he accepts that men are scum and women are saints. Mind you, that's James talking and I haven't met the woman.)

This Guard can't see what objection there could be to him going to Mount Melleray, apparently once the court case is over, the cops, technically speaking, have no more to do with it. And if we need the lad to identify anyone, he goes, we'll know where he is.

I get home and I broach the subject of the monastery with James. You think my reaction was anti? I leave his to your imagination. Ballistic doesn't cover it. Very little of it is printable.

I'm to forget it, he's not for a second going to go to any bleedin' bog-arsed monastery, no way José, forget it, *forget* it! That's just a small flavour.

Would you believe I find myself arguing with him, as if I'm in love with this notion? Could he at least think about it? Like, has he any better ideas?

I'll think about it all right, he says, in your dreams. It's my life, you know. At least it was when I looked the last time. *I'll* decide what I'll do and when I'll do it. Whose bleedin' looper idea was this?

Mine.

I've funked it again.

Bleedin' airhead, he yells. I'll decide, right? Not you or anyone else. He storms off into his room.

I go about the place like a dervish, tidying up. I should be the one to go to Mount Melleray, get a bit of peace for myself, leave him to his own devices, the pup. Does he not realize the pickle he's in, that everyone's only trying to help? I wasn't joking when I asked if he had any better ideas. I certainly can't come up with any. What are we going to do? Wait for the knock on the door? The next ambush in another laneway? I see now it was pie in the sky that the two of us should go and live in a cosy cottage someplace, with me in a new job. What am I qualified for? How many contract cleaning companies are there in rural Ireland?

I'm like a mad thing, pulling all the books off the shelves to dust them, squirting Jif over everything in sight. I throw the cushions off the bed-settee to clean underneath them — and there's one of Patsy's earrings.

I stop, calm down. In a way I'm glad I've found this, in a way I'm not. It means I'll have to contact her again to let her know I found it.

I want to see her because I can't bear to have bad blood between us, I don't want to see her because we'll never be friends again. At least, not like we were. I suppose I could post it to her in a Jiffy-bag . . .

I stand there looking at the golden circlet in the palm of my hand. It's in the shape of a dolphin, chasing its tail. Patsy has a thing about dolphins and Martin bought her these earrings for their tenth anniversary.

Yesterday afternoon when she comes back from the

phone box after ringing home, she's like a drowning kitten, her mascara is running down her face and her bouffant hairdo is as flat as straw. She's frantic. It rang and rang, she says, but there was no answer. Where are they all? I have to go home and see where they all are.

This is the person who was never going back, never, no way, who didn't care what they did, any of them. She'd even got the operator to try to make sure it was really ringing and that it wasn't out of order.

Hang on a sec, I say, you're soaked. I give her a towel to scrub her hair – this is obviously when the earring came off. She's scrubbing away and she's half crying. They should be there, we weren't going anywhere today – I have to go home right away. Sorry, Ange – I guess you think I'm really off the wall.

Not at all, Patsy, I say.

She's racing out of the flat. The front doorbell rings. She gallops down the stairs, me after her.

Yep. You're right. It's Martin. Half hangdog, half aggressive. Hey, Pats, he goes, I knew you'd be here. I have the kids in the car.

Splat! She gives him a box. Right in the face. Then she throws herself at him, arms around the neck, sobbing, all that, with the front door open and the rain creasing the pavement outside and me standing there like a third leg. If this is marriage you can have it.

I'm still looking down at this earring, I can't make up my mind. So I put it in one of the presses, safely inside a broken cup that we don't use.

Where is this place anyway? It's James, the door has opened without me hearing it. I have my back to him and I turn around. He's standing in the doorway with a belligerent face on him. I haven't a clue, I go, I'd have to buy a map.

Forget it. Don't bother. Slam! He's gone back into his room.

We're obviously making progress of sorts. If that's what I really want. Dammit, a monastery? Angela Devine? James Devine? How come I find myself on Pius Crawford's side? It's because I'm desperate, that's why.

I still hadn't rung him back by eight o'clock that evening and neither James nor I had brought up the subject of Mount Melleray again. Then the decision was made for us.

First, a brick came through the window. A half brick to be precise. I suppose because we're on the first floor a whole brick would have been too difficult to aim properly. We were watching television and things were fairly frosty between us. We were letting the telly do the talking.

I was getting fed up of it and as usual, I decided to make the first move in the ice-breaking department. I was walking across the room to fetch Adeline's photographs to show him when the window shattered. It seems he's destined never to see those bloody snaps.

The noise of a brick coming through your window is shocking, absolutely shocking. I wouldn't wish it on my worst enemy. It's like a bomb going off inside your head. This huge explosion and then all this glass crashing onto hard surfaces.

We both duck.

Then – I suppose this shows our different personalities – I run to the window in an effort to see who threw it, while James curses and swears and then barrels out the door and down the stairs.

To me, everything outside looks normal. People standing under umbrellas at the bus stop. Cars swishing by. Trees dripping dark green in the park across the

street. No one legging it as far as I can see . . . And it's a
cliché, I know, but where are the Guards when you need
them? I wouldn't mind but lately, particularly since that
journalist was murdered, they're foot-patrolling much
more than they used to around here.

I can't see James. Whoever it was must have run the
other way, towards Dorset Street. Immediately I find
myself worried sick that whoever James might be chasing
could have a knife. Even a gun. Guns are ten a penny in
Dublin these days. Any gurrier with a twenty-pound
note seems to be able to hire one for the night.

Have you ever noticed that if you drop even a small
drinking glass how much of it there seems to be when it
breaks? Huge chunks of the stuff had come in on top of
the sink, slivers of it have stuck into the soles of my
shoes, I can't see them but each step produces tiny
crunches.

Bits of brick had scraped off against the sides of the
sink, crumbs caught in the ruching of the curtains. I
realize the rain is squalling in through the jagged glass,
what's left of it, in the window, and I start looking
around for something temporary to patch into it.

James comes back without any further damage to
himself, thank God. Did he see anyone?

No.

He helps me clean up. With his good hand he fixes a
piece of a cornflake packet over the hole in the window
with Sellotape. Not that it's going to do much good in
this rain.

That was item one on the menu for the evening. It
wasn't long before we got to item two.

Guess who drops by unexpectedly, about forty minutes later. Our dear landlord, Mr Reddy, that's who.
May I come in? He has on his grave face and he has his
rent book in his hand. I know we're paid up to date so

I've no worries on that score. Behind me, James turns up the telly, an ad. That terrific one for Peugeot cars, search for the hero inside yourself. You'd have to laugh.

I'm not laughing, though. It's not convenient at the moment, I say, as firmly as I can. Reddy flushes up. Well, then, I'll say what I have to say out here, he says. I'm afraid I'm going to ask you to leave.

Leave?

Yes, leave. He has this naturally quavery voice and it's even more quavery than usual. I've had a number of complaints, he goes. And although I didn't know it until now – he's looking over my shoulder – I see you've broken a window . . .

Who were these so-called complaints from?

Never mind who they were from. I run a respectable establishment here.

Now why is that our Dwyer down the landing pops into my mind? He who just happens always to be on site when there's any trouble.

I know who the complaints were from, I say to Reddy, and however many there were, correct me if I'm wrong, I could take a wild guess that they were all from the same party. And all unjustified. Now, if you'll excuse me, I know my rights. I slam the door. Lean against it.

He's knocking again. I can feel the knocking against the middle of my back. I should have anticipated this, one of the other neighbours confided in me once on rent day that Reddy is a member of one of those super-Catholic outfits who lean to the right of the Ku Klux Klan. Maybe it's Pius Crawford's Catholic rights, ha ha!

Some Christianity he's showing at the moment, wouldn't you say?

I try to ignore the knocking. Stare at the telly. The Peugeot ad is over and here's one now for a programme coming up later in the week. It's for *Davis*. I don't watch

Davis often, even if I have charge of the television, but I wouldn't be too keen on it in any case because it's one of those panel discussion programmes about serious issues. At that time of night my brain is usually scrambled and I'm looking for something really naff where I don't have to think. Preferably with a few laughs.

Miss Devine, Miss Devine. I can hear Reddy's voice squeaking outside over Derek Davis's.

Derek Davis is staring at the camera from under his eyebrows. Date rape, he says, in a voice from the mummy's crypt. In the wake of the release on to the streets of James Devine—

James zaps the telly. He's sitting in his chair like it's Oul' Sparky and he's waiting for that switch to be thrown. Reddy is still knocking into my back. Miss Devine, I've every right – open this door. I've *every* right—

Shut up! I scream at the door, I hammer on it with both my fists, banging back at Reddy.

I'm going now but I'll be back tomorrow, he shouts through the door. Then he seems to wait. I hold my breath. The silence in the flat is deafening.

Next thing I can hear him walking away, going down the stairs. Our door thwacks a little as he slams the outside one.

I turn around and look at James. For all my big brave words, I know we're on a lost cause. I also know James knows – neither of us can stomach much more of this. He's trembling.

We can certainly fight being thrown out of our home if we have the guts for it. Tony Gregory is our local TD, he'd help us, he'd easily handle Reddy. And even though we haven't signed any contract, we've been here so long we have definite rights. Rights to proper notice, for instance.

What is the point, though, of staying in a place where

you're not wanted, where your neighbours want you out? It was different when I thought he might want to throw us all out in order to develop the place into yuppie apartments. That'd be easy to fight. But now we're pariahs. Now I know what it must feel like to be a drug dealer in the middle of the Concerned Parents' territory.

Will you get the hell down to that monastery, for God's sake? I say. Just for a while at least. (So much for principles . . .)

Eff off, he goes, I'm going near no monastery.

Leaving the time not exactly ripe for intimate discussions on the finding of fathers.

How I went to work the next morning, how I pushed that polisher around, I don't know. But, anyway, I did. I suppose when everything is crashing down around you it helps to keep to some kind of a routine. I did find myself going into daydreams, though. Like I didn't recognize my own hand at one stage. I gazed at it, this white, unfamiliar thing splayed against a yellow duster. Starfish?

To my astonishment, James is up and dressed when I get home. It's a different story this morning, every inch of bravado seems to have been sucked out of him. The telly isn't on and he isn't eating. He's sitting at the table staring into space.

What is it, James? Did something else happen?

Nothing happened.

What's up, then? Why are you just sitting there?

It's a free country, isn't it? But his heart isn't in it, he's as cowed as a whipped pup.

I put my bag down and glance with longing at the bed-settee. I'm so tired my eyes can't focus. I force myself to stay standing. James, I say gently, look at me.

He shakes his head. Gazes at his fists, balled on his knees.

I'm as sceptical about monks and monasteries as you

are, I say, but one thing I do know, they're lovely tranquil places. I'm positive you won't have to do the Catholic bit if you don't want to, they take everyone in — Muslims, Hindus, Jews, atheists — anyone who asks. They don't even ask you why. Think about it, James. You need a break from all this hassle. It won't be for long.

(If I'd thought last May, when this all started, that Angela Devine would be urging her brother to go to a monastery!) James doesn't respond or move. It's terrible to see him like this.

Slowly, he nods.

It's then I finally tell him about Pius. He listens quietly.

What do you think? I ask him at the end.

He's your da, he's nothing to do with me, is he? The hopeless expression in his eyes'd kill you.

By lunch-time that Tuesday a sort of recklessness has taken me over. I've pushed my tiredness into the background, I'm determined we're going to be well on our way out of Reddy's kip before he comes knocking again on our door.

Thank God it has at last stopped raining when I go down to the phone box to ring Pius Crawford. It'll have to be immediately, I tell him, tomorrow. There have been developments this end, and we have to leave our flat.

What kind of developments?

It'd take too long to tell you.

He'll be happy to make the arrangements. (I'll bet!) What time shall I tell them he'll arrive?

I'll have to find out about the buses, I say. Tell them sometime tomorrow afternoon or evening, that should cover it. Then I have to ask him where the blasted monastery is . . .

Angela, he goes, after he's finished telling me, please feel free to telephone me any time. His voice is hushed. We'll make arrangements to meet sometime soon, all right?

That'd be nice, I say.

He changes completely. Yes, thank you, I'll be in touch in the near future. Everything goes muffled, his hand has gone over the mouthpiece. He's talking to someone—

Here he is back, Thanks for everything, see you soon, God bless now, goodbye.

And, surprise surprise, I'm left with a dead telephone in my hand. This must be what it's like to be a married man's mistress.

Thirty-Four

The odd thing is, I find I'm not even upset about my father's reaction. Funny, isn't it? You spend half a lifetime wondering, and then when you galvanize yourself and get lucky enough to find him, it's like — well, what is it like?

I find I'm too exhausted to analyse my present feelings about Pius Crawford. I'm confused, certainly, but it's all too new. It took thirty-six years to get to this place, nothing is going to happen overnight and in all fairness he has to be given a bit of breathing space. On the other hand, he's not getting off the hook in the matter of my half-siblings. Sometime in the future I definitely want to meet my brothers and sisters. Definitely. That other Angela looked nice.

I decide I might as well take advantage of being in the telephone box. I ring Patsy and tell her she'll have to come and get her earring if she wants it, that I'd be afraid it'd get lost when we move.

She sounds shocked, as well she might. Move? What do you mean, move?

What I said. Move. You know, pantechnicons, packing.

Don't be like that. Why are you moving? Have you a place?

When I tell her no, to give her her due, she offers that James and I could stay with them until we get sorted out. Martin and I would love to have you.

I thank her for her offer but say we'll be fine. Hah! I'm thinking, Martin and I . . . Who was right? They're all lovey-dovey again. Until the next time.

I know what you're thinking, Angela, she says. You're thinking, what's going on with Martin and me — that there we were only yesterday—

I interrupt her. It's your business, Patsy. Look, I have to go, I've a lot of phone calls to make and I've to start packing. I'll be in touch. We'll be in tonight if you want to come for your earring.

I hang up.

For the rest of that day I couldn't shake off the feeling that James and I were making parcels of our lives. Putting everything in compartments and sealing them up, maybe even for ever.

Yet somehow, far from being momentous or tragic, the packing became gay. I should have been sad to leave, James and I had spent a long time in this place — James the greater part of his life. Bad and all as it was, it was home to us. Yet, despite all our problems and traumas, I was finding it a little exhilarating to think we were going to someplace new. I had got into a rut here.

I have to say that James did Trojan work, considering the plaster on his arm. And for the first time in ages we were working together as a team, the two of us having fun. We were consulting each other. What about this? (A raggedy cushion.) Nah! Out. Bam! The candlewick bedspreads? Uh-huh — gone! We became sort of feverish. Tearing papers, sweeping up drawersful of junk. This? (The Present from Tramore ashtray.) Out! Ornaments? All out. Why we ever needed ornaments — why anyone needs ornaments — I don't know.

When we'd cleared the bookshelves and stacked all the books in the middle of the floor, guess what fell out of *Macbeth*? My three-star scratch card in its envelope. I put it safely in my handbag.

I'd bought several packets of the jumbo-sized black rubbish bags. Leaving our clothes and toiletries until later – and my books because I'd have to get boxes for those – we reserved one pack to hold what we wanted to keep.

As it turned out, we didn't need the pack because everything we wanted to save fitted into two of the bags – yes, that's all, two! We divided our crockery and cutlery into what we needed to eat and drink and what were just spares. We kept four sets of sheets and four towels, a frying pan, our electric kettle and iron, our tin opener and a few spatulas, kitchen knives and serving spoons. James kept his precious CDs, his tapes and his ghetto-blaster. (And, would you believe, his baby toys. A rattle and a set of alphabet blocks I hadn't even known he had because they were buried so deep under the jumble of clothes in his wardrobe.) My lacquered tray, because wherever we end up, I don't want to give up my Saturday-afternoon deli snacks.

The whole process was most instructive. Two lives. Two whole lives totalling nearly fifty-six years and if you discount our clothes, the sum total of the possessions we really needed – or wanted – could fit into two jumbo-sized plastic bags. (Plus my books and it's arguable whether you need books. Certainly not at subsistence level – ask Mammy or any of her 'friends'.)

I look around. Are we sure we want nothing else?

I briefly consider Patsy's ruched curtains. No. A Present to Reddy.

The two of us do one last search but can find nothing more. What about the TV? All of a sudden, James is looking sad. What'll we do without a telly? And what about my bike?

The TV is Reddy's. If our new place, wherever it is, doesn't come with one we'll have to rent. Anyway, I tell him, you won't be looking at telly for a while where you're going!

All gaiety collapses. I could have bitten out my tongue. What about the bike? he's demanding now. I need that bike.

Look, you can get another one when your arm is better and when things settle down, I tell him. We can't keep it, you've got to see that. I'll ring the place you bought it from first thing tomorrow, tell them we can't keep up the payments. They'll take it back – thank God it's still in good condition.

He becomes really upset about that bike but what option did we have? I couldn't exactly bring a motorbike with me, neither could he, and it wasn't doing either of us much good chained up and attracting penalty interest on the payments.

Speaking of options, I'm in no position to have scruples about asking for help with the move – so who could I ask?

Guess.

James and I took turns that evening sitting by the window to watch for any bricks.

I finally gave him the photographs. He spread them out and looked at them but, as far as I could judge, they had little effect on him.

I'd been reading too much into what his reaction might be. He didn't know Mammy at all – I keep forgetting that and these were snaps of a long-ago little girl. Why don't you keep them, I suggest to him, bring them with you to Mount Melleray?

I'm thinking that maybe in the peace and quiet he'll be able to study them better and then they might begin to mean something to him. He simply shrugs, turns his attention back to the television. But I notice he bundles them as neatly together as a pack of cards.

At about ten o'clock, just before it got dark, I slipped out to go down to Ken Sheils's place. I wanted to ask him about moving us, I had a note ready to put in his mailbox in case he wasn't in.

I hadn't seen him since Birr and so much had happened in between that it felt like weeks and not just a couple of days — I mean, that trip had been on the Saturday and this was only the Tuesday evening . . .

I could see his window was open — it looks out on to the street. He was at home.

Hi, he says, after he buzzes me in. He's on the landing, hanging over the stairs. His voice is echoing in the stairwell even though he's talking just above a whisper so as not to draw the attention of the other residents.

Hi, I whisper back.

I'm breathless when I get up to his landing. (I don't like lifts. What if there's a fire?) I know it's late, I go, and I'm sorry to disturb you, but I was wondering if you would do me a favour tomorrow?

He hesitates. Birr again, is it? It'll have to be tomorrow night I'm afraid because I've a job.

No, it's not Birr. And tomorrow night would be perfect. We're moving out of our flat and I have a few bits and pieces that I'll need help with. I thought if you and your van were free . . .

I can't read the expression on his face, it's closed in. I assume he thinks this is a bit much to ask. I get embarrassed. Look, it doesn't matter, don't worry about it. I can get at taxi, it's not furniture or anything, we only have a few plastic bags, and books, they'll easily fit.

Of course don't get a taxi, he goes. Come in – would you like a cup of coffee?

It's on the tip of my tongue to refuse but then it flashes through my mind that I can't just keep asking this guy to do things for me while keeping him at arm's length.

Sam immediately jumps up on my lap when I'm in and sitting down. I stroke his silky little body. Ken goes into the kitchen section of the room, begins quietly to make the coffee. I'm really sorry about this, I go, I don't mean to keep using you like this just because you own a van—

I don't think you're using me at all.

It's just that, when I asked you, the expression on your face—

I was admiring how you looked. He doesn't turn around. He might as well have being telling me the price of coffee beans in Colombia.

I concentrate on Sam.

This guy invented silence. He feels no need to chatter when he has nothing to say. Whereas before, I guess, I found this to be rather an odd, even intimidating habit, now I find it restful. The quiet sort of radiates out from him.

All you can hear is the odd clink as he takes cups out, places spoons on the saucers. When he's silent like this, you don't feel you have to talk either. So I don't. (Quite a novelty for the Gabber Angela!) Inside, though, I'm giving myself a stern scolding. I'm telling myself I'll have to sort out the situation between Ken and me once and for all. All right, we're never going to be *Gone With The Wind*. But then, at my age, am I likely to find *Gone With The Wind*? I read stories all the time in *Hello!* about fifty- and sixty-year-olds who are head over heels about each other, *Romeo and Juliet* ('this one is for keeps'), so why not me?

Do I even want *Gone With The Wind*? I suppose

everyone does, to a degree – but we all know that it doesn't last and couldn't I settle for what seems to be on offer here? Good old-fashioned reliability, steadiness, companionship. And sex too. The sex was all right, wasn't it?

I can't see straight about this guy. I'm starting to depend on him too much and that's complicating things to the extent that I'm putting reins on myself – as you know, I hate being one tittle dependent on anyone. Yet every time I've hit a crisis lately, who was the first person I ran to? And it wasn't just because he had transport. Patsy has transport and I didn't run to her, did I? To and fro, pro and con, my brain starts to hurt from all this ruminating.

He brings the coffee over, pulls up one of the dining-room chairs to sit in front of me, takes Sam from me. You'll have to write down my telephone number, he goes, save you all this running down Gardiner Street in the middle of the night. This move is a bit sudden, isn't it? Where are you moving to?

I tell him about the brick and Reddy and Dwyer.

I'll say one thing for you, Angela, he goes, no one can say you lead a dull life. He sips his coffee. Have you considered that maybe that brick was unconnected with your troubles – could it be just a casual passer-by? Some little thug?

No, I say. It has to be connected. It's too much of a coincidence.

M-mm, he goes, as if he doesn't believe me.

I sip my coffee, which is lovely and mild. I saw the jar – he uses the Cap Colombie, it's very expensive. Maybe you have a point, he says then, in his slow way. Maybe you and James should move. These media hypes always die down after a little while but now, with these books—

What books?

He stares at me. You don't know? It was in the papers last Sunday.

What books?

His face creases, he's desperately uncomfortable. I sit up on the edge of the chair. Tell me, I go, please, Ken. What books?

He tells me. Apparently there are two journalists racing each other to see who'll be the first to get books out on the subject of date rape in Ireland. Star centre-piece (surprise, surprise), Rosemary Madden's case.

That'll teach me. I was getting too quiet, too relaxed. Thinking I have things under control. I put the coffee cup down on the floor beside me. Carefully, because my hand seems to have lost a lot of its strength. Did it say when these books are likely to come out?

No — I'm sorry, Angela, I've upset you now. I shouldn't have said anything about it but I thought you knew. Look, he puts his own cup down beside mine and takes my hands in his, try not to worry about it. Tell your solicitor. You might be able to take out an injunction.

I think about going through that whole rigmarole, widening all those wounds. And I have no idea whether or not free legal aid would handle injunctions to stop people publishing books.

I might, I say, I'll see. (I don't know what I'm saying here. I'm on automatic. But I do know one thing, I'm certainly not going to allow the two of us to be sitting ducks. Books take a while to come out, don't they? But if they're racing each other—)

Ken lets go of my hands, sits back again in his chair. Where are the two of you moving to? I tell him about James going to Mount Melleray. As for me, I say, I don't know where I'm going yet, but during the day tomorrow I'll find somewhere temporary, just for a few nights while I look around for a flat. I'll get one easy. The *Herald* is full of them.

Where temporary? he asks. You mean a hotel or something? Or have you a friend you could stay with, that friend, Patsy?

Something like that, I say back. I realize for the first time that I've got so carried away with the packing – and am so relieved about James being sorted out, temporarily at least – that I haven't thought through the question of where to go myself.

We don't actually have to go tomorrow, we have until Friday at the very least before the next rent money is due. But you know how once you make a decision to do something like that you have to do it right now. Then I remember that Gardiner Street, right here where we're sitting now, is full of hostels and bed-and-breakfasts further down towards the Liffey. I'll be fine, I say to Ken, I'll probably move into one of the bed-and-breakfasts down the road.

Why don't you move in here for the few days?

I know by his face that this popped out.

Ken! I go as if I'm totally taken aback – which, of course, I am – but my brain surges like a rocket. I have to be very careful here.

Sorry, he goes, that was a bit previous of me.

It would be so easy just to say yes. To have the decision made, to have someone look after me. But he has only one bedroom. One bed. And yet I don't want to hurt him.

Not at all, I say, don't be sorry, I just don't know how to react. You're a very generous man and I appreciate the offer very much—

But you're afraid I'll want to sleep with you again.

I stare at him. Thank God it's out in the open. Well, won't you?

Of course I'll want to, he says. He's being brave although it's obvious he's still mortally embarrassed. But only if you want to, too, Angela. I'm not a— He bites it off.

Rapist. He was going to say, I'm not a rapist.

For once I'm not offended, I'm really not. I could see he didn't mean any offence and he wasn't referring to James, it's just one of those things that people say.

It's all right, I say. But I'm glad you brought it up, we do have to talk about this. Even if this business of me staying here hadn't come up. You must think I'm a horrible person. After all, we have gone to bed together already and now here I am going all prissy. You must be asking yourself what the hell is wrong with me, was I just leading you on . . .

You are not a horrible person, Angela, he says slowly. And I know full well you were not leading me on. As a matter of fact, I've been asking myself if I've been the one who's been forcing myself on you.

Now we're both stuck for words. We're tiptoeing around each other, like a pair of little children meeting each other in the playground for the first time. We should be honest with each other, I say eventually.

Yes, we should. He shifts a little in the chair as though he's getting ready for some really big attack.

It's he who breaks it. So what do you want from me?

This is useless, of course. Gets us nowhere. Before I can answer it, he leans forward in his chair again. I'd do anything for you, Angela, he says, but the question I want answered is what I just asked you. What do you really want from me?

We're still tiptoeing. We're both afraid of our lives to do or say anything that could be used in evidence against us later. The first one to declare loses. It's time to be blunt. Look, Ken, I say, this isn't going to be helpful, but

I don't know what I want in the long term. I'm sorry but I don't. I do know what I want right now — a bit of peace. I can't keep up with what's happening to me or to James.

It's my turn to lean forward now, our heads are only inches apart although I don't really notice. I'm thinking so fast that my tongue can barely keep up. I'm blurting.

Look what's just happened to me this summer, for a start there's the James situation and what that has taken out of me — out of both of us, with everyone hounding us, the press, everyone. To tell you the truth, I feel absolutely cornered. But I'm the only one he has, Ken.

I'm so worked up I put both my hands to the sides of my head, because I feel if I don't it might explode. He's gazing at me like I'm some kind of lunatic, which is exactly what I must look and sound like. I can feel the little veins jumping in my temples.

Do you know what that must feel like? I ask him. To have no family at all, only one person? At least at one stage of my life I knew what it was like to have more than one person. You know, too. The fact that James and I don't get along all that well on the surface doesn't really matter. How could we? There's no one else for him to have a go at. He's had a raw deal in his life, he really has, and he has to be very angry inside.

What's more, there's the small detail of me meeting my father for the first time ever. How do you think I feel about that little development after all these years? And do you know what? I can't make up my mind whether I'm pleased or sorry we found him last Saturday . . . Maybe I should have left well enough alone. But it's too bloody late now, isn't it? Then there're my money troubles, not helped by the fact that I've dropped out of at least one, probably two of my four part-time jobs.

Also I'm being thrown out of the place we've lived in for years—

I run out of steam. To me, the chronicle of my life this summer reads like I should just go and jump off the nearest bridge as quickly as possible and stop wasting everyone's time.

Maybe now you can see how mixed up I am, I say in a quieter tone of voice. How I can't concentrate on whether or not we should sleep together. To tell you the truth, Ken, that's about the furthest thing from my mind. Sex, even the mention of it, seems irrelevant to me. It's absolutely nothing personal.

I understand. Ken's face is deadly serious now. I really do, Angela. But I do take issue with you. Sex can be very comforting—

I'm opening my mouth again when he shushes it with one finger. On the matter of beds, on staying here, my offer stands. That chair you're sitting on opens out into a bed. No problem.

I look back at him as though he had two heads. I don't understand you, I say. Are you St Francis of Assisi or what?

Thirty-Five

Ken Sheils flashes me a grin. I'm far from St anybody, he goes. You haven't a clue about me, you should meet the lovely Diandra — she'd fill you in sharpish. He looks sad all of a sudden.

I couldn't stay here, it wouldn't be fair.

What's not fair about it? I'll admit I would love for us to develop something together, but if it's not to be it's not to be. Listen, Angela, you've been through a very rough time and if it's peace you want, you couldn't be in a better place than here. Think of it as your personal Mount Melleray. I'll be out working. Sam'll be out with me. You'll have the place to yourself all day. You wouldn't believe how quiet these apartments are, all of us solitary worker bees in the little solitary cells of our hive. We're all dead scared even to say hello to each other in case we'd be thought to be minding the other fella's business. There's plenty of room as you can see. He waves an arm around the apartment. There's a whole empty wardrobe in there in the bedroom. My clothing requirements, as you can gather, are modest. He looks at his feet. And I think I wouldn't mind at all knowing you were here to come home to — even for just a few days and even if there was nothing more to it than a bowl of soup in the evenings. He holds up his hand like a lollipop lady – stop, stop! Don't get all panicky. I'm not presuming anything. We could simply play house for a few days, couldn't we, Angela?

He's niced me to death. I think of the peace, the cleanliness of the place. No Dwyer, no Reddy. All right, I say. For a couple of days. If you're really sure.

Am I sure? I'm obviously not the orator I think I am.

We smile at one another. I won't take up much space, I say, I haven't much stuff, my clothes and a few black plastic bags.

Great. Ken gets to his feet. Look forward to it – I'll get you the spare keys. And by the way, I won't hear a word of argument, the guest gets the bedroom. I sleep out here.

But—

I *said* – not a word of argument. He puts a finger on my lips to shut me up.

Thanks. I say it humbly because I mean it humbly. Being me, though, I'm still worried that this won't run as smoothly as is being offered. The nights are long and we'll be only a few feet away from each other. Still, it is only for a couple of days and I do get up very early in the mornings.

He's not finished. There is one condition, he goes. And that is that you start behaving like the gorgeous person you are. Do you look at yourself in mirrors at all? You're a beautiful woman, Angela.

I gape at him. No one in my life, not even Tom Bennett, has ever said that to me and I haven't a clue how to react. Mirrors? I don't have time to examine myself in mirrors. And when I do look into one, when I'm washing my teeth, all I see is a mole under the hairline on the left-hand side. I'm certainly not beautiful. No way. How – how do I behave? I stammer it. I – I need my hair cut . . .

Your hair's perfect, he says back quietly. Cut it if you like but it's perfect. And so is your face. He grins. And so is your body and so are your legs – as I so well remember.

Well, there was no answer to that, was there?

He insists on walking me home. But he doesn't kiss me like he did before. It's like he's now put an exclusion zone around me.

I was still half shocked as I climbed the stairs and then let myself back into our place, so out of it that I actually got a surprise when I saw the state it was in – the books piled in the middle of the floor, the bare look of the shelves above the sink, the scored surface of Reddy's table. During the time I was out, I'd semi-forgotten the clearout James and I had given it.

I noticed that Adeline's photographs were no longer where he had put them, on the draining board.

And here's James himself, not sitting by the window as he's supposed to, to watch for potential thugs. James has the attention span of a one-day-old kitten. Instead, he's hunched in the middle of it all, plastic bags to the right of him plastic bags to the left. Staring at Reddy's telly for the last time.

No point in recriminations. Any problems? I say to him.

Uh-uh! he goes. I flop onto the settee. James, we mightn't see each other for a while.

He doesn't remove his gaze from grand-prix racing. The noise is frightful. Look, I go, would you turn that down a bit? I want us to talk.

He gives this big exaggerated sigh and zaps the television off. Same old belligerent James. It's like the brick, the brief intimacy of us packing together, his genuine fear and misery of only a few hours ago have never happened. I'm tempted just to go to bed – after

all, I have to get up again in six hours' time, but I meant
what I said to Ken Sheils on James's behalf. It must be
awful to have just one person in your life.

It's in my mind to talk to him about everything
important that I haven't said to him, all our lives
together. But now that he's staring at me, I can't think of
any of it. I'm as inane as ever. Are you all set for Mount
Melleray?

He picks up the zapper again but before he can use it,
Look, I go quickly, what I really want to say is that I'm
going to miss you, James. I'm going to miss you terribly.

He's going to fall off his chair with surprise and
confusion. Then he stands up, I'll miss you too, muttered
so quickly and quietly that I would have missed it if the
place hadn't been so deathly quiet. Then he's gone into
his room.

It isn't much, I know, but to me it's unbearably
moving.

In bed that night, I can't sleep. It's my last night here,
his too. Our last night as a family, such as it is. I have the
deepest, strongest instinct that this night is like a
guillotine. We are about to be chopped apart. Even if he
stays in that monastery for only one day, for half a day,
this is the end of whatever chance we've been given to
develop a particular relationship. No more working on
that one. We were given nineteen years and our time is
up. From now on it has to be something else.

I always knew this night would come, I even wished
for it, for James's sake — and, to a lesser extent, for
mine, so that I could have a life too. But it's something I
never truthfully confronted before and now that it's so
unexpectedly here, the moment has struck with terrible
ferocity. Too soon, too soon, I'm screaming inside. Give
me another chance. One more month — one week? All
right, just one more day . . .

This hurricane is narrowed to this pinprick. James is leaving me.

Pictures. James in a blue babygro with a matching soother and hair like feathers. James terrified by the dark and unfamiliar surroundings and coming into my bed on the first night we slept in this flat – he was five, nearly six. All those long treks to the school principal when he was late, or forged sick notes, smoked, didn't have this that or the other homework done. All that MTV. His leathers everywhere. Coke cans. Crisps. Sodden towels. Lynx aftershave. Him arriving home with bunches of motorway daffodils, throwing them on the table without meeting my eye. My heart in my mouth every time I heard him vroom off on the bike. The whiteness of his face the day those two cops came in. His smile. His rare and dazzling smile.

I'm lying there just after four o'clock, looking at the ceiling and waiting for the time to get up. Through James's closed door I hear him sobbing.

I'm paralysed. I should go in, take him in my arms. But I know he'd reject the gesture. The moment passes. I don't hear him any more.

Next morning, when I come home to this flat after work for the last time, he's up again. Businesslike, as much as a boy with a mottled face can look businesslike. His bruising has faded quite a lot, though, and to be fair he doesn't look at all bad. If it wasn't for the cast on his arm he could even pass for someone who'd just had a small argument with a lamp-post or a door.

He certainly seems calm, resigned. Even friendly, which is not a disposition I readily associate with James. Given what I heard from his room last night, I would have expected him to be a bit more cut up. Maybe the upset is too deep to show on the surface. Get this thing over, that seems to be the mood for today. He's shaved. He's packed his gear. The facilities look bereft, you know the way they do, without all the cans and accoutrements.

What about money? I sigh, exaggerate, slip back for safety into my old ways. You'll need money.

I'd been worrying about this. I had no way of raising instant cash — certainly nothing left to hock — and the bonds take more than a week to come through for encashment. I hadn't even received the latest ones yet.

There are moneylenders, of course, but I'd sooner eat earwigs. One of the women at work is in desperate straits because of moneylenders. Would you believe, it all started with Communion outfits for her twins, she didn't want her kids to be outshone. The Vincent is trying to help her out but she just seems to be getting deeper and deeper in. Once those Shylocks get a hold of you they never let go.

The post office savings office is opposite Trinity College. Utilitarian. We got there at just after ten o'clock but even so, there was a big queue ahead of us. You had to take a number. The next number available was 39 and they were only on number 11 at this stage. We didn't have that kind of time.

Stay here, I go to James. He sits down on one of the chairs in the waiting area.

I'm so deep down distraught I don't care who thinks what of me. I march up to the counter and butt in on a transaction. Excuse me, I say to the woman customer (who's not amused), I'm terribly sorry, but this is very urgent.

I ask the clerk if I could see a supervisor immediately.

The customer sighs heavily and drums her fingers on the counter. I ignore her as the clerk rings someone. He puts down the phone, tells me to wait over at the side,

by a glass door. I don't even look at James, I'm sure he's
mortified at my snotty behaviour.

To make a long story short, the supervisor takes on
board what dire straits we're in and says he'll do what he
can. I'm not looking for the moon, I say firmly, in case
he hasn't got the message. Just nine hundred pounds.
And it's my money, after all. He gives me a funny look.
He looks at the bonds I've brought in. You're lucky, the
bonds are now computerized, he goes, come back in
forty-five minutes.

James and I use the time by going across the river to
BusÁrus to check the timetables. Maybe the crying last
night took away some of the poison. He's so docile it's
killing me. I want him to yell at me, balk at what I'm
asking him to do. BusÁrus is an extraordinary place. I
know it's for transients – it's where you get all the
country buses and the ones to take you to the airport –
but that's not why it feels so lonely. After all, the airport
is for transients too but it feels solid, exciting, outwards-
looking. BusÁrus feels as though the structure itself is
temporary, a bit hopeless, like nothing belongs there,
nor ever did, not the staff, the kiosks and shops, not even
the big tiles on the floor.

Today the place seems sadder than ever, although
there are young backpackers everywhere and busy knots
of sailors clustered around the area where you book the
tour buses. Town is hopping with sailors, especially
O'Connell Street and Grafton Street and, I believe,
Temple Bar.

We stop in front of the big timetable boards. The time
James and I have left together is now measurable.

Last week a big American aircraft carrier came in for
the Fourth of July celebrations. It was too big to anchor
in Dublin, had to stay a couple of miles out to sea. The
whole of Dublin was agog. Teenage girls were behaving

as if the sailors were Oasis but it wasn't only them. Would you believe 175,000 people (out of our tiny population) entered a competition run by the National Lottery for people to be able to go out and visit the ship? All the women at work, for instance. I meant to, I just didn't get around to it. Wouldn't it be lovely to have a life so uncomplicated that you could go bananas about the visit of five thousand American sailors to your city?

We find there's a bus he can get at twenty past one.

My stomach fills with that watery feeling. Now we know. One hundred and twenty minutes. You might think I'm cracked, thinking about sailors and the National Lottery at a time like this. That's me — busy busy busy!

According to Pius Crawford's directions, he has to go to Dungarvan and then take another bus to Cappoquin and then hitch or walk. Will you take that one? I ask him, as if what we're discussing is whether or not he'll have ice cream after his dinner.

He shrugs. Fine, it doesn't matter which one I take.

Well, they'll be expecting you.

Twenty past one is fine, fine . . .

What about the bike? I'm all biz. Will you be able to take it back to them if I ring them? You won't be able to wheel it with your bad arm, will you? Let me see now, if we took it down between us, one on each side? It's only a few hundred yards to the shop.

He fires up. Stop fussing, for God's sake. I'll be able to manage it perfectly.

You won't, James. How will you be able to manage with your—

Shut up. I will. You saw how I managed with the packing. Some of those bags with the crockery are heavy. He stops. Sees I'm not arguing any more. He looks at me with what could be compassion. It'll be grand, Angela.

I turn back to the timetables as if I haven't memorized the Dungarvan one enough.

There are phones in BusÁrus and I ring the shop while he heads home to finish his packing. The time is leaking away, I can't stop it.

There's aggro at first, from the fellow who answers the phone. But eventually he puts the owner on to me. He asks for further payment. I say no. We to and fro on it a bit while I have to feed in more coins. Then I say, Well, if you won't take it back, you'll have to sue us for the balance of the money because we're not paying any more.

There must have been something about the tone of my voice. He agrees to take the bike, provided it's in good condition and provided James signs X, Y and Z. He'll sign anything, I say, provided there's no more money involved. You'll get the bike back sometime this morning.

By the time I get back to the bonds office, they have the money organized. It's a draft, though, which means I then have to go and get it cashed 'in any post office, mam'.

For me that's the GPO. So I find myself running back across the bridge. And, wouldn't you know it, another queue. Jesus, come on, come on, time, time, how many minutes left now?

The way I'm carrying on, you'd think he was emigrating to Australia and not temporarily to another part of Ireland.

This is the first time either of us has ever gone away from the other. As I told you, he blew his one and only chance, that time when he wasn't able to go to the Gaeltacht, and I don't count the night he spent in the cells, or the all-nighters he pulled earlier this year at parties and suchlike.

I hear myself keening on and on like this, like Lady Macbeth. For Christ's sake, Angela. I force myself to get a grip. I march out of the GPO with more than a thousand pounds in my handbag. Nine hundred plus interest.

I arrange my face before I go into our flat. His luggage – a rucksack and a duffel bag – is piled by the door. The television isn't on. He's leaning against the draining board.

Oh, God, I wish he had the television on. You're ready?

He nods.

I mustn't give in to what I'm feeling. My throat feels like it's filling with ice. I look at the two bags by the door. Is that all you're taking? Very matter-of-fact. And is this what you want me to keep for you? Indicating a loose pile of stuff by the naked bed-settee.

Yes – very quietly.

Let's see now, it's five past twelve, you'd want to be getting a move on if we're to get that bike back and we're to catch that bus. I can't swallow.

Angela, I don't want you to come with me.

But I want to.

No. Vehemently. He stands off the draining board. No. Quieter. He seems to have matured ten years in the last five minutes. I can't read his mood properly. He's calm – but what else?

James—

No. Listen to me, I don't want you to come with me either to the bike shop or to BusÁrus.

But—

Leave it, Angela.

How's he going to wheel the bike with one arm? I don't ask him any more, I feel I've no permission. I can't look at him, I reach into my bag, grab a handful of twenties, pass them over. Here, take this — I thrust it into his hand.

I don't need all this.

Take it, take it, I go. My heart is frantic. If he doesn't take this money I'm going to crumble away into dust. Consider it your share of my winnings. Anyway, you'll need busfare, and I don't know whether you'll have to pay for your board and lodging at that monastery. I'd better give you the address where I'm going to be staying for a few days.

I root around in my handbag again and find a bus ticket. Then I lean too hard on it with the biro and the top snaps off. I have to find another piece of paper. Quick. Which rubbish bag did I put my notepaper and envelopes into? How is it you can never find *one* piece of paper when you're in a hurry?

Use this. He pulls a Lottery receipt out of the inside pocket of his jacket.

I didn't know you did the Lotto? It was something to say.

I scribble Ken's address on the back of the ticket, add his telephone number. I'm good at remembering numbers, but it's easy for me, I don't have to remember very many.

When I find a flat, I say, I'll let you know. I'll write to you at the monastery.

OK. He doesn't even look at the address, just folds the ticket again and puts it back in his inside pocket.

You'd better get going, James, or you'll miss that bus. I can hear my voice saying this hateful thing. Are you sure you'll be able to manage wheeling the bike by yourself with that arm? Are you sure you don't need any help?

It's cool, stop fussing.

The smell of Lynx is very strong. Let me at least help

you bring down your stuff — you can put it in the panniers while you're wheeling it.

He bends down, using his good arm to pick up the two bags. I rush to help him. Let me carry one down the stairs for you. Are you definitely sure you don't want me to take them down to the bus for you — meet you there? James?

He shakes his head.

Then, Cheerio, Angela. See you soon. As he looks full at me, his eyes, those wonderful eyes, hold something I can't read. I've always been able to read James. What's gone wrong? The feelings are like rockets pushing up inside me.

I crack, seize him and hug hard. He doesn't hug me back because he can't with the plaster cast and the bags but for one instant he does lay his rough cheek against mine. You read that emotional pain is like a knife. It's not, it's more like a slicer or a chainsaw.

Next thing I'm looking at an empty doorway.

I manage to hold back on the crying until he's well gone. I'm standing looking at Reddy's bare boards in the hallway outside our door and telling myself I'm being absurd. For God's sake, Angela, will you give over? It'll be two, three weeks *max* . . .

I cried so hard I slept, woke up, didn't know where I was, realized.

When I got up I smelt him everywhere, Lynx, runners, sweat. All I could do was sit. Draw the flat in around me like a womb.

At about three o'clock I roused myself a bit, enough to find stationery. I wrote to Justine and Nicola and, after a bit of hesitation, to Francesca, via her foster mother. I told all three of them the bare bones of the story — and that if they cared to know, their brother could be contacted at Mount Melleray.

I washed my face, walked down to the GPO to buy stamps and to post the letters. I couldn't tell you whether it was raining, dry, the Sahara, what. Yet I suppose it did me good because by the time Ken Sheils arrived, just after tea-time, I felt quiet.

I was still worrying, though, about how he managed with that bike . . .

Thirty-Six

All set? Ken looks down at the black bin bags, which I'd stacked neatly just inside the door. Is this all?

Yep. My landlord can have all the rest, bad luck to him. The furniture isn't ours.

And there was I rearranging everything in the apartment to give you space.

Sorry, Ken.

Angela, Angela — he takes my shoulders, gives me a little shake — will you stop all this apologizing? Seriously. You'd apologize for living. Someone soon is going to lose patience with you.

Sorry. It escapes before I can catch it. He sighs, lets me go. What are we going to do with you?

It takes less than quarter of an hour to move me out of the home James and I have lived in for fifteen years. More because I feel I should than because I want to — I'd seen it so often in films and on the television — I walk back in for one last look around. I feel very little. Or at least very little for the place itself. Only that I wish James was there sitting hunched in front of the television. And I'm all cried out on that one.

I decide to keep the keys, let Reddy have the expense of changing the locks. I never want to see him again, even to try to get our security deposit back. It was only twenty quid – a fortune fifteen years ago! Anyway, knowing him, he'd find some reason not to pay it back.

I remember the Daisy Market mirror over James's damage to the wall. I walk over and take it down, revealing the hole in all its glory. At least twenty quid's worth. I win!

When we were going into Ken's apartment with my clothes and belongings, do you know what? Not one person looked out of his or her door to see what all the rustling and kerfuffle was. I'd been defensive about this – after all, I didn't want anyone thinking that I was moving in to live in sin with someone. (Having already been to bed. Talk about inconsistent!)

This is par for the course, Ken says. I did tell you about this – bees, hives? Some weekends you'll hear stereos thumping at various parties but generally we all put feelers out first to make sure the way is clear.

Sam greets me like a long-lost friend, wagging his whole body in the absence of a tail. And Ken himself could not be nicer. When I get into the bedroom, I see he's put a bunch of flowers on a little table beside the bed.

In fact, he's almost too nice. He doesn't put a toe beyond the bedroom door. I'll leave you to get sorted, Angela. I'm making coffee. Come on out whenever you're ready – or don't come out at all. Just do your own thing. This is very important, all right? For as long as you're here, you're to come and go, behave exactly as you would in your own place.

I had pre-sorted the bags while I was packing, so finding what I needed immediately is easy and it takes me less than a quarter of an hour to get settled in. Here's more evidence of Ken's thoughtfulness. He'd told me the previous evening that he'd loads of space in his wardrobe. When I open it? Completely empty except for one anorak.

I go out into the living room. He's reading a newspaper. Where are all your clothes?

He gets up. I've a hall closet — they're in there. Are you ready for your coffee yet?

Sure, thanks. Are you sure I haven't inconvenienced you?

Angela, what did I say to you last night? Will you learn to accept people's good intentions? There's an art to taking as well as giving, you know.

Sorry.

He purses his lips. Grins. There you go again.

I sit down.

He diverts towards me on the way to the kitchen area, Before I forget, here are the keys. And I got another set cut this afternoon, I'd better explain to you how the alarm works.

I'm sitting listening to which key works what lock and what the combination of the alarm is and I don't know how to feel. No man has ever treated me like this before, as though I'm somebody they like, no big deal. I suppose where Tom Bennett was concerned I was a mother-substitute. I've been mother and father and sister and brother to James.

Ken Sheils seems to see me as me.

When we're nearly finished our coffee he looks at his watch. It's only just eight o'clock, he goes, and it's a lovely evening. I'm going for a walk for an hour or so, clear my head. You're welcome to come if you like — but don't feel you have to. You stay in, go out, anything you want.

This guy must have some faults. But apart from a stubborn temper (as seen in the row with the lorry driver on the way to Birr that first day), so far I can't see any. What was wrong with that Diandra?

He turns on the telly so we can watch the Lotto draw. The *Coronation Street* signature tune is playing and the announcer comes on to remind us that after this week's Lotto draw we can watch *Touched By An Angel*, then the *Nine O'Clock News*, then *Thou Shalt Not Kill*. Here we go, Ken says, glancing across at me. His eyes are lit up. I do Multi-draw so I'm in every week.

This reminds me that I have yet to send off my scratch card.

He gets three numbers. Nearly there, he goes, haven't had three for a while, I think it's a good omen. I know I'm going to win soon, I have this feeling . . .

All over the country half the population is saying the same.

I decide to behave like half the population. My world had shrunk so much, it was time to unshrink it. I think I'll come for that walk with you.

You could always buy a Section 23 apartment, you know, that's what mine is . . . It's half an hour later and we're moseying along the main drag of the Phoenix Park under the huge trees. Joggers, strollers, cyclists whizzing by us in the cycle lane, kids swinging out of their parents.

I couldn't afford to buy an apartment, I say automatically. Unless my scratch card comes good, the prospect of me as a homeowner remains as likely as me taking a hot-air-balloon ride with Richard Branson. (Hunky or *what?*)

We're passing the Monument, which Ken informs me is actually called the obelisk and which is a new one on me, we always knew it simply as the Monument. The usual gangs of youngsters racing up and down the wide, shallow steps, groups of teenagers lying around sipping beer or Coke. Sam is having a brilliant time, romping and saying hello to fellow dogs.

You probably could afford it, you'd be surprised, he says. All you'd need is about a thousand pounds' cash and with the tax relief and first-time buyers' grant and all the rest of it, you could probably get a one-bed for less than thirty-five pounds a week. And mortgages are so cheap now.

I'll certainly consider that, I say, so as not to seem rude, thanks for the advice. But I make a mental reservation. If and when James and I ever get close to having our own place, it'll be a roses-round-the-door job or nothing. I like Ken's apartment — but in an abstract way. It's clean and fresh but no way is it a home.

I give myself a mental kick. I'm still thinking of James and me together. Stop it. James is gone. I make a huge effort not to see that barren flat.

It's odd to find myself here. In present circumstances the Phoenix Park would be the last place I'd have chosen for a walk. I'm sure, though, that for one moment our connection with it didn't occur to Ken Sheils. I've got to realize that the whole world isn't hanging on the affairs of Angela and James Devine. The sun is still bright, everyone is in summer gear and, without doubt, not one of these hundreds of men, women or children is wasting a single thought on us. In my line of sight, not one person is reading a newspaper or listening to a radio. The Devines? Who? That was last week. What's next?

We walk on as far as the classy white entrance to the American ambassador's house before turning back towards the van. Ken's gift of silence allows all the other senses to operate. If I'd been chatting I doubt if I'd have recognized that lovely summer-evening smell of warm leafy air, or heard the whirr in time to look up at a flight of ducks overhead.

Whatever it is, rosy sun, faraway laughing of the kids, all that spacious greenery, I'm so relaxed now I feel as if it's almost possible to heal.

I got a bit of news today, Ken says, as the van comes in sight. Diandra says she's going for a divorce.

I don't quite know what to say. Although the referendum was passed, at this point no one has got a divorce yet in Ireland.

I try to strike a balance between being sympathetic and being nosy. I hope you won't be killed in the rush!

He picks up a twig off the ground and throws it for Sam. It's no big deal, I suppose. She can have whatever she wants from me, I'm not going to stand in her way. I hate the thought of lawyers and going to court.

Sure what can she get?

He shrugs. Who knows? The apartment. She has her own living arrangements now but who knows, once lawyers and money come into it? She could probably screw me into the ground.

Ah no, I say, she couldn't. It wouldn't be fair.

Well, I'm not going to lose any sleep over it. It's going to be a couple of years anyway, by the looks of things, so I won't have to evict you tomorrow.

It was strange driving past our old gaff, seeing the piece of cornflake-packet cardboard still in place in the broken window. And when we got back inside Ken's apartment I felt stranger still. Awkward.

It's very shadowy in the room because the sky is losing light outside. Do you want to watch a bit of television, he asks, or will you go straight to bed? He's being so correct he's stiff.

I hesitate. It seems rude just to go to bed straight away. I don't mind, I go. I'd need to be in bed by eleven at the latest — I've the usual early start tomorrow.

Fine, he goes. Any preference as to what you want to

watch? He uses the remote control to turn on the television and then excuses himself to go to the bathroom. There's the usual delay while the television warms up, then on comes *Davis*. I'd forgotten about *Davis*. I freeze. Before we go into our discussion, Derek Davis is saying into the camera, I want you to watch this clip of film.

Rosemary Madden's face fills the screen. Of course I'm co-operating with my author, she goes, I want my story to be told. And there's only one authorized version of my story.

From Ken's bathroom comes the sound of the toilet flushing as the camera pulls back from Rosemary Madden's face. Her brother is standing beside her, the older, thickset one. Why shouldn't she make a few shillings out of this? he goes. That scumbag has ruined her life.

Ken is out, sees the screen just as we're back to the studio and Derek Davis. Derek has cards in his hand and he looks up from them. There are a lot of issues surrounding this case—

Ken snatches up the remote control, zaps, up comes Trevor McDonald on *News At Ten*. The American presidential election.

I'm very sorry, Angela, Ken says. I didn't know.

Scumbag, the brother said. A lot of people use the term but to me it's now as clear as day. It was the brother who sent the letter. Probably the brick as well. Probably organized the beating.

I'm numb. I'm tired. I'll care tomorrow.

The next morning I have to leave Ken's apartment extra early because I have to be outside our flat, ex-flat, for the minibus to pick me up. The only iffy moment comes when I'm tiptoeing out through the little lobby towards the front door. Sam, who's in his basket, is awake and watching me and he makes as though to hop out. I shake my head hard and make a face at him. He's obviously a very intelligent little dog because he stays where he is. Ken is snoring lightly in the narrow bed-chair and I make it out without waking him.

Somehow I get through work – thank God none of the women mentions *Davis* – although every bone in my body feels as though it's been through a cement mixer. And when I get back to the apartment, it's empty. Ken has already left for work and the place is spotless. There's a note taped to the kettle.

I'm working in Malahide today and I'll be back at around seven this evening. Help yourself to the contents of the fridge. And here's the juicer, I didn't know whether you knew where to find it. See you this evening – K.

The electric juicer has two oranges beside it.

I'm too tired to eat or drink anything. I do what I haven't done in twenty years. I go back to bed.

I sleep like a zombie and don't wake up again until five past three in the afternoon.

At first I'm still in my dream, a light, airy one, something to do with the Isle of Man, a place I don't know a thing about. But it's a lovely place, sunny, happy, a bit like the Phoenix Park actually, now that I examine it.

But then a weird thing. I realize that it is myself who is light and airy. There's something missing and it's not just fatigue. There's no worry.

I sit up, test this.

The lightness is real. The cloud of agonizing and worrying has lifted. Not altogether, of course, but enough so as I can see out from under it.

I could go so far as to say I feel even a tiny bit happy.

Whoever first said 'out of sight out of mind' was a very clever person. James was not out of mind exactly, but he was certainly not sitting in every brain cell. He's safe down there in his monastery and no one will be calling him a scumbag. There'll be no telly so he won't even hear it from a distance. I see him walking through a lovely old cloister, or through a meadow. Like I always saw Mammy. Daisies et cetera.

I get out of bed, make it to Ken's standards, I hope, and go out into the silent living-room. He certainly told no lies when he said this place was quiet. The living-room window is closed and the noise of the traffic from Gardiner Street below is only a hum. We used to be crucified with road works on this street but Ireland has had the Presidency of Europe since the beginning of June and because Gardiner Street is on the way to and from the airport, there hasn't been a pneumatic drill down there since then. (All we get now are the sirens from the motorcades!)

I don't want to disturb the spotlessness of Ken's kitchen so I decide to go out for something to eat. Yes, I think, Bewley's. Like an ordinary person.

So I do. Everything seems new. Shiny. I love all the tourists. I love the waitresses with their old-fashioned uniforms. I even love the pushing and the shoving at the self-service rail where I queue up for egg and chips. Egg and chips for breakfast at half past three in the afternoon! Mammy'd turn in her grave.

And on the way back, guess what? I go to Carthy's and I redeem her garnet ring and her neck chain. I leave the video for another couple of days because I don't want to be seen hawking it up Gardiner Street. In that area I'd probably be brought straight in to Store Street or Fitzgibbon Street for questioning.

When Ken and Sam come home, I have the kettle on

and the table laid for tea. I've made a salad from what I found in the fridge and from a selection of deli meats I bought on the way home. He wants to play house? I'll give him house.

It really is like playing house, it's like Rock Hudson and Doris Day. He's arrived home exhausted in his work overalls having toiled for us, so my next move is I run over to him and say, Had a bad day, dear? And then I should help him into his steaming bath. And give him his highball. (Although I've never quite understood what exactly a highball is.)

I'm no Doris Day, alas. As he's standing there with his keys still in his hand, looking at all this domesticity, I find it hard to read his face. Being Angela Devine I say, I hope you don't mind? We've ice cream for dessert.

Mind? I love it! He means it too.

After our tea, we go for another walk – across the bridge, down the Quays, towards Alexandra Basin. He knows a lot about the ships docked along there, and the Isle of Man ferry, the container vessels. He explains that the huge steel cakestand on the deck of one of our Irish ships is for helicopters. In turn I can tell him about life on board the *Asgard*, which is also berthed there. It's the Irish sail-training vessel and a friend of Patsy's Martin has something to do with it. (Naturally, because he's a friend of Martin's, he runs it . . .)

I'm glad I can tell him at least something he doesn't know already. There's a certain imbalance in our knowledge of our native city. In the couple of months I've known Ken Sheils I've been more places and learned more about the area within a couple of miles of where I was born than I'd learned all those years of my life living in it.

I'm still testing the airy feeling I woke up with this afternoon. I wonder what James is doing right now, I say to Ken — and would you believe I can say it without choking up.

Probably mitching into the nearest big smoke to have a pint, he says it so easily I can see he's made a lot of progress in accepting James for what he is.

This must be what it's like to be on your holidays.

I test myself some more about James. Should I telephone the monastery? I ask Ken. Just to say hello, make sure he's all right?

It's up to you of course, he goes, but try to think back to when you were his age, flexing your independence. Would you have wanted people checking up on you all the time?

He could be lonely. He's had a very hard time.

He could. But being lonely is part of growing up too. Angela, he hesitates, please tell me to butt out if you want to but maybe he's never had the chance to be independent. Couldn't this be his first real solo flight? And should you trail after him so soon.

Echoes of Patsy.

He takes my hand. Quite casually, no pressure. Why don't you leave it until early next week? He'd welcome a call then. He'd probably see it as genuine concern and friendship rather than as you treating him like a child. He glances sideways at me. The breeze is from behind and his hair is blowing around his face. Tell me to shut up, that this is none of my business. It's just that I can vividly remember back to when I was his age . . . He lapses into his silence.

It's hard to take. He's right, though. Letting go is not physical — it's not them moving out. It's that you have to give them the gift of cutting off worrying about them. The pain kicks in, but I ride with it. I can deal with it. Fairly well.

We've come as far as we can go before we have to

turn in off the river. The East Link Bridge is busy, traffic flowing in both directions. We stand for a minute to look down towards the sea. There are yachts moored in the middle of the river on the far side, a graceful white cruise liner tied up at the quay. Listen, Angela, Ken says, on a related topic, I hope you don't feel you have to be as good as your word and find yourself a flat this week. You're welcome to stay as long as you like. You're a very easy house-guest. Feck it, he says, I'd *like* you to stay. Will you?

I don't look at him but I imagine he's blushing.

There's a show on at the Point on the far side of the river, cars milling around, streams of people converging, the water bus coming alongside. We're too far away to read the posters – it could be ballet or a musical or Christy Moore or some huge international rock act. Why don't I know? There's a whole world happening that I've let slide by.

Now is my opportunity to give my first small gift of freedom to James. Well, as it happens I've done nothing about finding a place so far, I say to Ken. Maybe I'll stay another week, if that's all right with you? (I said the first *small* gift!)

All right? It's more than all right. Ken grins. But be careful, Angela, you might even enjoy yourself. And then where would we be?

Thirty-Seven

That weekend I wrote a letter to James — I thought this would be a good half-way house between his need to strike out and mine to keep contact. So I was careful, wrote nothing significant, not a word about Rosemary Madden or her brother, or people racing each other to bring out books. Just work and Dublin and events and people I observed. I did tell him I missed him, but in a lighthearted way — I miss you, you clot, I'm suffering from withdrawal symptoms from all that passive smoking. Then I told him a bit about Ken. *He's the friend you met in the hospital and whose address I gave you — remember?* I described Ken's apartment and little Sam.

I finished up by asking him to drop me a line soon, to let me know all the news. That they must have some way of getting letters out of there!

I signed it 'all my love, Angela'.

I posted it on the Saturday evening — remembered to post the famous scratch card too — and then Ken and I went to see *Il Postino*, which I loved, even though I don't normally like subtitles. Afterwards we had ice cream. We chit-chatted about the movie.

Then Ken says, You know what, Angela, you're lovely when you relax. You're lovely anyway, but when you're relaxed you're more beautiful than Princess Di. Did anyone tell you you look a bit like her? He grins.

Go away out of that, I go, you charmer, you! (But who wouldn't be chuffed?)

Are you like your mother? he asks me then. Yes, I say, although I have my father's colouring. The minute I said it, it was like a plug being pulled. I started thinking about Pius Crawford. Uh-oh, Ken says, have I said the wrong thing?

No, not at all. It's just that—

It's just that your father is unfinished business. You find now that it's not enough just to know who he is.

I look across the table at him with new respect. How did he know this? Something like that, I say.

Well, maybe you should finish the business, he says.

No, I say quickly, I haven't the energy. Well, not just at the moment. What I mean is I haven't the courage. I change the subject rapido. What happened with you and Diandra? I ask him.

She couldn't live with me, he says quietly.

I can't believe that, I say. I can't imagine how anyone couldn't live with you. You seem so—

I'm not. I'm not so anything. Don't put me on a pedestal, Angela. That's a very dangerous thing to do.

Well, give me a hint. You know everything about me, after all.

He cocks his head to one side, like Sam does. All right, he goes. It's a pretty tawdry and commonplace little story. Diandra wanted things I couldn't give her. Or, in her opinion, wouldn't give her. She was ambitious for me, for us. For money, really. She wanted the big house, the fancy car. We had row after row about it.

He looks at me very seriously. I'm not ambitious, Angela. If you're looking for a high-flier you'll have to look somewhere else. I'm perfectly happy dandering along doing odd jobs at my own pace and earning whatever I need to live. In Diandra's opinion, I could have done this for a second income, as my nixer. I should have been heading up my own construction company or doing something, anything that would give me more money, or at least status. She used to say she had no intention of being known as the handyman's wife. I tried for a while, I worked for a big building firm, which did have promotional ladders. He grins. Sorry about the pun – but it was pretty good, eh? He becomes serious again, toys with his ice-cream spoon, moving it around the bowl of the sundae dish. Diandra always said I was living as though I was already retired. But, you know, to me that's the perfect way to live. To her I was the under-achiever of the century and in the end she despised me for it. In the end we despised each other, actually. I enjoy what I do, Angela, and I decide when and how I work. He gazes into the middle distance. That may all change now, of course, with the divorce. If she wins more money from me in alimony.

Rubbish, I go. You've no kids. And she can work, can't she? Isn't she able-bodied?

You don't know Diandra, he says quietly. He shuts down. I take the hint. Will we go back?

Speaking of under-achieving or, rather, under-earning, it occurs to me on the Sunday morning as I'm lying in bed, feeling decadent – I don't even want to know what time it is – that if Patsy wanted to find me for a gig or a wedding, she doesn't have this address.

It's not bad, I think, living this placid, mole-like life, where no one except James knows where to find me. (Or my father, in emergencies. And then he has to wait until a Saturday morning, in which case the 'emergency' will presumably have passed!)

I probe to find how I am about missing James this

morning. The all-encompassing hard pain of it has softened out for sure and has become more generalized. I'll love him until the day I die, that's not in doubt. To my surprise, however, because I never contemplated this before, I can certainly live a decent life without seeing him every day. Is that disloyal? I decide not. I decide it's just part of the next phase of both of our lives, I've to step sideways, let him pass me out and go forward. It was what my instinct was telling me the night before he left. Things will never be the same again.

It's not so bad. What's difficult to admit is that it may be better.

One definite improvement – waking up in this bed is like waking up to find you've nestled into a warm cloud. I've been sleeping on a bed-settee for far too long.

I listen for signs of life in the living room, hear none, wiggle my toes, snuggle down for another bit of kip. So if Patsy finds someone else for the act – no difficult task in this town – so be it. Anyhow, given our recent history together, I doubt if we could do a show together now without the cracks showing.

Then I admit that all of the above is just b.s., I'm enjoying myself, end of story. And I don't want the enjoyment to end. Shirley Valentine or *what*!

Ken has big wide breakfast cups. The day stretches ahead and I'm as close to being carefree as I've ever been.

What'll we do today? When we're finished, he collects the cups and brings them from the table over to the sink. Would you like to go for a drive in the country, the seaside, the mountains? But don't let me dictate. Maybe you have plans of your own.

Yeah, right. Plans.

I stretch luxuriously – that's how at home I am –

before I get up to help him. The question is, I say back, what would you be doing if I wasn't here, cluttering up your apartment and your life?

I'd be lonely as hell. I'd tell myself this was a great life, this life of the ascetic, but I'd be lonely as hell.

I'd meant the question facetiously but he has this trick, Ken has, of whipping the ground from under you with his directness. It takes a while to get used to it. James's idea of a long conversation, unless he's in extremis, like he was in the hospital, would be 'There's no food in this place' or 'I'll get the Nite Link' or 'Have you the loan of a few bob?' He doesn't ask many questions that don't relate to his finances or his digestive system.

Ken's still waiting for me to reply. What about it so, have you plans?

I thought I'd take a plane to London, see a show in the West End before I have to be back to clean out a few offices at six o'clock tomorrow morning.

He ignores this. Would you like to spend the day together?

Sure. Why not. What about Mass?

I went this morning. I hope I didn't wake you going out.

Again he takes my breath away. My question had been facetious, it had never occurred to me that he was religious. Hardly anyone I know goes to Mass any more – even amongst the women at work it's usually only the ones over forty.

There's no point in being sarky with this guy.

An hour later we're driving out of Dublin across the M50 toll bridge.

Free*dom*. No California beach babe in her convertible could have felt as free as I did. As well as the giddy notion that no one on earth would be able to find me, before we left I insisted on paying to fill the tank with diesel and he let me. So now I'm not even obligated. This trip is on me.

I roll down the window. Hundreds of feet below us, the cloak of trees and vegetation along the Liffey Valley and the Strawberry Beds is as green as you'd see in a travelogue about the Mekong Delta. It's cloudy, but ahead of us, you wouldn't believe it, the sun is shafting a shining handful of rays on to the Dublin mountains. Real rays. The cover of *My First Missal*.

All this symbolism. What with James in a monastery and Ken here turning out to be a serious Christian, maybe it's time I looked into my own soul!

Where are we going?

I'm not pushed, he says back. I thought we'd just drive, find somewhere to stop, by a river maybe, have a picnic. Drive some more, get back before the rush hour, how's that sound? (Tea-time on Sundays is nearly worse than it is on weekdays. All those Sunday drivers. I suppose it's an indication of all this new affluence we keep hearing about on the radio.)

I settle back, take Sam on my lap and wallow in my new life. I wish we could go back to the city and start again. And again and again, like Groundhog Day. I want this day to last for ever.

We have our picnic by the canal in a village called Rathangan, just off the Curragh in Kildare. It's a lovely place, which has a river as well as the canal. I'm lolling on one elbow, daydreaming at the sky. Then Ken says, Since we're this far, why don't we go on to Derrybride? Beard the lion in his den.

What? That brings me upright quick enough – talk about a douche!

Your father. We'll drop in. Say hello.

We will not. Some other time.

Angela, he says softly, you're putting it off. I'll go with you, I'll support you.

I'm getting angry now. You're damned right I'm putting it off. Look, Ken, I appreciate your inviting me to stay in your apartment and all this – I wave my arm around the general scenery – but I really think—

You really think what, Angela? That I've no right to make suggestions like that? Of course I don't – but it's only a suggestion. He rolls over on his stomach, picks at the short grass. I think you should do this, otherwise you'll never have peace. However, if you don't have the bottle—

That did it, of course.

In order to be fair to Pius Crawford, I insisted on ringing first. We went to the public telephone box in Rathangan and got the home number from Directory Enquiries.

The temptation to hang up became stronger with each ring.

I heard the receiver being lifted, my stomach turned. Click. A child's voice. Well rehearsed. This is Esther Crawford speaking, thank you for calling. Pius, Dorothy, Angela, John, Matthew, Mark, Esther, Luke or Ruth are unable to take your call right now, please leave your name and number. If you wish to ring Pius Crawford about a property, the number is—

I hung up. I already had his office number. I march out of the box, my heart whacking against my ribs.

I got an answering machine. There's no one home. Satisfied now?

He's sitting on the bonnet of the van. He's let Sam out and the dog is nosing around in the gutter beside him. Why are you so angry, Angela?

Look, I say to him, why did you push me on this? What's it to you?

Do you really want an answer to that?

Given what I've discovered about his directness, I suspect maybe I shouldn't pursue this. Try me, I say cautiously.

I want to ask you to marry me, Angela. But not until you're free. And you're not going to be free until you've sorted out all the relationships which preoccupy you twenty-four hours a day. Your father being one of them. He says all of this without a flicker in his voice or in his eyes.

A proposal? Of marriage?

I can't take it in – certainly not when it's delivered like this and when I'm in a lather. And by the way where's Beetroot Man? The guy in front of me is as cool as the Antarctic, he doesn't even get down from the bonnet of the van.

Are you serious? My voice is hoarse.

Deadly.

We drive home in silence. Not the grand, warm, easy silence of before. This silence is so highly charged as to be uncomfortable. On my side, anyway. He doesn't seem to be all that bothered, dammit, he's certainly not behaving as though he's bothered, driving with one elbow relaxed in the open window frame beside him.

Why did what I say make you feel so threatened?

We're back in the apartment and I've just said I'm tired and that I need to get to bed early. I'm hovering near the bedroom door. It's only half past six.

He's leaning against the window-sill of the living room and, with the sky behind him, I can't properly read his expression.

I can't say why, I tell him. It just does, that's all – and, anyway, who's to say I feel threatened?

It can't be because you're afraid of commitment.

You're the queen of commitment. Current decisions about sex aside, I know you're comfortable with me.

Am I?

Yes, you are. He lifts himself off the window-sill. You know you are.

Well, I'm not that comfortable with you at the moment, I can certainly say that for definite. And you talk about when I'm free. You're not free.

I will be – but you're right, it was probably too soon to bring it up.

He walks towards the kitchen. If you don't want me to say what's on my mind, Angela, you shouldn't ask. I believe in telling the truth – you can't develop a relationship on any other basis, can you? Or I can't at any rate. Apart from anything else, truth is easier. Lying is an exhausting business, all that remembering what you said. Are you too tired to have something to eat?

With anyone else I would have huffed off into the bedroom, standing on my dignity, all that. I'd learned to my cost, however, that there was no point in playing the smallest game with Ken. Actually, I say, I'm very hungry. I allow myself a small glare. I didn't get to eat much at our picnic.

I'll make pasta, he goes. Sit down – or would you care to have a nap and I'll call you?

I'll wait, I say. Then, Since we're into truth and being straight, can I ask you something, Ken Sheils? When we met first you were always blushing. That doesn't sit right with the person you're showing me now.

I'm very shy, he says back, as he's organizing saucepans and spoons. I genuinely am. But when I know what I want, no matter what it is, I'm not shy any more. You'll probably find that I'll continue to blush if you introduce me to someone new but I don't think I'll ever blush with you again.

He switches on the cooker, I turn on the telly. I couldn't tell you to this day what came up on the screen.

A second proposal of marriage.

Ten minutes later. There's another thing I've got to ask you, Ken. What about the age difference? Are you not concerned that I'm eight years older than you?

The look he gives me over the counter which divides off the kitchen area is mocking. Come on, Angela, I'm surprised at you.

I'm not deflected. What's more — you asked for honesty — there's your iffiness about James. There can be no question about anything — *anything* — between us of a, well, of a permanent nature, without him.

Do you think I don't know that? He stops sieving tomatoes for a moment. Where James is concerned, I apologize for my initial reaction, I admit it was tactless, but you wouldn't have thanked me in the long run, would you, if I'd pretended it didn't matter? It'd have to have come out at some stage.

Behind him, the pasta boils over and he lowers the heat. As far as I'm concerned, what James has done in the past, no matter what it is, has nothing to do with what he could do or be in the future. From what you tell me the chap really could do with a few lucky breaks. I wish him nothing but happiness.

You've an answer for everything, haven't you?

No, he says quietly, I don't. I've as many questions as I have answers.

This conversation is wearing me out. I raise the volume on the television and pretend to be absorbed in it.

The pasta, when it comes, is very good, angel-hair, with a tomato-based sauce he makes himself once a week and keeps in the freezer part of his fridge. (I told you the man is so perfectly self-sufficient he'd make you sick.)

Am I getting the impression we're seriously considering my proposal? He's pouring the coffee after we've finished.

Unexpectedly, my stupid heart does a small fandango. I don't know, I say. (Am I being as honest as he is?)

Well, I have to say it's better than a no.

With all that had happened — and the coffee too, to be fair — it took me ages to get to sleep that night. At about one o'clock in the morning, I gave up temporarily, stole out to the kitchen and, by the light of the fridge alone, poured myself a glassful of milk. I looked across at the bed-chair as I tiptoed back to the bedroom but it was too dark to know whether or not I'd wakened him. I couldn't hear him either — if he's not awake, he's a very quiet sleeper.

Back in bed, I sipped the milk and reviewed the events of the day. The awayday in the car. Emotional mangles. James, Pius Crawford. Most momentous of all, the proposal.

You do the strangest things in the early hours, don't you? Before I could second guess myself, I took a biro and an old envelope out of my handbag which, the habit of a lifetime, I always keep beside my bed. Poised the pen. Right, I thought, no messing. Do it quickly. And no cheating — no Kenneth Sheils or Angela Rose Devines if it doesn't come out right the first time. It's got to be straight. And only once.

K-E-N-S-H-E-I-L-S.

Underneath, A-N-G-E-L-A-D-E-V-I-N-E.

I look at it. Try to guess the outcome, discover to my horror that now I desperately don't want it to come out wrong.

Now I'm thinking maybe I shouldn't do it at all. The lengths look so unbalanced. Could I just make it Kenneth? After all, that *is* his real name.

No. You promised no cheating.

I started to cross off the common letters, I was back at eleven years old, sixth class. Me and Patsy. He was left with four. Love Like Hate *Adore*. My hand shook as I began my own. Seven. The full shilling.

Love Like Hate Adore Kiss Court *Marry*.

Jesus.

I tore it up. Finished the milk. Turned off the light and lay there.

Jesus.

I was walking along Gardiner Street on my way back to the apartment after work the next morning, and was just approaching the entrance door to the block, when I heard my name being called. I turned around to find two Guards behind me – one of them the nice one from Kerry or Cork to whom I first reported the assault on James, the other talking into the walkie-talkie fixed to the belt across his chest.

Miss Devine – the Kerry one comes up to me. We've been looking for you at the address you gave us on Mountjoy Square. You've moved?

Temporarily, I go. You're out specially looking for me? For how long? Have you got someone for the assault?

He shakes his head, he looks troubled. No, I'm afraid not. And don't get the wrong impression, we're not out this morning specifically looking for you, so don't get alarmed. We're just on our regular foot-patrol. I recognized you because you and I have spoken before. He looks up at the apartment block. Is this where you're living now? Could we come in for a minute? We need to have a word with you.

The keys to the apartment begin to feel sweaty in my hand. Please – is there something wrong?

The Kerry Gárda glances at his colleague, who has finished talking into his little machine. Probably not, he says then. We just need to talk to you. It would really be better if we came in.

I know Ken has to have gone. I'm not sure how he'd feel.

Come in.

They're huge in the little living room, even bigger than the detectives who loomed in Reddy's place. At least there were high ceilings there. What's this about? I look from one to the other.

We found a motorbike registered in your brother's name.

Where? When? I have immediate visions of James and his bike being fished out of the Liffey. Christ, where did you find it, tell me?

Don't be alarmed, please, Miss Devine. It could have been stolen. Where is your brother? He didn't miss it? He glances around the apartment.

You *know* where he is — I asked if it was OK for him to go to Mount Melleray.

Incomprehension on both faces.

Don't you write down these things? I went up and asked would it be OK if he went to a monastery for a while, because of the counselling he was supposed to have. When did you find the bike? Where?

Last Thursday evening.

Oh, God. (And I was out gallivanting . . .)

When did you last see him, mam? the other Guard asks gently.

On the Wednesday, around lunch-time. He was bringing the bike back to the shop where we bought it, or at least that's— He was wheeling it, he still had the cast on his arm — I knew I shouldn't have let him do it on his own. Why didn't you tell me until now? This is Monday morning.

We called to your place both on the Thursday night

and again on the Friday, Miss Devine. No one there seemed to know where you had gone.

I have to sit down. Already the recriminations are crashing around in my brain. Why didn't I mind him? Why didn't I see him to the bus? Why did I let my father talk me into this Mount Melleray thing in the first place? Why didn't I keep him safe by me?

They tell me that the motorbike was found fifty yards from our flat, around the corner outside Belvedere College. It was reported on the Thursday by one of the priests because it was partially blocking one of the entrance gates.

I grab on to this as good news. I'm being silly getting into a tizzy like this. Being James, he abandoned the bike because it was too much trouble to wheel it all the way to the shop. He's more than likely still snug in his bed in the monastery.

The Guards use Ken's telephone to ring Mount Melleray.

James did not show up at the monastery on that Wednesday. He is not there.

Thirty-Eight

Y ou can get used to anything.

That encounter with the two Guards happened on Monday, 15 July. Today is Thursday, 22 August and Ken Sheils and I are entering the school to find out what grades we got in Leaving Cert English. It seems highly irrelevant.

Dwayne, the so-called rock star, is in through the doorway just ahead of Ken and me. Mr Elliott is there, of course, and the other teachers. When he sees me, Éibhear Ó Súilleabháin, the Irish teacher — who, by the way, is *not* wearing a jumper today — comes straight over to me and sympathizes with my plight. Irish people are pretty good that way, I find. They're not embarrassed about genuine tragedy.

Ken gets a B3. I get a B1.

A B1 in English. It's practically unheard of. Mr Elliott is beaming at me and sympathizing with me all at once. Ken doesn't know what to say to me. I'd always thought he was much better than me at English. I'd been telling him that over and over again. But, to be fair, he seems genuinely pleased for me.

The piece of paper you get is a horrible flimsy thing. You can barely read the computer printing on it. All that sweat and worry and work and the outcome is this puny thing.

I can't take it in. B1. There's another B3 but she, Ken and I are the only Bs. The class got mostly Ds with a couple of C2s and one C1. There wasn't a single fail. I'm the star.

Let's go home, I say to Ken.

My first call that first day when we found out James had not turned up at the monastery was to Pius Crawford. He'd heard nothing. He tried to engage me in talk but I cut him off. I said I'd ring again. This time I left Ken's number.

My brain was speeding that morning, as you can imagine, as I was dialling the next number, Patrice Murphy's. An answering machine. It's still only half nine, said the Kerry Guard, these fellas keep bankers' hours, we'll try again in a few minutes.

I have to say that these two could not have been nicer or more helpful. They helped me to trace James's friend, Ferdia, through the computer world in Dublin, which is relatively small. (It helped that the boy's name was unusual.) Then, through Ferdia, I managed to contact all of the other members of their gang who hung around together. Including girls and their girlfriends. Nothing.

Meanwhile, the Guards trawled through all the places they usually trawl on occasions like this. Focus Point, Simon, the Samaritans, the Salvation Army, all the homeless hostels. Bed-and-breakfast registers — after I told them he had a fair amount of money when he left. Nothing. No trace.

They came back and back. Did he have a bank account — no — a credit card — no — anything at all, the use of which could possibly leave some sort of trail, passport? No.

James had vanished.

The holy all of it is that he is nineteen, he's of age. If he wants to disappear he is perfectly entitled to do so.

If the worst hadn't come to pass – and, of course, that was what we were all thinking but not saying – he could be anywhere within the European Union. Almost anywhere. They can still trace you going through borders, apparently. Except from here to the UK. Which made it the most likely.

The tabloids were predictable. SEX ASSAULT YOUTH MISSING. At least I didn't get as upset this time. Maybe I'm becoming immune.

Others aren't. As a sidebar (thank you, O. J. Simpson) guess who turned up at the deli one Saturday morning – I forget whether it was a week or two weeks ago.

I'm serving a Samantha. Over her shoulder I see this grey-faced man in a suit, unusual enough on a Saturday morning. He's neat but he looks wretched, puffy face, as though he's been crying. Which he probably has. It's Pius.

The deli owner lets me go on a break, although we're busy.

We go for a cup of coffee in a fast-food place a few doors down from where I work. Pius doesn't beat about the bush. Immediately we sit down, he shows me a newspaper – one of the local *Eagles* or *Bugles* or whatever it's called. CATHOLIC RIGHTS FOUNDER'S LOVE CHILD. Page One.

I read the first few lines. A bizarre twist to the mysterious tale of the convicted rapist who has now disappeared—

I give it back to him. I couldn't be bothered reading the rest. You ascend into the most extraordinary state when someone goes missing on you in unexplained circumstances, the best way I can describe it is it's like you're permanently dreaming. You don't believe it –

you simply can't believe it. It hasn't happened, he's been there all the time, you just haven't been able to put your finger on him. You wake up, you realize it has happened. Then nothing else matters, nothing else at all.

Pius is waiting for my reaction to his page-one story. I don't give a sugar about Pius. Maybe I will again in the future. After we find James.

That's dreadful for you, I say. I'm sorry that's happened.

You have to tell me who originally told you how to find me so I can go after the effer (he didn't say effer) who sold me out. I notice his accent has broadened.

Why? I ask him. What's the difference? It's not going to change the story – the story's true, isn't it?

He clutches my wrist. Please, Angela, in the name of God, please . . . I have to – I have to do something. I can't just sit at home and let them do this to me, my business, Dorothy.

I don't think I'm a hard-hearted woman but I find this tiresome. Isn't that weird? This guy has had sway over my emotions and my imagination since I began to think for myself. Thirty years or more. Right now, he could be Wallace or Gromit or Homer Simpson. A cartoon.

Nothing matters in my life now except getting from one day to the next and finding James. Or what happened to James. I'm sorry, Mr Crawford, I say, but as you know I gave my word.

It was that effer Mick Flanagan, wasn't it? I've traced it.

No! I told you.

A shred of memory concerning the police station. The younger Guard, all ears.

But maybe that's not fair. My experience with the Guards has been very good. Anyway, whether he did or he didn't is irrelevant. I'm sorry, Mr Crawford, I say

firmly, for the last time, I can't tell you who told me.
But now that we're talking like this, on neutral territory,
so to speak, can you tell me something?

What?

Why did you hide from my mother when she was
calling for you outside your house?

He stares at me, this big, handsome man. His eyes
protrude slightly, I hadn't noticed that the last time.
They're not ugly or anything, or even very remarkable.
Just something I observe now. I – I couldn't he goes. My
parents, my family—

I gaze back at him. I'm trying to get back those feelings
of urgency. My mother. My father. My mother and
father together producing me. This is who I am.

It doesn't work. Detachment is a terrible thing. I stand
up. We're awfully busy, I'm afraid I'll have to go back.

You're not going to help me?

I can't see what I can do – honestly, I really can't. I
won't make things worse for you by going near you again
if that'll help. Unless I need to for some reason. And I
certainly can't see any reason at the moment.

He stares up at me. He's baffled. Poor Pius.

I repeat it – I have to go now.

I leave the coffee shop. When I look back, he hasn't
stood up yet. I realized something I had up to then
refused to admit – I'd been holding off on it because
letting go of a lifelong fantasy is not easy. What I realized
took approximately one brutal second. It wasn't only
him, it was her as well. They were the exact wrong pair
to fall in love. One was as weak as the other.

It killed me finally to acknowledge what I'd probably
known deep in my heart for a long time.

No, that's an exaggeration, I was already going in the
door of the coffee shop. I didn't die.

I hope to God he can work things out at home. And

some time in the future I will contact him again. In better circumstances. As I remarked before, there's a whole family down there for me. I'd hate to let them go completely.

I kept going those first few weeks by being busy. Busy with James as a project. I still had a fair bit of money left so I took time off the cleaning job in order to concentrate. I have to say they were very understanding at the company. (Although Furry Slippers' reaction could only be guessed at . . .)

At my suggestion, RTE Radio put out an appeal at the end of their news bulletins for him to contact me – or for anyone who had any information about him to contact me or any Gárda station. Nothing. *Crimeline* will be doing a reconstruction of his last movements when it comes back into the autumn schedules. Isn't it ironic? Now I'm courting the media. Or some of it. The Guards are quite hopeful about the programme producing some results.

The days do turn into weeks. I'm back at work and still living at Ken's place. There's no point in moving now, he said to me, after he came home from work that first day, 15 July. Why don't you wait until things settle down a bit? Anyway, you'll need a base with a telephone. Next afternoon, he went one better, bought me a mobile phone and a spare battery. It hasn't been of much use to me so far but I change the batteries religiously and keep it on at all times, day and night. Stupid. James couldn't possibly ring me on it.

Ken's absolutely convinced James is still alive. I'm hanging on to that. You know how direct and honest Ken is. He wouldn't say it unless he believed it.

I don't know what to believe myself during my more lucid moments. Some days I get very down and think the worst. Horrible pictures lodge in my mind, he's being fished out of the Liffey, there's water spewing out of his nose and mouth. He's washed up on Dollymount Strand, missing fingers and toes, his skull grinning. He's bobbing about, all bloated, in the middle of the Irish Sea – you hear on the news about people going over the sides of ferries. I don't know why I keep seeing him in water. After all, fire is my big bugbear.

He's been murdered. Her brothers and her father were waiting for him that last Wednesday dinnertime. They ambushed him and now he's lying in a shallow grave somewhere in the Dublin mountains.

I mentioned this to the Guards and they said they'd keep it in mind. I gather they showed the anonymous letter to the Maddens – who denied all knowledge. Well, they would, wouldn't they?

I feel sometimes his disappearance is a judgement on me. I wasn't strong enough, good enough, strict enough, loving enough, something enough. God is whipping me back in line. Ken does his best to knock that out of me, sometimes he wins, sometimes he doesn't.

On my good days I see James walking free in London. Maybe working in a pub. (I refuse to contemplate him sleeping in a doorway . . . I utterly refuse. You know how I feel about the appalling vista of homelessness.) Maybe he got on a ship. Maybe he's in South America or Australia.

I rack my brains to try to remember anything he might have been interested in – by now his money would be gone and he'd need a job. Up to now I've been able to think of nothing except motorbikes and television. I tried all the courier firms, then all the motorbike shops in town. I rang RTE. Once I told them who I was and why I was enquiring, they were solicitous. But they'd hired no staff recently and they don't take unskilled people on spec. They recruit through advertising and they hadn't had any competitions that he could possibly have been eligible for. I wanted to ring the BBC but Ken talked me out of it. I mean, where would you start with the BBC?

In case he was lying low and needed simply a subsistence job, I trekked around the security firms (although, given his record, even I knew there was little chance there) and the all-night garages and shops. I spent one whole week walking around department stores and fast-food shops, showing a photograph of him that Ferdia gave me and asking the staff if they'd seen him.

For a while — and I still half harbour this notion — I believed that he'd won the Lotto and was going around the world in high style. Remember the receipt he pulled out of his inside pocket? The one on which he wrote Ken's address?

Well, why not?

I went into the National Lottery office in Abbey Street. Like everyone else I approached, they went out of their way to help, but no, there had been no anonymous winners fitting James's description.

I pray, sort of. It's probably just superstition. Mammy told me once (I think Francesca was there too) that a lot of people in all kinds of different religions believe that each star in the sky is a different guardian angel. So I've started praying to James's guardian angel and to my own, asking them to talk to each other, bring him home to me. Angel of God, my guardian dear, to whom God's love commits me here, ever this day be at my side, to light and guard to rule and guide.

Silly childish stuff, but it does help, particularly when I can't sleep. I concentrate on Mammy's face, ask her to look after him, to find him, make him safe. Starlight, starbright, Mammy, you didn't do much for him in life, please help him now . . .

Et cetera.

In the middle of it all, everyone else's life goes on, you

have to try to fit in. You have to go to work, you have to look at television and eat and talk about other things. You can't live on the edge twenty-four hours a day, not after the first few weeks anyway, it's just not possible.

I even went out to welcome home Michelle Smith and our Olympic team at the beginning of this month. One of the reasons I went was because, weather-wise, the day was probably the worst of this or any other summer, so I felt that very few would turn out for them. You'd hate to let them down.

I was right. Michelle, God love her, was such a game little soul – she's absolutely *tiny*, you know – all you could see was this streaming wet mophead peering out over the edge of the open-topped bus. You had to guess that she was holding up the four medals. Poor girl, she was wetter than she ever was in any swimming pool. And probably frozen. And for all her spunk, all she could see in O'Connell Street below her – at the beginning, anyway, where I was standing – was this row of empty crash barriers and a few hardy souls daring the elements from under a scattering of golf umbrellas.

You do all these ordinary things as if you're a living citizen of the world but you're doing them with the top millionth of your brain. All the rest of you is dead or concerned only with maybe this happened or maybe that happened, suppose we try here, we never thought of that before . . .

And the theories. The bloody endless speculation. Experts. Feature articles and interviews. Psychologists. Retired criminologists. As if you're not speculating enough yourself.

You also get into a state where you're constantly looking for signs, symbols and omens. For instance Ken has an English Usage book and in it, I came across the information that el or il at the end of a name means bright, shining or shining being. Or Angel. I started saying the angel prayers because I'm Angela. That was an omen – see?

Or I'd hear a song on the radio, California Dreamin', say. If I heard something about California on the news within a certain amount of time I'd remember the song, connect the two and be sure it would be a message that James was in California. I became so convinced for one whole day about this that I rang the American Embassy.

You get the picture. Believe it or not, I do find this kind of activity keeps me from going wholly insane.

You might imagine from what I said about the praying that the worst time is the middle of the night, but personally I find the worst time is when you're walking along a street and you see the back of some boy's neck and you're convinced it's James but when you run to catch up with him, there's no resemblance whatsoever. It's a sickening feeling. Or when you remember that we're talking about a boy who couldn't – *can't* – boil an egg for himself.

Some good things always come out of every situation, don't they, no matter how grim. The deep goodness of the people you ask to help. Support from unfortunate families in a similar situation with whom the Guards put me in touch. We all feel the same, you know. One woman's son has been missing for eighteen years – *eighteen years* – and still she waits for him to come home. She has total faith that he will. I hold on to that with her. James will come home.

Another good – or goodish – outcome was that Patsy heard the radio appeal and got back in contact with me.

She and Martin have done their best. He's utilized every contact he has, here, in the North, in Britain, even in Holland and Germany. He has a friend who's a printer – let's hope it's not Mr Madden, I didn't ask! – who printed up leaflets, and Martin and Patsy dropped them in every pub and club and fast-food restaurant in town. They keep inviting Ken and me up to their house for lunch or dinner, or just to drop in.

Patsy and I will never be as close as we were. We'll be friends, we are friends, and that'll never change. But although I've really tried to claw myself back emotionally to the time before the whole thing started so as to be able to pick up the pieces with her, it won't work. I keep seeing her face as she's holding out the original clipping about him and then her putting it on the table.

Eventually, only last week, she did go up to Reddy's house to retrieve her earring – I'd put it in an envelope and left it tucked in at the back of an old radiator in the hallway. I knew no one ever cleaned behind there. (Why didn't I just keep it for her? Remember the state I was in? And I didn't know if we were going to meet again – or even if I *wanted* to see her. Ever again.)

She came back, not only with the earring but with a couple of letters. One made me break down in floods. It was the letter I'd sent to James. Returned. Via Pius Crawford, to whom the Abbot had sent it. My father's note with it said he hoped I was all right and that he was praying for me.

When I managed to pull myself together, I could only stare stupidly at the other one. I nearly laughed, to tell you the truth. I'd been selected to go on *Fame and Fortune* with Marty Whelan. Several weeks ago. I'd forgotten to change Reddy's address to Ken's when I posted the bloody card.

I tore up the letter, which didn't cost me a moment's regret. (Anyhow, could you imagine me on television in my present state, giggling and laughing with Marty Whelan? And who's rooting for you at home, Angela?)

This is the most surprising revelation within a situation

like this. All inessentials fall away. All that stupid old guff about houses and roses around the door and winning the quarter of a million? All gone. If I had James back I'd live with him in a dog kennel. As for taking revenge on the Maddens? I don't *care* that they sic'd the media on us or if it was the brother who beat James up. I'd pave their garden paths with flowers if they could arrange it that I could see him slouching towards me across Mountjoy Square.

At least the Maddens had genuine cause for grievance. I do have difficulty forgiving some others, though – I'm sure I don't have to spell it out for you who they are. They just never let go, do they? The latest headline – I don't read the actual articles because they always regurgitate the whole story – was about Rosemary getting engaged. HAPPINESS AT LAST FOR SEX ASSAULT HEROINE.

Most times, I'm actually too busy to dwell on any wrongs done to us, real or imagined. If I become bitter, the biggest loser will be me, isn't that right? The world will move on and I'll still be stuck.

I still won't totally let go of my Lotto theory. I mean, if people are anonymous, they're anonymous, aren't they? The Lotto people might genuinely not know that he was the one. Ken and I discuss this endlessly. Or, rather, I talk about it and Ken listens. He points out, with good reason, that they have to make out the cheque to a real person. I believe, even though they say they don't do this, that if someone really insists on anonymity and demands it, that they can make out the cheque to cash.

You have to believe in something.

So that's where I stand at the moment. As for Ken and me? On hold. We did have sex a couple of times and it was successful enough, I have to say that. I was able to let go a bit and forget for a few minutes. He was right about one thing, it can be comforting.

But he still has his sleeping arrangements and I have mine. We've developed a routine, very quickly as a matter of fact, but where I'm concerned everything still centres around James. I think it always will – even after we get some definite news one way or the other.

Funnily enough, I think more so than if he was actually here. It's sort of a life sentence.

Ken still thinks that if I can come to terms with whatever has happened or will happen to James, and if I can sort out me and my father – which I intend to sometime in the future (I think) – we should get married. He also says I should go and get some sort of help. Psychological help, counselling or something.

I can't at the moment, I'm too busy.

He says he's prepared to wait a lifetime for me.

Who knows?

Maybe.

The next hurdle is the book – or books. Ken says he'll be there this time to protect me. And maybe, you never know, something good might turn up out of one or both of them in the end. Unlike radio and television pro-grammes, which are nine-day wonders, or newspapers, which end up as pulp for toilet paper, books generally have a long shelf life. I'd imagine they'll use that photograph of James, with or without the little coffin over his eyes. Someone might go into a library some day, somewhere in the world, and recognize him. Such developments do transpire, you know, you read about them every day.